DEFENDER OF HEARTS

KINGDOM OF WALLS BOOK TWO

TANYA BIRD

CHAPTER 1

$\mathcal{A}$stin felt the air shift before he heard the creak of the bow. His head snapped to the right, and every muscle in his body contracted beneath his uniform. He studied the shadows at the end of the corridor, where the flickering orange light cast by a torch faded into black.

Someone was hunting him.

One hand reached for his knife, the other for the hilt of his sword. His ears strained for any thread of noise to grab on to.

He was trained to hear it.

The air shifted again, and he drew his sword, spinning it once, twice. It was the only shield he had, and it did its job, knocking the arrow off course. He threw his knife in the direction of his attacker, and it disappeared into the shadows. A howl of pain rang out. Astin was moving then, his long legs stretching and his boots pounding the stone. A weapon flashed up ahead, and he threw himself to the ground, sliding as a knife passed overhead. He suspected it was his own knife but did not dare look back to confirm it. Into the darkness he went, sword swinging. Relief swelled in him when it connected with flesh and bone. Another wail of pain, and a bow dropped to the ground.

The familiar whine of the king's door opening drew Astin's attention. And there was King Borin peering around the edge of the door frame, fringe tilting, despite having been told numerous times to close his door if there was no guard waiting for him on the other side.

'Inside!' Astin called as he thrust his sword up between his attacker's legs.

A pained scream collided with the sound of the door slamming shut. The man collapsed, and Astin shoved him away so he could free his sword. The ground beneath him was slippery with blood as he rose, running his weapon across the man's throat.

Footsteps came at a run, and Astin reached for the bow on the ground before snatching up one of the scattered arrows. He loaded the weapon and took aim. His hands slackened around the bow when a defender stepped into the light, looking from Astin to the dead man on the floor.

'Check on the king,' Astin said, looking back at the corpse. His eyes travelled from the unkempt hair to the simple clothes, all the way down to the worn soles of the boots. This was no soldier, no sea warrior. This was a merchant man.

The door opened once more, and this time King Borin strode out. He was all bravado now that the intruder was dead. The other defender followed at his heel, scanning the corridor.

'You should stay in your bedchamber until the castle is secure, Your Majesty,' Astin said, positioning himself in front of the corpse.

Borin stepped around him and peered down at the man. 'Who is he?'

The answer was another merchant who wished his king dead. Another merchant prepared to sacrifice himself for a greater cause.

'I don't know,' Astin replied. 'And I don't know if he's alone, so I need you inside.'

The young king did not move. 'Look at his clothes, his hair. He is a merchant, is he not?' He knew his bodyguard was obligated to answer honestly.

Astin swallowed. 'Appears that way.'

'First my father, now they come for me. It seems they will not stop until my entire family is wiped out. And what does my mother say? Forget about justice. Let us all move forwards.'

It was revenge that the queen mother steered her son from, the kind that consumed a man whole and turned him into something unrecognisable. Borin had been possessed by revenge once before, and no one wanted to see a repeat of that.

'Your family is quite safe' was all Astin said.

Borin's face twisted, his stubby nose turning red. 'Brand him and hang him in the merchant borough. I want everyone to see what becomes of traitors. He can greet the merchants as they rise from their beds in the morning.' The king looked back at the corpse. 'And find out how in Belenus's name he got into my home. It seems we have defenders falling asleep at their posts.'

Astin gave a small nod. 'Yes, Your Majesty.'

The young king turned and padded back to his quarters, slamming the door closed behind him. The noise echoed along the corridor.

The second defender stepped up beside Astin. 'Your orders, sir?'

'You heard the king,' Astin said quietly. 'Brand him, then hang him on the wall.'

CHAPTER 2

The boar watched her through the gaps in the crate, daring her to hand over the coin nestled safely in her pocket. Lyndal's gaze fell to the sharp tusks, then moved over the dark woolly coat to the swollen belly.

'And you're sure she's pregnant?' she asked the ship merchant, who stood with one foot tapping.

He nodded. 'Just a few weeks off by the look of her.'

Lyndal regarded the man, trying to figure out if he was trustworthy. The last thing she wanted was to return to the nobility borough with the animal and have her family laugh at her. 'My sister is married to a commander, you know. So if no babies arrive within the next few weeks, you can expect him to be waiting here for you the next time your ship docks.'

The man did not so much as blink. 'If your sister is married to a commander, then how come a lady such as yourself is down here alone at the port?'

That was a very reasonable question. 'I'm free to go

where I please. Every merchant here knows of my connection, as does every defender watching you from atop that wall.' She gestured over her shoulder as she delivered the lie. Never mind the fact that Harlan had told her repeatedly not to enter the port without an escort.

'The sow will birth boarlets before my next visit.' The man straightened and crossed his arms. 'Now, ten shillings, or she goes to the man waiting behind you.'

Lyndal glanced over her shoulder to a balding man eyeing the boar. She swallowed, then pulled out her coin pouch, handing the ship merchant his money. He nodded his thanks and went to turn away. She grabbed his arm. 'Wait. How am I supposed to get the crate to the merchant borough?'

The man's eyebrows lifted. 'You don't expect my men to venture into an enclosed borough riddled with defenders, do you?'

Fair point.

'Perhaps you could leash the animal and I could walk it?'

The merchant chuckled. 'The sow will more likely walk *you*.'

Lyndal chewed her lip as he turned and walked away. Before she could come up with any more terrible ideas, a throat cleared behind her. She turned to find Astin Fletcher standing there rubbing his freshly trimmed beard.

Bodyguard of King Borin.

Harlan's best friend.

And the only man with the ability to instantly darken her mood.

For the love of...

She turned to him, chin raised. 'Defender.'

Those cool grey eyes of his looked from her to the sea merchant to the boar. 'I thought Commander Wright told you not to enter the port without an escort.'

'Harlan is my brother-in-law, not my guardian.' Her eyes narrowed. 'And what are you doing here?'

'I went to collect you from the shop. Birtle wasn't entirely forthcoming when I questioned him on your whereabouts, so I figured you were somewhere you shouldn't be.' His eyes returned to the animal in the crate. 'Tell me you're not considering buying that thing.'

'The deal is done,' Lyndal replied. She cleared her throat. 'Now I just need to get it off the dock.'

Astin assessed her. 'You do know that's a boar, not a pig.'

She rolled her eyes back in his direction. 'It's a domesticated boar.'

'Is that what the ship merchant told you?'

She scowled in place of a reply.

'Let's hope it's familiar with the concept of fences.' He looked in the direction of the ship. 'We're going to need some rope.'

Lyndal's shoulders relaxed. 'You'll help me?'

'I don't really have a choice.' He pointed at the ground. 'Don't move from this spot.' Then he walked off in the direction of the ship, returning with a length of rope.

A few expert knots later, he had a harness made for the animal. Carefully, he partially opened the crate and secured it around the boar before opening it all the way. The animal took off, squealing and growling in protest as the harness pulled tightly around her. Astin waited several minutes for her to settle enough to attempt walking with her.

'You right to carry the crate?' Astin asked, once the boar had given up fighting him.

Lyndal reached down and took a firm hold of it. It was heavier than she had anticipated, but she did not dare complain as she lifted it off the ground. 'Yes, fine.'

Astin looked sceptical but said nothing as he headed for the beach.

She had only taken a few steps when she was forced to place it down again. She wiped her hands on her blue cotton dress and reached for it once more.

'Step aside,' Astin said, returning to her.

She did as she was told, watching as he hoisted the crate in the air. He somehow managed to perch it on one shoulder as if it were a basket—all the while keeping hold of the boar.

'Shall I take the pig?' she offered.

He glanced sideways at her. 'And end up in the water?'

She played with the ends of her long hair to give her hands something to do. It was bad enough that he had found her at the port—alone. Now he got to play the hero, and she was forced to let him.

'Keep up, would you?' he called over his shoulder.

She glared at his back before following him down the dock.

Lyndal's sisters and mother stood in a line staring down at the crate with varied expressions. Blake's brow was pinched in confusion, and Eda's head was tilted as she curiously eyed the animal. Their mother's mouth hung open, but no words came out.

'In a few weeks, we shall have boarlets,' Lyndal said, trying very hard not to look at Astin, who stood leaning against the cart with an amused expression. 'And when they're big, we can slaughter them for the merchant families who are really struggling.'

'Boarlets?' Blake said, tucking her hair behind her ears. 'Not piglets?'

Lyndal swallowed. 'The domesticated pigs we're familiar with from our youth are rarely seen outside the farming borough nowadays. This is the next best thing.'

The boar squealed and thrashed as if poked with a hot rod. The crate rocked from side to side, then stilled.

'You'll need stronger fences,' Astin said. 'The pen you have at present won't hold her.'

'Yes, thank you, Farmer Fletcher,' Lyndal said, glancing in his direction. 'I know you're on duty tonight, so we shan't keep you.'

Astin had a way of speaking to her that made her feel like a child in need of supervision. And his stormy stare was so penetrating, she often found herself looking away despite efforts to the contrary.

The defender walked to the front of the cart and climbed up, gathering the reins.

'Lyndal,' Blake whispered. 'At least thank the man for collecting you from the dock.'

Thank him? She had endured a lecture on pig care for

the entire length of the journey. How a defender knew about such things she had no idea.

Drawing a breath, she called, 'Thank you, defender. Your help today was much appreciated.'

His gaze slid to hers, weighing her down once more. 'Can you do me a favour?'

'What's that?'

'Please don't go buying a wildebeest believing it to be a cow. I'll leave you on the dock next time.'

Lyndal's fingers curled closed as she drew a long, deep breath. But before she had a chance to respond, reins slapped the horse's rump, and the cart pulled away. When she looked back at her sisters and mother, she found them all smiling at the ground.

'Your laughter only encourages him,' she pointed out.

Blake pressed her lips together in an attempt to stop. 'When you give him the ideal reaction, that too encourages him. He says these things to get a rise out of you, and it works every time.'

Her mother, Candace, stepped forwards and took hold of Lyndal's arms. 'What on earth possessed you to buy a boar from a stranger?'

'Oh, I don't know. A decade of famine and rain that shows no sign of stopping? A new king who cares more about his appearance than his people? A distinct lack of meat in the merchant borough despite an ongoing supply? Take your pick.'

'You cannot fix all the problems in the world,' Candace said, brushing a thumb down her daughter's cheek.

'Which is why I'll settle for one borough.'

The boar thrashed in its crate, pulling the women's

attention. The harness Astin had made was now tangled around its neck and belly.

Should I get my bow in case this all goes terribly wrong? Eda signed.

They had hoped the youngest Suttone sister would have resumed speaking by her seventeenth birthday, but it had arrived and gone, and she continued to sign in place of speech—despite rather strong encouragement.

'We can handle one boar between four of us,' Lyndal said, pushing up the sleeves of her dress and staring down at the boar.

'Three of you,' Candace said. 'I am too old to wrestle wild animals.'

Blake approached the crate. 'Keep your eyes on those tusks.' She slid the door open enough for Eda to get her hand through and take hold of the rope. 'I'll open on three.'

Lyndal positioned herself next to Blake, ready to catch the animal if it tried to flee.

The family's duck chose that moment to join the fun, coming at a run from the house.

'Not now, Garlic! Go back inside.'

Garlic ran straight up to Lyndal's feet instead.

'Ready?' Blake asked, looking between them. 'One, two, three.' She tugged the crate open, and the boar flew out.

While Eda had some muscle on her, thanks to her obsession with weapons and sparring, she was no match for the pregnant boar. Her arms were almost pulled from their sockets as she hit the ground. She was dragged six feet before Blake leapt after her, catching hold of the rope. The boar came to a stop, squealing in protest.

'Goodness,' Candace said, hand pressed to her chest. 'I thought you said the animal is domesticated.'

Lyndal ran over to help her sisters. 'She is. That's why she's running away instead of trying to kill us.'

A horse approaching at a canter made them all look in the direction of the front path. And there was Lord Thomas, seated upon his tall chestnut gelding, face clean-shaven and hair neat despite the speed at which he travelled. He pulled up his horse in front of them, eyes immediately going to the boar.

'Uncle,' Lyndal said, her voice a few pitches too high.

Eda tried to brush some of the fresh mud off her dress but only managed to smear it more.

'For heaven's sake,' Thomas said, shaking his head. 'You have been living in the nobility borough for more than a year now, and still you present yourselves as the lowest form of peasant.'

Candace stepped into his line of sight, as if that might somehow erase the scene before him. 'My lord, we had no idea you were paying us a visit.'

'I see that.' He dismounted and walked over to his sister-in-law. 'The king and queen mother are coming to dine with us tomorrow, and the queen has asked that Lyndal attend.'

Lyndal glanced at Blake, whose surprised expression mirrored her own. 'Queen Fayre? I've never even met her.'

Thomas waved a dismissive hand. 'That is what happens when one makes a nuisance of themselves. They suddenly become visible.'

Eda crossed her arms and glared at her uncle.

'Nuisance?' Blake said, taking a step in his direction. 'The merchants sing my sister's praises. She spends more time helping people over that wall than here with her own family.'

Thomas looked down his straight nose at her. 'You say that like it is admirable to abandon one's responsibilities at home.' He turned his attention back to Candace. 'Regardless of the reason behind the invitation, Lyndal must attend. We wish to keep the queen mother happy.'

Candace looked back at Lyndal. 'I suppose she may attend if Queen Fayre has requested her presence.'

Thomas gave a curt nod. Then, turning back to his horse, he mounted, flicking his cloak out behind him. 'If rumour is to be believed, the match between the young king and the Toryn princess is no longer. The food situation in Toryn is worse than here in Chadora. Better His Majesty find a well-bred wife here in his own kingdom, where we have enough mouths to feed already.'

Candace and Lyndal exchanged a knowing look. It was no secret that Thomas wished to see a crown on his daughter's head. The Suttone sisters had no objections. They adored their spoiled cousin and wished her nothing but the best.

'I think we can all agree that Lady Kendra would be an exceptional match,' Thomas continued. 'She comes from a long line of nobility, is well-spoken, educated—but not so educated as to make the king appear a fool.'

The king did not need any help with that. His everyday actions spoke volumes about his intellect.

'And she is fertile,' Thomas added, despite having no proof of the fact.

Candace smiled. 'And compassionate. A true queen.'

Thomas cast a stern look at Lyndal. 'Compassionate when appropriate, mind.'

She wondered what he deemed inappropriate compassion.

'It is likely she will simply wish to meet you,' Thomas continued. 'Then you will be free to help in the kitchen or assist Lady Kendra if she should need you throughout the evening.' He adjusted the reins. 'It will benefit you all to show your cousin in the best possible light.'

Lyndal forced a smile. Anything to end the conversation. She needed him gone before the boar went rogue again. 'We would all love to see Lady Kendra with a crown on that clever head of hers.'

He nodded. 'And be sure to mention her charitable nature. She has, after all, taken her half-merchant cousin under her wing.'

Candace looked down at the ground. 'I suppose the occasional visit might be seen as charitable.'

'Shall we withhold food until tomorrow?' Blake asked. 'To give my sister that slightly starved look one expects from a merchant?'

Thomas levelled her with a disapproving look. 'Did your mother never teach you how unbecoming sarcasm is on a lady?'

Blake adjusted her grip on the rope as the boar pulled once more. 'She has certainly tried, my lord.'

Thomas shook his head. 'I will send for Lyndal in the

afternoon. My daughter will find something appropriate for her to wear.'

Candace bristled. 'Lyndal has plenty of fine dresses, my lord.'

His gaze drifted to Eda. 'And you. Are you speaking yet?'

Eda did not even shake her head. She liked to infuriate him by playing deaf as well as mute.

Lyndal spoke up on her behalf. 'Not yet, my lord, but I assure you we're all working towards the same mutual goal.'

Thomas all but sneered as he turned his horse, then cantered away without so much as a goodbye.

Only when he exited the gate did Lyndal turn to her sisters. 'With the Toryn princess out of the way, every noble man with a daughter will be parading their offspring before the king now. You watch.'

'We cannot blame your uncle for being among them,' Candace said. 'Kendra is a very competent young woman.

'With no understanding of the world outside her borough,' Blake said. 'I love her dearly, but she's a little out of touch for the role.'

'Can you imagine if Uncle succeeded?' Lyndal said. 'He'll be even more unbearable with that kind of power behind him.'

Candace brought her hand to her forehead. 'Let us not get ahead of ourselves.'

The boar thrashed and pulled Eda in the other direction once more. Lyndal and Blake both grabbed for the rope.

'Let's focus on getting the boar in the pen today,'

Lyndal said. 'And rebuilding the pen when she breaks it apart,' she added quietly.

Blake shooed her sister out of the way. 'And catching her when she escapes?'

Eda smiled. *Then you'll need to wash the debris, mud, and pig shit off you before you meet the queen mother.*

'Language,' Candace said, tutting.

I didn't say a word, Eda signed before dragging the boar away.

CHAPTER 3

Astin stood at the king's side, watching the disgruntled merchants gathered in the square before them. He studied their hands, expressions, distribution of weight, all while taking mental notes of the weapons concealed beneath oversized clothes—clothes that had likely fit once upon a time.

'This is how a good king deals with his people,' Borin whispered to him. 'Face to face, in their own setting.'

He was repeating what his mother had told him that morning. Queen Fayre was an excellent puppeteer, and Borin seemed content being the puppet—for now.

Men stood in groups watching the exchange between Borin and the merchants representing them. It was clear by their body language that they had not forgiven the king for the lockdown which had taken so much from them. Hundreds of merchants had died from lack of food and illnesses stemming from it. To make matters worse, Borin had then trapped the merchants in the square and instructed his men to shoot them, naively believing his father's killer would miraculously reveal himself.

The killer still had not been found.

Astin had a bigger problem at present. In the year since Borin's coronation, there had been four attempts on the king's life, ranging from poisoning to an attempted drowning in a bathtub. The problem with hatred of that kind is that it has the ability to seep through walls.

'I really do not understand the problem here,' Borin said, his chest expanding. 'There has been more meat in the merchant borough since *I* became king. Plus there are fewer people to feed now.'

Astin winced. The fact that there were fewer people should have been a matter of shame.

'That shows you how little there was before,' replied the man, 'not how plentiful it is now. I'm a butcher. I can't even speak directly with the farmers I'm to buy from.'

'That wall needs to come down,' said another. 'Or at the very least the gate should be opened for business.'

Borin's lips pinched as he looked between the men. 'I must balance the needs of the entire kingdom, not one borough.' He scoffed. 'You should be thanking me for what you have. Instead, you hold out your hand while complaining. You are free to buy directly from the sea merchants who come each month, because the wall you complain about protects our livestock from the diseases you will inevitably introduce. We have built something unique here, something that is the envy of many.'

The merchants stared back at him, brows creased and mouths downturned.

'Something unique all right,' said a man at the back. 'A prison camp.'

The merchants' hands twitched at their sides, signalling that it was time to go.

'Let's end it there,' Astin said quietly, all the while scanning their surroundings. If it were up to him, he would have come with a small army or not at all. He was by no means a fan of the king, but he took his responsibility to keep the man alive seriously.

Borin glanced at his bodyguard, then nodded. 'I believe the matter to be sorted.'

The merchants exchanged a look that would melt iron. One of the men went to follow the king.

'That's far enough,' Astin said, stepping in front of him. He remained there until Borin was safely on his horse, then looked around before following him.

'The famine is not over yet—for anyone,' Borin called. 'If you think the rest of Wales is fairing any better, you are wrong. Carmarthenshire is a muddy wasteland of skeletons.'

It was true that other kingdoms under King Edward's rule were no better off. Many people foolishly travelled to Chadora seeking refuge from the famine, then died waiting to be let in.

Astin mounted his horse and gestured for the king to start moving.

'You're killing us, one by one,' someone shouted after them. 'We were better off when Aymer de Valence controlled this land—and that's saying something.'

Astin shot the man a warning look, conscious that Borin was easily set off by the slightest suggestion that both he and his father were not superior to the 2nd Earl of Pembroke in every way. Their rivalry was the reason Pembroke became Chadora upon the earl's exile.

'You're not fit to be king!' the other shouted.

Astin blinked. 'Just keep riding.'

Borin turned in his saddle, mouth agape. 'Are you going to let them speak to me like that?'

'They're just blowing off steam. They're not real threats.'

'Go on, run back to your castle,' the man called, walking after them. 'You think you're safe there?'

And there it was. A threat to the king's life—punishable by death. Not a quick death either but the slow torturous kind, where by the time they were actually strung up on the wall, their own family did not recognise them.

Astin dismounted and marched over to the man, grabbing him by the front of the shirt and throwing him to the ground with such force that the air left him in one violent gasp. Making a fist, he punched the man in the face, ensuring he broke his nose for effect. Blood poured freely as the merchant writhed on the ground, cursing and blinking away tears.

The bodyguard prayed it was enough to satisfy the king.

Borin watched the man for a moment, then gave a satisfied nod before turning his horse away. Astin looked around at the other merchants, one glance making it clear no one was to move. A broken nose was better than a public execution, and they all knew it.

He marched back to his horse and mounted once

more. Then the pair made their way across the square towards the rising portcullis.

'Tonight I will be dining with Lord Thomas Welche,' Borin said, having already moved on from the violent scene. 'While he may be one of the more prominent figures in the nobility borough, his name is not without scandal.'

Astin had encountered the cocky lord enough times to form an opinion of him. He had seen the way he spoke to the Suttone family. He had even once seen him take a hand to the youngest of the sisters. Though only the once. A visit from Harlan had put an end to that. Even Lyndal tended to shut down in his presence, and she was as outspoken as they came.

'His wife's sister married a merchant,' the king went on. 'Four children. I believe the son died in the tunnels a few years back. And the daughters.' He shook his head. 'Beautiful trouble. The eldest married Commander Wright, as you know.'

Astin drew a long breath and prayed for patience.

'It shows what a tattered state his mind was in after he was removed from his post.' Borin tutted. 'Still, I will not speak too poorly of him. I am aware of your ongoing friendship.'

On and on he went, with his own unique version of events. Astin had learned long ago that there was no point trying to correct him. He was never wrong about anything.

'I suspect Lord Thomas wishes to present his daughter as a potential wife. She is well bred and in her prime so far as fertility goes. Though I cannot for the life of me picture her face. I suppose if she was a horse of a girl, I would surely remember that.'

That was true. He always remembered a person's faults.

'What say you on the matter?' Borin asked, looking sideways at him.

They passed beneath the archway into the royal borough.

'It's not for me to comment. Your mother is far more qualified to guide you on such things. But I pray whatever union follows is a happy one.'

That was mostly for his own sake. It was uncomfortable enough bearing witness to family fights. Couple fights would be a whole other headache.

'Or perhaps I shall simply take her as a mistress,' Borin said, sounding pleased with himself.

Astin stared straight ahead. 'Don't mistresses come *after* marriage?'

'Mother is always telling me to think ahead.'

The bodyguard was fairly sure she had not been referring to mistresses at the time but said nothing.

'You might be content with tavern whores and servant romps, Fletcher, but a king can select his conquests from any part of the kingdom.'

Astin was not sure which was worse, Borin using the word 'conquests' or the fact that the king was aware of his entanglements with maids. If the warden found out, Astin would be in a lot of trouble.

'Do you require additional guards for this evening?' Astin asked, moving the conversation along.

'I assure you I am quite safe in the nobility borough,' Borin replied with a chuckle. 'They all love me.'

Not true. Many were losing patience with his lack of direction and progress. They may have had more food than the merchants, but what they did not have was a strong leader to make them feel secure about their future. A boy guided by his ego was not adequate.

'If you aren't safe in your home, then you aren't safe anywhere,' Astin said.

The king adjusted his reins. 'Well, then it is a good thing I have you to be afraid on my behalf. My father always said fear is a waste of a king's energy.'

Brave words born of stupidity.

'Do try to relax this evening,' Borin said. 'You can be a bit of a wet blanket at these kinds of gatherings.'

'Due to my bad habit of saving your life?'

Borin chuckled again. 'You do know I kept you on as my highest-ranking guard for your jokes. You always know how to make me laugh.'

'While I appreciate that,' Astin said dryly, 'the other part of my job is to keep you safe.'

Borin kicked his horse into a trot. 'Why not find yourself a fresh maid to entertain you for the evening?'

Drawing a calming breath, Astin followed him.

CHAPTER 4

'Rubies or emeralds?' Kendra asked.

Lyndal turned away from the window and faced her cousin, who was holding two necklaces to her collarbone. She wore a cream gown, the bodice embroidered with tiny roses and the neckline and cuffs trimmed with gold fabric.

'My goodness. All you're missing is the veil.'

Kendra's face fell. 'Is it too much like a wedding gown?'

'Is that not the point?' Lyndal asked, walking over and taking the emerald necklace from her cousin's hand. 'Definitely the emeralds.'

Kendra turned, assessing her reflection in the long mirror while Lyndal fitted the necklace. 'I think the point is to be subtle, not throw a bride at him the moment he steps through the front door.'

Lyndal smiled to herself. 'Well, if King Borin doesn't immediately propose after seeing you in this dress, then he truly is mad.' She appeared behind Kendra in the mirror, squeezing her cousin's arm encouragingly. 'You look absolutely beautiful.'

Kendra's hand went over hers. 'I am pleased you are here. I do hope Father was nice when he extended the invitation.'

'Don't worry about me. I can handle dear Uncle Thomas.' She squeezed her cousin's arm again before letting go. 'It's nice to spend time with my favourite cousin.'

'Hardly a compliment. I am your only living cousin in Chadora.' Kendra turned to see herself from the back. 'I am sorry I have not spent more time with you all over the previous year. Father likes to keep my social life nice and busy, perhaps to get me out from under his feet. And you know how time slips by.'

Lyndal waved the apology away. 'Never mind that. I'm rarely in the borough anyway.'

'Yes, Mother keeps me up to date with all your charity work.'

Lyndal scrunched her nose up. Charity was a popular term among the nobility. The ladies loved to appear "charitable" before their peers whilst never actually stepping foot outside their borough.

'What *is* the plan exactly?' Lyndal asked, changing the subject. 'Am I to sing your praises before the queen and then vanish into the kitchen to help wash dishes?'

Kendra walked over to the wooden stool in front of the dressing table and sat. Picking up the powder, she began dusting her face for the eighteenth time. 'Father says he will be led by the queen's wishes. I assured him you are more than capable of carrying polite conversation. He frets you will bring up the almshouse.'

Lyndal played with the ends of her hair. 'Well, it would be the ideal audience to share some of my ideas.'

'But not the right time.' Kendra cast a stern look over her shoulder.

With a heavy sigh, Lyndal replied, 'Then you better find me a rich husband when you're queen. One way or the other, I'm getting my almshouse.'

She had been throwing the idea at anyone who would listen. A home in the merchant borough for those with nowhere else to go. The sick and hungry would never die alone on a muddy street again.

Kendra met Lyndal's eyes in the mirror. 'I am quite certain all eligible noblemen will overlook your inferior bloodlines if a crown does land upon my head.'

It was not intended as a nasty comment, so Lyndal let it slide past her. It was not her cousin's fault she was blinded by her own privilege. Her father was Lord Thomas Welche, after all. In fact, Kendra had come out surprisingly well considering the fact.

A knock at the door made them both turn, and a maid entered the room.

'The king's just arrived out front, my lady.'

Kendra rose, pinching her powdered cheeks as she faced Lyndal. 'How do I look?'

A lazy smile appeared on Lyndal's face. 'Like a queen.'

Astin dismounted, looking around the neat gardens of Cardelle Manor, then up at the windows above. It was tempting to assume the king was safe within the walls of the nobility borough, but the bodyguard knew there were no safe havens in Chadora for an unpopular king.

Even the farmers were now complaining.

Borin's ever-tightening control over the borough was not only destroying relationships with buyers but prevented farmers from slaughtering animals for their own personal consumption. Yet according to his sister who lived and worked there, livestock numbers were up from the previous year. So where was all the extra meat? Certainly not going to the merchants, who continued to pay exorbitant prices for scraps of offal and bare bones.

Borin slipped from the saddle and joined him on the ground. 'Remind me of the daughter's name again? It might help me remember what she looks like.'

'Lady Kendra,' Astin said, handing his horse's reins over to the waiting groom.

'Ah, now I remember.' He nodded as details returned to him. 'Fair girl, large cheeks.'

Astin glanced at the groom, who was very much within earshot. The problem with the king's descriptions was that they were rarely complimentary, and he was by no means selective with his audience. He had once described a lady as 'the droopy-faced woman with the witch nose' to her brother. The rest of that particular dinner had been rather awkward—even if King Borin had not been aware of the fact.

The royal wagon rolled to a stop a few feet away, and Queen Fayre peered out from beneath the rounded top, taking in the sight of the house. If there was a suitor being pushed in the king's direction, you could be sure the queen mother would be close by to evaluate her. While she had been keen for her son to marry the Toryn princess, Toryn's recent loss of herds to murrain had her rethinking her strategy.

'Shall we?' Fayre said, stepping down and walking past them towards the house.

Borin followed his mother, obedient son that he was. Astin drew a breath and trailed after them.

Inside, Lord Thomas waited in the foyer, his elaborately dressed wife and daughter standing stoically behind him. Astin's feet stopped when his eyes landed on Lyndal standing alone by the stairs. She wore a long-sleeved green dress, tailored at the waist. Her golden hair was in two tucked braids, lips painted pink. She was one of those women who drew a lot of attention with little to no effort.

As if sensing his eyes on her, she glanced in his direction, then straightened. He nodded a greeting before turning his attention back to the king.

'And you remember my daughter, Kendra,' Lord Thomas was saying.

The king looked her up and down as she lowered into a well-rehearsed curtsy. 'Yes, of course.' He tilted his head as he studied her face. 'You have grown up since I saw you last, thinned out in the face.'

Kendra responded to the backhanded compliment with her most brilliant smile. 'Very much a woman now, Your Majesty.'

Astin snuck a glance at Lyndal. She was watching the

exchange with equal amusement. Her smile was something else entirely, the kind that made people fall silent to watch it play out.

'And this must be the famous cousin I have been hearing so much about,' the queen said, looking past Kendra to where Lyndal stood.

Thomas stepped aside. 'My wife's niece. Born in the merchant borough. My daughter has been kind enough to take her under her wing.'

The queen looked Lyndal over. 'I assume the merchant girl has a name?'

Lyndal moved forwards and curtsied with equal grace to her cousin. 'Lyndal, Your Majesty.'

The king frowned at her. 'Well, well. Haven't you come a long way since you stopped me in the middle of the street and begged for my help?' He glanced at his mother. 'Naturally I obliged. I am the people's king, after all.'

Astin looked at the ground and swallowed down the cough in his throat.

'You have a good memory, Your Majesty,' Lyndal replied. 'Your help at the time was much appreciated.'

'And then we were reunited in the square the day you confessed to killing my father,' Borin added.

Thomas suddenly did not know where to look. His wife clasped her nervous hands together in front of her while Kendra's smile froze in a very strange position.

'Excellent memory, it turns out,' Lyndal said, her tone breezy.

The queen only laughed. 'Ignore him. Many merchants confessed to a crime they did not commit that day. That is what one does in order to protect the people they love from being shot dead.'

Borin's cheeks coloured a little. 'Perhaps if you had not shown up in a mood, we would know who the killer is.'

Queen Fayre ignored him, gesturing for her to move closer. 'Come here.' She took hold of Lyndal's face, gently turning it side to side. 'Such a pretty thing.' Letting go, she said, 'I have heard all about the work you are doing in the merchant borough. I wanted to meet you myself and see if the rumours were true.'

'What rumours?' Thomas asked.

The queen found a smile. 'All good things, I assure you.'

That should have made Thomas happy, but instead he glowered in Lyndal's direction.

'Your older sister married Commander Wright, is that correct?' Fayre asked.

Lyndal nodded. 'Yes. I'm afraid he got stuck with the entire litter.'

The queen's sharp eyes never left her. 'And yet you return to the merchant borough daily.'

'My family still has a shop there.'

Fayre nodded. 'But you do not go for the shop.'

Lyndal looked around at the people staring at her, Astin among them. 'I'm in a fortunate position. I can help those who are struggling by cooking a meal, running errands, or simply caring for an infant whose mother is ill. Very small things.'

'Small acts add up,' Fayre said.

Thomas cleared his throat. 'My daughter has played a vital role in teaching Lyndal the ways of a lady.'

Astin scraped his teeth over his bottom lip. He was fairly certain Kendra had not been to the merchant borough since the Suttone women moved out of there.

Nodding in agreement, Lyndal said, 'Lady Kendra is a fine example of what a lady ought to be. Though hopefully we can learn from each other.'

Borin smirked. 'And what is it you think a lady can learn from a merchant?'

Lyndal met his gaze. 'How to make one carrot stretch across six meals.'

It was meant as a joke, but there was no humour in her eyes.

'Join us for dinner,' the queen mother said, her eyes shining with something Astin could not identify.

Thomas twitched in irritation. 'I believe Lyndal was going to help out in the kitchen. A merchant cannot have too many skills nowadays.'

The queen mother looked at Thomas. 'I think your niece has enough skills, and I would certainly enjoy her company.'

Lady Victoria placed a hand on her husband's arm. 'Let her join us.'

'Fine.' Thomas gestured abruptly to the dining room. 'This way.'

'There really are no limits to my mother's charitable nature,' Borin said to Thomas as he followed him into the next room.

Astin stopped in front of Lyndal. 'As the king's guard, do I need to watch you with the cutlery this evening?'

Lyndal stared up at him. 'I'm honestly surprised you didn't immediately deem me a threat and haul me away.'

He leaned in, voice low. 'I thought I'd be nice and let you eat first.'

She tilted her head. 'The chivalry really never ends with you, does it?'

'It really doesn't.'

The hostility present during their early encounters had evolved into a squabbling siblings type of relationship. It was fun—some of the time.

Lyndal still had not moved. Seeing her hesitation, he said, 'Half merchant, half nobility. You're the perfect muse. Don't worry, the queen mother will forget all about you by tomorrow.'

Lyndal rolled her eyes before walking ahead of him into the dining room.

'Kendra also speaks Latin and French,' Thomas said, pushing his half-eaten meal away.

Lyndal stared across the table at it. There was still pork on the bone. If she could get to the kitchen in time, she could take the bones home with her. She would boil them up in a large pot of broth at the shop, encouraging families to come by and take some for soups and stews.

Her eyes moved from plate to plate, calculating.

'What about you, Lyndal?' the queen said. 'Do you speak any other languages?'

Thomas made a noise that resembled a snort but covered his mouth with a napkin to disguise the fact.

'A little Gaelic,' she replied, tearing her gaze from her aunt's plate.

Borin's eyebrows rose. 'Gaelic? That is hardly a sensible choice.'

'Not much of a choice,' Lyndal replied. 'Merchants learn what we must in order to conduct business. When French ships start docking in the port, I'm certain every merchant will soon speak French, Your Majesty.'

The queen mother bit back a smile and laid down her fork. 'My dear, you are such a breath of fresh air.'

Lyndal could feel the heat of her uncle's glare on her once again. She would pay for these compliments later if she did not bring the focus back to her cousin. 'Speaking of fresh air, you really should take a walk through the gardens after dinner. Lady Kendra's knowledge of plants and fauna will have you in awe.'

Kendra picked up her cup. 'I would be most happy to show you if you can tolerate the rain.'

'We must all tolerate the rain,' Borin said gallantly, despite the fact that whenever he appeared on the wall for one of his tone-deaf speeches, there was always someone holding a canvas umbrella over him.

Rising from the table, Lyndal said, 'Please excuse me. I'm going to see if the cook needs help with the pastries.'

'Good idea,' Thomas said, visibly pleased by her imminent departure.

She made her way into the kitchen, where the cook was filling a tray with custard and ginger tarts. Where the rich were getting honey from she had no idea.

'Do you mind keeping the bones for me?' she asked, popping up beside him.

He tutted. 'You trying to get me in trouble?'

'I'll take that as a yes.'

He shook his head, the beginnings of a smile on his aged lips. 'If his lordship finds out, I'll tell him you stole them.'

She leaned on the bench, smiling. 'And he'll believe you. That was plan B, by the way.'

A low chuckle came from the man, cut short when Astin entered the kitchen. He walked over and began inspecting the tarts.

'Don't you have a king to look after?' Lyndal asked.

'That's what I'm doing. I don't suppose you'll help me out by tasting a pastry?'

The cook glanced up at that. 'What for? They're excellent.'

Astin nodded slowly. 'That may be, but I should probably check they're free of poison.'

The cook only grinned when he should have taken offence at the suggestion.

'And what if someone has poisoned the food?' she asked, crossing her arms in front of her. 'Then I'll die.'

He searched her face, that semi-smirk of his making an appearance. 'That's a risk we're all prepared to take for the good of the kingdom.'

The cook chuckled once more.

'Don't do that,' Lyndal said, eyes going to him. 'If you laugh, you'll only encourage him.'

Astin moved closer to her. 'You know, your eyes go a vibrant green when filled with hate for me.'

She lifted her chin. 'A familiar shade, then.'

He winced. 'Ouch.'

More laughter from the cook, cut off when Thomas marched into the kitchen. He stopped in the doorway and looked straight at Lyndal. 'You are not stealing kitchen scraps again, are you?'

'Of course not, Uncle,' she said, taking a step back from Astin. 'The pastries are on their way.'

'The queen mother will depart soon but wishes to speak with you first. Can I trust you not to embarrass me again?'

'Again?' Astin asked, turning to him. 'When did she embarrass you the first time?'

Lyndal almost fell over when he came to her defence. Though it would not end well for him.

Thomas's eyes narrowed. 'Is there a reason you are standing in my kitchen, defender?'

'Yes, actually,' Astin replied.

Thomas waited for him to explain what he was doing. When Astin offered no further information, he mumbled something under his breath before marching back out the door.

Lyndal turned to Astin, an expression of gratitude on the tip of her tongue, but he spoke before she could.

'You better get out there.'

Then he was gone from the kitchen also.

She stared at the door he had disappeared through, a puzzled expression on her face. Glancing at the grinning cook, she said, 'Bones. Don't forget,' then followed them. Her eyes instinctively went to Astin when she entered the dining room. He was standing by the wall—not looking at her.

'Queen Fayre has invited me to court,' Kendra said, drawing her attention to the table. Her cousin's eyes were lit with excitement.

'That's wonderful.' Lyndal slipped back into her chair, eyes meeting the queen's. 'I assure you she's wonderful company.'

Fayre adjusted the tart on her plate. 'I would like it if you accompanied your cousin for the remainder of the season, as I suspect you are also good company.'

'Is that appropriate?' Borin asked with a mouth full of pastry. 'The girl's fortunes may have turned, but she is still a merchant by definition.'

'I must agree with the king,' Lord Thomas said, sitting forwards in his chair. 'We would hate to contribute to any scandal at court.'

The queen stared coolly back at him. 'I am quite capable of choosing the company I keep.' She pushed her plate away. 'Lyndal will join her cousin for the remainder of the spring, unless there are any *viable* objections.'

The uncomfortable silence that followed made Lyndal want to crawl under the table. She was still wrestling with the idea of 'spring'. Referencing seasons was pointless as Europe continued to suffer through a decade-long winter. Seasons were only differentiated by how heavy and often the rain fell. Though winter did bring an occasional dusting of snow that quickly turned to slush.

Realising that everyone was waiting for her reply, she said, 'That is a very generous invitation...'

'You are quite welcome,' the queen said, not giving her a chance to add a 'but'. She pulled her plate closer and picked up the tart, taking a small bite. Her eyes closed as she chewed. 'I am quite tempted to invite your cook along also.'

Kendra laughed, though it was a little on the awkward

side. Lady Victoria smiled politely while Thomas stared hard at his fork. Borin was helping himself to another tart. When Lyndal braved another look at Astin, she found him watching her with a dark expression she could not translate. He was likely unhappy at the prospect of her venturing into his territory.

She was going to need to ready herself for a long and frosty spring.

CHAPTER 5

astin walked the muddy road to the gate that separated the royal and farming boroughs, a large knot in his stomach. His sister only ever came to him with bad news. The last time had been twelve months earlier, when rinderpest had found its way to the herd. They tracked the disease back to a bull their stepfather had purchased from outside the wall. Thankfully, Presley had acted at the first sign of symptoms, isolating the sick to prevent spread to neighbouring farms.

Six months before that, it had been a wild dog attack. They had dug under the wall and taken the new lambs as they were being born.

Now Presley stood on the other side of the gate wearing her usual wary expression, auburn hair plaited to one side and dark circles enclosing her amber eyes. She worked harder than any man he knew.

Astin watched her through the portcullis as it rose, and she watched him right back. He walked beneath the archway and away from the guards. Presley tucked the piece of parchment she carried, which allowed her to ask for him at the gate, into her dress and followed him. She stopped a few feet from him when he turned to face her.

'You look well.' Her tone was flat. 'At least we know where all the food is going.'

It was an uncomfortable thought that he had more access to meat than the farmers producing it. He knew King Borin had men tracking every ear of wheat grown and every chicken hatched in that borough. When his family lost the lambs to the dogs, the king had sent defenders to the farm to investigate.

'Everything all right?' he asked. 'Rose? Mother?' The latter was the news he was expecting any day now.

'Cooper's finally done it,' Presley would say. *'He beat our mother to death.'*

'Rose is good.'

Rose was their half-sister who had been born a few years after he left the borough. He had only seen her a handful of times in her six years but always asked after her.

'And Mother's fine,' Presley added. 'And Cooper.'

'I didn't ask about Cooper.'

She studied him a moment, no doubt trying to read his mood before continuing. 'I'm getting married.'

Astin's eyebrows shot up, though he had no idea why he was surprised. She was twenty-two years old, and her friends were dropping babies all over the borough. 'Married? To whom?'

'Chadwick Wesleye.'

Astin leaned his weight on one foot. 'Royce Wesleye's boy?'

She lifted her gaze. 'He's not a boy anymore. He's twenty and three.'

Astin tried to picture the little thug as a man. 'He still throw rocks at sheep?'

She gave him a tired look. 'He was eleven when he did that.'

'I didn't catch any other boys his age doing it.'

She shrugged. 'Maybe you would have if you stuck around for longer.'

He did not miss the pain that flashed in her eyes. She was never going to forgive him for leaving, despite knowing his reasons. 'Do you love him?'

'Does that matter?'

'Not to anyone else, but it should to you.'

She wet her lips. 'His family produces ninety percent of Chadora's grain. It's a smart match.'

Nothing changed on his face. 'This match your idea or Cooper's?'

'I can barely remember.' She lifted her shoulders in a resigned shrug. 'He showed up, we courted, and now we're to be wed. I just thought you might want to know.'

He sucked on his teeth. 'So he asked Cooper for your hand?'

'Who else is he going to ask?' she said, her voice even. 'You?'

Fair point.

If Cooper had laid one finger on her, fifteen-year-old him would have found a way to take her with him. But for whatever reason, the old man had reserved his bad moods for his wife and stepson. Though Lari Brooke would never admit her second husband hurt her. She could be black and blue and still deny any wrongdoing on his behalf. That would mean admitting she had made a mistake in marrying the man mere weeks after burying her first husband.

'Well, congratulations,' Astin said. 'When's the wedding?'

'In the summer.' One corner of her mouth lifted. 'Whatever that means anymore.'

'It's your best chance of finding a flower for your bouquet.'

The faintest smile appeared on Presley's lips before she suppressed it.

Their childhood had been filled with jokes and knowing smiles, but it seemed those small moments had not added up to much. Now they were just sad reminders of a past life.

'Well, I should let you get back to the king's side.' She took a step away, mumbling, 'God knows he needs you there.'

Astin pretended not to hear that last bit. 'Am I invited to this wedding?'

She started walking backwards away from him. 'If you come visit us before summer, I'll consider it.' Turning, she headed off down the road.

CHAPTER 6

$\mathcal{L}$yndal stood on the back step of their home in the nobility borough, watching Blake angry-feed the chickens. Her sister was throwing scraps and water all about the place, her eyebrows knitted together in one determined line. She had not taken the news of Lyndal's departure to Eldon Castle well.

'Is it safe for me to approach?' Lyndal called to her. 'You're really swinging those pails.'

Blake glanced in her direction. 'Don't muddy up your shoes on my account.'

Lyndal exhaled and stepped down onto the soggy lawn, holding her skirts up as she walked. 'The wagon will be here any moment. Are you really not going to say goodbye to me?'

Blake picked up a few stray vegetable skins and threw them at the boar's pen before turning to face her sister. 'Fine.'

'Fine?' Lyndal laughed, walking straight up to Blake and pulling her sister to her. 'It's only a few months, not forever. The queen will probably tire of me in a few weeks and send me packing anyway.'

Blake relaxed against her. 'Or she'll see you as we see you and never let you leave.'

Lyndal pulled back to look at her. 'I assure you my merchant roots will shine as bright as the sun we can't remember.'

'Good.' Blake threaded her arm through Lyndal's as they walked towards the house. 'I'll await reports of unruly merchant behaviour from Uncle Thomas, then.'

'Though not too unruly or I shall never hear the end of it.'

Blake drew her closer. 'Just make sure you return to me the same person. I couldn't bear it if you came back a proper lady.'

'To even suggest such a thing…'

Their mother appeared in the doorway, wiping her hands on her pressed apron. 'The wagon is out front. Of course, you will have to squeeze in around all of Kendra's belongings. Anyone would think she is moving to the castle permanently.'

'I thought that was the plan,' Blake said, smiling mischievously.

'Has Eda returned?' Lyndal asked, looking past her mother into the kitchen.

Candace pressed her lips together, and Blake looked at her feet.

'Why's everyone acting like I'm never coming back?'

Blake sighed and looked up. 'It's a big change. Eda will come around.'

Lyndal stepped past her mother, shaking her head.

'Well, when she does, she'll have to put her apology in a letter. I can't stand around waiting for her to descend whatever tree she's hiding in.'

Out front, Kendra was waiting in the wagon, one foot tapping. 'Do come along,' she called. 'The queen mother awaits us.'

Blake took Lyndal's hand and squeezed. 'Better not keep the *queen* waiting.'

Lyndal kissed her cheek. 'Maybe you can come visit.'

'I'm sure Harlan would love that.' Blake's tone was pure sarcasm.

Candace stepped forwards to kiss her daughter. 'Take care of each other. Court can be tricky to navigate, but it will open doors if you can find a way to fit in. Then you will have no trouble finding a suitable husband.'

'Suitable' was the key word in that sentence.

'Be sure to tell Eda I left in tears so she feels guilty,' Lyndal said, ignoring the disapproving tuts of her mother. She almost stepped on the duck as she turned away. 'Garlic,' she said, crouching. 'Don't fret, my love. I shall be back before you know it. Make sure you watch over Pig for me.'

Traditionally all the animals were named after herbs and spices, but referring to the boar as a pig annoyed both Harlan and Astin, so the sisters had all agreed to bend the rules for the sake of maximising the joke.

Blake picked up the duck so it would not chase the wagon down the road.

'Off you go,' Candace said, eyes shiny.

Lyndal pressed a hand to her churning stomach as she walked away. The driver was waiting to take her hand as she stepped up into the wagon. It was surreal given a year earlier she had been eating insects while imagining her death. Now she was on her way to Eldon Castle.

'Is that what you are wearing?' Kendra asked as Lyndal settled herself on the seat opposite.

Lyndal looked at her. 'No. This one is a ruse. Just when Queen Fayre expresses her disappointment in my choice of dress, I shall whip it off, revealing a much nicer one beneath it.'

Her cousin squinted her disapproval. 'Very funny. This is my future, you know.'

Lyndal leaned over and squeezed her cousin's hand. 'No one's going to be looking at me.'

'But they *will* judge the company I keep. If I fail to win over the king, my father will remind me of the fact long after I have married someone who is *not* of royal blood.' She looked out as the wagon pulled away, head shaking. 'Sorry. That was unkind. Perhaps I am more nervous than I realised.'

Lyndal knew the kind of pressure Kendra was under. 'You're not a failure if you're not queen by the end of the spring. You do know that, right?'

'In my father's eyes I will be. He is still recovering from the disappointment of me being born a girl.' Kendra smoothed down the skirt of her gown, which fell perfectly around her legs. 'I once witnessed your father sing your praises about the way you hung laundry. I was eight at the time, and rather jealous.'

'And yet you never thought to try it for yourself.'

Kendra bit back a smile. 'I can safely say my father would have had a very different reaction to me hanging laundry.' Her expression turned serious. 'Listen to me complaining. At least my father is still alive. And you would look stunning wearing a wheat bag, by the way. Pay me no mind.'

Lyndal's eyes shone with mischief. 'Perhaps I'll test that theory.'

'Ah, no. Peasant clothing I will allow. Wheat bag I will not.'

Lyndal's mouth fell open. '*Peasant clothing*? My dear cousin, if you think this is what people are wearing in the merchant borough, then it's been too long between visits.' She looked down at her cotton dress with its pleated bodice and lace along the sleeve.

'You really do straddle two worlds,' Kendra said on a sigh.

'The Suttone women have invented a new class— peasant gentry.'

Kendra smiled as she turned to watch the passing scenery. The wagon swayed gently, the horse moving at a slow trot.

As they neared the gate, Lyndal pressed a hand to her stomach. The separation from her family was going to be the most challenging part. She had never been away from them overnight, let alone divided by a wall for weeks on end.

A horse cantered up beside the wagon, causing both girls to jump in their seats. It was Eda.

'Please stop the wagon,' Lyndal said to the driver.

The driver pulled up, and Lyndal's feet landed on the ground at the same time Eda's did. The girls wrapped their arms around each other, holding tightly for a few moments.

Eda was first to let go. *They better treat you well or I'm scaling that wall and coming for them.*

'What did she say?' Kendra called from the wagon.

Lyndal glanced over her shoulder. 'She's just wishing us a pleasant stay.'

'Right,' Kendra said, sounding sceptical.

The sisters exchanged a small smile.

'I'll see you at the Solar Festival,' Lyndal said, smoothing down her sister's hair. 'If not before.'

Across a rope? Eda signed.

'If you think a rope is going to keep me from you, then you don't know me very well.' She kissed her sister's cheek. 'Stay out of trouble.'

She turned away before the sting of tears became anything more and climbed back into the wagon. They rolled away, and she held her hand up in a long wave as they passed beneath the archway into the merchant borough. Her younger sister would be absolutely fine, but that did nothing to ease the pain of separation.

The gate closed behind them.

'At least you have people who will miss you,' Kendra said as they headed towards the merchant village.

Kendra had wanted a sibling her whole life. While her mother had had no problem falling pregnant, staying pregnant was another matter.

'Your mother will miss you very much,' Lyndal said.

'And my father will miss me because I kept her occupied and out of his hair,' Kendra replied with a playful smile.

They fell silent again, watching the road. Occasionally they passed merchants who would look in their direction. Lyndal felt like a fraud sitting up in that wagon, as though she were pretending to be something more. A year earlier she had walked everywhere, nearly falling down from starvation, just like they were.

They passed between the village and the forest, slowing when they reached the square.

'Oh my,' Kendra said, hand going to her mouth.

Lyndal followed her gaze to where a decomposing body hung on the wall. She longed for a similar reaction instead of the numb acknowledgement that resulted from years of desensitisation. She did notice the smell though. It was amazing how quickly one became accustomed to the fresh air in the nobility borough.

The two defenders at the gate approached the wagon as it rolled to a stop. The driver handed over a letter from the queen mother, an official invitation to Eldon Castle. The guards looked the young women over, then gestured for the portcullis to be raised.

'Here we go,' Kendra said, her words almost drowned out by the loud clank of the gate.

Lyndal pressed her damp palms to her thighs as the wagon lurched forwards. She had glimpsed Eldon Castle through the gate her entire life. Never did she imagine having reason to enter the royal borough—other than being locked in the tower. It was by no means a stretch for a member of her family.

They passed the barracks, where defenders trained with swords and poles. Others ran laps around them. Lyndal looked for Harlan. Her brother-in-law was in charge of the new recruits, and she thought seeing him might make her feel a bit braver. But he was nowhere in sight.

The stables were next, rows and rows of stalls bursting with horses of all sizes and colours. Grooms walked back and forth, carrying saddlery and pails of soaked barley. Next to the stables was a fenced yard. A handful of men stood with their boots resting on the bottom rail, watching a young rider try to saddle an unwilling horse.

'There it is,' Kendra said, drawing Lyndal's attention. 'Eldon Castle.'

Lyndal looked ahead to the pale sandstone construction looming over yet another wall. It was rumoured to be influenced by French designs, which she knew nothing about. To the far left loomed the tower, with its sharp roof and tiny windows barely big enough to frame a starved face. She immediately thought of Eda locked in there after being caught stealing a chicken. How on earth she had coped in such a place at only fifteen years of age Lyndal had no idea.

As they passed through the wide hinged gate, Kendra leaned forwards and asked, 'Is that King Borin's bodyguard?'

Lyndal's gaze went to the man waiting at the front entrance of the castle, and sure enough, it was Astin Fletcher in his black uniform and leather armour.

'Yes, it is.' Normally the sight of him had her groaning aloud, but his tall, familiar frame was oddly comforting.

When the wagon came to a stop, Astin moved forwards and extended a hand to Kendra before the driver even had a chance to exit the wagon.

'Defender,' Kendra said, stepping down.

'Lady Kendra.'

Not one to sit around and wait for help, Lyndal stepped down just as Astin turned back to her. He was far too close, but it fell on him to move away, because in order for Lyndal to retreat, she would need to climb back into the wagon.

'You all right?' he asked, searching her face.

She tried to mask her surprise. 'Genuine concern in place of an insult? What sorcery is this?'

His lips curled slightly. 'Harlan sent me.'

Of course he had. 'Oh.' She looked past him to where a servant was collecting their belongings. 'That was kind of him.'

Finally he stepped back, and she was able to breathe.

'I'm on duty shortly, but if you need anything, you can send word to me via one of the servants.'

'Send word to *you*? Why not Harlan?'

His eyes searched hers. 'You'll struggle to find servants prepared to travel outside the castle walls to deliver messages to the barracks.'

She felt her cheeks heat. 'Of course.' When he turned to leave, she said, 'I appreciate you popping by to welcome us.'

Those grey eyes bored into her a final time, and then he was striding away from them.

'Ready?' Kendra asked, her eyes shining with excitement.

Lyndal tore her gaze from Astin. 'As ready as I'll ever be.'

CHAPTER 7

*K*endra sat in one of the expensive chairs in the solar that connected the two bedchambers, occasionally touching a finger to the corner of her painted mouth. Lyndal, not used to being idle, paced the length of the room. Waiting around to be summoned by Queen Fayre was a special kind of torture for her. There was nothing to keep her busy in the meantime. Nothing to clean, no food to prepare or water to fetch.

No boars to wrestle.

'Oh do sit down,' Kendra said in a pained tone. 'You are wearing a track in the rug.'

Lyndal stepped off the rug onto the hardwood floor and resumed pacing. A knock at the door made her stop and turn.

Kendra rose elegantly from her chair and went to open it. A young servant boy stood in the corridor.

'Her Majesty Queen Fayre has requested your company in the garden terrace, my lady,' he said.

Kendra nodded and looked back at Lyndal. 'I believe we are ready to join her.'

The women followed the servant along the west corridor, down some stairs, and through a narrow door that opened to a large terrace. Lyndal paused when she stepped out, looking around at the trellis walkways and arbours, likely once used for shade. The garden beds were raised to prevent waterlogging. They were exploding with mature herbs and colourful plants. Exotic birds hung in cages along the castle wall—as trapped as she was. Immaculately trimmed hedges and wattle fences marked the perimeter.

'Do come along,' Kendra whispered over her shoulder.

Lyndal hurried forwards, spotting the queen alone by the fishpond in the middle of the terrace. A few yards past her, seven women were seated playing chess and talking among themselves.

'Your Majesty,' Kendra said as they neared the pond. She fell into a low curtsy, Queen Fayre's inquisitive eyes following every movement. 'What a lovely space this is. Was this your vision?'

Kendra was right at home in this setting, knowing exactly what to say. And Lyndal was happy to let her do the talking.

'Actually, my vision had a lot more citrus trees and flowers in it,' the queen mother replied. 'However, we must all make do without those things for now.' Her eyes went to Lyndal. 'I am so pleased you decided to join your cousin. What do you think of my home?'

Lyndal looked around the terrace. 'It's enormous. I'm certain I'll get lost—frequently.'

Fayre smiled.

'And you've still managed to create a colourful space without citrus trees and flowers,' Lyndal added, looking over her shoulder at the cages.

'Are you fond of birds?' the queen mother asked.

'I'm fond of them flying in the sky. Not one for cages, I'm afraid.'

'Well, I think they are a lovely feature,' Kendra said.

Queen Fayre watched the birds for a moment. 'I find their silence unsettling. However, the king is fond of them, so they remain. Imported all the way from Africa, I believe.'

That made Lyndal feel even more sorry for them. 'What must birds born of heat and sun think of our frigid temperatures and constant rain?'

The queen mother's eyes returned to her. 'I am certain they think us mad for living here and cruel for forcing them to suffer alongside us.'

The sadness in her tone made Lyndal swallow.

'Come,' Fayre said, suddenly upbeat. 'I shall introduce you to the other ladies, and we can hopefully squeeze in a few games of chess before the rain starts up again. Do you both play?'

'I love the game,' Kendra replied quickly.

'What about you?' Fayre asked Lyndal as they wandered to the small tables where the other women were gathered.

'I play, but not well, Your Majesty. I lack the patience required. Lady Kendra, on the other hand, is quite skilled.'

'My cousin exaggerates,' Kendra said, a hand going to her chest in a gesture of modesty.

Queen Fayre smiled at her. 'We shall soon find out.'

The other women looked in their direction as they approached, wearing smiles that did not match the top halves of their faces. Lyndal reminded herself to smile back as the women gleefully assessed her attire. Her mother's words came to mind.

If you can find a way to fit in, then you will have no trouble finding a suitable husband.'

Flashing her teeth, she offered herself up as prey.

Astin spotted Harlan standing in the far corner of the armoury, head bent as he inspected a shield. He walked over, stepping over the weapons laid out on the ground.

'Thornton thinks some extra weight in the shields will help build strength,' Harlan said when Astin appeared beside him.

Astin took the shield and tested the weight. It was surprisingly heavy. He flipped it over to find iron bars attached to the back. 'Clever.' He handed it over. 'You heading home soon?'

'The second I'm finished here.' Harlan turned to face him. 'You see Lyndal yet?'

'I was out front when they arrived.'

Harlan headed for the door. 'She seem in good spirits?'

'Given *I* was the first person she saw upon arrival, yes.'

Harlan chuckled. 'That was lucky timing. One might think you *planned* it that way.'

'Don't start. I saw the wagon. I was being nice.'

Harlan glanced sideways at him. 'Right place, right time. Got it.'

'You can't ask me to watch out for her, then throw shit at me when I do.'

'Why not?'

Astin bumped him into the door frame as they stepped outside. Harlan swore, righted himself, and followed him out.

'I appreciate you looking out for her,' Harlan said, catching up to him. 'Kendra tends to look out for herself.'

'Figured as much.'

The pair headed for the mounting yard, where Harlan's horse was saddled and waiting for him.

'The king tell you he went to the farming borough this morning while you were off duty?' Harlan asked.

Astin squinted in the direction of the castle. 'No. He failed to mention that. Any idea what he was doing there?'

'Your stepfather came to the gate earlier. I suspect that had something to do with it.'

Astin exhaled. 'Probably why he didn't bring it up.'

Harlan chuckled.

'He makes it really hard to keep him alive sometimes.'

'Only sometimes?'

When they reached Harlan's horse, Astin waited for the groom to leave before asking, 'Does the thought of those two men having direct dealings with one another fill you with as much fear as it does me?'

Harlan mounted and looked down at him. 'Safe to assume they're not sharing strategies on how to better help the poor. Talk to Presley about it next time you see her. She did say she wanted to see you before her wedding.'

'Not sure an interrogation is what she had in mind.'

'But not tonight,' Harlan said, swinging his horse around and nudging the mare forwards. 'Tonight, enjoy the fact that someone else is keeping the king alive and get some sleep.'

'That is such a married person thing to say,' Astin called to him. 'Perhaps I'll go to the tavern for a few ales.'

Harlan emitted a low laugh before kicking his horse into a canter.

CHAPTER 8

*L*yndal and Kendra descended the grand staircase into the courtyard, hoods of their cloaks pulled up to protect them from the mist of rain. In the middle sat a fountain, water bubbling out of the top and spilling down three tiers of stone. All that was missing from the scene was a summer sun and ladies in short-sleeved dresses, laughing into brass goblets. Lyndal remained hopeful she would see something like it again in her lifetime.

'Of course I had to let Queen Fayre win,' Kendra whispered as they passed the fountain. 'I cannot simply beat her at chess and expect us to be friends afterwards.'

Lyndal looked up at the smoky black sky. How she missed the stars. 'I think Queen Fayre is the kind of woman who would prefer to win on merit, not charity.'

'I was being polite.'

'I think the word you're looking for is deceitful.'

Kendra closed her mouth. 'Do you think she likes me?'

'What's not to like?'

'You literally just labelled me deceitful.'

Lyndal smiled. 'I simply want you to be yourself. It's a long charade if you do become queen.'

They passed the chapel and stopped at the entrance to the hall, peering inside. Guests stood in small groups in the middle of the room while others were seated at the long tables lining each wall. Trays of food sat untouched. Eggs, salted meat, roasted chicken, and colourful root vegetables. Guilt slashed through Lyndal like a knife. In the next borough, children were being put to bed with a cup of warm water, a trick to fool the stomach into thinking it had been fed.

'I do hope there will be dancing,' Kendra said. 'Perhaps the king will ask me.'

Lyndal's gaze drifted to the high table where Borin was seated, picking through a plate of food. His mother sat at his side, watching the room. The chairs around them were empty. Prince Becket had departed soon after the coronation, taking the number of royal family members in Chadora to two. It was no secret Queen Fayre wished that number to grow.

'Oh, there is Lady Henley,' Kendra said, smoothing down the front of her dress. 'We should take the seats nearest her. She is one of Queen Fayre's closest friends.'

Lyndal's feet did not want to move suddenly, or rather wanted to move in the other direction—towards her bed. But as neither bed nor lingering in the doorway for the remainder of the evening were viable options, she sighed inwardly and followed her cousin.

⌁

Warmed by ale, Astin followed the rain-soaked path around the castle, still trying to figure out why he turned down a barmaid's advances in place of a perimeter check. After all, if the king died on someone else's watch, it would be no reflection on him.

As he neared the south gate, some movement farther along the wall caught his eye. His feet stilled as he peered into the dark. The guard on duty at the gate looked between him and the wall.

'Something wrong, sir?' the defender called to him.

Astin held a hand up to silence him, then moved deeper into the shadows. He froze when he realised what he was looking at. It was a gently swinging rope, moving as if someone had not long ago released their grip on it. His heart sped up as he looked up and drew his weapon.

'Breach!' he shouted, turning away and breaking into a run towards the gate.

The defender on duty drew his weapon also. 'Breach!' he echoed.

'Open the gate!' Astin roared, approaching at a run.

It opened just wide enough to let him slip through, then clapped shut behind him. He ran along the bottom of the wall, searching for any signs of a descent. When he did not find anything, he stopped, cursing as he turned in a circle. A few more defenders had emerged from the castle to join the hunt.

'Find the warden,' Astin shouted at one. 'Where's the king?'

The young defender was struck in the left side of his face with an arrow before he got a word out. A scream erupted from him. Astin jogged backwards and pressed himself against the wall, breathing hard as he searched the shadows around him.

'Take cover!' Astin called to the other defenders.

But his warning was too late. An arrow came from the other direction, striking another defender in the side.

'Multiple shooters!' Astin shouted as he took off at a sprint towards the castle. His job was to get to the king, and yet it was Lyndal's face that flashed in his mind. Clever words would not save her from arrows.

A defender circled the fountain in the courtyard, hand resting on his weapon. He stopped when he saw Astin running towards him. 'What's going on?'

'Draw your sword, defender. We're under attack. Where's the king?"

'The hall, sir.'

Astin slowed to a jog when he reached the chapel, carefully moving along the wall towards the music. If music was still playing, then the king was still alive. The thought buzzed in his mind as an arrow whistled over-head, bouncing off the stone wall. He was out of time. Rounding the corner, Astin headed for the hall.

'Intruders!' he called to the defender at the door.

When the defender went to draw his sword, a figure emerged from the darkness, a blade glinting in his hand.

'Behind you!' Astin called too late.

The defender's throat was slashed, and he fell to his knees, clutching his throat. Astin tackled the man with the knife to the ground while driving his weapon into his stomach. He thrust it upwards before jumping to his feet.

'Defenders to the doors!' Astin shouted as he charged in. The music stopped, and all the guests, Lyndal and

Kendra among them, turned to look at him. 'I need everyone under the tables.'

Lyndal's eyes went to his bloodied uniform. Then she reached for Kendra, dragging her towards the closest table.

'All of you,' Astin said when no one else moved.

Stanford, one of Borin's other bodyguards, was already dragging the young king from his chair. 'Is there a threat?'

'You could say that.'

Borin peered around his bodyguard. 'What sort of threat?'

'You cannot expect Chadora's nobility to get down on their hands and knees,' Lady Henley said, appearing outraged by the suggestion.

Astin ignored her, stopping one of the defenders who went to pass him. 'Cover Queen Fayre. We don't know how many there are.'

'What do you mean, you do not know how many there are?' Borin asked.

Queen Fayre closed her eyes. 'Let him do his job.'

Panic broke out as the guests realised the seriousness of the situation, trays of food and jars of wine falling to the floor as people hurried to take cover. Astin's eyes went to Lyndal, who had reappeared to help Lady Henley.

'Quickly now,' Lyndal was saying, guiding her to the ground. Then, seeing there were still people out in the open, she returned for them.

While Astin admired her level head in a crisis, he was about to throw her under that table himself if she did not take cover.

The thud of an arrow hitting flesh made him turn. The defender at the door staggered backwards, and a moment later, a bow swung into view, a fresh arrow pointed right at Astin.

Raising his sword, Astin threw it at the sliver of a man pressed against the door frame. It spun through the air, destroying the bow. In two strides he reached Lyndal, all but throwing her to the ground. She sucked in a surprised breath before crawling beneath the table. The now bowless intruder drew his sword and marched into the room, jaw set and eyes ablaze. And Astin stood in the way of what he came for.

Just as Astin reached for the dagger strapped to his calf, another defender appeared behind their attacker, shooting him in the back. The man slowed, feet clumsy suddenly and eyes wide. Astin stepped up to him and kicked the weapon from his hand, sending it clattering to the floor. He cut the man's throat to spare him a worse fate than if he were to survive.

'Make sure no one comes through that door,' he instructed the defender. Then, turning back to the room, he asked, 'Is everyone all right?'

There was no reply from the guests. Even Lady Henley seemed to have momentarily lost her tongue.

'Another merchant?' the king asked, moving out from behind Stanford.

Astin looked down at Lyndal, who was crouched under the table holding her shaking cousin in her arms. She was completely still as she stared at the man bleeding out at his feet. 'Looks that way.'

Lyndal flinched at the sound of his voice, then met his eyes. He saw no fear in them, only heartbreak.

Walking over to the table, Astin picked up one of the linen napkins and wiped it over the blade of his sword before sheathing it. 'No one moves until the castle is secure.'

With that, he headed for the door.

CHAPTER 9

'How am I supposed to sleep after witnessing such... such grotesque violence?' Kendra asked Lyndal as she stared up at the roof. 'Every time I close my eyes, it is all I can see.'

Lyndal sat on the edge of the bed, having tucked her cousin in like one does a child. 'You won't be alone. I shall sleep at the end of your bed like a loyal dog.'

Kendra reached out and took hold of her hand. 'Thank you. What would I do without you here?'

'I'm certain someone else would have eventually dragged you under that table.'

Kendra pressed her eyes shut. 'I simply froze. My legs would not work.'

'That's a common response to fear.'

'Surely you must have been afraid also.'

Lyndal tucked Kendra's hand beneath the blanket and brushed hair back from her face. 'I'm a merchant. It's rarely an advantage, but living with fear is what we do best.'

A loud knock at the door made Lyndal jump and Kendra shoot up in bed.

'What if it is another intruder?' Kendra asked, voice cracking. 'What if they did not catch them all?'

'I doubt very much that they would knock before entering.' Lyndal rose from the bed and wandered over to the door. 'Who is it?' she called, hand on the door.

'It's Fletcher.'

Relief filled Lyndal. She had not seen him since he left the hall, and her mind had imagined all kinds of terrible outcomes. Glancing over her shoulder, she said, 'Go to sleep. I'll be back in a moment.'

She stepped out into the dimly lit corridor and pulled the door closed behind her, hugging herself against the cold. 'What are you doing pounding the door down in the middle of the night? I'm trying to calm Kendra down so she sleeps.'

Astin ran a hand down his blood-spattered face. 'I knocked on *your* door, but you didn't answer, despite clear instructions not to leave your bedchamber.'

Lyndal scowled up at him. Then, registering the exhaustion on his face, her expression softened. 'Well, I'm quite safe, as you can see. What about you? Are you hurt?'

His head dipped slightly. 'No.'

'How many intruders were there in the end?'

'Four.'

'All merchants?'

He nodded, went to speak, then stopped at the sound of footsteps. He had his sword drawn and his tall frame parked in front of her before the figure even came into view. Lyndal peered around him and saw the warden,

Shapur Wright, come to a stop. Astin immediately sheathed his weapon and stepped aside.

'Apologies, sir.'

'At least you did not throw your weapon at me.' His eyes went to Lyndal. 'Queen Fayre wants to speak with you.'

'Now?' Astin asked before Lyndal could reply.

Shapur nodded.

'Kendra is all but asleep,' Lyndal said, stepping out from behind Astin.

'Leave her. She only asked for you.'

Lyndal looked down at her creased dress and tucked the loose pieces of hair behind her ears. 'Very well.'

'Fletcher will escort you.' His gaze shifted to Astin. 'Queen Fayre wants a word with you also.'

The bodyguard shifted. 'Yes, sir.'

They watched the warden turn and walk off before looking at each other.

'You heard him,' Astin said. 'Let's go.'

Lyndal opened the door to check on Kendra, then quietly closed it again. She noticed Astin was glued to her side on the walk there, eyes moving over every shadow and nook they passed.

'You're rather on edge given the castle has been secured,' she said quietly.

'I know better than to be complacent, especially given we don't know how the intruders got into the borough.'

Lyndal looked up at him as they walked. 'Have you checked for tunnels?'

He sighed. 'I'm not really in the mood for your jokes.'

'Who's joking?'

They arrived at the queen's quarters, located in the east wing. The guard posted at her door disappeared inside to announce their arrival. He reappeared a moment later, nodding at Astin. The pair entered and found the queen seated on the lounge wrapped in a robe. A book lay open beside her.

After a formal greeting, Astin asked, 'Would you like me to wait outside?'

Fayre rose from the lounge chair. 'No, you should stay.'

Astin nodded.

The queen mother clasped her hands in front of her as she looked to Lyndal. 'You may have heard that all our guests will be leaving in the morning. The warden has deemed the castle unsafe at this time.'

Relief pulsed through Lyndal. In the morning, she would be going home. 'Well, the warden does know best.' She tried to keep the unbridled joy out of her voice.

Fayre watched her a moment. 'You know, I watched you closely this evening, in the hall. You did not panic. You did not make a fuss. You calmly followed Fletcher's orders and assisted others.'

Lyndal wondered where the conversation was going. 'I prefer to be useful in a crisis, though that's not to say I wasn't falling apart on the inside.'

'A woman's strength is measured by her ability to internalise that fear, because one slip and we are labelled as hysterical.'

Lyndal was not sure how to respond to that, so she waited for the queen to continue.

'I like to surround myself with strong women. I truly believe our kind draw strength from one another. And I

wonder, would you be open to staying under the circumstances?'

Lyndal saw Astin's weight shift in her peripheral
vision. 'Did you not just say that guests would be leaving
in the morning?'

'I did. But since you both only arrived a day ago, I am
hoping to keep you for a while longer. I am certain Lord
Thomas will agree as long as we take extra precautions
with your safety.'

'Have you discussed the matter with the warden?'
Astin asked.

Her eyes went to him. 'Yes. And with the king. In fact,
His Majesty even offered *you* as the ladies' guard for the
duration of their stay. The warden agreed.'

'Oh,' Lyndal said, her mind playing catch-up. 'But what
about the king's safety? Surely that's a priority.'

'The king has an entire army at his disposal. The fact
that the two of you are already acquainted will make the
arrangement more comfortable for everyone.'

Astin was oddly silent, no doubt thinking up clever
ways to tell the queen no, absolutely not. In the meantime,
it fell on Lyndal to speak up and save them both.

'Kendra and I couldn't possibly take the king's best
guard. Surely it's easier to send us on our way and allow
Astin—I mean, Fletcher—to do his job.'

She thought her logic was sound, but Queen Fayre
stared back at her as though she were speaking in
tongues.

'While I appreciate your thoughts on what is best for
my son, I have some opinions about that myself. I would
like to see him married—and soon. Lady Kendra seems

like a bright young woman, but I cannot wait months for confirmation.'

Lyndal looked up at Astin, willing him to object. How he looked so calm she had no idea.

'Are the orders effective immediately?' he asked.

Queen Fayre nodded, and Lyndal tried very hard not to click her fingers in front of Astin's face and ask if he had heard properly. She knew defenders were supposed to follow orders without question, but this was ridiculous.

'Of course, your guests will need to cooperate if the arrangement is to work,' Astin said, finally meeting Lyndal's eyes. 'I can only do my job if they're prepared to listen.'

That sounded much more like the Astin she knew.

'As long as your demands are reasonable, *defender*, then I can't foresee there being any listening issues.'

Queen Fayre looked between them. 'Good. Then it is settled. You and Lady Kendra will remain at Eldon Castle for the rest of spring, and Fletcher will be in charge of your safety for the duration of your visit. Now, I suggest you get some sleep. There has been quite a bit of sickness in the merchant borough of late, as I am sure you are aware. Fearing further spread, yesterday the king had those displaying symptoms removed. They are currently isolating in the lazaretto borough. I thought we might pay them a visit in the morning.'

The lazaretto borough was where the sick went *after* they died, not before.

'I've not heard of any contagious outbreaks,' Lyndal said. 'Scurvy is the biggest problem facing the borough right now.'

Fayre nodded. 'The symptoms reported are consistent with scurvy.'

'Then why remove people from their home for a disease that isn't contagious?' Lyndal asked, confused.

The queen mother blinked those sharp eyes at her. 'Why indeed? Good night, Lyndal.'

It took Lyndal a moment to register the dismissal. Lowering into her curtsy, she said, 'Good night, Your Majesty.'

Astin walked to the door, holding it open. Lyndal met his cool gaze as she passed him, marching straight off down the corridor. A second later Astin fell into step with her.

'Go on,' she said the moment they were out of earshot of the other defender. 'Say it all now so we can be done with it.'

He glanced sideways at her. 'Say what?'

'Tell me how my presence here has ruined your life, how the king will likely die because you're being forced to guard two women.'

He looked amused by the words spilling from her mouth. 'It's a temporary arrangement. We'll all survive it if you do as you're told.'

'You can just focus on Kendra. No one wants me dead.'

He sighed. 'I'll be following orders.'

'Merchants aren't breaking in to kill other merchants.'

'Don't be naive. Anyone can get caught in the crossfire of this strange war we're stuck in.'

They were silent a moment.

'This is what comes of you showing up and playing the hero at last night's feast,' Lyndal said, unable to let the subject go. 'Perhaps if you hadn't been there she might have chosen someone else for the job.'

'By "playing the hero", do you mean *not* letting the king die? You do understand keeping him alive is my job, right?' When she did not reply, he added, 'It won't be me all the time. I do sleep occasionally.'

They rounded the corner of the corridor. Clearing her throat, she said, 'We should probably lay down some ground rules.'

When they reached her bedchamber door, he turned to her. '*You're* going to lay down some ground rules?'

She faced him, making herself as tall as possible. 'Yes.'

'Such as?'

She gestured between them. 'Such as giving me personal space when we're together.'

Exhaling, he took a small step back. 'I need to know where you are at all times. If you need to use the garderobe, you tell me or the defender on duty first.'

She crossed her arms in front of her. 'I really hope you're joking.'

'I never joke about garderobes.'

'I recall at least three jokes you've told over the previous year involving a garderobe.'

His lips turned up. 'Really? You remember all three?'

'Yes, vulgar punchlines forever burned into my mind.'

'Well, I never joke about my work. I won't tolerate sneaking off. Like it or not—'

'Not.'

He tilted his head. '*Like it or not,* you're stuck with me now. Let's just get through the next six weeks in a civil manner. I'll respect your privacy so long as you don't give me cause not to.'

She searched his eyes. 'Sounds reasonable.'

Astin reached past her and pushed the door open. 'In you go.'

Arms still crossed, she replied, 'I'll be sleeping in Kendra's bedchamber tonight. I only stopped here because you did.'

Grunting his annoyance, he reached past her again, tugging the door closed. They walked side by side past the solar door that connected the bedchambers and stopped in front of Kendra's room. He let her open the door herself this time.

'There will be a guard patrolling the corridor,' he said. 'If either of you need to step foot outside this room overnight, you speak with him first. I'll be here in the morning.'

'Six weeks,' she said as she walked through the door.

'Six weeks.'

CHAPTER 10

'What in God's name happened here last night?' Harlan asked, dropping onto the seat beside Astin.

The bodyguard looked up from his bowl. 'And good morning to you too.'

'"Absolute carnage" were my father's words.'

Astin looked around the mess hall to check no one else was listening. 'Didn't help that I was half-cooked when I became aware of the fact.'

Harlan watched him a moment. 'I'm glad you were nearby for Lyndal's sake. I was going to call on her but figured she needed some sleep after last night's festivities.'

Astin pushed his empty bowl aside and rose. 'I'm about to head there now.'

Harlan followed him out of the mess hall and into the morning fog. 'Now I have the fun job of telling Blake that people were slaughtered at the dinner her sister attended last night.'

'Shame I'm too busy to bear witness.'

'Warden tells me Queen Fayre requested Kendra and Lyndal remain here under your protection.'

'More fun news to pass on to your wife.' He tugged the hood of his cloak up. 'Did your father also tell you it was the king's idea? I saved his arse last night, and then five minutes later he's pretending he doesn't need me.'

'Probably wants you out of the way so he can conduct his shifty business with your stepfather.'

It was meant as a joke, but the thought had crossed Astin's mind.

'Just make sure that bruised ego of yours doesn't interfere with your new responsibilities,' Harlan said.

Astin stopped walking. '*Bruised ego?* Are you drunk?'

Harlan stopped a few paces ahead and turned. 'I know you. You don't handle rejection well.'

'One can't reject something that's not on offer.'

Harlan laughed. 'Admit it. It kills you that she doesn't swoon when you walk into a room like other women.'

'I'll admit it bothers me that she gets up and leaves.'

'Because you normally walk in and say something like "What happened to your hair?"'

'A joke.'

'And what about the time she was nice enough to cook you dinner and you asked if she dropped the pork into the salt bag?'

'Another joke.'

'It was quail, by the way.'

'I know it was quail. That's why it was funny.' He threw his hands up. 'Eda laughed.'

Harlan exhaled. '*That's* your comedic gauge? I once saw that girl use a decapitated chicken as a puppet.'

The youngest Suttone sister was not without her quirks.

'The point is,' Astin finished, 'Lyndal's hair is always immaculate, and she's a solid cook. I make jokes because we all know they're jokes.'

Before Harlan could reply, the warden called to him from ten feet away. 'Is there a reason you are out here with Wright instead of doing your job, Fletcher?'

Both men turned. Then Harlan looked back at Astin, waiting for his response.

'There's a guard patrolling the west corridor, sir,' Astin called. 'The ladies know not to leave their room without an escort.'

Shapur's scowl deepened. 'Is that why the Suttone girl is wandering around the castle by herself at present?'

Astin's blood heated a few degrees. 'Perhaps I wasn't clear last night when I gave *very specific instructions*. I'll go there now.'

Harlan looked down at the ground in an attempt to hide his growing smile.

'Perhaps a clearer conversation is in order,' Shapur replied before walking off.

'Yes, sir,' Astin called to his back.

The second he was out of earshot, Astin shoved Harlan. 'Don't you have new recruit arses to wipe?'

Harlan only laughed as he walked off in the direction of the training yard.

~

Wallis, the kitchen maid, blinked in confusion. 'You want the whole jar?'

Lyndal stepped past Wallis to where jars of fermented cabbage sat in a neat row on the bench. 'Four jars should be enough.'

'Enough for what, miss?'

'Yes, enough for what?' came a stern male voice.

Lyndal almost dropped one of the jars as she spun around to meet Astin's thunderous stare. She found a smile for him. 'Oh, there you are.'

'Here I am.' He crossed his arms, waiting for an explanation.

'I forgot to mention that I'm an early riser,' she said, placing the jar she was holding back on the bench.

'So am I' was his rather unhappy reply. 'If you wanted to visit the kitchen, you should have sent the defender on duty to fetch me, or at the very least had him accompany you.'

'To the kitchen for some cabbage? That seems a tad dramatic.'

Astin reached her in a few strides, his tall frame looming over her. She made a point of not stepping back.

'This castle was attacked a few hours ago.' His voice was a growl. 'I thought you were supposed to be the sensible sister.'

She was very aware of the height difference in that moment. 'I *am* the sensible sister.'

'Then follow the few simple rules in place for your safety.'

Conscious of Wallis frozen in place watching them, she said, 'If I apologise, can we move on?'

'Spare me the empty apology and just do as you're told next time.' He finally stepped back from her.

'Very well,' Lyndal mumbled as she turned away from his glare to face Wallis. 'Might you have a basket?'

The kitchen maid glanced nervously at Astin before walking to the other side of the room to fetch one.

The defender picked up one of the jars and turned it in his hands. 'The queen's carriage will be out front in half an hour. Where's Lady Kendra?'

'Dressing.' Lyndal took the jar from him and placed it in the basket. Looking down at her blue dress, she asked, 'What does one wear when accompanying the queen mother to visit the sick?'

He stared down at her, not speaking for an unsettling amount of time. 'Are you seriously asking me for fashion advice?'

Rolling her eyes, she brushed past him. 'Forget it.'

'Lyndal,' he called after her.

She stopped and turned back to him with a tired expression. He looked very uncomfortable suddenly.

'That dress is elegant and practical,' he said. 'It's a fine choice.'

The corners of her mouth lifted. 'Was that really so hard?'

Astin followed the carriage on horseback, through the gate and into the lazaretto borough, located in the heart of the kingdom. Kendra sat opposite Queen Fayre, discussing the dire food situation in Ireland, trying to sound worldly. The queen mother's silence was a solid indication the strategy was not working.

Lyndal was by the window, holding on to her basket of cabbage, seemingly tuned out of the conversation. Her gaze was fixed on the rows and rows of graves, many of them fresh in that part of the borough. He knew her father and brother were buried somewhere—as was his own father. He made a point of not looking, because the visual of his father's grave never seemed to get any easier.

'What do you think, Lyndal?' the queen mother asked, pulling her into the conversation.

Astin's eyes should have been on his surroundings, but he found himself watching for her reply instead. Her blonde hair was pinned back and threaded with blue ribbon. She played with the end of it as she stared at the queen blankly.

'We were discussing the loss of livestock in Ireland,' Kendra said, helping her out.

Lyndal nodded. 'Yes. Any loss of livestock is tragic. But at least without walls, the Irish are free to hunt and fish wherever they please.'

Astin wished he could have seen the queen's face after that response.

'The absence of walls makes it easy for thieves,' Kendra said, 'and is the reason their animals got sick in the first place.'

'And *yet*, I've not heard of one Irishman requesting a wall be built,' Lyndal replied.

'Because they do not know any better.'

Lyndal looked away. 'Or perhaps they've learned from our mistakes.'

Queen Fayre spoke up at that. 'What is the answer, then?'

Lyndal's eyes went to her. 'I think history has proven, quite definitively, that no one cares for the opinion of a merchant on this subject.'

'But you are not like them,' Kendra said. 'You are just as much one of us as you are one of them.'

Lyndal's eyes met Astin's, and he saw how much that statement pierced her. She might have had meat back on her bones and some nicer dresses, but he understood that every inch of that beating heart was merchant. She had lived in that borough her entire life. Starved, suffered, grieved in it. She wore the trauma of that existence like a crown of thorns.

Astin pushed his horse into a trot and rode ahead of the carriage and other guards, past the muddy gravesites, stopping at the leaning huts at the far end. They were more like shelters built for animals. Risk of harm to those in his charge was low, but he still treated every man, woman, and child he passed with the same suspicion he would when guarding the king.

Wasting people emerged from the huts, pale-faced and wary. Mothers held tightly to the hands of children, relaxing a little when they laid eyes on Queen Fayre. She represented hope for a broken system. Her timely return to Chadora had made her somewhat of a hero.

The queen mother was first to exit the carriage when it rolled to a stop. As she stepped down, her eyes moved along the line of people staring back at her. There was no hiding her shock at the conditions these people were living in. Kendra was next, taking one look at the sick, then anchoring her feet where she landed. Lyndal looked like any other noblewoman as she elegantly took the driver's hand and joined her cousin on the ground. The flash of shock on her face was quickly replaced with a convincing smile as she moved towards the merchants.

Astin gestured for Kendra to follow, and she reluctantly moved to his side, using him as a barrier between herself and the sick.

'You don't need to hover the *entire* visit,' Lyndal whispered at Astin over her shoulder.

Normally the breeze in the lazaretto borough carried the smell of death, but Lyndal's floral scent seemed to have taken over the air.

'That's the point of a guard,' he replied without looking at her.

She slowed her pace. 'Must you look so serious, then? You're scaring people.'

Now he looked at her. 'Good.'

The queen mother wandered the length of the line, bowing her head and pausing occasionally to speak with people. She managed to maintain a sensible distance without being obvious about the fact. Kendra tried to mimic her gestures, holding a smile that did not quite reach her eyes.

Then there was Lyndal.

She walked straight up to the woman at the end of the line, taking hold of her hand and asking questions. Then she pulled one of the jars out of her basket and handed it to her. 'Share it around. You only need a spoonful each morning. The symptoms should start to settle within a few days.'

'What on earth is she doing?' Kendra whispered to Astin. 'Some of these people are literally bleeding from the mouth, and she just marches up and touches them.'

Astin's eyes never left Lyndal. 'It's scurvy. It's not contagious.'

'We do not know that. The king has isolated them for a reason.'

Yes, because he's an idiot, Astin thought. He said nothing as he followed Lyndal along the line, watching as she took hold of icy hands, squeezing encouragingly as she chatted away.

Towards the end, she crouched in front of a young boy, brushing hair off his face. His eyes were bloodshot, his gums swollen and protruding from his mouth.

'I don't like cabbage,' the boy said, his cracked lips stained with blood.

Lyndal tilted her head. 'You know, I'm not very fond of it either, but it's going to help you get better.'

Her genuine desire to help these people had Astin squinting in the other direction for fear she would see the admiration on his face.

Lyndal handed the final jar to a young girl with red curls springing in all directions. Pulling the blue ribbon from her own hair, she combed the girl's hair back with her fingers and tied it.

'Mother usually brushes it,' the girl said.

Lyndal looked up at the woman standing behind her. 'Is that your mother?'

The woman gave her a sad smile. 'She's back in the borough. The defenders only took those with symptoms.'

Lyndal rose and turned to glare at Astin as if he had

personally torn the girl from her mother's arms. 'Did you know about this?'

'That they were separating the sick from the healthy? Yes.'

'That they were separating children from their parents for a disease that isn't even contagious?'

He drew a breath. 'I don't work in the merchant borough.'

'No, you're just friends with all the men who do.' She let out a frustrated breath. 'Am I the only one who has a problem with this?'

Queen Fayre looked in her direction, then wandered over. 'What problem is that?'

Lyndal's feet shuffled. 'There are children here without family, Your Majesty.'

The queen mother looked to the woman standing behind the girl. 'Is this not your daughter?'

'No, Your Majesty.'

Fayre stared down at the small girl. 'How many children are here without family?'

'Four.'

Clearing her throat and straightening, Lyndal said, 'Your Majesty, I'd like to request that these children, who clearly have scurvy, be returned to their families.'

The queen watched her calmly. 'You mean the children who my son, your king, requested be removed and placed in isolation?'

'Isolation for *scurvy*. Sure, the symptoms are a little more confronting, but that's what comes of famine stretching on, year after year. Most merchants get it at some point. At fifteen my joint pain and fatigue were so bad I couldn't get out of bed. No one came to take me away. I was eventually cured by carrots.'

Kendra wore a look of horror. 'Father never told me you had *scurvy*.'

'Needless to say, the carrots did not come from him,' Lyndal said before returning her attention to the queen mother. 'These children don't need to be locked in with the dead. They need small amounts of the right foods—and their own mothers combing their hair.'

The sharp edge in her tone had Kendra looking nervously between the two women. 'Perhaps we should discuss this later,' she said lightly. 'Let the queen mother fulfil her obligations here.'

No one moved.

Astin was used to standing still and silent during tense moments, but he had a strong urge to speak up on Lyndal's behalf. The pained plea in her eyes made him look at the ground. It was the same look his sister had whenever she was forced to visit him.

Queen Fayre did not appear angered by the outburst but rather fascinated. 'You know, there is such a thing as being too honest.'

Lyndal released the breath she was holding. 'I apologise for the outburst, but for some, family is the only thing they have left. Must the king take that from them too?'

A tight laugh came from Kendra. 'I think we can all agree honesty is an admirable quality, but let us keep that honesty on a nice tight leash, shall we?'

Lyndal stepped forwards. 'And why are there walls for this borough at all? Why must we seek permission to bury loved ones? To visit their graves? Surely King Borin is happy to relinquish control once a person is dead.'

Before Queen Fayre could respond, Kendra walked over and took Lyndal by the shoulders. 'While you have made some very sincere points, I think we should—'

'In fact, I would like to request that all these people standing before you be allowed to leave,' Lyndal said, shrugging free of her cousin's grip. 'Simpler still to just put an end to the insanity. They're quite capable of isolating themselves if they truly believe they're a risk to their families.'

'Are you finished?' Queen Fayre asked, her tone even.

Kendra's lips were pressed together so tightly at that point that all colour had left them.

'Yes,' Lyndal said, her voice catching as her head caught up with the words that had tumbled out of her. 'I think that covers all the… relevant points.'

The queen turned to one of her guards. 'Have a physician brought in. If he can confirm that these people are not contagious, they are free to return to the borough. Say nothing to the king until I have spoken to him.'

Kendra looked heavenwards, releasing the breath she had been holding. The merchants were all staring at Lyndal as though she were a goddess sent to save them. For all Astin knew, maybe she was.

'Your Majesty,' Lyndal began, 'I—'

Fayre raised a hand, cutting her off. 'I came here to see the situation for myself. I always intended to send the merchants home if there was no need for them to be here.' A coy smile appeared on her face. 'But the cabbage was a nice touch,' she said as she stepped between the girls and headed for the carriage.

Laughter rose up Astin's throat, but because he was on duty, he swallowed it down and bit back the accompanying grin.

'Oh my goodness,' Kendra muttered, head shaking as she followed the queen.

Lyndal stared after them, her face slack. 'Not a word, defender,' she warned.

He raised his hands. 'I believe you've said enough for all of us.'

She cast a venomous look in his direction before dragging her feet all the way to the carriage.

CHAPTER 11

*L*yndal stepped out into the corridor and pulled the door closed behind her. 'Pig's in labour?'

'We've been over this,' Astin said from behind Harlan. 'It's a boar.'

'A boar the girls named Pig,' Harlan said.

Astin muttered something Lyndal chose to ignore. 'I really wanted to be there for the birth. Do you suppose I would be allowed to return home for a few hours? I could be back before dinner tonight.'

Harlan was already backing away from the conversation. 'You're going to have to ask your bodyguard about that. I've passed on the message, so my job's done.'

'Coward,' Astin said.

The commander made a crude gesture over his shoulder before strolling off down the corridor.

'Perhaps you could find a reason for us to leave?' Lyndal asked Astin, eyes pleading. 'Please. These boarlets are very important.'

He looked back at her with scepticism. 'I know for a

fact that Wright House has enough food to sustain your family.'

'The boarlets are not for us. They'll go to merchant families in need.'

Astin's resigned expression gave her hope.

He drew a long breath and said, 'You do not leave this room. Understand?'

'I swear before Belenus.'

Lyndal returned inside her bedchamber, pacing the length of the room and wondering what to do about Kendra. She knew her cousin would much prefer to remain at Eldon Castle than watch a boar give birth.

It was thirty minutes later when there was a knock at the door. She rushed to answer it, and Astin's eyes moved over her.

'You already have your cloak on,' he said.

'I'm a very optimistic person.'

He sighed. 'Horses are waiting out front.'

She clapped her hands together. 'I just need to speak with Kendra and—'

'Your cousin is playing chess with the queen,' Astin said. 'She will remain there for the afternoon. And if anyone asks, it was a family emergency of a private nature.'

Lyndal lifted her brows. 'Clever.' She pulled the door shut behind her. 'Not only will I be there for the birth, but I'll also get to see my family.'

His eyes searched hers a moment before stepping aside. 'I hope you can ride.'

'Of course I can ride. We owned a horse once, you know. Before the nobility wall went up.'

'So you were all of three years old?'

She jabbed him with her elbow. 'Ten, actually.'

Astin straightened when he caught sight of something up ahead. Lyndal followed his gaze to where a maid was walking towards them. The pretty young woman smiled up at him as they passed. 'Defender.'

Astin nodded a greeting but said nothing.

When they rounded the corner, Lyndal grinned up at him. 'Quite the man around these parts, aren't you?'

Astin gave her a blank look. 'I've no idea what you're talking about.'

'I've heard all about your little escapades within the castle.'

His eyebrows came together. 'And where would you have heard about such things?'

She shrugged. 'Blake, of course. There really isn't much that doesn't make its way to me eventually.'

Astin's jaw ticked with annoyance.

'Don't worry,' she assured him. 'Your secret is quite safe with me—for now.'

Astin shook his head. 'You have no idea what you're talking about.' When she glanced over her shoulder, he clicked his fingers in front of her face. 'Eyes forwards.'

She looked up at him instead. 'Is that your type?'

'What?'

'She's obviously very pretty.'

'I'm not talking about this with you.'

'And very... dark-haired.'

He quirked an eyebrow at her. 'So?'

'So I wonder if that's a preference.'

He watched her a moment. 'You're asking if I like brunettes?'

Her ears burned now. 'Never mind.'

'Yes,' he replied without hesitating.

She felt a bit winded by that response.

'And women with black hair. And redheads. And every shade in between. I don't care about hair colour.'

She noticed he did not say blondes. 'Oh, well, good to have options, I suppose.'

His gaze slid to her. 'Now that we're both thoroughly uncomfortable, can we never speak of this again?'

She nodded and fell silent.

Out front, two horses stood saddled and waiting. As Lyndal was preparing to mount, hands landed on her waist, gripping in a way that made her throat close. She did not have to look over her shoulder to know it was Astin. Then he was walking away before she had even landed in the saddle. She watched him mount and adjust his reins before looking in her direction.

'Ready?' he asked in the tone of a man doing his job.

Her gaze fell to her own horse. 'Ready.'

The moment they stopped their horses out front of Wright House, Blake appeared from around the side, arms open. 'You are the proud owner of two boarlets so far.'

Lyndal hugged her sister so tightly Astin thought he heard bones creak. Her eyes pressed shut before she released her sister. 'Be honest. On a scale of one to ten, how bad has the pining been within the house?'

Blake laughed. 'It's only been a few days. Though I was ready to steal you back when Harlan told me about the feast.' Her eyes went to Astin. 'Lucky you now have a tall, strapping bodyguard to keep you safe.'

'Yes, lucky me,' Lyndal said dryly. She was distracted by the sight of the family's duck racing towards her. 'Oh, hello, Miss Garlic.' She scooped the duck up in her arms, kissing its face. 'At least someone has missed me.'

'I never said I didn't miss you.' Blake looked at Astin again. 'Has she been unbearable?'

'Don't ask him that,' Lyndal said. 'He doesn't need further encouragement to wound me. He's quite capable of taking a knife to my feelings without prompts.'

Her words prickled over Astin's skin. 'When have I ever taken a knife to your feelings?'

'At my uncle's house recently you asked me to test food for poison.'

Blake sighed. 'I'm sure he was joking.'

'Of course I was joking.' Harlan's words came back to him, slapping him in the face. 'I'd never let you near the food if I thought there was the slightest chance it had been meddled with.'

'He's only saying that to appease *you*,' Lyndal said as she placed Garlic on the ground.

Astin made a mental note to reduce the severity of his jokes, since she did indeed appear to be taking them to heart.

'Lyndal!'

Everyone looked in the direction of the house as Candace rushed out to greet her daughter.

'What are you doing here?' she asked, kissing both of

Lyndal's cheeks.

Once upon a time, Astin's mother had shown that level of affection to her children. When his father was still alive. Cooper had done a proper job of blowing up family relationships when he arrived on the scene.

'Eda is at the shop,' Candace said. 'How long are you staying?'

Lyndal's disappointment was palpable. 'Not long, unfortunately.'

'We are more than happy to spare you,' Candace said, 'given all the good you have done in only a few days.'

Lyndal appeared confused. 'What on earth are you talking about? What good?'

'You don't have to play modest,' Blake said. 'We know all about your little speech in the lazaretto borough. The merchants have spoken of nothing else since you demanded their release.'

Lyndal blinked. 'Oh, that.'

'Yes, that,' Candace said, frowning. 'It was very brave.'

'Except that Queen Fayre intended to send them home anyway, so I could have saved my breath.'

Blake took hold of her hands. 'We're not praising you for the outcome. We're proud of you for speaking up at all. Queen Fayre is rather intimidating, and I had no idea you were so rebellious.'

'Her headstrong personality and opinionated tendencies weren't a clue?' Astin asked.

All three women turned to look at him.

'You do yourself no favours,' Blake said to him as she pulled her sister away. 'Ignore him and come, before you miss the birth entirely.'

Astin kept his eyes down as he passed Candace's disapproving stare. He followed the sisters around back to the pigpen, which had been newly reinforced to hold a boar.

Wood shavings were laid out in place of straw, which had long ago become a rarity. Lyndal dropped down beside the labouring boar without a thought to her dress, stroking its back as she watched the three suckling boarlets.

'And now there are three,' Blake said. 'They know exactly where to go when they come out. It's quite fascinating to watch.'

Lyndal reached out to touch one of the stripy boarlets. 'How are they so adorable?'

The mother twitched, head lifting off the ground, and out slipped another one.

'Clever girl,' Lyndal said, peering down at the slippery animal.

Astin found himself watching Lyndal's face in place of the birth. She was in awe of this wild animal, and her childlike excitement warmed his insides.

'Here comes another one,' Blake said.

Lyndal picked up the nearby towel and gently wiped at the boarlet still struggling to get up. It eventually toddled off in search of a teat.

'I heard they can have up to twelve babies,' Lyndal said as the animal twitched and squirmed once more.

Out came another boarlet.

'That's number six.' She wiped at it with the towel a few times when it did not move. 'This one doesn't appear to be breathing.'

Taking the towel from Lyndal, Astin picked up the boarlet and held it in his open palm, rubbing it vigorously with the towel. Still it showed no life, so he began pressing lightly on its chest. The girls watched on with worried expressions, until finally it began to wriggle and squeal.

'Oh, thank goodness,' Lyndal said, taking it from him. 'How did you know what to do?'

'I'd be more surprised if he didn't know what to do,' Blake said, 'given he was raised in the farming borough.'

Lyndal looked at her sister, brow pinched. 'What? Since when?'

'Since I was born and raised in the farming borough,' Astin said.

Lyndal's mouth hung open. 'But you're a defender. Defenders are selected from among the nobility.'

'You're a merchant living in the nobility borough,' he replied. 'Sometimes the rules just don't apply.'

She closed her mouth. 'I'm just surprised you never mentioned the fact.'

'You never asked.'

'And you do have a tendency to block out his voice when he speaks,' Blake said, a smile playing on her lips.

Lyndal continued to stare at Astin like she had no idea who he was suddenly. 'And what about your family?'

'Also farmers, if that's what you're asking,' Astin said.

She drew a breath. 'I mean are they alive? Do you have siblings?'

Reading his discomfort, Blake answered on his behalf. 'There's a sister, a half-sister, a mother, and a stepfather we're not supposed to mention.'

'So not an orphan,' Lyndal said.

'What made you think I was an orphan?' Astin asked.

'*You.* You made me think that. You and your life, and your… your lack of family. Every meal eaten here instead of in the farming borough made me think that.'

'Perhaps it has something to do with the stepfather we're not supposed to talk about,' Blake whispered.

'Here comes another one,' Astin said, grateful for the distraction.

Two more boarlets arrived in quick succession, bringing the total to eight. They waited for more, and when none came, the three of them sat watching them. After feeding, the boarlets all fell asleep, stacked neatly in a row. Garlic wandered over and jumped up onto Blake's lap, eyeing the new additions. Lyndal was leaning forwards, unable to stop touching the new arrivals.

'So much cuteness,' she said quietly. 'Have you ever seen anything so beautiful?'

Astin was no longer looking at the boarlets. He was watching her. 'No,' he said before looking away. His gaze met Blake's in the process. Those sharp eyes of hers did not miss much. Standing, he brushed wood shavings off his trousers. 'It's time to go. Say goodbye and meet me at the horses.'

Lyndal appeared taken aback by the abrupt departure. 'That's awfully trusting of you. Shouldn't you frisk Blake before leaving?'

'And have Harlan beat me to a pulp when he learns of it later?' he replied. 'No, thanks.' He nodded a farewell at Blake before turning away. 'Don't be long.'

CHAPTER 12

The next week passed in a blur of social gatherings and chess matches. Then suddenly they were six days out from the Solar Festival, having more conversations about dresses than Lyndal could stomach.

'What do you think of this one?' Kendra asked Lyndal. 'Too yellow?'

'We're celebrating Belenus,' Lyndal replied. 'There's no such thing as too yellow when it comes to sun gods.'

She was saved by a knock at the door, yet another invitation to play chess on the terrace. By the time the women left their quarters the rain fell heavy. Lyndal expected the gathering to be moved indoors, but when they arrived, she found Queen Fayre and the king seated comfortably beneath umbrellas the size of wagons. Servants held the umbrellas in place, blinking against the rain pounding their faces.

'Dear God,' Lyndal whispered to Kendra as they remained tucked in the doorway, taking in the scene.

Kendra pointed. 'Oh, look. Here come some more umbrellas. We will be fine.'

'We will, but what about the poor servants holding them?' She looked over her shoulder at Astin, whose expression matched her own. 'This is insanity,' she mouthed.

He stepped out into the weather without saying a word, taking his usual position against the wall. At least he was mostly under cover there. Kendra and Lyndal had no choice but to move beneath the waiting umbrellas and join the royal family for chess.

'Lyndal, you can play me,' Queen Fayre said, gesturing to the seat opposite.

Lyndal took a seat, the umbrella moving with her, then watched as Kendra floated over to the table where the king waited. Her cousin curtsied, said something that made him smile, then lowered herself elegantly into the chair opposite him.

'I know it is wet,' Queen Fayre said, reading her mind, 'but fresh air is very important.'

Lyndal snuck a look over her shoulder and found Astin watching her. It was comforting knowing there was one other sane person on that terrace. 'I believe it's your turn to go first,' she said as she faced forwards again.

'I believe you are right.'

They played to a chorus of rain splattering around them, her cousin's delicate laughter occasionally drifting in their direction. It seemed every word the king uttered amused her. There were sure signs of attraction from both parties. Lyndal could see it in the way he leaned in when he spoke, the way his eyes fell to Kendra's mouth when she replied.

'Checkmate,' Fayre said, sitting back.

Lyndal's eyes snapped back to the board, and sure enough, she had lost—again. She had yet to beat the queen mother, and it was not because she was letting her win.

'Time to change players,' Fayre said, waving her hand. 'You can switch seats with Lady Kendra.'

Lyndal glanced at Borin, who appeared annoyed by the suggestion. 'His Majesty seems quite happy with his current opponent.'

'Mother thinks you might have some magical ideas about how to win the merchants over prior to the festival,' the king said. 'She is putting you in front of me in hope that we discuss it.'

'Oh.' Lyndal did not move.

'I thought a flag parade might cheer everyone up.' The king was practically shouting to compete with the noise of the rain. 'Cheer people up.'

A flag parade? The merchants did not need cheering up, they needed food. 'A flag parade is one idea,' Lyndal replied.

'Off you go,' Fayre said, dismissing her.

Lyndal hesitantly rose from her chair. The servant holding the umbrella moved with her, his arm trembling from holding it up for so long. She glanced apologetically at him.

'Tell the king some of your ideas,' Queen Fayre said as she fixed the chess pieces.

Kendra and Lyndal exchanged a confused look as they passed one another.

'A flag parade is very patriotic,' Kendra called as she took a seat.

Lyndal wished Astin could hear the conversation. He would surely find the idea of a flag parade as ridiculous as she did.

'What about community garden beds?' Lyndal said as she moved her pawn.

The king cast a tired look at his mother.

'Hear her out,' Fayre said without looking at him.

Borin exhaled through his nose. 'Go on, then. Tell us about these garden beds.'

On the plus side, if he hated her suggestion, he might never speak to her again.

'There's a strip of land between the shops and the forest line. It gets plenty of light, but the grass has died. Now it's just a long stretch of mud with a few stepping stones to navigate it.' She took her next turn. 'There's plenty of room for some raised garden beds that could be easily maintained by the merchants.'

The queen mother looked in her direction. 'What has prevented the merchants from doing something with the space themselves? Lack of materials?'

'A lack of quality soil. With no animal manure or food scraps to speak of, there's no way to improve the quality of what's there.'

King Borin leaned back in his chair, regarding her. 'Nothing would make it to maturity. It would be snatched by the first greedy merchant to lay eyes on it. Or perhaps you expect me to provide defenders to guard the gardens?'

Irritation pulsed through Lyndal as she stared at him.

'True, there may be problems initially until people get used to the idea of regular food. But that's not for you to manage. The merchants are more than capable of dealing with it. We're quite self-sufficient when given the opportunity.'

The king watched her for the longest time. 'Do you honestly expect me to believe that if I supply some horse shit and a bit of soil, the merchants will change their opinion of me?'

She shook her head. 'No. It'll take a lot more than that. It'll take consistent acts that demonstrate you understand their situation and wish to help. You can't just deliver some materials and make some empty speech. You need to show up in a meaningful way.' She paused. 'Plant vegetables that will help with the scurvy problem they're facing. They'll not forget it.'

Borin leaned forwards in his chair. 'Feels a lot like grovelling.'

'It's not grovelling.'

'A peace offering, then,' he said, waving away her retort.

Lyndal's eyes met Fayre's, and the queen mother gave her an encouraging nod. She drew a breath. 'You know, a flag parade would be a splendid way to finish. You could be first to turn the soil, then lead the parade through the village.'

That got the king's interest. 'I shall consider the idea.' He tapped the board, making the pieces rattle. 'It is your move.'

Lyndal pushed her castle to the far end of the board, then glanced at Queen Fayre. The faintest of smiles played on the queen mother's lips. She nodded her approval before turning her attention to her game.

Astin stepped inside King Borin's quarters and bowed. 'You wanted to see me, Your Majesty?'

Borin held his arms out while a servant buttoned his silk tunic. 'Yes. Come in.' He shooed the servant away when he was done and turned to face Astin. 'I shall be heading into the merchant borough tomorrow to open a garden and will lead the flag parade afterwards. I have asked the warden to prepare the borough and ensure it is safe.' He turned to the mirror. 'I would like Lady Kendra and her cousin to accompany me for the event. Lady Kendra for her company and Lyndal for her newfound popularity within the borough. Turns out the peasants are rather fond of her. She can be my human shield, if you will.'

Astin's eyebrows came together in a hard line. 'I beg your pardon?'

Borin met his eyes in the glass. 'Relax, Fletcher. No one will be shooting arrows at me with her planted at my side. I can see you are still upset with me for assigning you to the women.'

'Not at all.'

'If you truly desire to be back in my service, all you need do is ask.'

Astin drew a breath. 'I'd prefer to follow orders, Your Majesty. I'll consult directly with the warden about the safest way to proceed.'

'Do not fret about me. The warden has assured me I will be quite safe with what he has planned.'

Astin's gaze fell to the ground. 'While that's a relief indeed, my focus is on the ladies under my protection.'

Borin waved a hand. 'I cannot foresee any issues with my best guard on the job.'

'Is that all, Your Majesty?' Astin asked, impatient to flee.

'Actually, there was another matter I wanted to discuss.' Borin turned once more and extended a hand for the servant to slip rings on. 'It is regarding Lyndal.'

That got Astin's full attention. 'Yes?'

'Pretty thing. Dull in conversation, however.'

Astin scraped his teeth over his lower lip and waited.

'I wish to know if her virtue is intact,' Borin said, lifting his jewelled hand and admiring it. 'I imagine she has been on her best behaviour since arriving here, but every woman has a past. Wright should be able to speak on the subject, though if I went to him directly, I doubt he would be very forthcoming given our history.'

Astin reminded himself to breathe. 'Why?' The word came out choked, prompting Borin to look in his direction.

'What do you mean, *why?*'

'What do you need that information for?'

Borin straightened and stared at him. 'Because I wish to know. A king is not required to explain himself to anyone.'

Astin wet his lips and glanced at the window. 'Lyndal is a lady in every sense of the word. To question that does her a dishonour.'

Borin took a step in his direction. 'What is the matter with you? I have asked something of you, and still you stand here. You are dismissed, defender.'

He knew his time was up when the king addressed him as 'defender'. Bowing his head, he left the room.

~

'He just keeps getting better,' Astin told Harlan.

They were standing at the edge of the training yard, watching Roul Thornton fight.

'He'll be warden before we know it,' Harlan said, turning to Astin. He looked him up and down. 'What's wrong with you? You look like a kicked puppy. Where are the girls?'

'Safely with the queen mother on the terrace. I've just been to see the king.'

'Ah. So you're pissed off at the king. What did he do now?'

Astin's mouth soured. 'He was asking about Lyndal's… history.'

A confused look came over Harlan's face. 'What history?'

Astin met his gaze, and Harlan's features hardened in response.

'He seriously asked you if she was a virgin?'

Astin nodded.

'I thought you said Kendra holds his interest,' Harlan said.

'She does. I've watched him closely with both women. He tolerates Lyndal's company at best.'

The commander's gaze shifted to the castle. 'So I don't have to worry about him taking her as a mistress?'

Just hearing the word 'mistress' in a sentence where she was the subject had Astin's feet shuffling. It should not have mattered to him either way, but apparently his protection of her was not purely duty related. Too much time spent together—that was the problem. Now he was behaving like an overprotective... brother? Friend? Any feelings beyond that were impractical and dangerous.

'The queen mother is probably thinking about suitors,' Harlan said. 'She's taken with Lyndal and probably wants to be of help in that regard.'

Astin watched as Roul disarmed a recruit in two moves. 'I doubt Lyndal will be interested in any man the queen mother recommends.'

'What makes you say that?'

He shrugged. 'She seems like the kind of woman who wants to pick her own husband.'

Harlan chuckled.

'What's so funny?'

Harlan's gaze slid to Astin. 'You. Jealous.'

'Here we go.' Though Astin wondered if the sensation resembling a stomach full of lead was indeed jealousy.

Roul was pairing the recruits up to spar and gestured to Harlan.

'I'm needed,' the commander said. 'Tell the king what you must to keep your head and nothing more. And pray Queen Fayre is playing matchmaker. That's better than any agenda the king might have.'

Shit. It did feel a lot like jealousy. It was climbing his throat and heating his palms. He was in big trouble if it turned out he had feelings for the woman he had spent the previous year tormenting. And Harlan would hang him from the nearest tree if he ever did anything to ruin her chances of finding happiness—and she deserved that happiness.

Pushing every rising feeling down to the pit of his stomach, he put on his defender face and headed for the castle.

CHAPTER 13

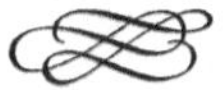

The merchants' expressions ranged from curious to pure hatred. Not only did they not forgive the king standing on the edge of the newly built garden bed, a shovel loaded with manure in hand, but many wished him dead.

'Let Prince Becket step up and have a go at leading us,' Astin had overheard men say at the taverns. 'He can't do any worse than the arse currently sitting on the throne.'

Becket might have been a viable option if he had shown any interest in the role at all. The fact that he fled Chadora the day after the coronation showed he wanted no part in any of it.

'I hope to see flourishing garden beds next time I visit,' the king continued, trying not to draw breath.

It was oddly satisfying seeing him press his nose to his shoulder every few moments to manage the smell.

He coughed. 'Cabbages the size of heads.'

The problem with that visual was that a decapitated head currently sat on a pike in the square. The merchant man had been caught atop the farming wall and had managed to kill two defenders before being caught.

Astin noticed Lyndal look down at her feet, no doubt thinking the same thing he was. He found himself doing that a lot. Someone would say or do something, and he would look to her for a reaction. Sometimes she met his gaze, sharing her private thoughts without speaking a word.

To King Borin's credit, he did actually place the manure into the garden and turn the soil over it—sort of. He then wandered between the new garden beds, feigning interest and deflecting questions about when more meat would be coming.

Queen Fayre wandered also, stopping to have the conversations her son was fleeing from. Her gaze always drifted though. To the wasting faces watching her. To her oblivious son. To Kendra, who stood balanced on a stepping stone, trying to keep her shoes clean. And to Lyndal, who walked through the mud without a second thought to her shoes or the hem of her dress. She was completely at home digging and planting alongside the other merchants. At one point she even handed out cups of water to the men doing the labour. Then she called the children over to help with the planting, telling them they were all responsible for keeping the garden alive.

'You can't pick vegetables until they're ready to be eaten, no matter how hungry you are,' she said as she pushed seeds into the dirt with her bare finger. 'And do you remember what you do after you pick them?'

'Replace what you take so more can grow,' said one of the girls.

Lyndal leaned down, touching her nose to the girl's. 'Clever girl.' She straightened and looked around. 'Now, I need some muscle for this next part.'

A boy stepped forwards, around five years of age judging by his height. 'I'm strong.'

'Excellent,' Lyndal said, handing him a pail. 'I need some more water from the well.'

All the while, the queen mother watched on, her expression stoic and unreadable.

When it was time for the flag parade, the king mounted his horse, looking like he was about to ride off to war. The merchants moved to the main street in preparation.

'Would you mind if I stayed here and finished the planting?' Lyndal asked Queen Fayre. 'It won't take long.'

Fayre glanced over her shoulder at her son, then turned to Astin. 'Take Lady Lyndal back to the castle as soon as she is done. Lady Kendra will accompany me.'

Lady Lyndal? Every merchant within hearing range looked in their direction, no doubt as surprised by the formal address as he was.

'Yes, Your Majesty,' Astin said.

When Queen Fayre was out of earshot, Lyndal leaned in and whispered, *'Lady Lyndal?* I'm glad the nobility weren't present for that blasphemous address. They might have thrown rocks at me.'

Astin took a step back from her. 'They'd have likely had their servants do it for them.'

'What was that?' she asked, angling her head.

'What?'

She pointed to his feet. 'That. Stepping back from me like I'm a leper.'

'You're covered in dirt and shit,' he said.

She let out a noisy breath. 'You've been in a foul mood all day.'

'Are you gardening or chatting? You'll have to return to the castle at some point, you know.'

The hurt in those jungle green eyes of hers made him want to take a fist to his own face. Bending, he picked up the small shovel and handed it to her. 'Sorry.'

'And I'm sorry you're stuck here with me.'

'It's not that. I'm just tired.'

Her eyes moved over him. 'Well, I won't be long. Then you can go take a long nap.'

'A nap, you think?' He shook his head and went back to standing guard while she dug away in his peripheral vision. After a few minutes, she began to hum to herself, and his eyes were drawn to her once more. She was always a pretty thing to watch, but happy was hard to look away from.

Straightening, Lyndal went to move to another part of the garden, but her heel slipped off the stepping stone. Astin could not get there in time. Down she went, her arm collecting the edge of the garden bed as she fell.

He was pulling her to her feet a moment later, eyes moving over her. 'You hurt?'

She began laughing. *Laughing.*

'Oh my goodness.' She wiped at her eye. 'My sisters are going to be *so* disappointed they missed that.'

He noticed a tear in the sleeve of her dress and took hold of her elbow. 'You're bleeding.'

'I am?' She was still laughing as she inspected it. 'It's only a scratch.'

Unbuttoning her sleeve, he slid it up her arm to see for himself. 'It's not a scratch.' He pressed a hand over it to stop the bleeding. 'Stop laughing.'

That only made her laugh harder. 'Stop. You'll dirty your uniform.'

He held tightly to her. 'Blood goes with the job.'

She took a few calming breaths. 'That's actually really sad.' Then she burst out laughing again. 'I'm so sorry. I don't know what's wrong with me.'

He sat her on the edge of the garden bed, waiting a good five minutes for her to finish laughing. 'You done?' he asked when she finally fell silent.

She let out an enormous breath and looked down at the bloodied hand covering her arm. 'I think so.' Her expression turned serious. 'I think I really miss them.'

He did not have to ask who she was talking about. He had witnessed the close relationship with her sisters first-hand.

Reaching inside his cloak, he pulled out a ball of fabric.

'You carry that around just in case?' she asked.

He began wrapping her arm. 'You'd be surprised how often we need medical supplies.'

'Would I though?'

A smile flickered on his face. When he was done bandaging the arm, he said, 'A few more weeks, and then you'll be home with your sisters. They can laugh at you then.'

Her expression softened. 'Honestly, I thought *you* would be first to laugh.'

'Not when it's my job to return you to the castle in one piece.' He pulled her to her feet by her good arm, keeping hold of her until he was sure she was steady.

'In the meantime, I have Kendra to lecture me and you to boss me around.'

His eyes moved between hers, and then he let go of her arm. 'Time to go.'

'But I'm not fin—'

'You're finished.'

She opened her mouth to argue, then closed it again. 'Can we at least go by the shop and see if anyone is there?'

'No.'

'Why not?'

He looked heavenwards. 'Because my orders are to escort you back to Eldon Castle when you're done.'

'But Queen Fayre doesn't know I'm done.'

He gestured for her to start walking. 'There's a flag parade going straight past the shop. Someone will see you.'

'So?' She did not move.

'So the woman has a firm grasp on your future, and she's expecting you to play by her rules.'

'Would it kill you to speak kindly to me? You're the closest thing I have to a friend right now.'

His lungs stilled. 'I know it might not seem like it, but this is me looking out for you. You need to keep Queen Fayre onside. She's the only friend who matters right now. Trust me.'

She stared at him for the longest time. 'All right. I trust you.'

CHAPTER 14

stin knocked on Kendra's bedchamber door—for the third time. The royal carriage had already departed, and Kendra and Lyndal were supposed to be in the carriage behind it.

Drawing a long breath, he called, 'Breaking down the door in three, two—'

The door swung open, and he was blinded by glinting jewels and bright yellow fabric.

'Really, Fletcher,' Kendra said. 'Have you no patience? This is my chance to truly capture the king's attention. I am hardly going to rush the process.' She stepped past him and wandered to the other side of the corridor.

He swore under his breath and turned back to the room, ready to drag Lyndal from it, then froze when he found her standing in the doorway. She wore an off-the-shoulder gown the colour of the sky as the sun sinks below the horizon. It was a colour he remembered from his youth. Pink and orange, all at once. The bodice moulded to her waist, embroidered with silver thread that resembled light reflecting off the water. The skirt fell in a way that drew his eye all the way down.

'I had planned to wear something else,' Lyndal said, looking down at the dress. 'But the queen sent this to my bedchamber, no doubt fearing I would embarrass her in my common clothes.'

Thank God she was talking, because Astin had lost his ability to speak. A single glance had siphoned the air from his lungs. She was the ultimate offering to Belenus. If the sun did not break through the clouds the moment she stepped outside, then he would fall down from shock.

'You hate it,' she said. 'It's too much, isn't it?' She waited for him to respond.

'You look…' He just had to pick a word. One more word. Any word would do at that point. 'Ready.'

Her eyebrows rose slightly. 'I look… ready?'

'Ready to leave.'

Something resembling disappointment passed over her face. 'Good. I am ready to leave.' She ran a hand over her neat hair, which was pulled back and tucked at the neck. Then she touched a finger to the corner of her painted mouth. 'Let's go.'

He gestured for her to walk ahead, then immediately regretted it when he saw her from behind. The dress was cut low, her shoulders and upper back on display. And whatever soap she had washed with that morning lingered in his path, causing his body to soldier up in all the wrong ways.

He was really going to have to pull himself together in order to do his job.

After loading the women into the waiting carriage,

they made their way to the gate, Astin following on foot. The portcullis rose on their approach, and the party passed beneath the archway into the farming borough, following the road all the way to the square located in the centre of the borough.

Celebrations were well underway by the time they arrived. Soggy red banners hung high above the crowd, the festive music competing with the buzz of conversation and laughter. Some were already dancing while others took advantage of the break in the rain, sitting with plates of black bread and oil balanced on their laps. A queue for ale ran adjacent with the crowd of farmers and merchants. The nobility were gathered in a separate section enclosed by heavy red rope.

A young merchant man approached the carriage as it rolled to a stop, a wide grin on his face as he eyed Lyndal. 'My, my. Haven't we moved up in the world?'

Astin stepped in front of the man. 'That's far enough.'

'It's quite all right,' Lyndal said, a hand landing on Astin's arm. 'Egbert is an old friend.'

'Don't you mean jilted lover?' he retorted.

Astin stiffened.

'Ignore him,' Lyndal said.

'Oh, I remember you,' Kendra said, stepping up beside her cousin. 'You are that belt maker who came to the house last year and asked for Lyndal's hand.' She looked to Astin. 'Father thought she could do much better.'

Egbert frowned. 'Ouch.'

'And now you're happily married,' Lyndal said. 'How is your wife?'

Astin continued to watch him.

'She's good. You should come for a dance later, for old times' sake.'

Kendra laughed. 'That is hardly appropriate.'

'Let's see how the day progresses,' she said, her tone apologetic.

Kendra threaded her arm through Lyndal's and began dragging her towards the nobility.

'If you see my sisters,' Lyndal called over her shoulder, 'will you tell them I'm here?'

Egbert gave her a wave before joining the ale queue. Astin threw a warning stare at him, then followed the women.

'It is very important that we position ourselves in sight of the king,' Kendra whispered to her cousin. But Lyndal was barely listening, her head turned in the direction of the dancing merchants.

Astin had seen her dance at the festival the year before. Her dress might not have been as impressive, but her smile always drew plenty of attention. He had watched her from across the rope, partly because Harlan had asked him to keep an eye on the Suttone sisters, but also because she was hard to look away from.

'Smile,' Kendra sang, nudging Lyndal in the ribs. 'Queen Fayre is looking in our direction.'

The queen mother might have been looking in their direction, but her eyes were on Lyndal.

'Behave,' Astin told the women. 'No one's to leave this area without telling me.'

Lyndal turned with a look of surprise. 'Are you not going to follow at our heel?'

'Do I look like a dog?'

She tilted her head. 'Is that a trick question?'

His eyes fell to her smart mouth. 'Behave.'

She lifted her shoulders in an adorable shrug before she was dragged off once more.

He watched from the rope boundary as they made their way over to Queen Fayre. After a few minutes of conversation, the queen mother slipped her arm through Lyndal's and led her away. She introduced her to Lady Petula, whose body language did not match the pleasantries coming from her mouth. The Lady of Sulgrave House was looking Lyndal up and down as though she were a mangy dog.

Appearing lost, Kendra eventually went in search of her parents. The three of them stood speaking in hushed voices, eyes drifting in the direction of the king, who was surrounded by bodyguards.

Astin turned his attention back to Queen Fayre and Lyndal, only to find that Lyndal was no longer there. His eyes darted between faces, searching for her. When he did not find her, he moved into the crowd, slipping discreetly between the guests. He eventually spotted her at the rope barrier, dress hitched up and one leg already over. All the defenders were looking in the other direction, because they were focused on keeping people *out*, not *in*.

Astin reached her in a few paces, and she jumped when he stepped up next to her. She let go of the skirt of her gown, but it did not fall to the ground as it should have, because she was straddling the rope.

'So my one instruction wasn't clear?' he asked.

Lyndal awkwardly stepped back over the rope and fixed her dress. 'I do hope you're keeping an eye on Lady

Kendra. Lord Thomas will never forgive you should anything happen to her on your watch.'

He crossed his arms in front of him. 'And do you suppose your sisters would forgive me if anything happened to *you* on my watch?'

'God, no. You'd be drawn and quartered before you could utter the words "It was all her fault."' She gave him a playful smile.

He glanced in the direction of the peasants. 'Do you even know where they are? Or were you just planning on wandering aimlessly about?'

'They'll be easy enough to find.' She looked out. 'Eda will be the one with the bulky dress, due to all the weapons she's concealing, and Blake will be hovering nearby, ensuring the day doesn't end with our sister locked in the tower—again.'

It was tempting to let her go. She was in no real danger with her own people, certainly not with her sisters around, but orders were orders. 'You know I can't let you wander off. Your safety's not open for negotiation.'

'I know this is hard for you to understand, but I miss my family.'

He leaned away. 'Why do you assume I don't understand?'

'Because you're estranged from yours.'

'So I can't miss them? Is that the logic?'

She watched him a moment. 'All right. Tell me what happened. Give me a reason to stay on this side of the rope. I'm guessing your father passed away given there's a stepfather involved.'

He guided her back from the rope. 'Are you fishing for a tragic story in hope of humanising me?'

'Oh, please. It'll take a lot more than a sad family story to do that.' Her eyes returned to the peasants, searching for her sisters among them.

He let out a resigned breath, then said, 'My father died from pneumonia when I was eight, and my mother remarried shortly after. We didn't get along.'

Her eyes went to him. 'So you just left the farming life behind you and became a defender?'

'The defender part was accidental. I met Harlan down at the port one day. He convinced his father to let me train with him. The warden offered me a bed at the barracks. I suspect it was more about keeping Harlan company than my skills at the time. Anyway, it seemed like a better alternative than sleeping on the street.'

'So you stayed, and you became the great defender who stands before me now.' When he did not respond, she said, 'Your stepfather must be a special breed of man to have you fleeing your own home.'

Astin met her gaze. 'Like I said, we didn't get along.'

'Does he get along with the rest of your family?'

He squinted in the direction of the dancers as a new song struck up. 'I think the women in my family are more forgiving than me.'

'Forgiving of what?'

The memory of a belt slicing his back had him rolling one shoulder. 'Story time's over.'

Lyndal's face filled with pity. 'I'm sorry.'

'For what?' The question came out more agitated than he intended.

'I'm a merchant. I know suffering when I see it.'

When he met her eyes again, his rigid shoulders fell a little.

'There you are,' Queen Fayre said, stepping in between them.

Astin had been so caught up in conversation he had forgotten that he was responsible for two women. His eyes went to Kendra, who was thankfully still with her parents.

'The king requires a dance partner,' Queen Fayre said. 'I think you might be the perfect partner for him on this day.'

Lyndal appeared horrified by the idea. 'You want *me* to dance with the king?'

'There is no dancing in this area, as you know, so who better to help the king navigate the common space than a woman who has danced in it every year.'

Astin glanced over his shoulder at the merchants. 'That's not a good idea. Parading him in front of drunk merchants will invite trouble.'

The queen mother looked at him. 'Hiding behind a rope is not going to solve the problem, Fletcher. My son has bridges to mend.'

While that was true, Astin did not want Lyndal anywhere near those broken bridges.

Lyndal cleared her throat. 'Perhaps Lady Kendra might be a more suitable partner.'

'If I wanted Lady Kendra, I would have asked Lady Kendra.' Fayre's tone was impatient.

Lyndal looked to Astin as though expecting him to do something—something other than follow orders.

'Wait here,' Queen Fayre said. 'I shall tell him you are ready.' Then she wandered off to whisper in her son's ear.

'My uncle is going to kill me,' Lyndal told Astin, her hands opening and closing at her sides. 'He'll read this as an act of war against his daughter.'

Every hair on Astin's body was now standing on end. 'He'll have to get through me first.'

A hush fell over the nobility crowd as the king made his way over to Lyndal. He stopped in front of her, looking inconvenienced by the whole thing, then extended one hand.

Lyndal stared at that hand for a moment before reaching up to take it. The rope was pulled back, letting the pair enter the main area of the festival. People stopped talking, stopped dancing, stopped mid-pour of an ale to watch the pair strolling hand in hand towards them. The music faded to silence, and people began moving out of their way, never looking from the strange sight. The king never ventured to that side of the rope during the festival —and he certainly did not do so with a merchant at his side.

Astin followed so closely on Lyndal's heel that he was certain she could feel his breath on the back of her neck. His eyes jumped between faces and down to the hands stuffed in pockets. Every one of his senses was working together to keep her safe as she strolled alongside a moving target.

The pair stopped in the middle of the dance floor, and the peasants slowly formed a circle behind the defenders, who stood with their hands on the hilts of their weapons.

'Something cheerful,' the queen mother called to the musicians as she strolled into the open space to watch.

The lute player nodded and said something to the others. The music began just as Lord Thomas stepped up to the edge of the circle with an expression close to disgust. Kendra and her mother appeared a moment later, looking from the king and Lyndal to each other with confusion.

Every muscle in Astin's body was like carved stone as Borin raised one arm and pressed it to Lyndal's. They circled one another, prompting the peasants to push up on their toes for a better view. Astin made his way around the edge of the circle, knowing any attack on the king would put Lyndal in danger. But he soon realised that was not his main concern. The approving smile on the queen mother's face was the most alarming sight of all. She was not only looking at the dancing couple but at everyone watching them. Wary expressions had turned to curiosity. Some of the women were even smiling. A merchant girl dancing with a king was not something they had ever witnessed before.

Astin stopped walking, eyes back on Lyndal. That hair. That dress. Those painted lips. She was straight out of a fairy tale told to children.

A realisation hit him.

It was all part of one of Queen Fayre's plans. It was the reason she sent that dress to Lyndal's bedchamber. It was all a clever charade. The question was, how far could it move the dial? What exactly was the queen mother's endgame?

The music stopped, and Lyndal stepped back from the

king and curtsied. Instead of retreating to the nobility section, Borin took hold of her hand and displayed her before the now applauding crowd. Astin looked around at the smiling merchants and farmers, and a cold sensation crawled up his spine.

Lyndal had not remained at Eldon Castle for her cousin's sake, nor for Queen Fayre's amusement. She was a pawn in a game she had no idea she was playing. She *was* the bridge. Kind, generous, achingly beautiful. Shining brighter than any sun these people could remember.

Half merchant.

Half noble.

If people did not know her name before, they would know it now.

'Lady Lyndal,' Queen Fayre had called her.

Astin swallowed down the acid rising in his throat.

As Lyndal looked around at the applauding crowd, her eyes stopped on him. He saw the uncertainty, the confusion. It was enough to make him want to march over there and usher her away. Instead, he was forced to stand idle and watch her life begin to unravel.

CHAPTER 15

When King Borin finally released her hand, Lyndal took a relieved breath. What in God's name was going on? People were applauding. Queen Fayre was watching them with an expression bordering on maternal pride. The bland stares coming from the nobility were the one thing preventing Lyndal's head from exploding.

'Are you coming?' Borin asked her, impatient to flee the crowd.

She shook her head. 'In a minute.' She needed to see her family more than she needed air.

Borin strolled off, and her uncle followed, his eyes so loathing she thought he might go up in a bonfire of hatred. Lyndal caught sight of the backs of Kendra and her aunt as they retreated also.

A hand landed on her shoulder, and she gasped. It was Blake.

'What in God's name is going on?' Her sister was not one to beat around the bush.

Eda and her mother were standing behind Blake wearing the same worried expression.

Lyndal forced a smile. 'What was what?'

'That,' Blake said, pointing in the direction of the king. 'You and the king. All cute together.'

'It was just a dance.' But it was not just a dance. It was a test of some kind—one she had apparently passed with flying colours.

Candace brought a hand to her forehead. 'They are already lighting the bonfires for the ceremony. We do not have time for these games.'

Lyndal shook her head. 'What game is that?'

'That man will ruin any chances of you finding a husband,' her mother continued. 'He will use you up and discard you the second he feels the slightest bit bored.'

It took Lyndal a moment to register the conversation. 'What exactly are you asking me here?'

'How could you lie with that man?' Blake blurted. 'Have you forgotten that he once locked us up, starved us, then shot arrows at us?'

Astin appeared at her side, his presence dominating the space. 'Easy,' he said to Blake. 'It's not what you think.'

Lyndal closed her mouth. 'But thank you for assuming that, dear sister.'

'It seems we are missing a vital piece of this story,' her mother said quietly.

Lyndal took her mother's hand. 'The dance was Queen Fayre's idea, a ploy to win over disgruntled merchants. Nothing more.'

Candace stared at her daughter for the longest time, as

though trying to find truth in her eyes. 'So you will be home in four weeks as planned?'

'Absolutely. Nothing has changed.' She was reassuring herself also.

If you don't return to us in four weeks, Eda signed, *I'm coming for you.*

Lyndal stepped up and pulled her sister to her. 'Don't go starting wars just yet.'

'Lady Lyndal,' a voice called.

All five of them turned in Queen Fayre's direction.

'It is time to go,' the queen mother said. She offered a smile to Lyndal's family before making her way to the nobility section.

Lyndal released her sister, trying not to let her growing uneasiness show on the outside. 'I'm sorry.'

'*Lady Lyndal?*' Blake repeated. 'How does a merchant claim such a title? Did they baptise you in meat or something?'

Lyndal shifted her body to block Queen Fayre's view. 'Stop it. She'll hear you.'

'Let's go,' Astin said, taking her by the elbow.

Candace grabbed her other arm, looking her straight in the eyes. 'Do not let that man take anything you are not prepared to give him. You owe him nothing—king or not.'

That only made the uneasiness inside her surge. 'No. No, he doesn't want anything from me.' She looked to Astin for confirmation, but he was looking away. 'It was just one staged dance,' she said, turning back to her mother with a bright smile. 'I'll see you all in four weeks.'

She felt something dig into her side and looked down. Eda held a sheathed dagger in her hand.

If he tries to get into your bed, Eda signed by way of explanation.

'Put that thing away,' Astin said, pushing it out of sight. Then he was whisking Lyndal away. 'Let's go.'

The girls' father had taught all his daughters how to use various weapons when they were younger, but Lyndal had never had cause to use those skills with Blake and Eda around.

She tripped on some uneven ground as she watched her family over her shoulder. Astin righted her without breaking stride.

'I want to go home,' she said, looking up at him.

His throat bobbed. 'I know.'

The rope opened for them, and then they were back among the nobility. Lyndal eyed the crowd and found many of them looking in her direction. 'Tell me I'm being paranoid, that they're not looking at me.'

Astin moved in front of her, shielding her from their stares. 'Don't worry about them.' He looked over his shoulder. 'Lady Henley has Queen Fayre occupied, so take a moment to collect yourself while I go and find Kendra.'

She nodded, the action heavy.

'Wait here.' He dipped his head so he was eye level with her. 'Don't move from this spot.'

Another nod. 'All right.'

Then he was gone from sight.

Lyndal closed her eyes and exhaled slowly through her mouth, trying to calm her racing mind.

'What the hell are you playing at?'

Her eyes snapped open at the sound of her uncle's voice. 'Uncle.'

He grabbed her arm tightly and brought his face close to hers. 'You are lucky we are in a public place, or I would knock that smug expression off your face, you little harlot.'

'What?' She tried to pull free of his grip, and he tightened his hold on her.

'Do you really think he is going to let a little half-breed like you in his bed?'

Her arm began to throb. 'I assure you I've no intention of getting into anyone's bed.'

'You are a *merchant*.' He hissed the last word at her. 'A thief by nature. I just never thought you would steal your own cousin's future—a future she has worked her whole life for.'

His words lit a fire in her stomach. 'I've stolen nothing. And I suggest you let go of me before Queen Fayre happens to glance in our direction. She has a low tolerance for this kind of behaviour.'

His fingers tightened like a clamp, making her gasp.

Before he could get a word out, Astin stepped into view, two storm cloud eyes narrowed at Thomas.

'Either you remove your hand or *I* remove it. You have one second to decide.' His tone was pure ice.

Thomas released Lyndal's arm and turned to the defender. 'This is a private family conversation. I suggest you go watch my daughter.'

Astin did not move. 'The private conversation is over.'

Lyndal released a shaky breath and backed away. 'I'm going to find Kendra.'

'We're not done here,' Thomas said through his teeth.

Astin stepped between them. 'Yes you are.' He gestured for Lyndal to start walking. 'Go.'

She did not have to be told twice. She fled with her head pounding and vision blurring.

'Where is she?' she asked Astin when he fell into step with her.

'In the carriage. She's not feeling well. I've informed Queen Fayre that I'm taking you both back to Eldon Castle.'

Lyndal's eyes close with relief. 'You shouldn't have intervened.' She looked up at him. 'He's not an enemy you want, and I can handle him.'

'Was that you handling him?'

Her hand went to the tender spot on her arm. 'Suttone women are not made of glass.'

'I'm your bodyguard. I'm not about to stand idle while he breaks your arm. And I don't care what you're made of. It doesn't change the job.'

Up ahead, Kendra waited in the carriage looking close to tears. She turned her head in the other direction when she spotted them. The damage done by one dance was unthinkable.

Astin offered his hand, and Lyndal took it. So much strength in such a gentle grip. So much warmth.

Her eyes met his. 'Thank you.' Not only for the gesture but for everything that had come before it.

He kept hold of her hand until she took her seat, then rapped his knuckles on the side of the carriage to signal the driver to go. The carriage lurched forwards, leaving Astin behind and Lyndal to face the fallout alone.

'Queen Fayre wishes to speak with me upon her return,' Kendra said, not looking at her.

Lyndal watched her cousin for a moment. 'That's good news.' She tried to make her tone upbeat.

Kendra finally dragged her eyes to Lyndal. 'How is that good news when she has done her best to avoid me all day?'

There was no mistaking the resentment in her eyes.

Leaning forwards, Lyndal took her hand. 'I'm on your side.'

Kendra stared at her, eyes shiny. 'You do not get it, do you? Your side does not matter.'

Lyndal paced the length of the solar, back and forth, hugging herself tightly. She accidentally squeezed the bruise on her arm left by her uncle and cursed aloud. It had been thirty minutes since Kendra had been summoned by Queen Fayre. If chess was involved, she would likely be gone for hours.

Footsteps out in the corridor made her turn towards the door. It burst open, and Kendra stepped inside the room, black tears streaking her face. She had spent a startling amount of time thickening her eyelashes with tea leaves that morning. Now she was turning in frantic circles, shaking out her hands like she had just committed a murder.

'What on earth happened?' Lyndal asked, going to her.

Kendra stepped back. 'I am to go home.'

Relief poured out of Lyndal in one enormous breath. 'Thank Belenus for that.'

Kendra's eyes widened. 'What?'

'I'm sorry,' Lyndal said quickly. She spotted Astin outside the door, watching their exchange. 'It's just that… I would really like to go home.'

Kendra licked tears off her lips. 'Well, that is too bad. It seems you are to remain here—without me.'

At first Lyndal thought she must have misheard. 'What did you say?'

Astin knocked on the door frame.

'What is it?' Lyndal asked, a hand pressed to her slowing heart.

His expression was apologetic. 'Queen Fayre wants to see you in her quarters.'

A meeting in her private quarters meant she did not want anyone else overhearing—not even her guards.

Lyndal's lungs squeezed. 'I'm a little busy, as you can see.'

'It is not a casual invitation,' Kendra snapped. 'She is ordering you to go to her. Is that really so difficult for you to grasp?'

Lyndal's hand dropped to her side, her eyes burning. 'All right.' She nodded and looked around the room. What was she looking for? A reason to stay, perhaps. She forced her feet to carry her forwards. 'We'll talk when I get back.'

'I will not be here,' Kendra said, hands fisted. 'Do you not understand what is happening right now? I am in the way.'

'Whose way?'

'Yours!'

Lyndal's breathing was so shallow she feared she might faint. 'I don't understand—'

Kendra threw her hands up and headed for the door that led through to her bedchamber. 'I need to pack.'

Lyndal went to go after her, but a hand landed on her shoulder. She turned to Astin. 'What's going on?' Her eyes welled up as the question fell out of her.

He gestured for her to follow him out into the hall, then pulled the door closed behind them. He looked both ways before saying, 'I don't know, but I suspect Queen Fayre will answer all your questions.' He signalled with his head for her to start walking. 'You need to keep it together. Understand?' When she did not respond, he added, 'You're known for your level head, so stay level for me.'

The 'for me' part made it sound like he genuinely cared. 'She wants something from me.'

'She does. And you're about to find out what that something is.'

They rounded the corner of the east wing, the steady rhythm of his feet blending with her erratic steps. When they reached Queen Fayre's quarters, the defender on duty went inside to announce her arrival.

'Level head,' Astin said, voice low. 'I'll be waiting right here for you.'

She nodded, then stiffened when the door swung open again. When she entered, she found the queen mother seated comfortably on the lounge. The fire was ablaze with fresh wood, making the air stifling.

'Please,' the queen said, gesturing to one of the chairs. 'It is best if you are seated for this conversation.' She offered a smile no doubt intended to ease nerves.

Lyndal walked over to the chair and lowered herself into it, pressing the tips of her fingers into the expensive fabric.

'Level head.'

She raised her chin. 'I'm listening, Your Majesty.'

CHAPTER 17

'It's been three days,' Harlan said. 'And still she's not said a word to you?'

Astin shook his head. 'Not one word.'

'And she's not left her bedchamber?'

'There's a guard posted outside her door every minute.'

They were seated at a table by the tavern window, watching the merchants come and go from the dock. The air smelled of salt, blood, and manure. While more livestock was arriving on the ships each month, at least half of it never made it out of the port borough due to disease. Sick animals were slaughtered on the beach and thrown into the water. The merchants would wait in the shallows with spears and catch the fish that arrived to eat the contaminated carcasses.

'We can't help her if she doesn't tell us what's going on,' Harlan said, taking a swig of his ale.

Astin was technically off duty but refrained from drinking. He wanted a clear head when Lyndal finally decided to exit her room. He had thought he was doing the right thing by giving her space and time, a few hours to digest whatever it was Queen Fayre had told her. He never imagined that would turn into three days.

'We just ignore the rumours, right?' Harlan asked, looking down at his cup.

'She's not sharing the king's bed, if that's what you're asking.'

Harlan nodded. 'I think their little dance at the festival gave a different impression. The nobility are losing their mind at the mere thought of a merchant mistress.'

'And the merchants are practically celebrating in the streets.'

Harlan emptied his drink. 'Shame we can't peer inside Queen Fayre's devious mind and see what's really at play here.'

'We'll find out soon enough.'

The warden appeared at the tavern window, looking between them, then down at Harlan's empty cup. 'Early finish?'

The men rose and stood to attention.

'I'm off duty and about to head home,' Harlan replied. 'You should come for dinner.'

'Some of us work full days,' Shapur replied before turning his attention to Astin. 'Any reason you are here when the woman under your protection is out on the terrace?'

'The guard was supposed to fetch me if she emerged.' Astin knocked his chair backwards as he jumped out the open window instead of using the door.

'Perhaps he did not think to check the *tavern*,' Shapur fired back.

Harlan spoke up at that. 'He hasn't been drinking.'

'I'll head there now, sir.'

'Fletcher,' the warden said, stopping him in his tracks. 'Stay alert. Big news is about to break, and a lot of very powerful people are not going to like it.'

Astin exchanged a glance with Harlan, then saluted before jogging off in the direction of the castle.

'I am pleased you took a few days to think things over,' Queen Fayre said as she moved her bishop along the chessboard. 'It is a skill to push emotions aside when making decisions.'

Lyndal moved her castle sideways on the board and leaned back in her chair. 'I basically lay on the floor the entire time staring at the roof.'

'It is all right for a woman to lie on the floor sometimes—as long as she does not remain there.' Fayre looked up from the board. 'I imagine you have lots of questions.'

Lyndal watched her make her move. 'Questions *and* requests.'

'Go on.'

She moved her pawn, considering her next words carefully. 'Firstly, there's the matter of the almshouse in the merchant borough.'

Queen Fayre laughed lightly. 'Yes, I have heard all about this almshouse. If you are still here at the end of the month, I shall fund the project myself.'

And just like that, Lyndal had an almshouse. It almost

seemed too easy, but then she remembered what she would be giving up to get it.

'What else?' the queen mother asked.

The next question had been at the front of her mind for the past few days. 'The king… is he agreeable to all this?'

Fayre looked up. 'He trusts me.'

'That's not the same thing as being agreeable.'

The queen let go of her bishop. 'He wants to live a long life without looking over his shoulder all the time. He wants to be liked by his people.' She placed the piece down. 'He is agreeable.'

Lyndal chewed her lip. 'He was rather fond of Lady Kendra.'

'Yes he was.'

When Fayre did not expand on that, Lyndal said, 'And you sent her away.'

'She was a distraction.'

'She was perfect for him.'

Fayre was silent a moment. 'It is true, she will make a wonderful wife. But what this kingdom needs is a queen.'

'Why not Kendra?'

Fayre reached for her cup, taking a sip of water before answering. 'I think you know why. She can only relate to one portion of the population.'

'That's true of me also.'

'Yes, but you can relate to the largest portion, and more importantly, they can relate to you.' She tapped a finger on her cup. 'In time, you will grow accustomed to a more privileged life. Then you will be able to relate to both.'

Queen Fayre was dangling a crown in front of her, a crown she had no business reaching for. Three weeks, the queen mother had told her. Three weeks to get to know the king. Three weeks for him to get to know her. Three weeks to see if they could learn to work together and to gauge the temperature of the kingdom. All going well, Queen Fayre would announce their betrothal to the world.

Lyndal would be Queen of Chadora.

So she had spent three days making a list of everything she could do with a title like that. The almshouse was only the beginning.

'You have more questions?' Fayre made her next move.

'I can barely fathom the life you're offering, let alone think of intelligent questions.'

The queen lifted her gaze. 'So much of that life will depend on your resilience and commitment.'

'Commitment to your son or to the role?'

'They are the same thing. He is the reason the role exists at all.'

Lyndal stared at the board, contemplating her next move. 'What of *his* commitment? Taking a wife because you told him to is hardly a strong basis for a happy marriage.' She took a chance and moved her king.

'A happy marriage? Is that what you want?'

Lyndal drew a breath. 'That's what every woman wants.'

Queen Fayre watched her a moment. 'I thought you wanted meaningful change in our kingdom.'

'I do.'

Fayre moved one of her pawns. 'Check.'

Lyndal stared at the chessboard. 'I'll never be as good as you.'

'In chess or the other game you find yourself playing?'

Lyndal looked up. 'Both.'

Queen Fayre folded her hands in her lap. 'Give me until the end of the month. I can teach you both. I can even teach you how to handle my son. In time, and with the right woman at his side, he may grow into the man we all need him to become.' She gestured to the board. 'It is your turn.'

Lyndal glanced up at the heavy clouds above, then moved her knight.

Fayre moved her queen in response. 'Checkmate.'

'How surprising.' Lyndal sat back, studying the massacre before her. 'Would we grow to like each other? Is that how it works with arranged marriages?'

Fayre pondered the question. 'It is more important that you grow to trust one another and remember that you are playing for the same side.'

Lyndal bit the inside of her cheek to stop from speaking.

'Go on,' the queen mother said. 'You want to know if my husband and I were on the same side. Is that it?'

Lyndal nodded.

'We were for a long time.'

Lyndal bit her lip, unsure how far to probe. 'Until the day you left?'

Fayre brushed invisible lint off her sleeve, not meeting Lyndal's eyes for the first time. 'Oswin was headed down a dangerous path. I could not in good conscience follow him, and I could not stop him. I thought it best to quietly remove myself.' She finally lifted her gaze. 'I suppose you think me a terrible mother for leaving my children behind.'

Lyndal shook her head. 'I don't pretend to understand the workings of a monarchy, especially one in crisis.'

'It would have been irresponsible for me to take the princes away. They are this kingdom's future. The people needed to see them grow up here in order to trust them.' She paused. 'But I see now that I stayed away for too long. While I cannot change the past, I can do my best to steer Borin in a different direction than the one his father took.'

They were both silent a moment.

'Do you really think people will accept a merchant as their queen?' Lyndal asked.

'You are not *only* a merchant, are you? That is why this arrangement could work.'

'But the nobility only see a merchant.'

A nod. 'It is true that you will need to win the nobility over.'

'I have nothing to buy them with.'

'You can only buy their cooperation, not their loyalty.' Fayre's expression turned serious. 'You will need to watch your back over these coming weeks. News will spread of the courtship. Some will be unhappy about it.'

The word 'courtship' burned her eardrums. She preferred 'trial'. It sounded far less intimate.

'It is not a bad thing,' Queen Fayre continued. 'It helps us know where we stand. If for some reason the arrangement does not work out, we will reduce the entire thing to rumour and part as friends.'

That was the only reason Lyndal was even considering it—because she still had an out.

Fayre studied her over the rim of her cup for a moment. 'It was always you, you know. From that very first meeting. Lady Kendra was simply a means to you, the merchant girl with the enormous heart and impossibly high expectations.'

Lyndal fought to keep her foot still, a nervous habit. 'There's still the matter of meat.'

The queen mother laughed at that. 'Let us take one thing at a time. Right now you must focus on winning over my son.'

Lyndal's eyebrows came together. 'I thought you said he was agreeable.'

'He is agreeable to my plans, not yours. You have your work cut out for you, so I suggest you use the next few weeks wisely.'

The sound of approaching footsteps made Lyndal look over her shoulder. There was Astin, breathing heavy like he had come at a run. He glared in the direction of the defender standing by the wall, the one Lyndal had instructed *not* to fetch his superior because she feared he would talk her out of what she was about to agree to. Guilt hit her as their eyes met across the terrace. He had been there for her since the day she had arrived at Eldon Castle, despite their differences. And she had repaid him by shutting him out.

'Good timing, Fletcher,' Queen Fayre said, gesturing him closer as she rose from her chair.

He appeared next to the table, his hard stare on Lyndal as she stood also.

'So we are in agreement,' Fayre said, concluding their conversation. 'Three weeks.'

Lyndal's mouth was dry, but she found herself nodding. 'And if it doesn't work out, we part as friends.' She needed to hear that part again.

Fayre only smiled. 'I have complete faith in you.' She turned to Astin. 'Now, I thought perhaps you could take Lady Lyndal down to the butts. King Borin will be heading there shortly for practice, and I thought she might like to watch.'

Astin bowed his head.

It all felt a bit rushed suddenly, but time was ticking. If the queen mother thought applauding the king while he shot a few arrows was the best way to proceed, then she could do that.

'Lady Lyndal and the king will be spending a lot of time together over the coming weeks. I am counting on you to keep her safe during that time.'

Lyndal lifted her eyes to gauge Astin's reaction to that and met his hurricane stare. It seemed he was filling in the blanks well enough.

'Of course,' he said. 'Are you ready, *Lady Lyndal?*'

She fought the urge to be sick on the ground. 'Yes.' She curtsied before the queen mother.

'Meet me here at the same time tomorrow,' Fayre said. 'One cannot improve their game without practice.'

Lyndal nodded. 'Very well.' She avoided eye contact with Astin as she stepped past him.

'Fletcher,' Queen Fayre said behind her. 'Guard her like you would a queen.'

CHAPTER 18

$\mathcal{A}$stin walked a pace behind Lyndal down the corridor, trying to calm himself. Three days she had shut him out, ignored his requests to speak with her, accepted trays of food from the maid before closing the door in his face. He had been patient, despite a persistent urge to break the door down and shake the words from her.

'Guard her like you would a queen,' Fayre had instructed him.

It was abundantly clear that the part Lyndal was to play was bigger than any of them could have fathomed. When she slowed her pace to walk beside him, he lengthened his stride, not ready to hear the words from her mouth.

She emitted a large sigh before running to catch up with him. 'So, I have news.' She lifted her skirts higher so she did not trip in her efforts to keep up with him. 'Can you slow down please?'

'We don't want to keep the king waiting.'

Another sigh, her feet moving faster still. 'Queen Fayre has it in her head that I could… that I could be queen. Isn't that crazy?'

He was practically jogging now.

They exited the castle and headed for the steps that led down to the butts. He flew down them so fast, he was surprised she did not fall in her effort to keep up.

'Can you stop a moment?' she said at the bottom, out of breath.

He did not stop.

'Astin!'

He spun around, forcing her to pull up fast. 'It's *Fletcher*. That's how you'll refer to me from now on. That's how it works in this world you're diving into.'

She swallowed hard but kept her head high. 'I thought we were past all the hostility and silly games. I thought we were friends.'

'Is that why you ignored me for days on end, then went and made a life-changing decision without saying a word about it?'

'I'm telling you now.'

He crossed his arms, and she shrank back from him.

'She's luring you into a life of misery with a shiny crown and promises she can't keep.'

'She wants to help the merchants, and she knows I want the same thing.'

'She knows you're naive and can be easily manipulated.'

Lyndal's eyes widened. 'She's grooming me, I'll give you that, but I need grooming for this to work.'

He leaned in. 'Can you hear yourself? She's putting

you in bed with her son, all the while whispering instructions in your ear.'

Lyndal's face fell. 'It's not like that.'

'So what's it like, then? Tell me. Are you not about to show up at the butts and be all charming and seductive, stroke the king's ego, then something else later?'

Her face fell, and he hated himself.

'I've spent three days going over and over this in my mind, going crazy with indecision.' Her words were breathy. 'And for you to stand there and cheapen this situation…'

She stepped back from him and looked like she might retreat to the castle. Instead, she set her jaw and marched ahead of him in the direction of the butts. He had no choice but to follow her. It was his job to protect her, and she needed his protection now more than ever. She would be a walking target the moment the nobility got whiff of this plan.

'You're discharged, defender,' Lyndal said over her shoulder.

He exhaled and caught up to her. 'It doesn't work like that, genius. You don't have the authority to send me away.'

She laughed, a short sharp noise. 'Not yet.' She looked up at him without slowing. 'Do you think this is easy for me? Do you think I just woke up this morning liking that man?'

Rhetorical questions, so he did not reply.

'Every time I look at him, I see a red-faced boy screaming "traitor" from atop the wall—and I want to claw his face apart.' Her voice broke. 'And we stood in that square, unarmed, just trying to keep each other alive for a moment longer.'

'Stop walking,' he said quietly.

She marched on. 'And I've been handed this opportunity to do something, to help, perhaps stop anything like that ever happening again.'

Mud sucked at her boots, trapping one of her feet. She fell forwards as she tried to yank it free. He caught her with one hand and righted her, and they both fell silent. She was panting and clutching her skirts, eyes on the ground between them.

'I have three weeks to see if this can even work,' she finally said. 'My family will lose their minds when they learn of this. The nobility will likely come after me with pitchforks.' She lifted her eyes to him. 'But I owe it to the merchants to at least try.'

Rain began to fall, fat drops landing in place of the tears she was holding back.

Astin reached out and tugged her hood up, then looked in the direction of the empty butts, wishing he could take back the things he had said to her. 'Harlan will handle your family. I'll handle the pitchforks.'

Laughter came out on an exhale. 'Thank you.' She licked rain off her lips and glanced in the direction of the castle.

'Still want to go to the butts?' he asked.

She brought her red hands to her mouth and blew into them. 'I'm guessing the king will still practice if it's raining?'

'He will if he has an audience.'

She took hold of her wet skirts once more. 'Then I shall be his audience.'

Thirty minutes they had been waiting in the rain for King Borin to grace them with his presence. Lyndal's eyes kept returning to Astin, who was watching their surroundings with a serious expression. If someone did appear with a pitchfork, he looked ready.

At least he was no longer angry at her.

Her eyes went to the archery supplies that had been brought out in preparation for the king's arrival. 'Do you suppose I could have a turn while we wait?'

Astin looked in her direction with a surprised expression. 'Do you even know how to shoot?'

'I'm a Suttone. What do you think?'

The bodyguard wandered over and collected the long bow and a handful of arrows. 'If the king shows up, we were under attack.'

'Got it.' She blew into her icy hands, trying to get some blood circulation happening, then took the bow from him. He handed her one of the arrows and watched her load it. 'It's been a while.'

'And here come the excuses.'

She pressed her lips together to stop from smiling, then took aim at the mound at the far end of the muddy lawn. Upon release, she winced. It had made the distance but missed the target completely.

Astin chuckled behind her.

'All right,' she said. 'So I'm a little out of practice.'

He stepped up and handed her another arrow. 'A little? Did you notice the targets at the end?'

With a roll of her eyes, she loaded the bow and took aim once more.

'Wait,' he said, moving behind her. He hooked two fingers under her elbow, lifting. 'Don't let it drop.' His other hand went around her to the riser, adjusting her grip.

She watched his callused hand move over hers, hoping he did not notice the change in her breath at him being so close. She released the arrow, this time grazing the edge of the target.

'Better,' he said, arms falling away.

She turned. 'I would be much better if my hands were warm.'

'Really?' Taking the bow from her, he placed it on the ground and took both her hands in his. 'Let's test that theory, shall we?'

He rubbed her hands between his rough ones for a full minute, then brought them to his mouth. Warm breath engulfed her skin, making goosebumps break out on her arms.

'Try now,' he said, letting go and picking up the bow for her.

Her cheeks were hot against the rain as she met his turbulent stare. She had always read that expression as annoyance, inconvenience, impatience. But none of those things fit with the situation they found themselves in.

'I was hoping the rain might ease,' the king called to them.

Lyndal jumped, and Astin stepped back. Thankfully, he still had hold of the bow.

'Goodness,' Borin said, stopping in front of Lyndal. Two defenders flanked him. 'You look like a drowned rat.'

Lyndal forced a smile. 'The downside of being punctual, Your Majesty.'

His gaze went to the bow in Astin's hands. 'I see Fletcher has been showing you a thing or two.' He clapped the defender on the back as he took the weapon from him. 'It is a lot more difficult than it seems.'

Astin moved aside.

It was strange to be in someone's company for less than a minute and feel done, but there she was, already wishing her time with the king was over. 'I look forward to seeing what you can do.'

He clicked his fingers, like one does when gaining the attention of a dog, and held out his hand. Lyndal blinked in confusion.

'Arrow,' he said, his tone impatient.

Oh. He meant for her to fetch one for him. Slowly, she picked up one of the arrows lying by his feet, handed it to him, then moved aside. Borin loaded the weapon, aimed, and released, hitting the target's edge.

'Bow must need aligning,' he said, clicking for another arrow.

Lyndal had never felt more like a merchant as she stepped forwards again to do his bidding.

The king reloaded the bow and took another shot, which was only slightly better than his last effort. 'The rain,' he explained, gesturing overhead. 'Would you care to have a try?'

That seemed like progress—unless he drove the arrow through her neck at the last minute.

She took the bow, and he moved behind her as Astin had done. Arms went either side of her as he positioned her hands. He was not gentle—nor was he warm. The overpowering scent of perfume choked her, a contrast to Astin's earthy scent, a scent she found herself leaning into.

She caught that thought.

That was only because he was more familiar to her. Perfectly natural after spending so much time together. When her eyes flicked to the bodyguard, she found him scowling, his jaw clenched. He was as uneasy in the king's presence as she was—or perhaps uneasy on her behalf.

'Elbow up, elbow up,' Borin said, tapping her arm with two sharp fingers.

She was relieved when he finally stepped back. Looking down her arrow, she slowed her breath and let go. The arrow pierced the middle of the target. She knew it was a mistake the second she turned back to the king.

'Beginner's luck,' he said, snatching the bow from her hands. 'Very common.'

Why had she done that? Much better to miss completely than to wound his pride. She moved aside, eyes meeting Astin's in the process. He winked at her before looking away.

Borin never offered her another turn. He spent the next hour showing off while she smiled and feigned interest in his mediocre skills.

She studied his showy gestures. Listened carefully to the words coming from his mouth. All while trying to picture herself as his wife, her hand in his as they took vows to love and be faithful to one another.

Lies.

She would not love him, and he would not be faithful to her. How could she ever love a man who put vengeance above all else? Though love had never really been on the cards for her anyway. Her uncle expected an advantageous marriage—though never in place of his own flesh and blood. Thinking back to their conversation at the festival, she suspected Thomas had known what was coming.

Dropping the bow on the ground, Borin turned to her suddenly. 'I know Mother has already spoken to you of her wishes, so I shall not go over the details of the arrangement again. She assures me you will be cooperative over the coming weeks, compliant.'

Compliant? If her sisters had been present, they would have fallen to the ground in a fit of laughter, clutching their aching stomachs. It was the strangest commencement of a courtship speech she could fathom.

'And we shall see what comes of it,' he concluded.

She suspected there was a middle part she had missed.

'Perhaps we could dine together this evening,' she suggested. 'Get to know one another a little better.'

He stared at her. 'You think I do not know you?'

'We've barely exchanged a handful of words.'

'Sometimes that is all one needs to form an opinion.' He looked in the direction of the castle. 'I will be travelling to the farming borough tomorrow for business. Mother thinks it might be a good idea if you accompany me, let people get used to seeing you at my side.

Fletcher can keep you out of trouble while I am taking meetings.'

Another string pulled by his mother.

'We merchants do love our trouble,' she said lightly.

'I am well aware of the fact,' he said without humour. 'If this union does indeed go ahead, let us pray our sons take after me and are born sound of mind.'

Lyndal had no idea whether to laugh or throw mud at him. The things that spilled from his mouth should have remained private thoughts.

She fell into a curtsy, wanting the conversation to be over. 'Until tomorrow, Your Majesty.'

'If this is truly a courtship, there is no need for such formalities. You may address me as "Your Grace".'

Lyndal bit her top lip to stop the laughter rising up her throat. 'Until tomorrow, Your Grace.'

'That went well,' Lyndal said to Astin as they made their way back to the castle.

He took in her rounded shoulders as they climbed the steps. 'What were you expecting? Sonnets?'

'I was expecting manners. The man has a mother.'

They entered the castle and made their way along the shadowy corridor. When they reached her quarters, Lyndal turned to him.

'Can I show you something?'

He nodded and followed her into the solar, leaving the door open behind him. Lyndal went to the table by the window and picked up a stack of parchment, handing it to him. He ran his eyes over the first page. It was a list of projects with potential dates next to each one.

'What's all this?' he asked.

'These are all the things I'll do if I become queen.'

He flicked through the pages until he reached a detailed sketch of an almshouse.

'Queen Fayre has already agreed to fund that,' she said.

'So long as you marry her son and play by the rules.' He continued sifting through, page after page of ideas, ideas that would be inevitably shot down by the king. He stopped when he arrived at a sketch of a lavender bush. 'Lavender?'

'To attract bees.'

He looked at her. 'When was the last time you saw a bee in Chadora?'

'They'll come if there's lavender. I'll plant it everywhere.'

'And where will you get this lavender from?'

She tipped her face up to him. 'Queen Fayre has a pot of it on the terrace.'

'That bush never flowers.'

She took the parchment from his hands and placed them back on the table. 'Must you defenders always be such wet blankets?'

He watched her. 'So that's what you did in here for three days? Planned out all your post-wedding activities?'

'I was trying to figure out if the sacrifice would be worth it.'

'And you think it will? That you'll miraculously be happy with him?'

She breathed out. 'One can find happiness outside their marriage.'

'Give me one example,' he shot back.

'Queen Fayre.'

A laugh fell from him. 'Queen Fayre fled to Toryn the moment her sons were old enough to fend for themselves. Is that your big plan? Give him an heir and a spare, then run?' He pointed at the stack of parchment. 'I didn't see that in your notes.'

Her cheeks heated.

'Plus,' he continued, 'you come across as the kind of woman who would be painfully involved in her children's lives, not absent.'

Her mouth fell open. *'Painfully involved?'*

'You know what I mean. It's a compliment. You'll be a great mother.'

That appeared to ease her agitation. 'I'll admit, I always pictured a very different sort of father for these imaginary children. A hard worker with useful skills to pass down. A man who taught respect by example.'

A strong work ethic was important to merchants.

'Well,' he said, 'King Borin can teach your children to shoot a bow instead.'

'As long as his bow is properly aligned.'

'And there is no rain to throw his aim.'

She laughed that pretty laugh of hers, and he fell silent as he watched it play out.

'I should go,' he said. 'Leave you to write that letter to your family explaining the whole "you're about to be their queen" thing.'

She sighed. 'You might need extra security at the gate post-delivery.'

He grinned at the ground as he backed away.

'You think I'm making a mistake, don't you?' she asked, all humour gone from her voice.

'It doesn't matter what I think. It's not my place to comment on who you marry.'

'But I want you onside.' She shook her head, embarrassed. 'What I meant is—'

'I know what you meant. You want a friend this side of the wall.'

Her eyes searched his. 'Do I still have to call you Fletcher?'

'I think we can drop the formalities now. You can address me as "Your Superiorship".'

He turned to the door, and her laughter was the last thing he heard as he pulled it closed behind him.

CHAPTER 19

'I have some business to tend to in the merchant borough,' King Borin said through a baricade of guards as they headed for the wall.

Lyndal was supposed to accompany the king on horseback while he conducted business in the farming borough. A visit to the merchant borough had not been part of the plan. She knew there was only one reason for such a detour—and she was not prepared for it. The packed square waiting for them on the other side confirmed her fears.

Her mare stepped sideways as the portcullis rose. 'Easy, girl,' Lyndal said, knowing the animal was feeding off her nervous energy.

'You don't have to watch,' Astin said quietly beside her. 'We'll wait at the back.'

Apparently her bodyguard was a mind reader. 'Trial or execution?'

Astin nudged his horse forwards. 'Both.'

As they entered the borough, her eyes went to the

three men lined up against the wall, their hands tied in front of them.

'I shall address the crowd, and then we can leave,' the king told her through a gap in his guards. 'It can be a long wait for them to die, and we have a schedule to keep.'

Lyndal pressed her eyes shut.

It was time for one of Borin's infamous speeches.

As the king strode off, she tried to imagine a lifetime of his speeches. Perhaps he would write some just for her. Daily lectures detailing all the different ways she had disappointed him.

'Your sisters are here,' Astin said, pulling her from her thoughts. 'And judging by the looks on their faces, I think they received your letter.'

Heart thudding, Lyndal searched for them amid the hungry faces, spotting them at the edge of the square. It was clear they had not come for the execution.

As soon as the king was out of sight, Blake and Eda approached the horses.

'Are you going to dismount willingly, or shall we drag you from your mount?' Blake asked.

Lyndal looked to Astin, who was waiting for her reply. 'She threatens to drag me from my horse and you just sit there?'

He shrugged. 'If they pull a weapon on you, I'll be sure to lend a hand.'

Exhaling noisily, Lyndal dismounted and went to face her sisters. She braced when Blake came at her, but then her sister surprised her by pulling her into her arms, holding so tightly Lyndal teared up. As much as she wanted to fix the broken kingdom, the personal cost would be enormous.

'Imagine my disappointment,' the king shouted out over the crowd, 'discovering that the people I work so hard to protect choose to fight me every step of the way.'

Lyndal led her sisters away from the crowd so they could speak. Astin followed with the horses, leaving enough distance to allow them privacy. Years of guarding the king had taught him how to be close and invisible at the same time.

So it's true, then? Eda signed. *You're really going to marry him?*

'Nothing's official. It's a trial, of sorts.'

Blake was staring at her like she had antlers. 'So you're courting?'

How she hated that word. 'Courtship makes it all sound so pleasant. Right now we're just trying to get along.'

Then why do it at all? Eda signed.

'Your letter was a little light on details,' Blake said, glaring. 'I'm guessing this was one of Queen Fayre's bold ideas.'

Lyndal chewed her lip. 'Her reasoning is sound.'

'Sound for whom?' Blake said. 'You do understand what marriage entails? You'll share a bed with him, birth his monstrous babies, and spend your leisure hours watching him hang people just like us.'

Lyndal let out a shaky breath. 'If I'm queen, I'll be able to help people like us.'

Mother was too upset to come, Eda signed.

Lyndal rubbed her forehead where a headache was

starting. 'She was the one who wanted me to go to court. She said it would open doors. Well, a door opened.'

Blake grabbed hold of her arms. 'When the door to hell opens, you slam it shut, not step inside.'

Lyndal pulled out of her grip. 'Look around you. People are still dying. As a merchant, I can help a handful of them at best. But if I'm queen, I can lift the entire borough.'

Eda swallowed and looked away.

'Have you forgotten what he did?' Blake asked, her expression pleading.

Lyndal shook her head. 'How could you ask me that? The reminders are everywhere—and these people are still living it.' She looked in the king's direction. He was wrapping up his speech, which meant she was almost out of time. 'I'm going to help these people, and it would be really nice if you had my back. Don't stand there and tell me I'm stupid. Tell me I'm brave.'

When Blake did not reply, she turned away, eyes stinging. 'Tell Mother I said hello.' She headed for her horse.

'Don't marry him,' Blake called, following her. 'We'll find another way to help these people.'

Astin stepped in front of Blake. 'If you make a scene, your sister will pay the price.'

When Eda went for Astin, Blake blocked her with one arm. 'Easy, sister. He's just doing his job.' Though she stared daggers at him as she spoke the words.

'Ladies,' Astin said, turning to mount his horse.

A strangled cry made them all look in the direction of the square. One of the men was being hoisted up, the soles of his shoes scraping stone in a vain attempt to ease the pressure around his neck. Then came the familiar cries of a heartbroken family. Loved ones were shoved back as a barrier of defenders stood their ground.

When Lyndal looked at her sisters, she saw their trauma matched her own. Nothing was going to change unless someone actively tried to change it.

She could be that person.

She could win the king's trust, become a puppeteer.

Filled with a newfound determination, she watched Borin stride back to his horse, completely unaffected by the scene behind him.

Her sisters retreated to the safety of the crowd, watching her with heartbroken expressions.

Stand tall and strong, warrior, Blake signed to her.

It was what their father used to say to them when they were young, and she imagined him saying those words to her now.

The king trotted past with his circle of guards, not bothering to check if she was ready to depart.

'Ready?' Astin asked in his place.

I love you, she signed to her sisters before turning her horse away. 'Ready.'

The king's guards fell back when they entered the farming borough, enabling Lyndal to ride at the king's side. Astin followed a few paces behind them, listening as Lyndal asked Borin questions about the farms they passed. The king edged his horse closer to hers as he explained things as though she were an imbecile. She nodded along to everything he said, like he was the most interesting man alive. And even though he understood the game, jealousy reared inside him.

Every now and then, she would look over her shoulder, checking that he was still behind her. It showed she was afraid—and that fear was justified. King Borin was the one man Astin could not protect her from.

The first farm they called upon had once been known for its barley. Now chickens roamed in place of failed crops. Borin presented Lyndal to the farmers like she was a prize sheep, watching their reaction as she moved between them, smiling and asking questions. She even crouched down to speak with the younger children. She was pure sunshine, the epitome of everything missing from their farming lives.

Satisfied, the king went to speak privately with the owner. Lyndal wandered along the boundaries of the paddocks with the owner's wife, nodding thoughtfully as she absorbed each response. Astin tried to give them as much space as was safe for her, as the farming borough was considered neutral territory for both her and the king. But that was not to say the farmers were content with how things were being run.

When the king returned to the horses, they all mounted and rode out.

'Would you consider that one of the larger farms in the borough?' Lyndal asked the king as they exited.

'I would say average in terms of size and produce. Why do you ask?'

She looked to the mass of chickens scratching in the muddy fields. 'I was just curious.'

When they headed west instead of north, dread filled Astin. The next farm they would arrive at was *his*. King Borin had failed to mention it was on the agenda. It was probably because people no longer connected him to the farm. He was a defender now, and the farm had fallen into Cooper's hands long ago.

The moment they entered the property, his stepfather exited the house, squinting in their direction. His mother remained by the door as she removed her apron and smoothed back her hair. It had greyed considerably since the last time he had seen her.

'Home sweet home, right, Fletcher?' the king said over his shoulder with a smirk.

Lyndal looked back at Astin. 'This is where you grew up?'

'He was not much of a farmer,' Borin said. 'Or so I have been told.'

Astin wet his lips and kept silent. Cooper Brooke had likely painted a picture of him, and now was not the time to correct it. Astin met his stepfather's eyes as he dismounted, the darkest shade of brown he had ever seen on a man. He had always thought them black as a child.

'We just passed your lambs,' King Borin said, walking over to him.

'Born a week back, Your Majesty,' Cooper said, bowing to the king. 'All healthy as horses.' His eyes went to Lyndal, assessing her for the longest time. 'This must be the lovely Lady Lyndal I've been hearing about.'

Astin fought the urge to move in front of her.

'Lady Lyndal of Cardelle Manor,' Borin said. 'Lord Thomas's niece.'

Her title just kept getting longer.

Lyndal made no move towards him. She simply nodded a greeting before looking past him to where Astin's mother stood. 'And you must be Fletcher's mother.'

Lari glanced at Cooper, then offered her a tired smile. 'Please to meet you, my lady.'

'Shall we take a closer look at these lambs?' the king said, cutting the greeting short.

'Can I trust you to behave in my absence?' Cooper asked Astin.

'We haven't trusted one another in the past,' Astin replied. 'Why would we start now?'

Borin tutted. 'Come, come. Let us all be civil.'

Cooper gave Astin a hard stare before leaving with the king.

When the men were out of earshot, Astin looked to his mother. 'Where's Presley?'

'She's in the north paddock with Rose.' She never quite met his eyes anymore.

Clearing her throat, Lyndal said, 'Shall we take a walk and find them? It would be a shame to come all this way and not see your sisters.'

'It's a bit of a walk. We'll take the horses,' he replied.

Lyndal lifted the skirt of her dress, revealing her boots. 'Merchant feet. I can walk for miles with a pail of water in each hand.'

He loved the way her eyes shone with pride when she spoke of her roots.

'I could fetch her,' his mother offered.

He gestured for Lyndal to start moving. 'We'll walk.'

His mother took another step towards him. 'Astin—'

'It's Fletcher. I'm on duty.'

Lari nodded and looked down at the ground. 'Did Presley tell you she's to be married?'

'She did.'

Lari kneaded her apron between her fingers. 'I made some horse bread, and we have butter. Why don't you come in for some refreshments first?'

'I don't think Cooper would like that.' Then he was walking away.

Lyndal hurried to catch up to him, holding her skirts off the ground as she attempted to match his pace. Registering her struggle, he slowed.

'Want to talk about that very awkward exchange with your mother back there?' she asked, looking over her shoulder.

'Nothing to talk about.'

She watched him. 'She's not the first woman to marry the wrong man, you know. Are you really going to make her pay for that mistake for the rest of her life?'

'You don't know what you're talking about, so leave it alone.'

She sighed. 'I can see she's carrying a lot of guilt.'

'And yet nothing changes.'

'What would you have her do exactly?' Lyndal said on a laugh. 'The man is her husband. If he truly is a monster, he won't take kindly to a change of heart.'

He met her eyes. 'Speaking of family, what did your sisters have to say about your marriage choice?'

'Oh, I think you can hazard a guess.'

'Do you think showing them your lavender drawing might help?'

Her mouth fell open, eyes laughing. 'I take offence to that, defender.'

'As is your right, Lady Lyndal of Cardelle Manor.'

She shoved him playfully with little effect.

'Didn't I once hear you say you're named after your grandmother?' he asked.

'So you *were* listening at dinner all those times I thought you were blocking out the sound of my voice. Your point being?'

The corners of his mouth lifted. 'That makes you Lady Lyndal the second of Cardelle Manor.'

She laughed. 'Actually, I would be Lady Lyndal the *third*. My grandmother's grandmother was also named Lyndal.'

He chuckled lightly, the tension leaving his shoulders.

'It's really peaceful here,' she said, looking around at the muddy fields. 'I can almost picture the green paddocks before the rain arrived and stripped this place of its beauty.'

His eyes swept their surroundings. 'It really was something back then.'

Lyndal was silent a moment. 'Do you ever wonder how your life would have turned out if you'd stayed here?'

'I would have been dragged off to the tower for murdering my stepfather, then hung on a wall.'

Lyndal winced. 'It was that bad?'

'It was that bad.'

A hand landed on his wrist, and he followed it all the way up to that pretty round face.

'I'm sorry,' she said. 'I know what it is to grow up without a father, but I can't even fathom a terrible replacement.' Her hand fell away. 'I imagine your mother had no choice but to remarry. She had young children and could hardly be expected to run a farm this size by herself.'

His eyes went to the open gate up ahead. 'She doesn't need your excuses. She has enough of her own.' He gestured for her to stop and looked around.

'What's the matter?' she asked.

He pointed ahead. 'That's the paddock we keep the bull in.'

'The one with the open gate?'

He nodded and continued walking. 'Stay close.'

She took hold of his arm. 'Is it a charging bull by any chance?'

His eyes went to where she was gripping him. 'Not usually, but that's a very bright shade of blue you're wearing.' He smiled to himself when her grip tightened.

Astin relaxed when he spotted his sisters with the bull up ahead, his expression turning to one of amusement as he took in the sight of Presley knee deep in a bog, resting against the bull's rump. Rose was tugging on a rope attached to the bull's halter. She stopped when she spotted them approaching, likely wondering who he was. It had been nearly two years since he had stepped foot on the farm.

'*Now* you choose to visit?' Presley said.

Astin stopped at the edge of the bog. 'Good to see you too.'

'It's all right, Rose. It's just your silly brother.'

His youngest sister's expression changed from wary to curious. 'Is that your wife?'

Lyndal immediately let go of Astin's arm. 'Fletcher remains blissfully unwed.' She walked over to the girl and bent down, gently squeezing her bicep. 'Just as I suspected. Much stronger than your brother.'

Rose giggled.

'I'm Lyndal, by the way.' She extended a hand, and Rose took hold of it.

'He's stuck really good this time.'

Lyndal turned to face the exhausted bull. 'I see that.'

'You going to help or what?' Presley called to Astin.

'I'm in uniform.'

She let out an exasperated breath. 'We couldn't have a defender muddying up his boots, now could we? Do they still regularly sweep the wall walks so you can stroll debris-free up there?'

Astin was about to reply but stopped when he spotted Lyndal unlacing her boots. 'What are you doing?'

She tugged one off. 'What does it look like I'm doing? I'm going to help.'

Presley's eyebrows rose. 'I like her.'

'This is Lady Lyndal the third of Cardelle Manor,' Astin said.

Presley flattened her palms on the bull's rump. 'Fancy.'

Lyndal threw the second boot *at* him. 'Except I've never lived at Cardelle Manor.'

'I've heard about you,' Presley said, pushing. 'You're the merchant girl everyone's been talking about. The only woman to capture the king's short attention span.'

'You'll have to forgive my sister for speaking poorly of our king,' Astin said.

Lyndal began unbuttoning her skirt. 'Don't worry. I have very selective hearing.'

'Stop,' Astin said. 'If the king finds you standing in the mud with your clothes off, he won't be pleased.'

Ignoring him, Lyndal stepped into the mud and sucked in a breath. 'Goodness, it's colder than I realised.'

Rose was watching Astin, waiting to see what he would do next. With a heavy sigh, he removed his boots and socks, rolled up his trousers, and followed them into the mud.

'What do you weigh?' Astin asked Lyndal over the top of the bull. 'You're probably the equivalent of two sacks of flour?'

'That's a very rude question to ask a lady.'

'This bull weighs at least fifteen times that. I'm just doing the math.'

'Ready?' Presley asked.

Lyndal reached a hand around the bull, and Astin reluctantly took hold of it. 'Speak up if anything doesn't feel right. I don't want you injured.'

'He dislocated my shoulder once,' Presley said.

'By accident.'

His sister leaned closer to Lyndal. 'Defenders are notoriously violent.'

Lyndal smiled. 'You are so much funnier than your brother.'

Astin shook his head and looked up at Rose. 'Ready?'

The girl nodded.

'One, two—'

'Wait,' Lyndal said. 'Are we going on three or after three?'

He squinted across the bull at her. 'On three.'

'And we're pushing forwards, not up?' Lyndal asked, shoulder pressing into the bull's rump.

'Correct,' Astin said. 'We're not trying to lift the fifteen-hundred-pound animal out of dense mud. We want him to walk himself out.'

Lyndal took a few breaths, readying herself. 'All right. On three.'

Astin tried not to look at his grinning sister. 'One, two, three.'

The bull groaned as they pushed. Eventually, the exhausted animal lifted one of his front legs and took a step towards the edge.

'Good,' Presley said, slumping against the bull. 'Now we just need to do that over and over until he's out.'

Lyndal reached for Astin's hand once more. 'Let's not dilly-dally, then.'

The mud was knee deep, and her chemise had soaked up the layer of water sitting on top of the mud, making the fabric cling to her thighs. Astin tried very hard not to stare across the bull at her.

'Are you still with us, brother?' Presley asked, suppressing a knowing smile.

Heat crawled up his neck as he leaned into the bull again. 'One, two, three.'

This time both of the bull's back legs moved. The next time both front legs. Another back leg. Then finally, the bull was at the edge of the bog.

'This is it,' Presley said. 'Once he feels that firm ground beneath him, he'll go, so take the rope off now, Rose, and hop out of the way.'

Lyndal wiped the back of her hand over her sweaty brow, smearing mud over her face in the process.

'What?' she asked when she found him watching her.

'Nothing. Let's go. One last effort.' He took hold of her hand again, enjoying the sensation of her clammy skin a little too much.

That would need to stop.

Presley counted them in this time. 'One, two, three.'

They all gave one final mighty push, and the bull staggered up the muddy slope, falling to his knees before righting himself and trotting away with a defiant bellow.

Lyndal held on to her knees as she caught her breath. 'Thank goodness. That's all I had left.'

He had a clear view of her now, soaked from the waist down. He could not look away, even going as far as imagining the top half of her wet.

She straightened and brought a hand to her forehead, adding more mud. The hand fell away when she saw his face. 'What's the matter?'

Before he could think of a sensible response, Rose said, 'Is that the king?'

Astin's head snapped in the direction of approaching horses.

Shit.

The three of them scampered out of the mud, snatching up clothing and boots and wrestling them on as quickly as they could.

Borin looked between them as he pulled up his horse. 'What on earth is going on here?' His eyes settled on Lyndal, moving over her. 'I know merchants love their mud, but this seems a bit much.'

Lyndal dropped her gaze.

'Our bull was stuck, Your Majesty,' Presley said. 'Your companion was kind enough to help.'

The king was still staring at Lyndal. 'Well, next time she better leave it to the farmers.'

'It's just a bit of mud, Your Grace,' Lyndal said as she smoothed down her crinkled skirt.

'You forget who you ride beside,' the king shot back.

Astin's fingers curled into fists. 'My fault, not hers. I let her get in.'

The king looked at him. 'While that is noble of you, your job is to guard her, not keep her clean. Escort her back to the castle.' He swung his horse around. 'Cannot have the farmers mistaking her for a pig.'

They watched him ride away. Then Presley gave Lyndal a sympathetic smile as she went to collect Rose.

'Let's get you cleaned up,' she said, taking her sister's hand.

Astin and Lyndal remained there, not looking at one another.

'You did warn me,' she finally said.

He exhaled, nodded, then began walking. 'Let's go.'

CHAPTER 20

The next day, Lyndal accepted the king's offer to have dinner together in the privacy of his quarters. She listened to him talk about himself and his accomplishments for two hours while pushing the same piece of duck around her plate. It was never a good thing when your food reminded you of your family pet. She kept picturing Garlic roaming free around Wright House, despite objections from Harlan—which she suspected were for show.

'My mother told me that what a woman puts in her mouth greatly impacts reproduction,' the king said, pushing his empty plate away. 'Good nutrition should be the priority of every woman of child-bearing age.'

Lyndal's fork stilled. 'Sorry. It's an awful lot of food for two people.'

'A merchant's perspective.' He picked up his cup and drank, red wine staining above his lip, where stubble should have been.

Lyndal glanced at the door, wishing Astin were inside the room instead of out in the corridor. They could have exchanged knowing looks.

'You know, the birth rate in the merchant borough has dropped significantly,' the king went on.

Lyndal closed her eyes and laid down her fork. 'It's not by choice, I assure you. Though after seeing all the new lambs and calves in the farming borough today, I feel quite hopeful. How long until they'll make their way to the butchers?'

Borin swirled the liquid in his cup. 'It is too early to talk numbers, and it is certainly not for you to worry about.'

There was little that came out of that man's mouth that did not grate on her. That was about as far as her tolerance could stretch for one evening.

Looking down at her plate, she said, 'I'm afraid I'm rather exhausted. Do you mind if I retire for the evening?' She rose from her chair.

'I thought you might visit me in my bedchamber this evening.'

'What for?' As soon as she asked the question, she realised she knew the answer. 'Oh.' Surely he was not expecting her to visit his bed before they were wed. 'I might be half merchant, Your Grace, but I'm also half lady.'

His scratched his nose and straightened the cutlery on his plate. 'I assumed you would be equally as curious about the extent of our compatibility.'

She did not know where to look. 'Of course. It's just

that… our engagement is not even official yet. If we were to change our minds—'

'Very well.' He waved a hand in her direction. 'Off you go.'

She could see she had wounded his pride. 'It was an enjoyable dinner,' she lied. 'I hope we can do it again.'

He lifted his gaze to her. 'Perhaps next time you will eat.'

Nausea rolled through her stomach in place of food. Curtsying, she headed for the door.

Astin turned to her when she stepped out into the corridor, eyes moving over her.

'What's wrong?' he asked as the door clicked shut behind her.

She closed the distance between them, then whispered, 'Am I expected to lie with him *before* we're wed?'

Astin pulled her away from the door, nodding at the defender on duty as they fled. He waited until they were out of earshot before saying, 'You don't have to do anything—yet.'

'Yet?' she asked.

His eyes went to her. 'If you marry the king, you can be sure the entire kingdom will be waiting for an heir.'

She was silent a moment. 'The offer threw me. I think I hurt his feelings.'

'He'll live.'

'Perhaps I should have said yes, find out what I'm getting myself into.'

Astin tripped on his own foot, then looked accusingly at the floor behind him. His expression was eerily stern beneath the yellow glow of torches. 'If you *want* to share his bed, that's another matter.'

'I don't *want* to. It's just that I can't think of any examples in history where women have captured a king's heart with clever ideas on how to help the poor.'

'Lifting one's skirts is a classic technique.'

They arrived outside her bedchamber, and she turned to face him. 'I'm sorry.'

'For what?'

'For using you in place of sisters. I've no one else to talk to except Queen Fayre, but this particular topic might be somewhat awkward.'

He looked off down the corridor. 'As opposed to this very comfortable conversation?'

She suppressed a smile. 'If I do wed the king, then I'll have my ladies-in-waiting to bother instead.'

'Just be careful who you trust.'

Her eyebrows rose. 'I wouldn't select women I didn't trust.'

'You likely won't select them at all. The women usually come from noble families in favour with the king. I wouldn't count them as friends just yet.'

She had assumed she would have some say. 'I had thought Eda would join me here, but that might be a stretch.'

'Because she's mute?'

'Because she despises the king and walks around heavily armed at all times.'

Astin crossed his arms, studying her. 'And with Blake desperate for a child, you'll have no luck luring her away from Harlan.'

Lyndal blinked. 'What did you say?"

'I'm certain your sister has mentioned the fact that she wants children.'

'Yes, but you said desperate for it?'

Astin's arms fell to his sides. 'She was upset when I called past the house the other day. It's only been a year. Her body's still getting used to the idea of regular food.'

'You shouldn't be discussing my sister's body.' She was not angry at him but the fact that he knew something about Blake she did not. The separation was cruel. 'Sorry.' She shook her head. 'It's the kind of thing she would normally talk to me about.'

He exhaled. 'I'm sure she wishes she could.'

Lyndal scrunched her nose up when her eyes began to burn. 'You must be exhausted from following me around all day.'

'I can stay awhile if you want me to.'

'I'm fine. Go get some sleep.'

'I'll collect you in the morning,' Astin said, glancing off down the corridor. 'Duck shooting with the king, I believe.'

She paused halfway inside the door. 'Where do these mystical ducks live? Certainly nowhere near the merchant borough or port.'

'They live in crates, greatly inhibiting their ability to fly. The king prefers them that way.'

'Of course he does.' She leaned against the door. 'Well, goodnight, Your Superiorship.'

He bowed his head. 'Goodnight, Lady Lyndal the third.'

Lyndal woke in the night with a sharp cough, eyes snapping open at the bitter taste in her mouth. Sitting upright, she looked around the bedchamber, blinking hard. She could not see more than a foot in front of her. Coughing ensued, the air utterly unbreathable.

Smoke.

The room was full of it.

Pushing back her blankets, Lyndal leapt from the bed and headed for the door, arms outstretched in front of her. She felt around for the doorknob, frame, anything familiar to get her bearings. The darkness was not helping matters. Finally, she felt the smooth wood of the door beneath her fingers and reached for the handle. She turned it, but the door did not budge. She grabbed hold of it with both hands and yanked as hard as she could. When it did not open, she pounded on it with a fist.

'Open the door!'

The door was never locked. And where was the defender who patrolled the corridor overnight?

She coughed, gagged, her eyes burning and vision blurring. She made her way over to the solar door. Pulling it open, she immediately slammed it shut again when she saw the furniture engulfed by flames, reaching all the way to the ceiling.

Her mind raced.

The window.

She ran to it, tripping over a stool and landing on hands and knees. She crawled the rest of the way, feeling her way along the outer-wall. Coughing and crying, she rose and fumbled with the shutters before tearing them open. She pressed her face to the iron bars, but the air was no cleaner. Smoke poured out of the window, making it impossible to breathe.

'Help me!' She screamed the words as loudly as she could, but they dissipated in the smoke.

She moved to the bottom corner of the window, daring a look in the direction of the solar. The door glowed red now, but she knew the smoke would kill her before the flames did.

Back on hands and knees, she crawled to the bed and grabbed the woollen blanket from atop it. She dragged it to the door, jamming it in the gap at the bottom. The smoke still seeped through the top and sides though. By the time she got back to the window, she did not have the energy to stand. She lay flat on the floor, eyes pressed shut and hand over her mouth as if that might somehow filter the smoke.

So this was how she would die.

Not surrounded by people who loved her as she had imagined so many times during the lockdown, when death had hung over their house like a heavy cloud. Instead, she would be alone. The other people in the castle would not grieve but they would be inconvenienced by the disruption to their plans.

And what of her own plans? Her terrible drawings that Astin made fun of? They were now ashes.

A loud bang shook the room, and Lyndal opened her eyes, expecting to see flames.

'Lyndal!'

Astin.

She would recognise his voice anywhere.

Here, she yelled, then realised it was only in her head.

Her eyes sank shut, and she heard the pounding of boots through the floor. Then he was beside her, lifting her, telling her to hold on. She *wanted* to hold on, but she was no more than a rag doll in his arms. He clutched her head to his thudding chest as they fled the bedchamber.

A flurry of servants and maids passed pails of water in the corridor, dousing the flames in the solar. Astin flew by them, down the stairs, and out into the clean air of the fountain court. The sudden change seemed to prompt her lungs to start working again. Coughing resumed in violent fits.

'That's it,' Astin said, sitting her on the ground. He removed his cloak and wrapped it around her.

Her head pounded, and her nose and eyes ran. She struggled to move her arms.

He pressed two fingers to her neck. 'Your heart is racing.' When he sat her up, she slumped forwards again. His large palm spanned the width of her collarbone, holding her steady. He lowered his forehead to hers. 'You're all right. Cough. Throw up. Cry. Do whatever you need to—just breathe.'

She wanted to lie down, but he kept her firmly upright.

'I need to wash your eyes out,' he said, carrying her to the fountain. 'And get some water into you.'

She nodded, barely, as he placed her on the edge of the fountain. He scooped up water with his spare hand and angled her head, splashing it into her eyes, all while she continued to cough.

'Blink for me,' he said. 'That's it.'

After cleaning her eyes, he gathered more water and brought it to her mouth. She drank greedily, the cold soothing her aching throat.

'You gave me a fright,' he said.

She tipped her head up to look at him. 'The door was locked.' Her words were so hoarse she did not recognise her own voice.

He brushed tears from her cheek with his enormous thumb. 'The defender on duty is going to have no skin left on that back of his by the time I'm through flogging him.'

She rested her head against him, eyes closing. 'Thank you.'

He did not reply.

Boots sounded beneath the archway, and a few seconds later, the warden appeared in front of them, eyes moving over Lyndal.

'Everybody all right?'

Astin stood, keeping one hand on her shoulder to ensure she did not fall. 'She'll need a physician, sir.' He paused. 'The door was locked when I arrived—from the outside.'

Shapur's jaw ticked. 'I will send for the physician. Take her to the queen mother's quarters. Her Majesty is expecting you.'

Lyndal looked up, no longer afraid of him as she had once been. She had gotten to know him since the wedding —as well as one could know a closed-off man. She had managed to win him over one meal at a time.

She rose on unsteady legs, Astin keeping a firm hold of her.

'Shall I send word to your family?' the warden asked.

She shook her head. 'Not unless you want a riot at the gate.' A violent cough followed.

Astin held her steady.

'I'm feeling much better,' she assured him, willing her knees to hold. She took a dizzy step, her heart pounding in her ears.

'Hold on to me if you want to be spared the embarrassment of being carried,' Astin said.

She took hold of his arm, and they slowly made their way to the queen's quarters.

Fayre was watching the fireplace when they arrived, playing with the ends of her long plait that fell down one shoulder. She turned as they entered, her eyes moving over Lyndal. 'Dear God.' She walked over and cupped a hand to Lyndal's burning cheek, her lavish red heraldic gown slipping down her arm. 'My maids are making up a room for you. They are filling a tub as we speak. No one is to enter your bedchamber without Fletcher's approval. You will have my personal maids at your service. They will be the only people allowed near you until we figure out what happened.' She hooked a finger beneath Lyndal's chin, lifting it. 'You keep that head high if you hope to balance a crown upon it.'

Lyndal swallowed.

'Warden,' Fayre said, turning to him, 'I am trusting you to handle this.'

He bowed his head. 'I recommend all food be tasted prior to consumption in the interim.'

A food taster seemed a tad dramatic. But then if

someone was prepared to burn her to death, poison was not such a stretch.

'Fletcher,' the queen mother continued, 'I will leave it to you to hand select a guard for night duty, given the current one was clearly not up to the job. Has he been found?'

'My men are on it,' Shapur said. 'Shall I rouse the king?'

Fayre shook her head. 'I shall update him in the morning. You know how he gets when his sleep is disturbed.'

Lyndal looked down at her bare, blackened feet. The castle was still on fire, and no one wanted to tell the king for fear of waking him. What sort of king could not cope with a crisis without a full night's rest first?

'I imagine Lady Lyndal would prefer to see him after she has cleaned up,' the queen mother added.

Lyndal's appearance was the last thing on her mind, but she nodded in agreement. The mere thought of dealing with him was too much.

Shapur bowed. 'Your Majesty.'

He left, passing a maid in the doorway on his way out. The older woman stepped aside, then made her way over to Lyndal, offering a warm smile.

'Goodness, my lady. You're ashes and soot, head to toe. Let's get you cleaned up so the physician can take a look at you.'

Lyndal had not realised how tightly she was holding Astin's arm until the woman tried to pull her away. She did not want to let go.

'I'll be outside your bedchamber soon,' Astin said, as though reading her mind. 'Go. She'll take care of you.'

She forced herself to let go.

'I've got you,' the maid said lightly. 'Come along.'

Lyndal's eyes remained on Astin as she was led away. Only when they stepped out into the smoke-hazed corridor did she look away.

CHAPTER 21

'Stop before you collapse,' Harlan called to Astin. 'I'm not carrying you inside.'

Astin leaned on his knees, trying to catch his breath. Since sleep continued to elude him, he had opted for laps of the training yard instead.

'What exactly are we running from?' Harlan asked, walking over to him.

He was trying to run off his anger after someone had locked Lyndal in a smoke-filled room two nights earlier. It was also possible he was running from other feelings, feelings that seemed to be multiplying each time he laid eyes on her. 'I'm just doing my hours.'

'She's alive,' Harlan said, seeing through the lie. 'You did your job.'

He straightened. 'If you had seen her when I found her, you would know how close I came to losing her.'

Harlan looked in the direction of the castle. 'I hear the defender on duty was dragged naked from a bed in the servants' quarters. Must have been having a real good time.'

'He swears he never locked that door.'

'You think he's telling the truth?'

Astin threw his hands up. 'There's no motive. Plus it doesn't make sense that he would set the castle on fire and then stay there, knowing he would either burn to death or be caught.'

All they had was a defender scratching an itch and a maid who claimed the fireplace in the solar was down to embers when she checked on it before retiring.

But someone locked that door.

'Thanks for loaning me Thornton,' Astin said. 'I need someone trustworthy who'll remain at his post.'

'He should have waited until he was off duty, like you do.'

Astin did not even register his words. 'I was hoping the fire might be enough to scare her home, but Queen Fayre's still whispering promises into her ear.'

'Wow.' Harlan watched him a moment. 'No pithy comeback? This is worse than I thought.'

Astin squinted in his direction. 'What are you talking about?'

'This is real. You have genuine feelings for Lyndal, and I'm at a loss at what to think about it.'

Astin ran a hand down his face, not bothering to deny it.

'And now she's going to marry the king.' Harlan tutted. 'That's quite the mess you find yourself in.'

Astin paced a few steps, then stopped. 'Let's say you're

right. Say an attachment has formed. What do I do? How do I sever it?'

Harlan clapped him on the back. 'You're asking the wrong man. In my experience, it can't be done.'

Astin closed his eyes and exhaled. 'This is going to end badly.'

'Have you told her how you feel? It might be mutual.'

'God, listen to you. No, I haven't fallen at her feet and sung of my undying love.'

Harlan's eyebrows lifted. 'Is that how you think it's done?'

'And it makes no difference if it's mutual. If she's prepared to sacrifice her family for this noble cause of hers, I'm irrelevant.' His eyes went to the tower, which was alive with activity. 'Do I want to know what's going on over there?'

Harlan leaned his weight on one foot. 'Riot in the merchant borough this morning. Tenth day straight with no meat or eggs at the market. Fifty-plus merchants locked up.'

Astin swore under his breath. 'I'm surprised they have the energy to riot. They should be applauded, not locked up.'

'King's orders. Even my father disagreed.'

'Then I should go have a wash,' Astin said, wiping sweat from his face. 'Lyndal's with him on the stone court porch as we speak. If there's been a riot, he'll be in a mood.'

'Don't you mean *Lady* Lyndal?'

Astin shook his head. 'I'll throw your arse to the ground in front of the recruits if you push me to it.'

Harlan only grinned. 'Send Thornton to me.'

'I hope you're going to let him sleep.'

'Yes. *After* he's trained.'

Astin mock saluted him. 'Yes, sir.'

Astin heard their argument before he saw it. Lyndal and King Borin were standing by the north wall, the king gesturing wildly while she clutched the skirt of her dress.

'What's going on?' Astin whispered to Roul when he entered the court.

The defender glanced sideways at him. 'She wants the prisoners released. Apparently the butchers were promised a supply yesterday. Now the king is saying it'll be at least another two weeks.'

'Half won't survive another two weeks.'

Thornton nodded. 'That's what she's telling him. And she's *really* telling him.'

Astin exhaled. 'She sleep last night?'

'Nope. She came out twice asking if I could smell smoke, and she won't let the maid light the fire in her room.'

Astin squinted in her direction, listening.

'They're allowed to feel angry,' Lyndal said, letting go of her skirt. 'Those people are living moment to moment, and every day no meat arrives brings them another day closer to death.'

As tempting as it was to intervene, Astin knew there were no grounds for it. 'You go,' he told Thornton. 'Commander Wright's waiting for you in the training yard.'

Roul nodded, then quietly stepped out.

Queen Fayre appeared a moment later, striding towards the pair with a concerned expression. 'What on earth is going on here? I can hear all the way inside.'

Borin turned in a circle, attempting to calm himself. 'I will tell you what is going on. Because of you, I have a merchant telling me how to run my kingdom.'

Lyndal shook her head, her green eyes ablaze. 'It doesn't make sense. I've done the math.'

Borin jabbed a finger at her face. 'This is not your concern.'

That was enough for Astin. He walked over to them, positioning himself in front of Lyndal. 'Hand down, Your Majesty.'

Borin's eyes widened, and his mouth twisted. 'Is this a joke? I am your *king*.'

'And Lady Lyndal is the job I was assigned. My orders were to protect her as I would a queen, so hand down, Your Majesty. Then I'll move aside.' He kept his voice calm.

Borin sniffed and retreated to his mother's side. Then Astin stepped back.

'Let us all take a breath. I gather this is about this morning's riot?' Queen Fayre asked, looking to Lyndal.

'We were in the farming borough just a few days ago,' Lyndal said. 'Every farm we visited reported higher yields and a decrease in mortality rates year on year. Yet the merchants are getting the same amount of meat as two years prior—which is none.'

The queen mother's eyes shone with something resembling pride. 'You really have been paying attention.'

'It is not simple math,' Borin snapped. 'The needs of the merchants have to be balanced with the needs of other boroughs. The nobility require meat also.'

Lyndal stared in disbelief. 'Yes, I know all about their needs. While the nobility are always complaining about something, I assure you it's not the lack of meat.'

'The farmers were supposed to deliver carcasses to the butchers yesterday,' Fayre said to her son. 'Why the delay?'

Borin shifted his weight and looked away, which Astin knew meant whatever came out of his mouth next would be a lie.

'The heifers and ewes are to be kept for breeding. That is how one grows a herd.'

Lyndal blinked in confusion. 'There must have been some males among them.'

Borin turned to his mother. 'Do you see the lack of respect? How is this to work when she questions me so?'

Fayre placed a calming hand on his arm. 'Lady Lyndal is still recovering from a very traumatic experience. Her mind is likely still impaired from the smoke.' She looked to Lyndal for confirmation.

Lyndal exhaled. 'Yes. Forgive me, Your Majesty. I'm in need of rest.' Her tone lacked any conviction, though the dark circles enclosing her eyes did support the lie.

'So we are done with this conversation now?' Borin asked. 'I am a busy man.'

Lyndal went to the king and took his hand. Astin felt a pull of jealousy at the intimate gesture. God help him if she did make it to his bed while he was forced to stand guard outside.

'Please,' she begged, 'let the people locked in that tower go home. Don't punish them for being hungry.'

Borin pulled his hand free. 'They are criminals. They took axes to the wall that my father built.'

'They were desperate to gain your attention, to be seen and heard—and it worked. *Please.* Let them return to their families who are already suffering more than you can imagine.' Seeing his hesitation, she added, 'You could do it. You could go to that tower and release them yourself, be the hero of the story. They'll not forget it.'

He searched her eyes for a moment. 'If I do that, they will think they won.'

Lyndal stared at him in confusion. 'Your Grace, you're on the same side. It's not you against your people, it's Chadora against the famine. Their win is your win. But right now the merchants are losing, which means we're all losing.'

Astin's throat thickened, and a realisation hit him hard. She really was the queen Chadora deserved. He had been too lost in his jealousy to truly see it.

Borin looked to his mother. 'And what am I supposed to say to these criminals? Am I expected to simply pardon them and open the gate?'

'Yes,' Lyndal said immediately. 'That's how an act of mercy works. Maybe it'll result in one less riot down the track, or maybe it won't. But you do it anyway.'

Borin tapped a foot on the ground, looking between the two women.

'I think you should listen to her,' Fayre said after a long silence.

'And be seen as weak?'

Fayre shook her head. 'Acting out of pride and anger is weakness. Showing mercy takes incredible strength.'

Borin huffed like an angry bull. 'Fine. Let us go to the tower before I come to my senses.' He looked at Lyndal. 'You will stand at my side so I can blame you when they turn on me.' With that, he marched off in the direction of the gate, two guards flanking him.

'Off you go,' Fayre said to Lyndal. 'You do not need me.' The corners of her mouth lifted slightly when she said that.

'Do hurry up,' Borin shouted over his shoulder, prompting Lyndal to start walking.

Astin ground his teeth together and followed them.

When they arrived at the tower, Astin trailed Lyndal up the winding narrow steps, to a cell halfway up where all the prisoners had been packed in. Lyndal stood at the king's side while he addressed them in a slightly less obnoxious tone than usual. It was interesting to Astin that the prisoners were not watching the king but were looking at Lyndal. And when the cell door swung open, they continued to look at her, as though they did not trust what the king had said.

'There's nothing to fear,' Lyndal reassured them. 'The defenders will escort you to the gate. You're going home.' She moved back, going to stand with Astin.

Slowly and cautiously, the merchants filed out, each one pausing to bow or curtsy before descending the steps.

Borin lifted his chin and pushed out his narrow chest, visibly pleased by the show of respect.

'At least he's happy,' Lyndal whispered to Astin.

'Until he realises the truth.'

'The truth?' She looked up at him.

The young king was not the only one who was clueless about what was happening at that moment. Leaning in so Borin would not hear, he said, 'They're not bowing to their king. They're bowing to *you*.'

CHAPTER 22

*L*yndal pushed the covers back and swung her legs over the edge of the bed. She looked around the dark, empty room, then went to the window and pulled the shutters open, taking in greedy lungfuls of air. She stilled when she caught sight of the sky. There was a gap in the clouds, and a handful of stars shone down at her. A smile spread across her face. It had been a long time since she had seen stars.

Walking over to the door, she pulled it open. Roul appeared in front of her before she had a chance to step outside, his solid frame illuminated by torchlight.

'Everything all right, my lady?' he asked, looking past her into the room.

'I would like to go to the fountain court.'

'Now?'

She nodded.

Roul glanced down the corridor. 'I don't think that's a good idea. Fletcher would prefer you safe in your bedchamber.'

She rolled her eyes. 'History has proven that my bedchamber is the *least* safe place for me.'

He released a heavy breath. 'All right.' Looking her up and down, he added, 'Cloak? Shoes?'

Ah. She slipped on some boots and put on her thickest cloak. Tugging the hood up, she stepped past Roul and headed for the stairs.

The air in the courtyard was still and crisp as she stepped outside and looked up at the sky. 'When was the last time you saw stars, Thornton?'

'Yesterday during training.'

She laughed quietly as she made her way over to the fountain and lay down on the edge. Clasping her hands over her stomach, she stared up at the sky. The running water was loud in her ear, exactly what she needed to drown out her thoughts. Roul stood a few feet away with the same serious expression Harlan always wore.

'I can't sleep,' she confessed. 'I'm so tired, but my mind won't stop.'

At first she thought he did not hear her, but then he said, 'Are you afraid of fire?'

She blinked, and tears slid into her hair. 'I'm afraid I'll die alone in that room.'

He nodded. 'Well, you're not in that room now—and you're not alone. So sleep if you want to.'

Her eyelids felt like they weighed a hundred pounds suddenly. She blinked a few times and found she could not keep her eyes open. 'If the stars can break through this eternal cloud cover, then why can't the sun?'

She never heard his reply, because sleep took her.

Lyndal woke to blinding daylight and running water. She turned her head, registering the fountain, then sat up with a gasp.

'Good sleep?'

Her head whipped around, and there was Astin standing five feet away, watching her. She looked down at the rolled-up cloak that had been placed under her head as a pillow. Picking it up, she held it out to him. 'You didn't have to freeze on my account.'

He stepped forwards to take it. 'You were sleeping on stone.' He continued to watch her as he put it on. 'Thornton tells me you were out here most of the night.'

'And some of the day, it seems.' She stood and stretched her arms luxuriously above her head, feeling rested for the first time since the fire. 'Did he tell you that we saw stars?'

'Oddly, that was not part of his debriefing, no.'

She smiled at the ground. A few weeks earlier, they had barely tolerated one another's company, and now seeing him each morning was one of the highlights of her day.

'The king and queen mother have asked to see you,' he said.

She stilled. 'Together? Am I in trouble?'

He angled his head. 'Not to my knowledge. Unless there's something you wish to confess.'

She shook her head. 'Not if you don't already know about it. I suppose I should go get cleaned up.' She looked down at her nightdress, visible through the split of the cloak.

'Probably a good idea.'

Astin stood outside her bedchamber while she washed and dressed, then escorted her to the terrace, where Borin and Fayre were playing chess.

'Finally,' Borin said, rising from his chair.

Lyndal curtsied and found a smile. 'Apologies for keeping you waiting, Your Grace. You wished to see me?'

The queen mother rose also, going to stand beside her son with a coy smile. 'The king has a gift for you.'

'A gift?' That was the one possibility she had not considered. 'How thoughtful.'

'This way,' Borin said, marching away.

He never offered her his arm or gestured for her to go ahead. He was forever in a rush in her presence. She always felt like an inconvenience. But she followed dutifully, glancing once over her shoulder at Astin, who remained at the edge of the terrace.

'Down there,' Borin said, pointing over the balustrade.

She approached slowly, peering over the edge. Below was a one-horse wagon carrying a dead cow. Its throat was cut, and its tongue hung out. The head dangled over the back at a strange angle.

'Oh. It's a… dead animal.'

'Bled out and ready for butchering,' Borin said. Registering her confused expression, he added, 'For your charity work. Mother told me you like to feed the poor.'

He said that like it was an unusual leisure pursuit of hers. 'Yes, I'm quite partial to keeping people alive.'

The joke blew past him. 'Well, do with it as you wish.

You are free to go to the merchant borough. The kitchen staff should be able to assist you with whatever you need.'

It was the nicest thing he had ever done—even if it was his mother's idea. He appeared to be trying, so she took the olive branch he was offering her. 'Perhaps you would like to accompany me.'

He snorted. 'Do you honestly expect the king of Chadora to ladle soup into bowls for the poor? I do not even ladle soup into my own bowl.'

She had dined with him enough times to know that was true.

'Oh, and I have invited your uncle to dine with us tonight. He is keen to see how you are getting on.'

Lyndal tried to keep her face neutral.

'You will join us for dinner this evening,' he said. It was an order, not an invitation. 'And make sure the plebeians know where the meat has come from. Credit where credit is due and all that.'

Her smile seemed to have frozen on her face. 'I shall sing your praises from their eroding rooftops, Your Grace.'

With a curt nod, he strode off in the other direction.

Queen Fayre walked over to Lyndal, looking rather pleased with herself. 'He is a better man already because of you. Someday, he will be a better king.'

Lyndal peered over the edge at the ox again. 'A generous gift, yet he's no fonder of me.'

'Give him time. His pride is likely wounded from the dinner you shared the other night.'

Lyndal looked back at her with a questioning expression.

'When he asked you to join him in his bedchamber,' the queen mother explained.

Lyndal felt the colour drain from her face. 'He told you about that?'

Fayre's eyes shone with amusement. 'He does not take rejection well, and he needs to be reassured that he is not the problem.'

'Does that make *me* the problem?'

The queen mother suppressed a smile. 'You were the perfect lady, but you must learn to say no in a way that does not wound his fragile ego. It is an art form, one I can teach you.'

That would be a fun lesson.

'Fletcher,' Fayre called.

Astin made his way over to them. 'Yes, Your Majesty?'

'Lady Lyndal will be travelling to the merchant borough. Take a few extra men with you. The nobility can access the borough at any time, so better to take precautions.' She turned back to Lyndal. 'We still have a few weeks left to win them over.'

Lyndal released a breath. 'Good to know.' She lowered into a curtsy. 'Your Majesty.'

Fayre bowed her head before following her son.

'Did you know about this gift?' Lyndal asked Astin once they were alone.

'I did, yes.'

She began walking. 'A simple "the king is gifting you a dead animal" would have been a nice heads-up.'

'It's not my place to ruin his romantic surprises.'

She looked up at him. 'Would it be possible to get

word to my sisters and mother that I'll be in the square today?'

He nodded. 'I'll send someone to the house.'

When she looked back at the ground, she noticed their steps were perfectly in sync. Sometime over the previous few weeks, he had started shortening his stride, and she had started lengthening hers. Now their feet hit the earth in unison, and that made her chest feel light and her bones hum.

'Watch where you're walking, not down at your feet,' Astin said.

She met his gaze. 'A few weeks ago, you would have laughed hysterically if I had collided with something.'

'You mean before I was responsible for your safety?'

They entered the castle side by side. Clearing her throat, Lyndal said, 'You know, we haven't really spoken properly since the fire. I hope you know how grateful I am to you. Not only for saving my life but for all the kindness you showed. You truly did go above and beyond duty.'

He was silent.

She glanced up at him. 'Did you hear me?'

'Yes.'

'You're supposed to say something nice back.'

'You're welcome.' He did not look at her when he spoke.

Her brow furrowed. 'Have I missed something here? Done something?'

Taking her hand suddenly, Astin pulled her into a doorway. She held her breath as he dipped his head to speak.

'What exactly are you fishing for here?' His voice was laced with irritation.

She stared up at him. 'I was simply thanking you. You guard me as you would the king. I see it, and I appreciate it.'

He let go of her wrist. 'You know, I don't tend to cradle the king in my arms.'

She searched his eyes. 'Why not? I'm certain he would like it.'

Astin raked a hand over his short hair, then brought his face closer to hers. She did not know whether he was going to reprimand her or kiss her. Of course he was not going to kiss her. So why did her lips part and her heart speed up?

'The plan hasn't changed, has it?' he whispered. 'You want the crown.'

He was so close she could feel his breath on her face. She leaned into the sensation, and he drew back, waiting for her answer.

'What I want is to help the merchants,' she said.

'So you'll marry the king.'

Her heart threatened to burst through her ribcage now. 'Yes.'

His gaze fell to her lips, lingered there for a long moment, and then he stepped back out into the corridor. 'Then let's go.'

She took a moment to drift back down from wherever she had floated off to, then joined him in the light. She found herself unable to look up at him. 'If there was another way, I would do that instead.'

He nodded, hands on his hips. 'You don't have to

explain. I get it. Doesn't mean I have to like it though.' He gestured for her to start walking.

She obeyed. This time when they walked, she had to lengthen her stride to keep up, and her feet hit the floor out of time with his.

CHAPTER 23

While the carcass was being skinned and butchered, Lyndal tried to convince Wallis, the kitchen maid, to join her on a quest to the merchant borough.

'The king said I could ask the staff for help,' Lyndal said when Wallis responded with "No way."

Wallis continued chopping onions. 'So ask someone who wants to go.'

Lyndal glanced over at Astin, who was leaning in the doorway *not* looking at her, then returned her attention to the maid. 'When was the last time you left the royal borough? Don't you miss the hustle of the merchant borough?'

'I heard there are dead bodies on the street.'

'Bodies that will have likely been collected by the time we get there.' Not her strongest argument but worth pointing out. 'And you have the opportunity to be part of the solution. Fewer dead bodies tomorrow because of your good deed today.'

Astin coughed—his only contribution.

Wallis picked up a turnip and washed it in a bowl of water. 'I've got enough work to do here.'

Lyndal tried another approach. 'I understand. I'll ask someone else. The king might have some fresh suggestions for me.'

When she went to turn away, Wallis stopped her.

'Wait.' She let out a resigned breath. 'Are the rumours true? About you and the king?'

Lyndal backed away from the bench. 'I'm really not at liberty to speak about it.'

'Fine. I'll do it. But you better remember this good deed if those rumours prove true.' She placed the knife down, hands going to her hips. 'What do you need?'

A smile spread across Lyndal's face. 'I'm going to need some very large pots and as many vegetables as you can spare.'

Lyndal did not know how to fix what had broken between her and Astin that morning. He walked beside the wagon, still refusing to look at her. Acknowledging feelings of any kind seemed like a bad idea, but pretending the conversation had never happened did not seem helpful either.

'So serious, defender,' she said. 'Any potential threats identified?' If humour did not work, she could always throw a piece of onion at him.

No response.

'We haven't even left the borough yet. What could possibly have you so preoccupied?'

His gaze drifted in her direction. 'We're in shooting range of the wall, and you're an easy target right now.'

She refused to let him spook her. 'Are you suggesting there's a defender atop the wall who wishes me dead?'

'Any one of those men has the skill to carry it out on another's behalf.'

That shut her up.

She glanced nervously up at the wall, then behind her to the six cast-iron pots filled with meat and vegetables. There were another two filled with bones and organs, as well as an assortment of bowls and spoons. She decided to focus on the task ahead.

When they passed through the gate into the square, Astin's hand went to the hilt of his sword. He signalled something to the other defenders who had travelled with them, and they dispersed.

Once the wagon rolled to a stop, Lyndal and Wallis stepped down to set up. They asked some merchants to help build the fires for cooking, then went to fetch water from the well. Within the hour, two pots of soup simmered away.

Lyndal kept an eye out for her family, and just when she thought they were not going to show up, she spotted Blake and Eda at the edge of the square. Candace was not with them.

'I'll be back in a moment,' Lyndal told Wallis before making her way over to her sisters. Astin followed at a distance.

The three sisters stood in awkward silence for a full minute before anyone spoke.

'Is Mother all right?' Lyndal finally asked.

'She had some things to take care of at the shop,' Blake lied.

Lyndal nodded and played with the end of her hair. 'I gather she still hasn't come around to the idea of me with the king?'

Blake chewed her lip. 'Harlan told us about the fire.'

'It was quickly brought under control,' Lyndal replied. 'Shame about the furniture though. Very comfortable chairs.' She barely knew what she was saying.

You look so tired, Eda signed.

Lyndal's eyes began to sting. 'I've had a bit of trouble sleeping since.'

'Not surprising,' Blake said. 'Someone did lock you in a room and set the one beside yours on fire before leaving you to die.'

Lyndal crinkled her nose. 'I gather Harlan spared no detail in his retelling?'

'Do you think I gave him a choice?'

Silence.

Still going to marry the king, then? Eda signed.

She was the second person to ask that question that morning. 'I really think I can do this.'

'You mean if you can survive until the wedding?' Blake said.

More silence.

'You've always been incredible in a crisis,' Blake admitted. 'And this is the biggest crisis the merchants have ever faced. But he doesn't deserve you, which makes giving you up even more difficult.'

Lyndal's stomach fell. 'Please don't give me up. I couldn't bear it.'

Eda looked down and began rolling up her sleeves. *Enough. How can we help?*

Lyndal pulled her sisters to her, kissing their faces before letting go. 'We have soup for the children and offal and bones for everyone else.'

We'll spread the word, Eda signed. *Tell people to bring a pot with them.*

Blake was looking over at Astin with a thoughtful expression. 'What's the matter with him?'

How to explain something she was still getting her head around.

Let me guess, Eda signed. *He's figured out he fancies you— too late.*

Lyndal's mouth dropped open. 'Why would you say that?'

Blake's eyes returned to her. 'Maybe because the man has spent the past year asking after you when you're absent and staring at you when you aren't.'

'That's not true' was Lyndal's immediate reaction. 'If he was looking at me, he was likely thinking up his next insult.'

Blake tilted her head. 'Didn't you ever wonder why Eda never *accidentally* tripped the man or dropped soup onto his lap? She saw it before I did.'

Lyndal looked over at Astin, who continued to survey their surroundings as though an army of assassins were about to descend at any moment. 'Why did neither of you say anything?'

Blake's eyebrows rose. 'What for? You made it abundantly clear you couldn't stand him.'

She *had* given that impression. It had been a matter of pride. He was always noticing other young women and never her, so she made a point of not noticing him right back.

Except he had noticed her.

When she turned back to her sisters, she found them watching her with an amused expression.

'Why are your ears turning red?' Blake asked. 'Is it possible the attraction is mutual?'

'Louder,' Lyndal whispered back. 'I don't think he heard you.'

Eda pursed her lips. *That's quite a pickle you find yourself in, Lady Lyndal.*

Lyndal took a step back. 'Off you go. Bring me some children to feed. I'm here in the square with food enough for two hundred people because I've agreed to wed the king.'

The smile fell from Blake's face. 'And we'll stand by you through the entire disastrous marriage.'

Unless he hurts you, Eda signed. *Then I'll cut off his—*

Lyndal grabbed hold of her sister's hands. 'Best not to finish that just in case.'

'In case of what?' Astin said, appearing beside her.

Lyndal let go of her sister's hand. 'Oh. We're talking again.' She turned her younger sister in the other direction and gave her a gentle push. 'Off you go. Many mouths to feed.'

'There's already a line,' Astin said.

Lyndal turned back to the fires and saw he was right. The smell of simmering meat had lured people from every crevice of the borough.

'Keep order,' Astin instructed a nearby defender.

'For goodness' sake,' Lyndal said as they walked over. 'People are quite capable of forming a line without defender supervision.' She stopped in front of the bubbling soup pot and peered inside. 'This one ready?'

Wallis added a handful of salt, then gave it a stir. 'Now it is.'

'Bring your children forwards,' Lyndal called to the crowd. 'Everyone else is welcome to broth if you have something to take it home in.'

They removed the pots from the heat and placed two more over the flames.

The two women found their rhythm, Lyndal ladling soup into bowls and reminding people to return them so they could be washed and reused, and Wallis doing the washing while handing out the bones and offal.

'May Belenus bless you,' people said as they took the steaming soup from her.

Other common sentiments included 'Can we expect an announcement soon?' and 'He's a fool if he doesn't marry you.'

Lyndal was aware of Astin's gaze constantly flicking in her direction. That combined with the heat from the fires had her feeling hotter and hotter by the minute.

'The line's only getting longer,' Wallis whispered.

Lyndal looked down the growing line as she handed a

bowl to the eldest of four boys. 'You're responsible for bringing the bowls back to me. All right?'

He nodded, eyes never leaving the food.

'Halve the portions to make it stretch further,' Lyndal whispered to Wallis when the family stepped aside. 'And one bone per family.'

Wallis frowned. 'That's not even enough to—'

'I know,' Lyndal said, wiping her brow with the back of her hand.

She turned to a young mother holding a girl around three years of age, stilling when she caught sight of the girl's face. Her eyes were closed, her skin grey and lips blue. Lyndal stepped around the pot and carefully placed a hand on the girl's chest.

No heartbeat.

No movement at all.

She pulled her hand back as though burned. 'I'm so sorry.'

The woman stared at her with bloodshot eyes. 'She'll be all right once I get some food into her. Please.'

Lyndal swallowed. 'Your daughter is dead. I'm sorry.'

The mother shook her head, eyes watery. 'She was crying all morning, said her stomach hurt. A bit of soup will fix her.'

It was not the first time Lyndal had encountered mothers unable to accept the loss, mothers who had sacrificed every morsel of food so their child could eat, only to discover it was still not enough.

'I'll have someone help you,' Lyndal said quietly.

'You shut your mouth!' the woman fired back, clutching her daughter as tears spilled over and fell down her cheeks. 'I'm not leaving until you hand me a bowl.'

Astin stepped between them. 'Lower your voice,' he told the woman, signalling to another defender.

'My daughter has as much right to this food as anyone else here,' the woman screamed.

Astin took her by the arm and pulled her out of the line. 'Your daughter is dead, and the food is for the living.' He handed the woman over to the waiting defender. 'Find out if she has family in the borough, and take care of the girl.'

The defender nodded and led the woman away.

Wallis dropped the bowl she was holding and pressed a hand to her chest. 'She's really dead?'

Lyndal bent and picked up the bowl, brushing it off and handing it back to her. 'That's why we're here. Keep going.'

Wallis took the bowl from Lyndal's trembling hand and turned back to the pot.

'Everyone all right?' Astin asked when he returned.

Lyndal forced a smile and faced the line. 'Who's next?'

They continued filling bowls until every pot was empty. Then they added a little water to each pot to collect the fat around the edges, handing that to the next family in place of soup. An older man took the final bone, and then there was nothing left to hand over.

A woman was next in line, a girl clinging to her leg and another on her hip. Her face collapsed when she realised the pots were all empty, and a hand went over her face in an attempt to hide the devastation from her children.

It broke something in Lyndal.

If she was hot before, she was boiling now as she tried to keep her emotions contained. 'I need some air,' she said, moving away from the fires.

'Are you all right?' Wallis called to her back.

Lyndal covered her ears to block the growing noise coming from the line of people. Anguish poured out of the merchants, filling the square.

Black spots danced in her vision, and just as she felt herself begin to tilt, Astin appeared, catching her around the waist. 'Clear the square,' he shouted to an approaching defender. 'And help the maid.' He pressed a hand to Lyndal's burning cheek. 'Let's get you cooled down.'

She wanted to object, tell him she was fine, but the numbness in her body suggested otherwise. 'It doesn't make sense.'

'What doesn't make sense?'

She swallowed. 'Mothers carrying their dead children around the village when there's meat on the other side of that wall.'

He said nothing.

'When will this end?' Her voice broke.

He drew her closer, an arm still wrapping her waist. 'Stop talking, and breathe for me.' He nodded to the defender on duty as they passed through the port gate. A few minutes later, they were across the sand and standing at the water's edge.

'Look at the water,' he told her. 'Don't worry about what's happening behind you.'

She slowed her breathing and watched the waves roll in, grateful for the cooling breeze that blew in off the sea.

Astin bent and dipped his hand in the water, then brushed her hair to one side, placing it on the back of her neck. Her eyes closed at the sensation.

'Better?' he asked.

She nodded. 'Better.'

He withdrew his hand, leaving droplets of cold water on her neck. Opening her eyes, she stared out past the waves to the horizon.

'Can I ask you something?' she said.

'Yes.'

She took a moment to select her words. 'Before all this, when I was just a merchant buying a boar I couldn't transport down at the port... did you see me?'

He turned to her. 'I don't understand.'

'Did you *see* me?' She swallowed. 'Or was I just Blake's irritating sister? Easy prey for your jokes?'

He was silent a long moment, and then he brushed a finger down his nose. 'I saw you the day you marched out into the middle of the road and blocked the king's horse, demanding he help you get a letter to your uncle.' He shifted his feet. 'I saw you when you came to your sister's defence in the port a few weeks after that. I saw you stare down arrows in the square and confess to a crime you never committed. I saw you unable to stop crying at Blake and Harlan's wedding, because their happiness was your own. I saw you very clearly when you danced with all those men at last year's festival. I saw you laughing at the things they said.' He paused and took a breath. 'I've been trying to un-see you ever since.'

She was utterly speechless for a full minute. She stared

up at him, expecting him to tell her it was another one of his jokes, but he remained silent. 'Oh.'

Reaching up, he ran a knuckle down her cheek. 'Look at you. You're the only sunshine left in this place.'

Her skin prickled and her pulse quickened. Talk about bad timing. The merchants were depending on the match with the king to go ahead. She could not be acknowledging feelings for another man at this point in the game —especially one she could not escape.

'Astin' came a familiar voice.

His hand fell away, and they both turned to see Presley walking towards them.

'Sister,' Astin said. 'What are you doing here?'

'Looking for you.' She closed the distance between them. Then, drawing a breath, she checked her surroundings. 'There's something I think you should know.'

CHAPTER 24

For dinner with the king, Lyndal changed into a blue dress with an embroidered bodice and sharp neckline that had Astin looking everywhere but at her. Her golden hair was bundled atop her head like a halo. He watched her from behind as they walked towards the hall, where everyone was waiting for her.

'You can't say anything,' Astin warned her for the seventieth time. 'The king can't know we suspect anything.'

She looked over her shoulder. 'It's all right. I'm not about to throw your sister under the wagon. Besides, speaking up won't really make a difference. The king's not going to suddenly develop a conscience because he was caught.'

'We need more information before we start drawing conclusions.'

Lyndal sped up. 'A bit hard not to. He purchased forty head of cattle and gifted one to me. Are we not to assume the other thirty-nine animals went to the nobility while merchants continue to die of starvation before his very eyes?'

When they reached the hall, he grabbed her arm and pulled her to a stop. 'You need to be very careful.' His voice was a whisper. 'This is not just about my sister. You're in a very vulnerable position.'

She plucked her arm free from his grip. 'Isn't Thornton supposed to be watching me?'

'It's been a rather big day. I'd prefer to see you through the dinner.'

She searched his eyes. 'You don't trust me to keep your sister's secret.'

'I don't trust anything about this dinner—especially your uncle.'

She patted his arm. 'Have a little faith, defender. And I think I shall have a little wine.' With that, she turned and entered the hall.

Blinking slowly, he followed her in.

King Borin and Queen Fayre were in their usual seats at the high table. In front were Lord Thomas, Lady Victoria, Lady Henley, and Lord Wilfred.

'There you are,' Borin said when he caught sight of Lyndal. 'I am relieved you found time to wash and change.'

Lyndal curtsied before the high table. 'Your Majesties.'

Astin positioned himself by the wall on the other side, watching as she greeted the other guests. That was when he noticed she had been seated beside her uncle.

'Niece,' Thomas said, not bothering to stand.

'Uncle.' She bowed her head before reluctantly taking her seat.

'You look so well,' her aunt said, leaning forwards in her chair.

'Amazing what a bit of food can do for one's complexion,' Lyndal replied, smiling at Lady Henley across the table. She slid her plate farther away from her uncle's in the process.

'His Majesty was just telling us that you have been out doing charity work *all day*,' Lady Henley said. 'How tedious.'

'Not at all, my lady. Going years without adequate food, now *that* is tedious.'

Lady Henley exchanged a look with her husband, Lord Wilfred.

When Lyndal went to reach for the wine, a food taster swept in to sample it. Lyndal's fingers twitched on either side of her plate as she then waited for the wine to be poured. Thanking the servant, she picked up her cup and emptied it in a few solid mouthfuls. The servant immediately stepped forwards to refill it.

'The king gifted Lady Lyndal a carcass to help those most in need,' Queen Fayre said.

Thomas looked up at that. '*Lady* Lyndal now, is it?'

Fayre finished chewing her food, then placed her fork down. 'Her mother had a title, did she not?'

'She did. However, she traded the title for a merchant husband, Your Majesty,' Thomas replied.

Lyndal had another long drink of wine, then said, 'She never regretted it. A happy marriage is not to be sniffed at.'

Lady Henley raised her eyebrows but did not comment.

'How did it go today?' her aunt asked with an encouraging smile.

'I'm afraid one cow can only stretch so far.'

Borin glanced up from his food. 'It was a very large cow.'

'It's a very large borough' was Lyndal's reply.

Fayre placed her fork down again. 'Well, I am certain the merchants were grateful nonetheless.'

Lyndal nodded in agreement. 'They were—except for the lady carrying her dead daughter around the borough. We were one day too late for her.'

Astin drew a slow breath.

'Can we speak of something more uplifting?' Borin said.

Lyndal smiled. 'Of course. How's Lady Kendra?' she asked her uncle, picking up her cup and finishing what was left in it.

'Very well, given the circumstances.' He said that last part so only she would hear it.

Lyndal reached for the tray of roasted vegetables in front of her, only to have the food taster appear beside her again. With a sigh, she said, 'We're all eating from the same trays, are we not?'

Thomas tutted, then said, 'I gather from this you are not making a lot of friends here.'

Astin imagined all the things he might do to the man under a dark sky with no witnesses around.

'It is simply a precaution,' Fayre said, replying on Lyndal's behalf.

'No one else has died on their plates,' Lyndal said, shooing the young man away. 'So I'll take that as a sign all is safe, thank you.' The second he was gone, she reached for the wine and filled her own cup this time.

Lady Henley leaned over the table and whispered, 'Perhaps you should have some food.'

Lyndal nodded. 'Excellent advice.' Then she drank instead.

'It is good to see pork and mutton returning to the nobility borough, Your Majesty,' Lord Wilfred said, sitting up straight in his chair. 'Any idea when we can expect to see some beef?'

The smile fell from Lyndal's face, and her eyes snapped to Astin. He shook his head ever so slightly.

Borin shifted, visibly uncomfortable. 'Two months, the farmers are telling me.'

Astin and Lyndal stared at one another, a realisation settling between them. The remaining thirty-nine head of cattle had not gone to the nobility borough, which raised a much bigger question.

'Do eat up,' Queen Fayre told Lyndal. 'I imagine you are famished.'

'I would skip the chicken, however. It is a little dry,' Borin said, poking at his plate.

'My niece will not notice,' Thomas said, waving his fork. 'Merchants have a different palate.'

Lyndal closed her eyes, and Astin fought to keep his feet still and his face neutral.

Lady Victoria placed her knife carefully on her plate and cleared her throat. 'Did anyone catch the break in the clouds a few nights back? Some reported seeing stars.'

Lyndal's eyes opened. Slowly, she reached for the jar of wine and refilled her cup, drinking the entire thing before turning to her uncle. 'How is our palate different?'

Everyone stopped talking and looked in their direction.

'He meant no offence,' Victoria said, playing the peacekeeper.

Lyndal's eyes never left her uncle. 'I'm simply curious. It's clear to all that the nobility have better clothes and houses, more wealth and food, greater health, and more promising futures. But how is it that your palate is also superior?'

Queen Fayre glanced in Astin's direction. 'Lord Thomas did not say superior.'

Lyndal emptied her cup yet again and reached for the jar.

'I think you have had enough,' Thomas said, moving it out of reach.

She laughed, but it was not her usual pretty laugh. It was venomous. 'You people. Always deciding when we've had enough. Enough wine, enough food, enough freedom. I'm always surprised when I enter the merchant borough and find no wall around the well.'

'That is enough,' Borin said, throwing down his fork.

Thomas looked up at the high table. 'I must apologise on behalf of my niece, Your Majesty. I believe she was attempting humour and it fell flat.'

Lyndal stared at him, tapping one finger on the table. 'I wonder if that's because you have a more sophisticated sense of humour than I do.'

Thomas's face twitched.

'Fletcher,' the queen mother said, clicking her fingers.

'Would you see Lady Lyndal to her quarters? She is tired and in need of a good night's sleep. I shall have some food sent up.'

'Excellent suggestion,' Borin agreed.

Lyndal rose on unsteady legs. 'Let's hope no one sets the room alight.'

Astin did not get there quick enough to stop that one. Taking hold of her arm, he leaned in and whispered in her ear, 'Bid the king and his guests goodnight.'

'Have a wonderful dinner, everyone,' she said, falling into a leaning curtsy. 'That chicken will be fine in a soup. Heat it low and slow.'

Borin narrowed his eyes. 'Are you drunk?'

Fayre gestured for Astin to take her away while Lady Henley and Lord Wilfred looked on with disapproving expressions. Lyndal reached for the jar of wine on the table when Astin turned her.

'Absolutely not,' he growled, steering her sharply away from the table.

Thomas glared after her while Victoria stared down at her plate.

Astin was forced to keep hold of her as he guided her across the room and out of the hall. Thankfully, she waited until they were out in the corridor before tripping over her own feet.

'Well, that went about as well as I was expecting.'

Lyndal pulled out of his grip, almost falling over in the process. 'See? I didn't say a word about the cattle or your sister.'

Astin walked at her side, ready to catch her. 'Yes. Well

done, you, for the two things you didn't say during your verbal spewing.'

'It wasn't *that* bad.'

'You may feel differently tomorrow.'

When she tripped again, he caught her arm, and she did not pull free this time.

'Where do you suppose he's hiding the rest of the cattle?' she asked. 'And how does one hide animals that size? Someone knows where they are.'

Astin drew a breath. 'I'm not talking about this now.'

'Should we see if there are any stars visible tonight?' she asked, already moving on.

'Queen Fayre told me to take you to your rooms, so I'm taking you to your rooms.'

She pouted at him, and it was oddly adorable.

'But I'm not tired.'

He dragged her forwards. 'Give the wine a chance to do its job. You only finished guzzling it a minute ago.'

Only when they were standing outside her bedchamber door did he let go of her. She leaned against the frame, staring at up him with an expression bordering on adoration. He was immediately wary.

'Do I dare ask what's going on in that mind of yours?' he asked.

A slow smile spread across her face. 'I was just recalling our earlier conversation. You *see* me.'

He looked off down the corridor, ignoring the change in his pulse. 'Food should be here soon. Can you get yourself inside?'

She tilted her head. 'The real question is can I get myself out of this dress?'

His eyes returned to her. 'Stop. You have enough to regret in the morning.'

She presented her back to him. 'Can you at least help with the buttons?'

He stood there, not touching her. 'What are you doing?'

'Asking for your help. They're just buttons.'

Blinking slowly, he reached up and took hold of the top button, careful not to touch the bare skin visible above.

'This is always the cruellest part of the day,' she said quietly.

His fingers continued to work down the row of buttons. 'Why's that?'

'That bedchamber is empty. There's no sisters in there to lie beside, to laugh with and share secrets with in the dark.'

'Done,' he said, hands falling away from her exposed back.

She turned, her smile gone.

Feeling sorry for her, he said, 'Soon you will have a husband to tell all your secrets to.' He had to stop his mind there for his own sanity.

'I wouldn't trust the king with my secrets.' She hesitated. 'I trust you though.'

Swallowing, he reached past her and pushed the door open. 'In you go.'

She did not move. 'Don't you want to know if I saw *you*?'

He shook his head. 'It doesn't matter now.'

'You saved Pig's baby. How could I not see you?'

It took him a moment to figure out what she was talking about. His hand went to his brow. 'Ah, the boar.'

'I was always supposed to marry up, but not this far up.' She laughed. 'This whole thing is ridiculous.'

He said nothing.

'And now I'm thinking back to every time you came to the shop, to the house, to the dock, and I'm wondering why I never saw it.' She pressed her lips together and looked away.

His chest felt heavy and his hands restless. He gestured to the bedchamber. 'Go inside before someone sees you standing out here with your dress unbuttoned—with *me*.'

She covered her face with her hand. 'And now you reject me.'

'You're drunk.' He pulled her hands down and dipped his head to hers. 'Tell me to help you out of your dress when you're sober, and you might get a very different response.'

He saw her swallow as he stepped back.

It was perfect timing, as the rattle of a tray announced the arrival of a maid.

'I'll send for Thornton,' Astin said. 'Get some sleep.'

Lyndal stepped aside to let the maid pass and lost her balance.

Astin caught her again and walked her inside, sitting her on the bed. Turning to the maid, he said, 'Help her change, make sure she eats, and don't leave her side until she's asleep. Understand?'

The older woman nodded. 'Yes, sir.'

Then he marched out without a backwards glance.

CHAPTER 25

yndal peeled her eyes open and blinked away the fog of wine. Someone or something was shaking her.

'Lyndal,' Astin whispered.

She lifted her pounding head off the pillow and found him crouched next to the bed. 'Is the room on fire?' She looked around the still dark bedchamber as she asked the question.

'No.' He rose and grabbed the cloak off the nearby chair, dropping it onto the bed. 'Put this on and come with me.'

'Come where?'

He was fetching her boots. 'I want to show you something.'

She rose, pins and needles prickling one arm after sleeping in the same position for too long.

'How do you feel?' Astin asked as he swung the cloak around her.

'Fine,' she lied, looking up at him. 'Where's Thornton?'

'Probably back at the barracks by now.'

He gestured to the boots. She stepped into them and bent to tie the laces. 'Am I in danger?'

'Never when I'm with you.'

She followed him out into the empty corridor, where grey light was now filtering in. It was a little before sunrise. 'What are you doing up so early?'

'I've been training.'

She looked up at him. 'When do you sleep?'

'Before training. Unless the castle's on fire.' One corner of his mouth lifted.

He led her down an uneven stone path towards the gate, and she was grateful that it was not raining. A rare treat.

Looking up at the sky, Lyndal stopped.

'What's the matter?' Astin asked, looking back.

She exhaled and smiled as she gazed up at the clear sky. 'I see actual sky.'

He walked back and took her hand, pulling her along. 'We have to keep moving or we'll miss it.'

'Miss what?'

'You'll see when we get there.'

She hurried to keep up, enjoying the sensation of her hand wrapped by his. When she realised they were heading for the outer-wall of the borough, she slowed. 'Astin?'

He kept a hold of her hand. 'Almost there.'

They walked along the edge of the path, trying to avoid the worst of the mud. The curtain wall loomed ahead. At its base, Lyndal spotted a defender standing in front of a small door. The defender nodded to Astin, then turned to remove the drawbar, pulling open the heavy door.

'Watch your head,' Astin told Lyndal, ducking and following the defender into the dark hole.

Lyndal hesitated.

Astin looked back. 'Always safe with me, remember?'

Drawing a breath, she followed him. Ahead, she heard multiple drawbars being removed. She held tightly to Astin's hand as they waited to be let through. Finally, light split the door, and the defender moved aside so they could exit.

Lyndal froze when she found herself standing six feet from the edge of a cliff, then jumped when the door banged close behind her. The scrape of drawbars going back into place set her into a panic.

'Don't worry,' Astin said, pulling her away. 'He'll let us back in when we're done.'

'Done with what?' Her eyes went to the turbulent sea below. 'I'm not climbing down.'

He chuckled. 'Come. We'll get a better view farther along.'

She reminded herself to breathe and focused on the hand holding hers. It felt like the most natural thing in the world.

'Here it comes,' Astin said over his shoulder.

When she looked up, her feet stopped once more. Behind Astin, a pink line marked the horizon. All air left her lungs in one beauty-stricken, reminiscent exhale. Tears prickled her eyes as hope appeared on the skyline before them.

'I didn't want you to see it from behind a wall,' Astin said.

Neither of them spoke for the next few minutes. The only movement was the rise and fall of their cloaks with the ocean breeze. Then Astin walked over to the wall and removed his cloak. He laid it on the ground and gestured for her to come and sit. A smile spread across her face as she realised he had brought her through the wall to watch the sunrise.

'It's even better than stars, yes?' he said when he caught her smile.

'Yes.' She walked over and sat down on the cloak beside him. Her arm pressed into his as they leaned their backs against the wall. The warmth from him made her shiver. 'A nightdress isn't very practical for a clifftop walk.'

Astin turned and wrapped her cloak tighter around her, tucking it in place. 'Better?'

It was better, but she knew admitting that would mean the end of his efforts. She shook her head, and he wrapped an arm around her. She rested her head on his shoulder and shuddered with the instant warmth and comfort.

'Better?' he asked.

She nodded, scared to speak and ruin the moment. Then they sat in one of the most comfortable silences she had ever experienced, watching colour take over the sky.

'Look,' she said, finally breaking the silence. 'The first hint of orange.'

He made an appreciative noise, and his hand slid down her arm a little. 'What's your last memory of the sun?'

His breath on her hair made tiny bumps break out on her skin. 'I think I was around eight. It had rained the entire week, and then the sun broke through the heavy cloud just before it set. Never in a million years would I have imagined I wouldn't see it again for more than a decade.' She turned her head to look up at him. 'What about you?'

'I would have been thirteen. In the north paddock with my sister. I remember her hand pressed to her brow, shielding her eyes from the sun.'

Lyndal turned back to the sunrise. 'It didn't take us long to miss it. Constant wet stockings and muddy hems. And every time one of us complained, my father would say, "The rain can't fall forever". He said that every day for five years, right up until the day King Oswin stood upon the wall and told us all to abandon our god and pray to Belenus. I heard Father tell Mother that night that only a man with no faith left seeks out a new god. It's the only time I remember hearing fear in his voice.'

'Well, I don't think Belenus heard our prayers either.'

She shivered, and Astin's arm tightened around her, muscle shifting beneath his uniform. Closing her eyes, she committed the moment to memory.

'You can't watch a sunrise with your eyes closed,' he said into her hair.

She opened her eyes and took a breath. 'Any moment now.'

Colour splashed over the sea right before a spot of radiant gold appeared on the water's edge.

'There it is,' Astin said.

She watched in awe. 'I can almost feel its warmth.'

'You know, your hair is something else in this light.'

She looked up at him. 'As are your eyes. It's like the sun is rising in them.'

He swallowed, and his eyes travelled down to her lips. 'I should get you back before anyone notices you're gone.'

'I don't want to go back.' Never in her life had she wanted a man to kiss her more than in that moment. She was certain he would taste of sunrise. 'I want to stay at the edge of the world with you.' She remained perfectly still.

'We need to go now, before I do something foolish.'

Her body felt hot and cold all at once. 'I see you, defender. Do you see me?'

'I can't see anything but you.'

She wet her lips. 'The clouds will eventually return, and this moment will disappear with the sun. Do you really want to walk away before it's over?'

He dipped his head, so slowly she thought she would combust beneath his tender gaze. His lips hovered just out of reach, his breath on her lips.

'Last chance,' he whispered.

His words sent a shiver along her spine. Unable to wait any longer, she reached up and pulled his head down until his mouth met hers. So much sensation all at once. Warm breath, orange hues of light, and his sweet taste. Her mouth opened and her toes curled in her boots as she reached up and took hold of his face with both hands.

'You're freezing,' he whispered into her open mouth.

'Sorry' was her only response, because she wanted his mouth on hers again.

Pulling back, he looked into her eyes as he lifted his undershirt a few inches and placed her icy hands on his warm stomach. She immediately began to tremble, partly from the warmth but mostly due to the intimacy of the gesture. She tentatively ran her fingers over his warm skin and firm muscle. His mouth found hers once more, and she was dizzy with sensation then.

She had been kissed before. Mostly eager dance partners knowing full well it was all they would get from her. But this was different. A foreign hunger travelled all the way down to her belly, making everything below the hips clench. She explored lower, running her fingers along his trouser line, and his breath quickened in response. Leaning in, she pressed her thudding heart to his.

Closer. She needed him closer.

'We have to stop,' he said.

She shook her head, dismissing the suggestion. 'No. I don't want to.' She pulled him to her again.

His resolve dissipated, and he lifted her off the ground and onto his lap. Fingers trailed up her ribcage, caressing her skin through the cotton. Never had she resented fabric more than in that moment. Pulling up her nightdress, she guided his hand to her bare leg. A soft exhale came from her as she tipped her head back. He withdrew his hand and dropped his forehead to her collarbone, panting.

A throat clearing nearby had Astin leaping to his feet. Lyndal would have gone flying, but he caught her at the same time he drew his sword.

'Shit,' Astin said when he saw who it was.

Harlan stood ten feet away with his arms crossed, looking between them.

'Commander Wright,' Lyndal said, weirdly formal as

she adjusted her cloak. Colour flooded her cheeks. 'We were just kissing the sunrise.'

Harlan's eyebrows rose.

'Watching the sunrise,' Lyndal corrected, her ears now on fire.

He nodded. 'I see that. Well, I'm sorry to cut the viewing short, but Queen Fayre is looking for you. I wanted to find you both before my father did.'

Astin pinched the bridge of his nose. 'Appreciate that.' He was unable to look Harlan in the eyes. 'Let's go.' He gestured for Lyndal to walk ahead.

She pulled her cloak tighter around her and headed in the direction of the small door. There was no hand holding on the walk, only awkward silence as they stood waiting for it to open. Lyndal was first through, her chest heavy as she emerged into the royal borough on the other side. She looked up at the clouds now closing in. The sun was gone. The moment was gone.

Harlan said a few words she did not register before heading for the barracks.

'I'm sorry,' Astin said, appearing next to her.

He was sorry. Perhaps she was supposed to be sorry also.

'Let's get you inside,' he said, walking ahead. 'We need to beat the warden back to your rooms.'

She followed him. 'Why did you apologise? I wanted it. I'm not sorry.'

'Doesn't matter. We're this side of the wall now. Nothing that happened out there changes anything in here. Am I wrong?'

She was still lost in all that had happened on the other side of that wall. 'Astin…'

'I'm not here to make more messes for you to clean up.'

She grabbed hold of his arm, forcing him to stop and look at her. 'You're not another mess. I just… I just need a moment to think, and you're already shutting me out.'

He searched her eyes. 'You don't get both. You know that, right?'

'I know.' She swallowed hard. 'I know that. Surely you understand that I'm in a position to help, so I feel morally obligated to do so.'

Astin scraped his teeth over his lip, nodding. 'I understand.' He was quiet a moment. 'And hopefully *you* understand that if I remain your guard, I'm morally obligated to stand outside the king's bedchamber every night while you fulfil other obligations.'

Tears gathered in her eyes, but she blinked them back. 'Please don't hate me. I can handle anything except for that.'

His expression softened. 'I don't hate you.'

'Fletcher!' The warden's voice boomed across the open space.

Astin turned. 'Yes, sir?'

Shapur looked between them. 'Take Lady Lyndal to the terrace—now.'

Saluting, Astin watched him stride off before turning back to Lyndal. 'Keep your cloak closed. Don't let Queen Fayre see your nightdress.'

CHAPTER 26

Queen Fayre moved her castle along the chessboard, then looked up at Astin. 'I believe the warden would like to speak with you in private, Fletcher. Lady Lyndal is quite safe here with me until Thornton arrives.'

She knows. Heat crawled up Lyndal's neck at the realisation.

Astin bowed his head. 'Your Majesty.' His eyes met Lyndal's as he turned away.

She fought the urge to stand and follow him out, instead trying to focus on the board. She could feel the queen mother's eyes on her.

'Loyal, skilled, *and* handsome,' Fayre said once Astin had exited the terrace. 'Fletcher is quite the catch.'

Lyndal wiped her hands on her cloak and forced her eyes up. 'He's an excellent guard.' She reached for her bishop.

'Spectacular sunrise this morning.' Fayre shifted one of her pawns. 'I cannot remember the last time I saw colour like that in the sky. I imagine it was even better outside the wall.'

Lyndal held the tip of her bishop, trying to remember which way she was going to move it. Giving up, she let go. 'I imagine it was spectacular from any viewing point. So much hope in just a few fleeting moments.'

Fayre was watching her, not the board. 'It would certainly make a big difference if the sun was to return. Successful crops. Reduction in murrain and healthier livestock.'

'And flowers.' Lyndal moved her knight. 'Which means the return of fruit.'

Fayre glanced at the board and slid her pawn forwards. 'Check.'

Surprised, Lyndal studied the board, aware that her heart was beating so hard it was visible through her cloak. She moved her king out of danger.

'If only that were the answer to all our problems,' Fayre said, taking her next move. 'But it is not that simple. Now is not the time for careless mistakes. You are playing the long game here. Get the crown, produce an heir, save the merchants from a lifetime of misery.' She leaned back and looked at Lyndal. '*Then* you will be free to indulge. Take a lover, if that is your wish. So long as you are discreet.'

Lyndal tried to slow her breathing.

'Please do not risk your safety and the future of this kingdom by messing with the order of things.'

What was she supposed to say in response to that?

'And we cannot have a repeat of last night. The king is in a mood this morning. You embarrassed him—and yourself.' She reached for her queen, dragging it to the other end of the board. 'Checkmate.'

Lyndal looked down. Surely it was not that easy for her to win.

'Eat something,' Fayre said, gesturing to the plate of hard-boiled eggs. 'You need to keep up your strength.'

Lyndal wet her lips, where Astin's mouth had been less than thirty minutes earlier. 'So I can produce all those heirs?'

The queen mother smiled. 'You are at the very beginning of this fight. There is a long, tiresome road in front of you. Embracing it makes the journey much easier. Trust me. I am twenty years in, still fighting, and I am exhausted.'

Lyndal's brow pinched. 'I'm still trying to figure out what you're fighting for. Sometimes I think it's the people and other times I think it's your son's success.'

Fayre nodded. 'The people's survival depends on my son's success. If he fails, everybody suffers.'

Lyndal pressed her lips together in an attempt to hold in the words she had promised not to speak. But she trusted the queen enough to know she would not go after the source. 'Forty head of cattle left the farming borough yesterday. One was a gift to me. It made it to the merchant borough because I took it there myself. I'm curious where the rest went if not to the nobility?'

Queen Fayre's eyebrows came together. 'I am not privy to that information. However, that does explain your mood last night. You are upset they did not go to the merchants.'

'We should all be upset about that.'

Fayre reached for the food, placing a few slices of cheese and a boiled egg on a plate and sliding it towards Lyndal. 'You will not get anywhere behaving as you did last night. If you want information, then you will need to gain the king's trust.'

'And how do I do that?'

Fayre leaned back. 'Perhaps you can watch the next sunrise with *him*.'

Lyndal swallowed. She refused to regret the time spent with Astin or anything that had happened between them. 'The king trusts you. Can you not simply ask him?'

'For that reason I must tread more carefully than anyone. If I start poking around in business he means to keep from me, then all progress we have made will be lost. He is not in love with you. In fact, he is still learning to like you. So I suggest you choose your battles very wisely for now.'

It was not new information, but it was brutal to hear aloud.

'I want you to return to your bedchamber,' Fayre said, leaning back. 'Put on the dress that is laid out on your bed. My maid will help you get ready.'

'Get ready for what?'

The queen mother clasped her hands in front of her. 'You shall see in due course.'

Astin stood with the warden outside the mess hall, trying very hard not to drop his gaze.

Shapur had his arms crossed, staring him down. 'What

is it about the Suttone sisters that have sensible men behaving so foolishly? You cannot take the king's betrothed for a rendezvous outside the wall.'

'With respect, sir, they're not betrothed yet, and she was quite safe.'

'Safe from what exactly?' Shapur fired back. 'Do you think me a fool? She is to marry the king.'

'There's been no formal announce—'

'Shut your mouth, defender. You know as well as I do that is irrelevant. She is off limits.' He shook his head. 'What am I to do here? Tell me.'

Astin did not have an answer because he was utterly confused.

'I want you to take the rest of the morning to get your head together. Think long and hard about whether you can put your precious feelings aside, like you have been trained, and do your goddamn job.'

Astin saluted. 'Yes, sir.'

'Now get out of here.'

Astin went straight to the stables and requested a horse, then travelled to the only place he could think of to clear his head: the farming borough. He had thought he was riding aimlessly until he found himself out front of the family farm. He did not enter but remained on the road watching the sheep in the front paddock. It was not until he heard a horse approaching that he broke from his trance.

'Thought that was you,' Presley said, approaching on her mare. 'What on earth are you doing out here?'

Looking up at the sky, he saw it was nearing noon. 'I'm supposed to be clearing my head.'

'And how's that going?'

'Not well.'

'Then it's a good thing I spotted you and not Cooper.' She pulled her horse up a few feet away and exhaled. 'Did you see the sunrise this morning?'

He nodded. 'Seems the banning of Christianity and forced worshiping of a sun god no one really believes in is finally paying off.'

Presley laughed. 'Seems that way.' She looked around. 'The farm was stunning washed in colour this morning. I wish you could have seen it.'

He adjusted his grip on the reins. 'I can imagine.'

Presley exhaled and watched him a moment. 'I always thought you would come back eventually. I don't know why. Logically, I know any man who becomes a defender remains a defender, but you once loved this life.'

'I did. Before Cooper.'

She nodded. 'Before Cooper.' Her eyes drifted to the house. 'Doesn't seem fair.'

'What doesn't?'

'He gets to live your life. As the youngest of four brothers, with no inheritance, he should have ended up a farmhand somewhere, barely a penny to his name.'

Astin looked away. He did not like to think about what might have been. Yes, he could have returned to the farm when he was of age. He could have even kicked his stepfather off the land. But the man would have taken the rest of the family with him, and his sisters and mother would have paid the price for Astin's so-called heroic moment.

'Hayley Akerse lives a stone's throw from the nobility gate,' Presley said, changing the subject. 'She said no cattle have left the borough via that gate in some time, excluding a carcass here and there.'

'Seems they didn't go to the nobility borough either, which only leaves one other possibility.'

They both turned to look at the outer-wall.

'People are going to lose their minds if they find out he's selling meat elsewhere,' Presley said.

Astin struggled to imagine any king doing something so reckless, so damaging. But Borin was a special breed of king.

'Tread carefully,' he told his sister. 'I don't want you caught up in all of this.'

'A bit difficult given the cattle came from our farm. They're marked with our brand.' Presley glanced at the grazing sheep. 'If it comes to light they've been sold outside the wall, it won't be King Borin who takes the fall.'

She was right, of course. Borin would claim ignorance and happily feed a crooked man like Cooper to the dogs. The rest of the family would be eaten up alongside him. Astin was going to need to make sure his mother and sisters were protected.

'Where are you off to?'

Presley clicked her tongue. 'To the square for the announcement.'

'What announcement?'

She pulled her horse up, eyebrows coming together. 'Aren't you supposed to know before me? The king will be on the wall at noon. Everyone is expecting news of his betrothal.'

No. It was too early.

Then a realisation hit him like cold water. If the queen mother sensed a threat to her plan, she would act swiftly.

He swung his horse around. 'I have to go.'

'I might be wrong,' Presley called to his back.

Digging his heels in, he did not wait around to find out.

CHAPTER 27

The steps inside the turret were narrow and difficult to navigate. Lyndal clutched the skirt of her yellow gown, eyes moving from her feet to the light spilling in through the open door above. The dress was the most expensive thing she had ever worn, a fact that made her hands tremble and her feet miss their mark.

Roul caught her arm when her foot slipped from the step for the third time, saying nothing. He did not bother to ask if she was all right, because he already knew the answer. Lyndal had asked him to send word to Astin when she had left the queen, but no one had been able to locate him.

'Still no news of Fletcher?' she asked over her shoulder.

'Not since you asked two minutes ago.'

A few more steps and she was at the top, emerging into blinding daylight and flinching at the sound of a crowd below. She blinked a few times, spotting King Borin and Queen Fayre on the wall walk ahead.

'Come along,' the king said, running a hand down his tunic. 'The merchants have already gathered in the square.'

When Lyndal's feet stopped, Queen Fayre walked over and took her arm, encouraging her forwards. 'I will be right beside you.'

'What are we doing up here?'

Fayre led her to the embrasure, and the moment the merchants caught sight of her, cheers erupted.

'Some things are better experienced than explained,' Fayre said, patting her hand before letting go. She gave the crowd a wave. 'Smile, dear.'

Lyndal took hold of the embrasure to steady herself. 'What is this?'

The king stepped up beside her, eyes moving over her face. 'Goodness. You are not going to be sick, are you?'

Probably. 'Can someone please tell me what we're doing up here?'

Borin peered around her to his mother. 'I thought you told her.'

'Told me what?' Lyndal asked.

'Mother came to me this morning and suggested we make it official,' Borin said, looking out at the cheering crowd. He took Lyndal's hand and placed it on his arm. The crowd responded with deafening applause.

Lyndal stared at her hand resting on the king's twiggy arm and felt sick.

'It begins with this moment,' Fayre whispered into her ear. 'Look at them. They are counting on you.'

Lyndal could barely draw breath. Her eyes went over her shoulder, searching for Astin. He was not there. Roul stood in his place, watching her with a concerned expression. She looked back at the crowd, eyes moving from face to face, searching for something or someone familiar to anchor herself, but her vision kept failing her.

The king gestured for quiet. 'I have chosen a queen. Not only for myself but for all of you. I hear your approval loud and clear.'

Lyndal watched his mouth move, trying hard to register the words coming from it. She kept hold of his arm because she did not trust her legs.

The next few minutes passed in flashes of sight and noise. Her future had been decided without her consent— and it was too late to stop it. She looked to Fayre for confirmation of that, her head shaking in place of words.

The queen mother took hold of her spare hand, squeezing tightly. 'You can do this,' she mouthed.

She could do this. But did she *want* to do this?

Turning back to the crowd, she took in the hope-filled faces of the merchants. They wanted this. They *needed* it.

Lyndal slowed her breathing, slowed everything. She wet her tingling lips and slowly rediscovered her ability to smile. Of course she would do this. She had *planned* to do this before the sun appeared and Astin kissed her.

That kiss had changed her, marked her. It had ruined her. Was she supposed to ignore the fact?

She looked around again. Where was he?

'Wave,' Fayre said. 'They need to see you happy.'

Somehow, Lyndal lifted her hand and forced a smile. The vocals below vibrated off the walls and drifted up to her.

'I do not think I have ever witnessed so much adoration for a king,' Borin said beside her, a grin splitting his face.

'Imagine how proud your father would be right now,' Fayre said, knowing exactly what he needed to hear.

'I gather you all approve of your future queen?' Borin shouted, taking Lyndal's hand and presenting her to the merchants.

The crowd responded with more whistles and cheers.

After a few torturous minutes, the king stepped back from the wall and dropped her hand. 'That was the easy borough. Let us see what the farmers have to say on the matter.'

'The farmers have no objections,' Fayre said. 'They are already gathered, eager to hear the news.'

'And the nobility?' Lyndal asked, trying to bring volume to her voice.

'Tonight they will join us for a feast,' Fayre said. 'That way they feel a part of the celebration.'

Borin brushed his fringe forwards and looked at Lyndal. 'You must dazzle this evening. We cannot afford to lose their favour or respect. Let us not have a repeat of last night's carriage wreck of a dinner.

'Come, come,' Fayre said, gesturing for them to start walking. 'This is a time for celebration.'

With an impatient grunt, Borin walked off ahead, not bothering to wait for Lyndal. Five defenders marched after him. The cheering below had died, replaced with the hum of conversation.

'You should have asked me first,' Lyndal said to Fayre.

'So that you had time to talk yourself out of it? It was better this way.'

Her eyes went to the queen mother. 'Better for whom?'

'For them.' She pointed to the merchants below. 'I spoke with your uncle days ago. He gave his blessing once he realised Lady Kendra was not a contender.'

Of course he had. His need to be in favour with the king outweighed her inferior birth.

They fell silent when Astin emerged from the turret, out of breath. He looked around, then stilled when he spotted Lyndal.

'You will thank me one day,' Fayre said. 'Do not keep the king waiting too long.' With that, she followed Borin, acknowledging Astin with a nod as she passed him.

Lyndal took in his stormy expression as he stared at her. 'Where were you?'

He came at her, then pulled up six feet away, as though he did not trust himself to come any closer. Roul looked between the pair before wandering farther away to give them some privacy.

'What the hell is this?' Astin said, his eyes like two storms.

'I've been trying to find you.'

He linked his hands atop his head. 'To tell me the happy news? Sorry I missed the big announcement.'

A sob rose in her throat. 'I didn't know.'

His hands fell to his sides. 'You didn't know *what*?'

'The king just announced it. No one asked me.'

He blinked. 'What didn't you know? You didn't know that the most powerful family in Chadora can do whatever the hell they want? You stayed in their home. You joined in their games. What the hell did you think was going to happen?'

Her hands went over her face.

'You can cry until there's nothing left inside you,' he said, tone venomous. 'The only thing these people care about is that you do it in the privacy of your quarters.' Shaking his head, he walked off.

'Wait!'

He turned abruptly. 'Whatever you're about to say, I don't want to hear it.'

She closed the distance between them and lowered her voice. 'Queen Fayre told me it's acceptable for a queen to take a lover after having children.'

The disgust and disappointment on Astin's face made her immediately regret her words.

'I'm sorry,' she said, shaking her head. 'I don't know why I said that.' It was the panic talking, her fear of abandonment. Astin was a man with principles. He would never settle for such an arrangement, nor would she if the roles were reversed.

'Go,' he said, his tone defeated. 'You don't want to keep the king waiting.'

Her eyes widened. 'Are you not coming?'

'No.'

She searched his eyes, confused.

'Seems we both missed some important news. You see, as of today, I'm no longer your bodyguard.'

Her stomach fell. 'What?'

Astin did not stick around to explain. He marched away, disappearing into the turret. She listened with her heart in her throat as his footsteps descended the stairs.

CHAPTER 28

Shapur Wright was staring at Astin with fatherly disappointment. In many ways, the warden was the closest thing he had to a father, which was tragic.

'I'll go anywhere,' Astin said. 'You can stick me on the wall for night duty if you like.'

They were standing outside the armoury. Harlan was inside fiddling with a shield, pretending he was not listening.

Shapur cursed under his breath. 'I cannot banish you to the wall without the king wondering why. I can hardly tell him that you do not trust yourself around his future wife.'

Astin recoiled from the term. 'You wanted to know if I can do the job, and I can't. Tell him whatever you need to, so long as Lyndal's reputation is preserved.'

'Noble of you,' Shapur replied, sounding far from impressed. He turned to Harlan. 'Is Thornton up to the job?'

Harlan turned to them. 'Yes, sir.'

Shapur exhaled, looking Astin up and down. 'You will train for the rest of the afternoon. In fact, you can do the cliff climb and swim out to flat rock. Then you can do it again. Maybe by the time you are done I will have this mess sorted.'

Astin nodded. 'Yes, sir.'

With a shake of his head, Shapur strode off in the direction of the castle.

Harlan walked to the door, leaning on the frame. 'Is there anything I can say or do that will be of any help?'

'I think the less said in this instance the better.'

A young defender approached them at a jog. 'Commander, there's a woman waiting for you at the nobility gate.'

Harlan pushed off the door frame. 'My wife?'

'No, sir.'

Harlan grew impatient. 'What's her name, defender?'

'That's the thing. I don't know. She refuses to speak, but she handed me a piece of parchment with your name written on it.' He gave it to Harlan.

'Eda,' Astin said, his feet already moving in the direction of the gate.

Harlan followed. 'That's her handwriting all right.'

When Astin arrived at the gate, he saw Eda had been detained by a visibly annoyed defender on the other side. At her feet was a canvas bag with items of clothing spilled out.

'She pulled a knife on me,' the defender told Harlan through the latticed wood. 'Any other borough and I would have taken her hand off.'

Astin laughed through his nose. 'Good luck with that. Commander Wright trained her.'

The defender looked between them, confused.

'Let her go,' Harlan said.

The defender released her with a shove, and Eda turned to glare at him as she snatched up her bag and stuffed the spilled contents back into it.

'Does Blake know you're here?' Harlan asked her.

Eda shook her head as she approached the gate, signing something Astin could not interpret. Harlan seemed to understand though, because he replied with 'Even if I was to let you in, they'll never let you stay.'

More signing.

Harlan took a step back. 'If you want to help Lyndal, go home.'

Eda pounded on the gate with her fist, prompting the defender on the other side to come for her again.

'For God's sake,' Harlan said. 'I'll lock you in the tower myself if you make a scene.'

She signed something before the defender detained her once more.

'What did she say?' Astin asked.

Harlan rested his hands on his hips, replying quietly, 'She said, "Open the gate, or he dies, and then I open it myself."'

Astin's eyebrows rose. 'Right.' Harlan was looking at him like he had the solution. Lyndal needed somebody right now—he knew that much. 'Take her to Queen Fayre. Explain who she is. Be ready to translate.'

Harlan nodded slowly and cast a warning glance at Eda. 'Open the gate.'

A knock at the door forced Lyndal to drag herself from her oversized bed. She had not long returned from the farming wall, and she just wanted a few minutes to process everything before she had to face the nobility.

There stood Roul with his usual serious expression. Every defender was the same.

'Queen Fayre wants to see you in her quarters,' he told her.

Lyndal wanted to cry. 'I literally just left her side. What does she want?'

'I don't know. I'm just following orders.'

She closed her eyes and took a moment to collect herself. 'Fine.' Stepping out into the corridor, she said, 'Let's go.'

When they arrived at the queen mother's solar, they were let straight in. Lyndal sucked in a breath when she spotted Harlan and Eda standing there. She ran to her sister, all propriety gone. She hugged her so tightly she might have busted ribs if Eda had not been covered in a healthy layer of muscle. 'What are you doing here?'

Eda pulled away and signed, *We were in the square earlier, for the announcement. I figured you needed me.*

'And Mother and Blake let you come?'

She shrugged. *Mother said she would handle Blake.*

Candace might have disagreed with Lyndal's decision, but that did not stop her from being a mother. Now she had two daughters in the wolf's den and another who was going to be very unhappy when she found out.

The queen mother watched Eda with fascination.

'What is remarkable is not that you can speak with your hands but that both Lady Lyndal and Commander Wright understand you.'

'You learn it like any other new language,' Lyndal said. 'Though we hope not to need it forever.'

'It seems your sister is keen to stay here at Eldon Castle,' Queen Fayre said, amusement in her voice. 'Perhaps even insistent, though Commander Wright chose not to translate that part.'

Harlan glanced at her. 'Some parts were not appropriate for present company, Your Majesty.'

Fayre studied Eda for a long moment. 'The muteness poses a problem. The king will certainly have no tolerance for it. However, if the company will be helpful to you, she may stay until the wedding.'

Lyndal turned back to Eda and signed, *You will be miserable here.*

Eda shrugged. *We can be miserable together.*

A smile spread across Lyndal's face.

'You are free to return to the barracks, Commander,' Fayre said. 'Lady Eda will be remaining with us for now. I shall have a maid prepare the adjoining room.'

'Your Majesty.' He bowed, winking at the girls as he passed.

After he had exited the room, Lyndal thought she would use the opportunity to bring up Astin's dismissal. 'While I'm very appreciative, I did want to discuss you removing Fletcher from my service without speaking to me first. If I'm to be queen, I should have a say.' She felt braver with Eda at her side.

Fayre blinked and straightened. 'My dear, I removed

no one. Fletcher requested the reassignment. I only learned of it myself before you walked in.'

A cold sensation crawled up Lyndal's spine. 'Oh.' He had abandoned her, and she did not blame him one bit.

'Now, you have a feast to ready for,' Fayre said. 'Lady Eda can assist you in getting ready before she retires. I am afraid we cannot have a mute girl wandering among the nobility. She will remain in her quarters for the evening. Tonight is very important for the king, so we must all do our part.'

Lyndal nodded absently, knowing Eda would much prefer not to attend. 'Fletcher truly requested a change in assignment?'

Fayre reached up and ran the back of her finger down Lyndal's cheek. 'Eyes on the prize, dear. Your focus should be on making sure every guest tonight leaves in absolute awe of you.' Her hand fell away. 'And be on time.'

She was being dismissed, so she had no choice but to exit the solar. Curtsying, she headed out into the corridor, Eda on her heel. She stopped in front of Roul. 'Thornton. I can't recall if you've met my sister, Eda?'

'Not formally.' He nodded a greeting at her.

'She'll be staying here at Eldon Castle for a while.' She began walking, then cleared her throat. 'Do you happen to know where Fletcher is at present?'

'I believe he's in the water, my lady. The warden assigned him some extra training.'

Of course he had. Shapur Wright would make him pay for showing signs of weakness. She had two choices at that point: she could allow herself to fall apart, be distracted and draw negative attention, or she could return to her bedchamber and prepare for the most dazzling display of queenship she could muster.

Should we go find him? Eda signed.

Lyndal shook her head. 'No. I have a feast to prepare for.' She took her sister's arm. 'I can't tell you how much it means to me that you came.'

Blake wanted to come but—

'Harlan.'

He wasn't even going to let me through. I had to threaten to kill a man to get inside.

Lyndal winced. 'You'll need to be on your best behaviour while you're here. The king has a very short fuse right now.'

I can't believe you're actually going through with this.

Nor could she.

Are you going to tell me why Astin's no longer your guard?

Lyndal brought her sister's hand to her mouth and kissed it. 'So many questions, but this is not the time or place for that conversation.'

Eda glanced over her shoulder at Roul. *Is he the famous recruit the warden found living on the streets?*

Lyndal looked back at Roul. 'She's asking if you're Commander Wright's famous recruit.'

Roul eyed Eda. 'I was going to ask the same question of her.'

Lyndal smiled as she faced forwards again. 'You better watch yourself, Thornton. You were trained by the same commander.'

This was better. Her sister would fill the gaping hole Astin had left. Lyndal was sure of it. Eda would be safe company. Trustworthy. Funny. She would be that person to lie beside and spill her secrets to.

Eda was what was missing.

These were the lies she fed herself as she prepared for the biggest lie of all.

CHAPTER 29

*A*stin pulled himself from the icy water, shivering so violently it made the short walk to the cliff face difficult. He glanced down at his knee, which was bloodied and purple. The current had been strong and the sharp rocks below the surface devious. He paused at the bottom of the vertical climb, mapping out his path before starting. He had done it enough times to know the areas to avoid.

It took him twenty minutes to reach the top, then another five minutes to get up the wall.

'Get yourself cleaned up,' the warden said the second his feet hit the wall walk. 'The king wants to see you.'

He held his knees, catching his breath. 'About?'

'About returning as his personal bodyguard.'

Astin licked his lips, tasting blood. 'I don't think that's a good idea.'

'It is not a request, defender. It is an order.'

Astin bit his tongue, knowing he would be in a better

position to help his family if he kept in favour with the king. 'Yes, sir.'

Shapur looked around. 'King Borin was expecting you to grow restless in the role, so I suggest you play along with his narrative.'

He nodded, wiped a hand down his face, then watched Shapur walk away.

After a wash and a visit to the infirmary to have his knee bandaged, Astin went to see the king.

'Well timed,' Borin said. 'You may escort me for the evening.'

Astin stepped aside as the king exited the room, then followed him out.

'You should have come to me directly,' Borin said, slowing to walk beside him. 'I know her to be tedious.'

It took Astin a moment to realise he was referring to Lyndal. 'I thought it best to think about a more permanent arrangement for Lady Lyndal since she'll be remaining at Eldon Castle long term.'

'She is a handful, no doubt about it,' the king said. 'From what the warden has told me, however, Thornton can handle her.'

Astin kept his eyes trained ahead, teeth pressing hard together.

'Fear not,' the king went on. 'You are back at my side now.' He paused. 'Though you will not be escorting me to the farming borough for business. I cannot have your family squabbles interfering with the important work we are doing.'

Astin's eyes went to him. 'Business with Cooper Brooke?'

A nod. 'I know you two have history.'

'I wouldn't trust that man as far as I can throw him. You should watch your back.'

Borin tutted. 'I find him to be a very progressive sort of man.'

That spoke volumes.

'Tonight's guests are not thrilled at the recent news of my engagement,' Borin continued. 'And who can blame them? We are breaking with tradition. However, the merchants like her, and anything that gets them off my back is a good thing.' He stopped when they reached the entrance to the hall and looked at Astin. 'Goodness gracious. You look positively miserable. It is a feast, for heaven's sake. It seems you returned to me just in time.' He tugged his tunic straight, then stepped inside.

Borin strode in with his chin jutted out and one arm tucked behind his back. He was under the illusion that certain poses made him appear more mature than his twenty years, when in fact they only made him look like an even bigger fool.

'His Majesty King Borin of Chadora' came the announcement. The room fell silent to watch the king enter.

Astin walked over to Thatchere, another bodyguard who was already inside. 'Make sure everything is tasted before it comes into this room. And I want eyes on every door.'

Thatchere nodded.

Then Astin did what he did best: he made himself invisible for the evening. He took note of the guests in attendance, any weapons displayed or concealed, and made a mental note of anything or anyone the slightest bit suspicious. He watched carefully as the king moved about the room, greeting guests and accepting their lukewarm congratulations. Lord Thomas Welche was, of course, in attendance with his wife and daughter. Astin noticed that the guests offered their congratulations to him also, as if Lyndal's achievement was somehow his doing. The lord accepted the sentiments, all the while presenting his daughter at every opportunity. With her cousin betrothed to the king, Lady Kendra was now prime picking for eligible lords.

When Lyndal appeared at the door, the room fell silent again, guests casting both curious and judgemental glances in her direction. Astin could hear them quietly scrutinising everything from her gown to her gait as she went to greet the man she was to marry. She did not seem concerned by the negative attention, her face calm and always a smile upon it. But he expected nothing less from her.

Astin did not let his eyes linger on her for long. The memories from that morning were too fresh for that. He could still feel the weight of her on his lap, recall the exact temperature of her mouth, and hear her exhale when his hand had climbed her thigh. Her hair had been loose, soft golden waves falling down her shoulders. Now it was pulled tightly back, so she was all painted lips and coloured cheeks. A pearl necklace hung around that pretty neck of hers. Even without the crown, she was a true queen.

Astin tried very hard to focus on other things, but his eyes kept returning to her. When her gaze drifted in his direction, he saw all the confidence drain from her face. He hated being the reason for her deflation, so he looked away.

Keep the king safe, see him back to his quarters, then return to the barracks. He had done it a thousand times before. So why did the job feel like such a slog suddenly?

Roul came to stand beside him, eyes sweeping the room.

'Keep an eye on Lord Thomas,' Astin said. 'I don't trust him.'

Roul glanced in the lord's direction. 'Noted.'

He knew he should not ask, but he did it anyway. 'How did she seem this afternoon?'

'Better since her sister arrived. She was a mess after the announcement.'

Astin blinked slowly and said nothing.

A moment later, Lyndal's soft laughter rang out, drawing the attention of everyone around her. And there was that smile that could bring any man to his knees—except the king, apparently.

Turning his attention back to Borin, he tried his best to shut her out.

Lyndal tried very hard not to be sick all over herself in the middle of the crowded room. She had no idea how she was supposed to survive the evening under such intense scrutiny. Borin had a way of making her feel no better than the servants bringing out the food—extra problematic because she *was* no better than the servants bringing out the food. She was as common as they came, and everyone there knew it. She may have been more educated than some due to her mother's extraordinary effort, but nowhere near as accomplished as the other women in the room. It was unfortunate that she was the only one with a plan to help the merchants. It meant she had to swallow down her nausea and keep that frozen smile on her face. Except every time her eyes drifted in Astin's direction—which was far too often—it became harder and harder to maintain.

It stung how easily he had slipped back into his life before her. But that was defenders for you. If only she could switch her feelings off so easily. He had a way of dominating the room by simply being present. It was partly due to his height but mostly his confidence. Why did he have to be so easy on the eye? Why did her insides float at the sight of him in his black uniform and leather armour?

Lyndal spotted Kendra alone at the food table, so she excused herself from the conversation between Borin and Lady Petula. The two cousins had not spoken since Kendra's sudden departure, and she could not stand the thought of there being bad blood between them.

'I was hoping to see you tonight,' Lyndal said, her stomach in knots.

Kendra turned in surprise. 'Cousin.' She found a smile. 'Congratulations. What happy news.'

'Thank you.' At least she was being civil. 'I just wanted to say how sorry I am.'

'For what?'

Lyndal tilted her head. 'You know what.'

Kendra exhaled with relief. 'It is me who should be apologising. I left you here believing I resented you. I do not resent you, I envy you. Every woman in this room envies you.'

Lyndal had not been expecting that. 'What?'

'I understand if you no longer wish to—'

She pulled her cousin to her, holding tightly. 'I didn't know about any of this before coming here. I swear to you. I was rooting for you.'

'I know you were.' Kendra pulled away. 'Now, we must not set tongues wagging with emotional displays.'

Lyndal exhaled. 'See? You're a better queen than me already.'

'Nonsense.' Kendra waved a hand. 'I am simply more experienced in navigating this particular crowd.'

Lyndal saw her uncle making his way towards them, his eyes fixed on her. She held her breath.

'Niece,' he said by way of greeting.

She knew there was no chance of him calling her Lady Lyndal. Post-crown would be an interesting time. 'You look well, Uncle.'

He smiled, but it looked wrong. 'I hear congratulations are in order.'

She bowed her head. 'Thank you.' Her eyes went to the wall where her bodyguard was watching the exchange. She expected Roul to be keeping an eye on her—it was his job. But she found Astin watching her also. It seemed he was unable to break the habit.

'I am pleased you could make it this evening, Lady Kendra,' the king said, joining the group.

Lyndal jumped at his sudden appearance. It was an

unsettling thought that the two men standing on either side of her held all the power to make or break her between them.

'Your Majesty,' Kendra said, curtsying.

Borin's eyes moved over her. 'My betrothed will soon be selecting her ladies-in-waiting, and I do hope to see you among them.'

There was something in his tone that made Lyndal look at the ground.

'I am honoured by the invitation,' Kendra replied.

Lyndal wondered if Kendra knew what she was really agreeing to. Then she wondered if she was supposed to turn a blind eye to those things already. The answer was probably yes.

'You do not have a drink,' Borin said, turning to Lyndal. 'And this is a celebration.'

There were two reasons for that: the first being she could not stomach it, and the second being the thought of someone appearing to sample everything she put into her mouth.

'Shall I fetch someone?' Kendra said, looking around.

Thomas stopped her with a shake of his head. It was likely his pride could not take it.

'No need.' Borin gestured to a servant by the wall. The boy came forwards with a tray, a single cup of wine on it. The king picked it up and handed it to her.

Lyndal was relieved when no one raced up to taste it on her behalf.

'To the happy couple,' Thomas said, lifting his goblet.

Lyndal raised her cup, then drank.

Astin was supposed to be watching the king or watching the room, not watching her. But she had a way of holding his full attention. It had been that way since the beginning, even if he did not care to admit it. It was even more difficult to look away when she had the king on one side of her and Lord Thomas on the other. She was a fish between two sharks.

'Isn't someone supposed to sample that?' Roul asked, straightening.

Astin watched as she lifted her cup in an awkward toast. 'Everything's tested before it's brought in. That's the best we can do at gatherings like these.'

She drank and looked into the cup. It was subtle, but he saw her recoil at the taste. She sniffed the drink before turning her attention back to the conversation going on around her.

Astin narrowed his eyes. He had seen her drink enough wine to know she was no snob when it came to quality. He also knew King Borin's collection was one of the finest in Europe.

Astin's eyes shot to the servant walking away with the tray. Every hair on his body stood on end. Then his feet were moving. Slipping between the guests, he snatched the cup from Lyndal's hand.

Her mouth fell open. 'Excuse me.'

He brought it to his nose, then turned to Roul, who had followed him. 'Hemlock. Find the servant.'

Lady Kendra's face paled. 'Hemlock? Is that not highly poisonous?'

Lyndal brought a hand to her lips.

'You can tell that from *smell*?' the king asked, keeping his voice low so as to not draw attention.

Astin did not stick around to explain the extent of his training. Taking Lyndal by the wrist, he pulled her towards the door.

'I drank it,' she said behind him.

He dodged between the guests, pulling her faster still. 'I know.' The moment they stepped out into the fountain court, he turned to her. 'Bend over and open your mouth.'

Her eyes widened slightly. 'What?'

'Do it!'

She bent, leaning on her knees. He pushed two fingers into her mouth until he felt her gag, then withdrew them. She managed to take a few steps in an effort to get away from the door before being sick on the ground. Straightening, she wiped her mouth with the back of her hand.

He led her to the fountain. 'Clean your mouth out, but don't swallow the water.'

Again, she did as she was told.

He noticed her hand was trembling when she scooped up the water. 'How's your heart rate?' His own was elevated. 'Salivation? Any nausea?'

She looked up at him. 'All of the above, but it's not from the wine.'

He reminded himself to breathe.

'I just thought it was bad,' she said, 'and I didn't want to embarrass the king. I'm fine. Really.'

It took all his effort not to go to her. He wanted to cradle that head of hers, sit beside her with his fingers on her pulse just to be sure. But he did none of those things.

'What in heaven's name is going on?' Queen Fayre asked as she rushed over to the fountain. 'The king said something about poisoning.'

Astin took a step back. 'I'll have it tested, but it smelled like hemlock to me.'

'I barely drank any,' Lyndal said, standing to prove she was fine.

Fayre looked between them. 'Where's Thornton?'

'He went after the man who served her,' Astin said.

Fayre's eyes moved over him. 'Are you not supposed to be guarding the king?'

'He was just about to head back in,' Lyndal said.

Astin looked in the direction of the hall. 'I expected him to follow me out given his betrothed was poisoned right in front of him.'

The queen mother did not even blink. 'His Majesty must remain with his guests to prevent damaging rumours. I am here in his place.' She turned to Lyndal. 'I think it best if we have the castle's physician check you over.'

Lyndal frowned. 'The king will lose his mind if I abandon his guests.'

'Let me worry about that. We have a wedding coming up, and I need you healthy.' Fayre turned to Astin. 'How did you know there was something in her drink?'

How was he supposed to answer that? Should he admit to watching her all night instead of the king? Confess to knowing every expression of hers and what each one meant? He could translate every crinkle of her nose.

'Thornton asked me if the wine had been tested, and I noticed she had a reaction to the taste.'

'How very lucky for her.' The queen looked over her shoulder. 'I better have that mess cleaned up before someone steps in it.'

'It's my mess,' Lyndal said, moving to leave. 'I'll clean it up.'

Astin caught her arm, then immediately let go. 'You need to be checked by a physician.'

'He is right,' Fayre said. 'I shall have a guard escort you to your bedchamber. Thornton and the warden will handle the investigation and report back to me when they have all the facts.' Her eyes went to Astin. 'Thank you for your assistance, Fletcher.'

He was being dismissed, and he had no choice but to leave her.

'Your Majesty,' he said, bowing his head. He did not risk another glance at Lyndal before striding away, unclenching his fists and stretching out his fingers before disappearing into the hall.

CHAPTER 30

'For goodness' sake, put that sword away and stop pacing,' Lyndal called to Eda from the bed. The physician had left after declaring her fit and healthy, but apparently that was not enough for her sister. She was out for blood now. 'How on earth did you smuggle that thing in here, anyway?'

Eda turned to look at her. *Someone wants you dead, and that's what you want to talk about?* She resumed pacing. *And I didn't smuggle it in. I stole it once inside.*

Lyndal threw her hands up. 'Why would you tell me that?'

A knock at the door had Eda marching over to answer it.

'Eda!' Lyndal called. 'Don't you dare.'

Too late.

Eda yanked the door open, not bothering to hide her weapon. Roul drew his sword the second he realised she was armed. But when he moved to disarm her, she slipped around him. She knew every defender trick in the book because Harlan had taught her every one.

'Drop your weapon,' Roul said calmly, positioning himself in front of Lyndal.

When Eda did not comply, Roul tried another tactic, managing to get a hold of her wrist and twisting her arm until the sword fell to the ground. That should have been the end of it, but Eda threw her elbow up, connecting with the defender's chin.

'Eda!' Lyndal said, pushing between them. 'What on earth has gotten into you? Thornton's my bodyguard.'

Eda stepped back, panting. *Then why did you almost die?*

Roul stepped around Lyndal and kicked Eda's sword out of reach. 'If she ever answers that door with a weapon in her hand again, I'll take off the hand. Make sure she understands.'

I'm not deaf, Eda signed.

'She understands,' Lyndal said, hands raised as she tried to bring some calm to the room. She looked at Eda. 'I thought you came here to make life easier.'

You trust too easily, Eda signed.

'She making threats?' Roul asked.

Lyndal held her head. 'No. No one's making threats. I'm sorry. My sister's sorry.' She looked to Eda again. 'Aren't you?'

Eda looked far from apologetic as she gave a reluctant nod.

'Now, what is it you wanted?' Lyndal asked.

Roul eyed Eda for a moment longer before speaking. 'It was hemlock in the wine. Seems someone's unhappy about the announcement.'

'Yes,' Lyndal agreed. 'Everyone in attendance, which doesn't help you much. I gather no one else got sick or died.'

'No. Fletcher's questioned the servant who gave you the wine.' He hesitated before continuing. 'Now he's speaking with the rest of them.'

Lyndal's brow creased. 'Is he now?' She knew exactly what the questioning entailed when it was coming from defenders. 'Where is he?'

'He won't want you anywhere near it,' Thornton said straight away.

Lyndal crossed her arms in front of her. 'You can either tell me where he is or I can search the whole castle looking for him.'

'That's not safe.'

'Then the first option might be better.'

Roul exhaled, shook his head, and turned to the door. 'Your sister stays here.'

Eda went to object, but Lyndal raised a finger. 'Not a word. I only need one bodyguard.'

Eda threw her hands up and walked over to the chair, dropping down into it.

Roul took Lyndal to the north end of the castle, descending the steps into the bustling kitchen below. They exited the small door at the far end, passing a sobbing woman on their way out.

'That's never a good sign,' Lyndal said as she followed Roul. It took her eyes a moment to adjust to the dark, and then she spotted Astin pacing a few feet away. Blood splattered one side of his face.

He stilled when he spotted her. 'Why the hell aren't

you in bed?' His accusing eyes went to Roul.

'The physician said I'm healthy as a horse.' She walked over, noticing his reddened knuckles. 'What are you doing? The servants aren't to blame and you know it.'

'They are if a poisoned drink made its way to your mouth.'

She exhaled. 'So your answer is to beat up all the men and make the women cry?'

Astin looked past her to Roul. 'Leave us.'

The defender nodded before retreating to the kitchen.

When they were alone, Astin met her eyes. 'I need you to let me do my job.'

'This isn't your job, remember? You're no longer my bodyguard. *You* made that choice.'

He ran a hand down his face. 'I had to step away. You know I did.'

'So step away.'

He turned in a circle. 'I can't bear to be near you, and I can't stand being away from you. So what the hell am I supposed to do?'

She looked down when she felt the sting of tears. 'I'm sorry for that. It was never my intention to come here and mess up your life.'

'I'm responsible for my mistakes, not you.'

Mistakes. She hugged herself against the frigid air. It was nearing midnight, and the exhaustion of the day had well and truly caught up with her.

'I should have kept my feelings in check,' he continued. 'I should have focused on the job—cared less. And I should never have taken you outside that wall.'

That one tore.

'I'm in this position because at some point I stopped being a defender.'

'And started being human?' she asked.

'I can't afford to be human.' He exhaled slowly. 'You don't understand. How could you? You weren't built for this life, so you have no idea what it entails.'

She swallowed. 'That's not fair.'

'Do you really understand what you're up against? Who you're marrying? He doesn't care about you. That's not going to change. In fact, it's going to get worse. And you're *choosing* that.'

Her heart was thudding hard in her chest now. 'I'm choosing to help thousands of people, putting their needs ahead of my own. And instead of applauding me, you stand there belittling me and making me feel stupid.'

'Women who marry into these roles spend their entire lives preparing for them, and you think you can just wake up one day and push all your values and feelings aside and save everyone?'

'I'm not having this conversation with you again.' She raised her chin. 'I came to tell you to leave the servants alone and to let Thornton do his job. And now I'm leaving.'

'Because I hurt your feelings? You better get used to that. You'll be the king's emotional punching bag for the rest of your life.'

Her feet stopped. Returning to him, she shoved his chest with both hands. His feet did not move.

'That's enough!' Hot tears fell down her cheeks. 'I'll be his emotional punching bag, because that's the job. I expect it from him. But I won't be yours.' A sob tore from her. 'It's like a knife in the stomach, and I can't bear it.' She took a second to collect herself. 'I never expected it from you.'

Astin's face fell. He raked a hand over his head, suddenly looking lost. 'Lyndal—'

'No.' She backed away to the door. 'No more.'

CHAPTER 31

*L*yndal managed to avoid Astin for four whole days. She planned her time with the king around the times he was off duty and even found herself ducking into rooms she did not need to enter in order to avoid him. Of course, he knew exactly where she was due to the fact that Roul and Eda were usually standing awkwardly in the corridor waiting for her to re-emerge, but he did her the favour of continuing past without saying a word.

She passed time playing chess with the queen, writing letters, reading, or outdoors trying to prevent her sister from going insane from boredom. This existence worked, right up until the night the king requested she dine with him in his private quarters.

Leaving Eda in her bedchamber, Lyndal walked the dimly lit corridor to the east wing of the castle. She was surprised to find Astin standing outside the king's door but said nothing when his gaze drifted in her direction. It was the first time she had come face to face with him since their fight. She stopped a few paces from the door, careful not to meet his eyes. Without saying a word, he disappeared inside and returned a few moments later.

'The king will see you now,' he said, moving aside.

Her gaze flicked to his, and she immediately regretted it. All the feelings she had pushed down rose to the surface in a single glance. All the anger, the hurt, along with all the other ones she did not want to acknowledge.

'Are you going in?' Astin asked.

That was when she realised her feet had failed to move. Clearing her throat, she said over her shoulder, 'No need to wait, Thornton. It might be a late evening. I'll send for the night guard when we're done.' She saw Astin's jaw tick in annoyance, but instead of feeling triumphant at the small win, she felt sick.

Roul bowed his head. 'I'll see you in the morning.'

Astin kept his eyes ahead, promptly pulling the door closed the second she stepped through it. She jumped at the noise.

'I am absolutely starving,' Borin said, waving her in. He took a seat at the small table and gestured for the servant to start filling his plate.

He always said things like that despite the fact that she was always on time.

Curtsying, she went to join him. And so began two tedious hours of Borin talking about everything from the superiority of his horses to complaints about his new boots.

'I have a wide foot,' he explained, 'but it has never been an issue before.'

Lyndal listened, nodded, and chewed her food without

tasting it. She praised him, encouraged him, and laughed when he attempted humour. She never criticised, never offered her opinion. She did everything Queen Fayre had told her to do. She was the perfect companion.

His ideal queen.

'I wanted to speak with you about what will happen after the wedding.'

Lyndal perked up at that. 'Good, because I have lots of ideas. I think it's important the merchants see our passion to help them goes beyond providing for them.'

Borin placed his fork down and looked across the table at her. 'I shall stop you there. Your focus will be on producing an heir. A fertile existence demands a much quieter life than the one you are currently living.'

Lyndal stared back at him, trying not to let her disappointment show. 'I was keen to volunteer my time at the almshouse, schedule permitting, of course.'

He pushed his plate away. 'Mother has mentioned this idea of yours to me, and I must say, I am not in favour of it.'

All the food she had eaten felt like it was wedged in her chest suddenly. 'May I ask why?'

'We need people to be self-sufficient, not relying on handouts. Almshouses indulge the lazy.'

'I disagree.'

He laughed. *Laughed.* 'You would. It does not matter. You can disagree all you like, so long as you listen. We must address the bigger problems we are facing.'

'Bigger than mass starvation and death?'

'The solution to that is to invest in our farmers.'

She tried *very* hard to remain composed. 'What good

will that do if the meat doesn't reach the hungry?'

His face hardened. 'It will, when there is adequate supply.'

She knew she should have stopped there, changed the subject, done something Queen Fayre would have approved of. Done anything else. Instead, she said, 'There must already be adequate supply given the nature of the deals currently being made.'

'What are you talking about?' His tone was impatient.

'I'm talking about forty head of cattle that were sold outside our walls.'

She saw it then, a flash of something that confirmed what she knew. He recovered quickly though, plucking his napkin off his lap and dropping it on the table. 'I do not appreciate the accusation in your tone.'

'Can you clarify what you mean when you speak of investing in our farmers?'

The king looked over at the servant by the wall. 'Leave us.'

All of Lyndal's bravery left her. She sensed a change in him when the door closed.

'I will not discuss business with you,' he said, leaning forwards. 'Even when you do become my wife, you will remember your place. Do you understand?'

She nodded.

He rose, extending a hand to her. 'Come. Let us go to my bedchamber.'

She stared at the outstretched hand, her stomach churning. 'I don't want to go to your bedchamber.'

'I beg your pardon?'

Heat filled her face 'We're not wed. I'm not required to

produce an heir yet.'

His hand fell. 'It was not a question.'

'It should have been.' She rose from her chair. 'Good-night, Your Grace.'

'You are not dismissed,' he said, raising his voice.

'I am not one of your servants.' She took a step towards the door. 'I wish to leave.'

He was surprisingly quick as he positioned himself between her and the exit. 'Perhaps my mother failed to tell you that what you want is irrelevant. Now, because I am a patient man, I am going to ask you politely, once again, to join me in my bedchamber.'

She was trembling now. 'And because I am a lady, I will politely decline. Please move out of my way so I can leave.'

He approached her so fast that she stepped back in a panic, knocking her chair backwards.

'You will leave when I tell you to,' Borin shouted.

The door flew open, and Astin stepped into the room, looking between them.

'What is it?' Borin roared.

Astin replied calmly, 'The night guard is here to escort Lady Lyndal back to her room.'

'Then tell him she is not ready!'

Lyndal thought she would take advantage of the opportunity and slip past the king, but he seized her by the wrist as she passed, yanking her backwards. Her feet could not backtrack fast enough, and she fell, her arm twisting awkwardly. Before she even had a chance to register the pain, her arm was freed and she was back on her feet.

'You dare lay a hand on your king!' Borin shouted at Astin, his voice oddly high-pitched.

Astin pulled Lyndal behind him before unhanding the king.

'Move aside, Fletcher,' Borin said, his face bright red. 'I shall deal with you in a minute.'

Astin shook his head. 'I can't do that, Your Majesty. It's my job to protect you and that includes preserving your reputation. To let you continue down this path would be negligent.'

The king's eyes flashed. 'This is a private matter, and I am telling you to step aside.'

'And I'm telling you no.' Astin's words were slow and even. 'Your father never laid a hand on your mother. It's one of the reasons you looked up to him.'

Borin's face twitched a few times. Looking at Lyndal, he said, 'This conversation is not over.' He tugged his tunic back into place. 'Get her out of here before I do something I regret.'

Astin ushered Lyndal through the door, pulling it closed behind them. They fled down the empty corridor. Lyndal's trembling had grown to shaking, and she could do nothing to stop it.

'It's the fear working its way out of your body,' Astin said quietly. 'It'll stop in a few minutes.'

She was vaguely aware of him stopping to give instructions to another defender, and then they were walking again. Lyndal tried to form words but found herself choking on them.

'It's all right,' he said, reading her mind. 'Just walk.' He kept a firm hold of her arm.

When they rounded the corner, she stopped walking and looked up at him, eyes brimming with tears, but still no words.

His eyes reflected the flame from the torch above. 'Just give yourself a minute.'

'I'm sorry.'

'Don't say that.' He smoothed her hair, then held her face. 'Don't say sorry.'

'But now he's angry at *you*.'

'Shh. Don't worry about that. I can handle him.' He peered into her face. 'Did he hurt you?'

She shook her head, blinked, then wiped away the fresh tears. 'No.'

He took hold of her arm again and continued walking. 'Let's get you to your sister.'

'We can't tell her,' Lyndal said. 'You know what she's like.'

Astin glanced sideways at her and exhaled. 'I have to go back. If the warden learns I left my post—'

'Of course. You should go.' When they reached her door, she looked up at him. 'I'm so sorry.' She said it with a smile, yet tears continued to fall.

'Stop.'

'It's my fault though. I said things.'

'It doesn't matter what you said. He shouldn't have put his fucking hands on you like that.'

She knew he was at the end of his tether if he was using that language in front of her.

Before she could respond, her new night guard walked into sight, nodding at them both.

Astin shifted his weight and closed his eyes for a

second.

'Go,' she said, managing a smile. 'Please.'

He nodded, then left without another word.

She watched him until he turned the corner, then gave her night guard, whose name she could not remember, a weak smile before heading inside. She closed the door and leaned on it, sliding all the way down to the ground. Drawing up her knees, she cried silently into them. Astin had been right. She was not cut out for this life. The merchant blood was too strong in her veins, leading only to rebellion instead of necessary compliance.

What was the point of her misery if everything the queen mother had promised would not come to fruition? Borin would block her at every turn. It was clear now that he would never respect her enough to value her input. She would always be a merchant in his eyes, nothing more. He would tolerate her at best, so long as she stayed quiet and birthed a few boys who would likely grow to have blunt fringes that matched their father's.

She remained on that floor for hours, chewing her fingernails and thinking through every possible avenue she had at that point, every possible outcome. There were so many reasons why it was too late to change her mind. Yet the feeling in her gut, the one telling her to flee, grew stronger by the second.

Picking herself up off the floor, she turned and pulled the door open. Her night guard raised one eyebrow in question.

'I'd like to go for a walk,' she said, aware of what a mess she must have looked like.

'Now?' he asked, visibly confused.

She nodded and stepped past him.

'Your cloak, my lady?'

She was not feeling the cold at that point, so she continued walking. She knew Astin would be at the barracks by now, so she exited the castle and headed for the wall.

'You can't leave the castle grounds,' her guard said, voice firm. 'Those are my orders.'

She was halfway to the wall at that point, fighting the urge to run. But there were defenders at the gate ahead, and she knew she stood no chance of getting past them. She wanted to get to Astin, to tell him he was right, that she was sorry.

Her feet stopped and her face fell.

'I need to get you back to your room,' her guard said.

She pressed her palms hard against her eyes.

'Lyndal?'

Her hands fell away at the sound of Astin's voice. She turned, searching for him. He stood halfway between them and the castle, staring at her.

'What is she doing out here?' he asked the bodyguard.

'She wanted to go for a walk.'

Lyndal moved towards Astin, her pace quickening the closer she got. She half fell, half flung herself at him, wrapping her arms around him and burying her face in his soothing scent.

He peeled her off him, holding her at arm's length. 'What happened?'

She blinked, hating that she could not for the life of her stop crying. 'I... I've changed my mind.'

She saw the slow hardening of Astin's face as her

words sank in. 'Shit.' He looked at the other defender. 'I'll watch her for the rest of the night. You can return to the barracks.'

The night guard hesitated. 'But the warden—'

'I'll deal with the warden.'

The guard looked between them, nodded, then headed for the gate.

Astin relaxed his grip when he realised he was still holding her at arm's length. 'Where's your cloak?'

'I didn't bring one.'

He swore under his breath and turned her towards the castle. 'Let's go.'

Her chest felt like it might explode with all the things she wanted to say to him, with all the things she *felt* for him. She was undeserving of his devotion, of that she was sure. But she needed him to know he was utterly worthy of hers.

They walked in silence with space between them. They would already get in trouble if anyone saw them, so she did not want to make matters worse by clinging to him.

When they reached her door, she turned to him. 'Come in?'

His expression was tortured. 'That's not a good idea.'

'I know.' She watched the indecision play out on his face, then slowly reached for his hand, pulling him across the forbidden threshold.

'You changed your mind,' he said once he was inside the room, repeating her words from earlier.

She nodded. 'I changed my mind.'

He threaded his fingers through hers and brought the

back of her hand to his mouth, kissing it. It felt like his lips had landed everywhere at once. Then his mouth was on hers, and she was pressing against him. She could not get close enough. Picking her up, he turned, pushing the door closed and pressing her back against it. She wrapped her legs around him, melting against the hard muscle beneath his uniform. His hand was between her head and the door—always the protector.

She felt hot and breathless as she tilted her hips up, seeking sensation.

'Tell me if you want me to stop,' he said into her mouth.

Was he insane? She responded by kissing him deeper.

'Lyndal—'

'Don't,' she breathed.

He groaned into her mouth, one hand venturing beneath her dress. 'He'll know.'

She gripped his face with both hands and looked into his eyes. 'No he won't, because he'll never lay a hand on me.' She could see he did not trust her, and she did not blame him.

He searched her eyes. 'It's going to be a mess.'

'It's already a mess.' She kissed his stubbly cheek, then his other one, then his forehead, nose, chin. She kissed him until he believed her, until his mouth was on hers once more, even hungrier than before.

'Get me out of this dress,' she said, breaking their kiss. 'I need your hands on me.'

He lifted her off the door and carried her to the bed. 'You're sure?'

'I'm sure.'

CHAPTER 32

$\mathcal{A}$stin peeled his eyes open as he registered a banging noise. He had fallen asleep. Lyndal stirred in his arms, one bare goddess leg draped over his and the rest of her tucked neatly against him. Light was now filtering in around the shutters, casting stripes of light over her.

'Lyndal,' he whispered. 'Wake up.'

Her eyes blinked open, and the sweetest of smiles spread across her face. 'Good morning, defender.'

As much as he wanted to lie there bathing in her smile, they needed to deal with whoever was standing outside in the corridor. 'I need you to get up and answer the door.' He kissed her rosy cheek. 'And not look so pleased with yourself. Do you think you can do that?'

She startled when the knock sounded again, harder this time. 'It's probably Thornton.'

He kissed her back as she slid from his arms, plucking her robe from a nearby chair. As quietly as he could, he rose and gathered his clothes.

'You can leave via the solar,' she whispered, 'but be on guard in case Eda jumps you at the door.'

Astin stumbled around the room trying to get his boots on. 'I'm on duty at noon,' he told her. 'Try to wait until then before speaking with the queen. I want to be nearby for the fallout.'

'There may not be any fallout,' she whispered back. 'The king may end things himself after last night's disaster dinner.'

Astin pulled on his second boot and went to kiss her swollen lips.

'It's Wright' came Harlan's voice. 'Open up.'

The pair looked at the door, then at each other.

'He's going to find out sooner or later,' Astin said, belting on his weapon.

Drawing a breath, Lyndal went to open the door. 'Good morning, Commander.'

Harlan looked between them, then stepped inside the room, closing the door behind him. 'I'm not going to ask.'

Lyndal shrugged. 'I wasn't going to tell. Is everything all right?'

He crossed his arms and looked at Astin. 'Your sister came to the gate looking for you. When I couldn't find you at the barracks, I asked her if I could pass on a message.'

Astin's eyebrows came together. 'And?'

Harlan hesitated. 'She found out where the livestock went. Seems this is bigger than we realised. The animals went to King Edward.'

Astin took a moment to let that sink in.

'My guess is his mother is driving the entire thing,'

Harlan said. 'And for reasons I can't understand, King Borin agreed.'

'What is it with kings unable to say no to their mothers?' Lyndal asked, walking off her frustration.

Astin pinched the bridge of his nose. 'Every kingdom and country in Europe is desperate. The demand for healthy livestock has never been higher. Edward will play along in order to get what he needs, as any king in his position would.'

Harlan shifted his weight. 'Slightly surprising that Borin *agreed* though.'

'Chadora's army might be the most highly trained, but England's army outnumbers ours six to one,' Astin said.

Lyndal appeared surprised by that number. 'While that's an uncomfortable statistic, it doesn't change the fact that we have people starving to death while our king hands over the little food we have. If the merchants find out, there will be a revolt like nothing this kingdom has ever seen. No number of defenders will be able to stop them.'

The adjoining door opened, and Eda walked in. She paused when she saw the three of them standing there, her eyes darting between them.

'Now that it's officially a family meeting,' Harlan said, leaning against the wall, 'do you two want to let us in on what's happening here? Is there to be a royal wedding or not?'

Eda's eyebrows lifted. *What have I missed?*

'A slight hiccup in wedding plans,' Lyndal said.

Harlan rubbed his forehead. 'I gather the "no bride" part is the issue.'

Lyndal crinkled her nose. 'Turns out we're ill-suited. Who knew?'

'Everyone,' they all said.

There was another knock at the door. 'It's Thornton,' Roul said through it.

Lyndal moved to open the door. 'Come in. Everyone else has.'

His eyes went to Eda, and he remained where he was. 'Queen Fayre has requested an audience with you in the solar.'

Astin released a breath. 'Looks like we don't have the luxury of time after all.'

'Good,' Lyndal said, trying to appear brave. 'The sooner I break the news, the sooner I can go home.'

'You're leaving with me,' Harlan told Astin, pushing off the wall. 'You need to be as far away from this castle as possible. One sniff that you're a factor in this decision and you'll be drawn and quartered.'

'He's right,' Lyndal said. 'Go.'

Astin looked at her, his expression serious. He gave a resigned nod. 'All right. You have this. I'll see you on the other side of the wall.'

Her nervous smile was the last thing he saw before he exited the room.

Lyndal thought she was prepared when she entered Queen Fayre's solar, but then she saw King Borin standing by the fireplace. He watched her like a snake as she entered and curtsied.

'Your Grace. Your Majesty.'

'It seems we have a quarrel to work through,' Fayre said, looking between them. 'I hear some heated words were exchanged last night.'

Lyndal's gaze drifted to the glaring king. 'If by heated words, you're referring to your son almost pulling my shoulder from its socket in his effort to prevent me from leaving, then yes.'

'*You* were behaving like a spoiled child,' Borin spat, moving closer. 'And then you turned on me like a feral cat.'

'I said no to going to your bed, and *you* behaved like a wounded predator.'

Queen Fayre raised a hand, demanding calm with one simple gesture. 'Let us not get stuck on the details. The question is what is it you both need in order to move forwards?'

Lyndal's heart was thudding in her ears. That was her cue. Clearing her throat, she said, 'I no longer want to do this. We're ill-suited to a partnership of any kind, and marriage would be a disaster for both of us.'

The relief she felt at speaking those words aloud was short-lived. Borin descended on her like a ravenous dog.

'You do not get to make that decision! It is not your choice!'

Fayre stepped in front of Lyndal, forcing him to pull up quickly. 'I want you to step out of the room and let me handle this. Please.'

The veins in Borin's neck were bulging. 'This is what I was saying to you! She thinks she can do as she pleases with no regard to propriety and tradition. And now I have thrown away the respect of the nobility in choosing her as a *wife*.'

Fayre made herself taller. 'The nobility will come to respect a king who puts the needs of his kingdom ahead of his own vanity. Now, please, leave us.'

Borin stared hard at Lyndal before striding from the room, slamming the door on his way out.

Lyndal clasped her hands in front of her so the queen would not see that they were trembling.

'You should not have said that,' Fayre said, turning to face her properly. 'It was very confronting for him.'

Lyndal glanced at the door. 'I can't marry that man. I'm sorry. He's made it abundantly clear that he will not support the merchants, queen or not, so I see absolutely no benefit in going ahead with this insane idea.'

Queen Fayre drew a long, calming breath and smoothed back her hair despite not one strand being out of place. 'You will be in the best position to help, I promise you that. But you must take your time with this. You cannot simply hold out your hand. He will willingly give you all that you desire if you take your time and build rapport first.'

Lyndal's shoulders fell. 'He's cruel.'

'He can be, yes. He can also be very sweet in the right hands.'

'These are not the right hands.' She held them up. 'I know that now.'

Fayre never looked away. 'I must ask if this change of heart is really due to your quarrel last night or a certain defender who spent the night in your bedchamber?'

She felt like a pail of ice had been thrown over her. Of

course the queen knew. She missed nothing. 'If you're suggesting that—'

'The absolute worst thing you can do right now is lie to me. I am the one person who has your back through this marriage.'

Lyndal looked down at the ground. 'All right. You deserve honesty. Yes, Fletcher was in my bedchamber last night.' She swallowed. 'But I knew before that it would never work with the king.'

Fayre stared at her with motherly disappointment. 'That is the one and only time that will happen. Are we clear on that?'

Lyndal blinked. Had she not been listening? 'I just told you I can't do it.'

'Whatever doubts you are having, whatever fears you are drowning in, you must fight to rid yourself of them. You have a job to do.'

'I don't want it.'

'That is too bad, because the opportunity for a change of heart has passed. The plan is already in motion, and now it is my job, my *duty*, to ensure the match is a success.'

Lyndal shook her head. 'I don't need to marry him in order to help people.'

With a rare sigh, Queen Fayre walked over to the fireplace and watched the flames. 'This is what is going to happen. We are going to forget about everything that happened last night. It is done, and we cannot change it. I am going to give my son a long and painful lecture about how he speaks to you and how he treats you. Despite what you are thinking right now, I care very much about your well-being. There will be no violence in your marriage on my watch—I promise you that.'

Lyndal's breathing quickened as the target shifted in front of her.

'You are going to tell Fletcher that the affair is over, and you are going to mean it.'

Lyndal shook her head. 'No.'

'Yes.'

'I won't do it.'

'Yes you will,' Fayre said confidently. 'Because if you do not, I will have Fletcher taken into custody and locked in the tower.'

Lyndal's arms were heavy at her sides. 'He has committed no crime. He's been nothing but loyal to the king, despite everything.'

Sharp eyes assessed her. 'The king will not see it that way.'

'I love him.' The words fell out of her.

'I do not doubt that for one second given the enormity of the risk you took last night. But whatever fairy tale you have conjured in that optimistic little mind of yours, you must now dismiss it. You are engaged to the king of Chadora.'

Lyndal pressed a hand to her chest, struggling to hold back tears.

'I am sorry,' Fayre said, her voice cracking around the edges. 'I understand the pain you feel. However, this is the safest option for the pair of you. If you really care about him, you will need to tell him you have changed your mind.'

She blinked a few times, her thoughts fragmenting. 'He won't believe me. He knows me too well.'

'You must make him believe you. If he senses you are trapped, he will play the hero and end up dead. If he believes this is your choice, he will return to the king's side and continue his service.'

Lyndal brushed a hand over her wet cheek.

'The king will not be made a fool of,' Fayre said, gently this time. 'He will have you killed before he ever lets you walk away. I say this not to scare you but to make you see that turning away at this point is not an option. Tell me you understand that.'

Lyndal looked up at the roof as she attempted to stop crying. 'I understand.'

Fayre patted her arm. 'The pain will ease, I promise you.'

Lyndal stepped out of her reach, not meeting her eyes.

'Now I will go speak with my son,' Fayre said. 'If you are to be queen, you must be treated as such. He is not accustomed to having to work for a woman's affection. That is the problem when you grow up being handed all that you desire.'

Lyndal licked tears from her lips, saying nothing.

'And do not fret about your wedding night,' Fayre continued. 'There are tricks to ensure a successful consummation, tricks many women have used before you. He need not know that another beat him to it.'

Nausea rose inside Lyndal. 'I can't think about that right now.'

'Of course not. Take some time to collect yourself. Then go to Fletcher and tell him of your decision.'

Lyndal was still a moment, then finally lifted her gaze. 'Did you know your son is selling livestock to King Edward?'

It was clear by Fayre's expression that she had no idea. 'You are mistaken. King Edward has no hold over Chadora.'

Lyndal lifted one shoulder. 'I really hope you're right. Can you imagine the uprising if it were found to be true?' She left the room without bothering to curtsy.

$\mathcal{A}$stin knew when Lyndal sent for him that her meeting with the queen had not gone to plan. Her tear-stained face and puffy eyes confirmed it. While he knew with every fibre of his body that he was not going to like what she was about to tell him, he was patient as they stood outside the castle wall, away from prying eyes.

'Just tell me you're still leaving,' he said. 'That's all I really need to hear right now.'

She looked away, giving him his answer.

'What happened?'

Lyndal bit her lip before replying. 'We both knew it was too late for a change of heart.'

He moved sideways to catch her eye. 'After the wedding is too late. Now is just a very unfortunate time.' She took a small step back, which bothered him. 'What did she threaten you with? Whatever it is, I can help if you tell me.'

'It wasn't like that.' She shook her head. 'She assures

me my vision for the merchant borough will come to fruition. I was being pushy, trying to rush through a process that can't be hurried.'

He closed the distance between them and took hold of her arms. 'This is horse shit. What are you talking about? *Pushy?* The man's a lunatic.'

'I'm sorrier than I can put into words. The last thing I meant to do was hurt you.'

'Look at me.' He shook her. 'This isn't about me. We're getting you out of here for *you.*' Registering the shock on her face, he let her go. 'I'm sorry. I'm just… I'm trying to understand what happened in there that has you moving in the complete opposite direction.'

'It's the same direction I was always moving in,' she said, gripping her dress. 'Queen Fayre simply steered me back on course.'

He stared hard at her, trying to read her but failing. 'So, to be clear, your plan is to remain here, marry the crazy man, and play the virgin bride on your wedding night? *That's* your plan?'

Her ears turned red. 'The queen mother won't let him get away with bad behaviour again. She's speaking to him right now about last night, and he listens to her.'

He brought a hand to his forehead. 'Your naivety actually astounds me at times. I thought you were smarter than this.'

He saw a flash of hurt before she blinked it away.

'So it's fine for you to serve and protect a madman year after year, which is of no benefit to anyone, but when I come in with an actual plan that will help people, I'm naive?'

He drew a slow breath. 'I'm a defender. It's my *job.*'

'And when I'm queen, I too will have a job.' She crossed her arms. 'You never did tell me *your* plan. Were you going to get me out, then continue to be his guard dog?'

He dipped his head so he was eye level with her. '*My plan?* My plan was to step aside and let you dig your own grave. Then you came to me, crying, telling me you've changed your mind, and I fell into bed with you like an idiot.'

She looked away. 'I was confused and scared.'

'And now you're fine? Queen Fayre made it all better?' He began to pace, eyes on his feet. 'You know, I'm not doing this dance with you over and over again. If she's forcing your hand, you need to speak up, so I can help you. If you're actually choosing this for yourself, then you're on your own from now on. I'm not coming in that room next time to save your arse.' He paused. 'And you should know, the other defenders follow the rules around here, so if the king tells them to step aside so he can do as he pleases with you, they'll step aside.'

He faced her again, registering the hurt expression.

'Well, it's comforting to know just how deep your feelings run, defender. You care for my well-being so long as I follow your list of conditions.'

'We're back to "defender" now?'

'Appropriate given the direction the conversation has taken.'

He leaned in, speaking through his teeth. 'I'm going to ask you one more time if this is what you want. If it is, I'm done. It'll fall upon your sister to cover up the bruises.'

She looked so crushed by his words that he became

hopeful he might have actually gotten through. He was wrong.

Nodding thoughtfully, she said, 'I think that's for the best anyway. Any interference by you will only raise suspicions and cause problems for both of us. Better that we agree here and now to stay away from one another. You focus on your job, and I'll focus on mine.'

He blinked, his chest tightening. 'That's your answer?'

She looked him straight in the eye. 'I hope I was clear. Chadora can't have a stuttering queen.'

He took a few calming breaths as he stepped back from her. 'Loud and clear, *my lady.*'

Astin packed up his vile mood and rode to the farming borough to find his sister. Yes, he needed to speak to her, but he also needed a chance to clear his head before reporting for duty. He hoped the ride might reduce the probability of him breaking the king's jaw.

As he turned off the road and headed towards the farmhouse, he glimpsed his sister out front with a man he did not recognise. He thought it might be Chadwick, but they stood too far apart to be lovers. Presley's shoulders were rounded, her eyes downcast. The man's voice carried all the way to Astin, his gestures too big.

The pair looked in his direction when he appeared. Then Presley straightened, and the man lowered his hands. Astin stared hard at him as he pulled his horse up and dismounted. Only when he was standing beside his sister did he look to her for an introduction.

'Brother,' Presley said. 'You remember Chadwick.' She looked between them. 'And I'm sure you remember my brother, Astin.'

The men nodded, sizing one another up.

'What are we discussing?' Astin asked, eyes on Chadwick.

'A private matter' was the man's reply.

That made it official. Astin did not like his sister's soon-to-be husband.

'Wedding things,' Presley said, playing the peacekeeper. 'Boring things.'

Astin's gaze never left Chadwick. 'I'd like a private word with my sister, please.'

'We're to be married,' Chadwick replied, lifting that square chin of his. 'We don't have secrets.'

'Well, *I'm* not marrying you.'

Chadwick's face hardened. He went to say something, but Presley beat him to it.

'I'll see you tomorrow.'

Chadwick looked between them, nodded, then went to fetch his horse, which was tethered in front of the house. Presley watched him mount and ride away while Astin watched her.

'What is it with smart women marrying idiots?' he said. 'Of all the men in the borough…'

She turned to face him, arms crossed. 'Is this about Chadwick or *Lady* Lyndal? Because the look on your face when you arrived made it clear you weren't here to make friends. You could have tried.'

'I could hear him yelling at you from the road.'

She glanced in the direction of the house, where Rose

was peering out of the window at them. Astin followed her gaze and waved at his youngest sister. The curtain immediately fell back into place.

'The uniform has that effect on children,' he said.

'So does never visiting.'

His eyes returned to her. 'Where's Cooper?'

She began walking. 'Due home any minute, so you should probably leave.'

Astin fell into step with her. 'I got your message.'

She slowed, not speaking for a while. 'I may have snooped through some of Cooper's private letters.'

'It wasn't a one-time deal, was it?'

Presley shook her head as they walked beneath the bare trees that were once an orchard. 'I think they're under the illusion that they can keep it from the rest of the kingdom.'

'And the fallout will be disastrous.'

'What's happening in the merchant borough is already disastrous. So much preventable death. I hope the new queen has a plan.'

'Oh, she does.'

Presley watched him for a moment. 'Of all the women you could have fallen in love with, you had to go and fall in love with her.'

He stopped walking. 'You drew that conclusion based on what?'

She sighed. 'Seeing the two of you together.'

'For all of five minutes?'

'Well, you made up your mind about Chadwick after two.' She looked away, shaking her head. 'I don't have a ton of choices like you did.'

That last part got to him. 'What are you talking about? I never had choices.'

'You *chose* to leave.'

'You think that was a choice? Was I supposed to wait around until he beat me to death?' When she did not reply, he said, 'If this is about me leaving, surely you understand that I couldn't take you with me. I was hardly going to take you from the comfort of your home to live on the streets.'

Her eyes snapped back to his. 'The comfort of my home? Is that how you remember it?'

Astin's hands went to rest on his hips. 'You know what I mean.'

'No, I don't.'

'I would have been taking you from your mother, from regular food, from a warm bed—'

'You would have been taking me away from *him*.'

Astin searched her tear-filled eyes. 'If he had taken his belt to you even once, I would never have left you behind.'

She blinked. 'His *belt*? You think he needed a belt to hurt me?' Shaking her head, she stepped back. 'You should go. If he sees you here, Mother will be the one who pays.'

Astin did not move. 'If there's something you haven't told me—'

'I'm not doing this.' She began walking in the direction of the house, arms wrapping her like a shield.

'Presley.'

She picked up her pace, so he jogged to catch up. 'Tell me he never laid a hand on you.'

She turned to him, panting. 'It doesn't matter now. Your question's years too late. He never flogged me with his belt, never hit me, never kicked me in the face or held my head underwater. He never did those things to *me*. Happy?'

Astin felt sick as a realisation hit him. 'Oh shit.' He linked his hands atop his head, turning in a circle. 'I'm going to fucking kill him.'

'And what will that change? The damage is done.'

'You should have told me. I would have protected you.'

She started to cry. 'I couldn't. He said if I told anyone he would kill our mother—and I had every reason to believe him.'

Astin stopped moving. 'He doesn't still—'

'No. He hasn't touched me since I was fifteen, since the day Mother found out.'

He stared at her, his stomach rolling. 'Why have you stayed here all these years? I could have found you work, somewhere to live.'

She looked up at him. 'Why do you think?'

'Rose.' His hands fell to his sides. 'You stayed to protect her.'

'Yes, I stayed to protect her, because that's what a good mother does.' Presley wiped fresh tears off her cheeks and looked in the direction of the house. 'I stayed because she's my daughter.'

CHAPTER 34

Seven days. Seven days without one word from him. Seven days without his warmth, without his eyes on her. Seven torturous days.

Lyndal spent those days on the terrace and in the gardens. She walked, she sat, she watched the sky. She was waiting for the sun to return, but every day the clouds gathered. And every day it rained. She refused to retreat from it though, hopeful that it might cleanse her of the guilt she had carried every single day since standing in front of Astin and breaking both their hearts.

On day seven, she leaned on the balustrade of the terrace, face turned up to the sky. The colder the drops that fell the better.

Eda and Roul watched her from the doorway, letting her do whatever she needed to in order to be able to face the king for an evening.

Lyndal had confessed everything to her sister, cried out every ugly truth before swearing her to secrecy. No one could know. If Blake found out, Harlan would find out, then Astin. She knew he would never stand for it. He would die trying to free her from that life if he caught even the slightest whiff that it was not of her choosing.

So what exactly is your plan now? Eda had asked.

'To stop people dying' had been her response.

To stop Astin from dying.

She would find a way to exist within these walls, because she was a merchant. Internalising pain was a part of life.

So each night, she dined with the king and his guests. Smiling. Behaving. Never looking in Astin's direction. She pushed beef around her plate, watching Borin's thin mouth while he talked and studying his hair, wondering what he put in it that made it sit so stiff. That would lead her to think about Astin's hair, how it was a little longer than the average defender, how it had a slight wave in it. It was pure silk to touch. And his mouth full, his lips slightly upturned, like he was about to tell a joke and was already laughing internally. But those lips had sat in a hard line of late—her fault.

In return for all these unsaid things, the king did not lay a hand on her or ask her to sleep with him again.

Eda appeared next to her on the terrace when the rain stopped, a concerned expression on her face. *Apparently you have a dress fitting. Should I have the maid run a bath?*

Lyndal let go of the balustrade. It was only a week until the wedding, and she resented every small task to do with it, even if it was simply standing still for the seam-stress. 'No. Let's take a walk instead.'

Eda and Roul exchanged a look.

'You always like going to the stables to see the horses,'

Lyndal said, pushing back the hood of her cloak. 'Let's go there instead.'

They exited the castle and made their way down to the stables outside the wall. When a groom approached asking if he required a horse, Roul shook his head. The women strolled the length of the stalls, stopping to pet the horses. When they emerged on the other side, they spotted King Borin returning from the farming borough, Thatchere flanking him. Likely not a coincidence that Astin did not accompany the king on those occasions.

Lyndal checked over her shoulder to ensure Roul was not within hearing range. 'No doubt plotting their next external livestock deal.'

I'm tempted to tell the merchants what's going on, then join their fight, Eda signed. *Would solve a number of problems.*

'And kill a lot of people.'

Borin caught sight of Lyndal as he walked. She saw him sigh before he offered a wave. He had clearly planned to skip any awkward and unnecessary conversation, which suited her perfectly, but then a commotion at the merchant gate made him stop and turn.

Lyndal looked to Roul. 'Did something happen in the merchant borough?'

He glanced in that direction, then gestured towards the castle. 'Better get you inside.'

Borin was now marching towards the merchant gate, his bodyguard following at his heel.

'Let's go,' Roul said.

The women looked at each other, then followed the king.

'You're only going to piss him off,' Roul called to them.

The girls ignored him and continued on. As they drew closer, Lyndal saw there was a decent crowd gathered at the gate, pushing and shouting. Two defenders stood at the front, shoving them back.

'What in heaven's name is going on here?' the king shouted. 'Get those merchants back from the gate at once.' He turned when he heard Lyndal approaching behind him. 'What are you doing here?'

She was so used to his rude tone now that it barely registered. 'Seeing if there's anything I can do to help.'

He scowled, turning back to the merchants.

A woman pushed between the guards and flung herself at the gate. 'Is it true?' she screamed, eyes on the king. 'Did you sell our food to outside the wall?'

Borin paled. 'Take your crazy accusations elsewhere, and get off my gate.'

Lyndal's heart slowed. They knew. It had only been a matter of time before people found out the truth, and that time was now.

'You come here!' the woman screamed. 'You come out here and look at what you've done.'

Lyndal rose up onto her toes to see what the woman was referring to, and her chest squeezed when she spotted three dead children laid out at the defenders' feet. Her heels dropped to the ground, and she turned to Roul. 'I need you to go inside and tell Queen Fayre what's happening out here. Take my sister with you. She's safest with you.'

'I'm not allowed to leave you unguarded,' Roul said.

Lyndal pointed to the defenders on their side of the

gate. 'Do I look unguarded? Go. Queen Fayre will know what to do.'

I'm not leaving you, Eda signed, but Lyndal was already walking off in the direction of the gate, where a defender had drawn his weapon. He was hitting the woman through the latticed wood with the hilt of his sword.

'For the love of Belenus,' Borin shouted. 'Get back.'

'Stop hitting her,' Lyndal called to the defender. 'Can't you see she's grieving? She's unarmed.'

'He killed them!' the woman said, her bloodied knuckles around the wood. 'He's going to kill us all.'

Borin marched forwards. 'You dare slander my good name.'

Lyndal moved closer to the gate, hands going over the woman's icy fingers. 'I'm so sorry for your loss.' When she heard the king approaching behind her, she whispered. 'Move back. They're going to hurt you if you don't move back.'

Misery-filled eyes locked with hers. 'This is our fight, not yours.'

Lyndal flinched when a spray of something warm hit her face. She wiped at her cheek, then looked down at her fingers.

Blood.

It was not until her eyes returned to the woman that she noticed the blade through her throat. Lyndal followed it all the way up to Borin's twisted face. She gasped when he yanked it free, then watched as the woman slumped against the gate and slid to the ground.

Lyndal blinked, unable to move.

Then noise poured in. Screaming, cursing, weeping.

The merchants on the other side were holding their heads in disbelief.

'She was unarmed,' Lyndal said, her voice barely carrying.

Borin brought his face close to hers. 'This is what comes of your interference.'

She strained to hear him over the buzzing in her mind. A man made it through the defenders on the other side, only to be speared with a sword by a defender this side of the gate. More blood. More death.

'Tell them to stop,' she begged.

'Have you completely lost your mind?' Borin said. 'My men are doing their job.'

She made a move for the gate, but he grabbed her arm, fingers digging in. She tore free. 'Do not touch me.' Turning back to the gate, she shouted, 'They're unarmed.'

Borin took hold of her once again, spinning her around. 'Listen to me,' he roared, flecks of spit hitting her face. 'You will return to the castle this instant or I will throw you back into that borough where you belong.'

Lyndal blinked, trying to focus. 'You're disgusting. What sort of monster kills an unarmed, grieving woman?' She spat in his face, all self-control gone.

Borin grabbed her by the throat, squeezing.

'Go ahead,' Lyndal choked out. 'Let everyone see.'

His eyes flicked to the gate, and then he threw her at his guard, Thatchere. 'Get her out of my sight!'

Thatchere caught her, but she pulled free, coughing. Who else would speak up if not her? She fixed her eyes on the king, who was now shouting instructions to the defenders on the wall.

'Kill any man or woman who refuses to leave the square.' He stepped up to the gate. 'You want to behave like animals? Then you better be prepared to be slaughtered like one!'

Footsteps pounded on the wall above her, archers loading their longbows. Then came screams as the first round of arrows was released into the crowd.

'Tell your men to stand down,' Lyndal called to the king, leaping sideways when Thatchere reached for her. 'You're making it worse.'

He turned, eyes like two raging fires. 'I told you to leave!'

'Not until you call off your men. Please. I'll help you. I'll speak to them.'

He closed the distance between them, then drew a knife from a sheath that Lyndal had always assumed to be decorative. So she was quite surprised when she felt the sharp blade against her neck.

'I should have shot you in the square that day,' he said, his voice just loud enough for her to hear.

She stopped breathing, not because there was a knife pointed at her neck but because the hate in his voice was as thick as the blood running beneath the gate. She turned her head a fraction to meet his eyes, feeling a slight sting as she did so. 'Call off your men. If you don't, no army will be able to suppress their fury.'

She felt the pressure on her neck ease.

'You are lucky I need you alive,' Borin whispered. 'For now.'

The fire in his eyes dulled to embers as he withdrew the knife. But just as it left her neck, a body slammed into him, and he went hurtling to the ground, sliding all the way to the gate. Lyndal watched in shock as Astin climbed on top of the king and raised a fist, bringing it down on his face, once, twice. Two defenders reached him before the third punch, dragging him off.

'You piece of shit!' Astin shouted. 'You pull a knife on her?'

Borin groaned, slowly getting onto all fours, then spitting blood on the ground. He lifted his head to look at Astin, who was barely restrained. 'You traitorous bastard. You of all people know how this ends.'

One of the defenders kicked the back of Astin's knee, and he dropped to the ground. Puffs of steam came from his mouth with every breath. His eyes met Lyndal's, unafraid and unapologetic.

She struggled to process what was unfolding in front of her. Reaching up, she fingered the sticky blood on her neck. It glistened on her fingers. That was when she became aware of the silence. The unruly crowd on the other side of the gate had reduced to murmurs and shuffles of feet. The merchants were watching them, as were the archers atop the wall. All eyes were on the king as he slowly rose to his feet. Borin drew his bloodied sword, and the two defenders restraining Astin exchanged a look.

'What are you doing?' Lyndal said, her feet carrying her forwards. 'Your Grace.'

Borin glanced in her direction. 'For God's sake, will someone get her out of my sight?'

Thatchere came forwards, but before he reached her, Lyndal bent and snatched up the dagger Borin had dropped on the ground. The defender stopped short of her, not because he was afraid but because he seemed unsure how to proceed.

'Lyndal.' Her name was a warning growl from Astin's lips.

Borin's eyebrows lifted in amusement. 'What exactly do you plan on doing with that? Are you going to start killing people?'

She brought the blade to her own throat. 'If you kill him, we both die, and every merchant on the other side of that wall will have another reason to hate you.'

Astin's eyes widened. 'Put the knife down.'

She shook her head. 'No.'

Footsteps came at a run, and a moment later, Queen Fayre appeared in her line of sight, Eda and Roul with her.

'Lyndal,' the queen mother said, her voice slow and level. 'I need you to put down the knife and come to your sister. She is very distressed.'

Clever. She was hitting Lyndal in her most vulnerable area. 'If anyone hurts him, I swear before Belenus, and every god before and after him, that I'll cut my own throat.' Her eyes went to the gate. 'And you will all know who drove me to it!'

'Are you trying to start a war?' Borin hissed.

The war had already started.

Eda took a step forwards, but Roul caught her arm. She stood there with a helpless expression.

'Lyndal,' Astin said, his voice strangled. 'Please put the knife down.'

Borin looked between them, and a realisation dawned on his face. 'Ah, now I see it.' He slowly nodded. 'I must say, I expected more from you, Fletcher. You were the last person I thought would fall prey to her. I guess you were not as smart as I thought.'

'Son,' Queen Fayre said. 'Have Fletcher taken to the tower, and the three of us will move inside and deal with the matter privately. This is not the place.'

'No,' Lyndal said. 'I don't trust you not to kill him.'

Fayre moved slowly, walking out to stand directly in Lyndal's line of sight. 'What do you think will happen to all those people on the other side of the gate if you take your own life?'

A ragged breath escaped Lyndal. 'I want your word he won't be harmed and that the archers will stand down. No more killing.'

Fayre searched her eyes, then nodded. 'You have my word. No more killing.'

'That is not your decision,' Borin squawked behind her.

She rounded on him. 'Have you learned nothing? I am still trying to clean up the last mess you made.' She lowered her voice. 'Look around you and *think*.'

Borin looked in the direction of the gate, then threw his sword on the ground in a tantrum. 'You heard her. Take Fletcher to the tower.' Then to Lyndal, he said, 'You tell the merchants they have exactly one minute to leave the square before my archers start shooting again. Any further deaths will be on *you*.'

The second Lyndal lowered the knife from her throat, Roul stepped forwards to take it from her.

Borin walked over to Astin as he was pulled to his feet. 'This is not over, *traitor*.' With his hands balled into fists, the young king strode off, shouting, 'I want that square clear!'

Astin was led away, and Lyndal had no choice but to let him go. He was alive. That had to be enough for now.

Her eyes went to the gate, where the merchants waited to see what she would do. She knew she had the power to fan the flames of civil war or contain them.

You're bleeding, Eda signed, appearing next to her and inspecting her neck.

'It's nothing,' Lyndal replied.

He'll pay for this.

Lyndal headed for the gate. 'He will, but not at your hand.' She stopped in front of it and said, 'I'll not sit idle while you starve. Let me fight this side of the wall first. Go home. Please.'

The defenders kept a firm hold of their weapons as the merchants looked around, deciding what to do. Slowly, the people collected the dead and began to disperse. Two men came forwards to lift the dead woman off the gate.

'This is our fight, not yours.'

Those had been her last words before Borin killed her. Now, as Lyndal prepared herself for war, she realised how many others were waiting in the wings—hungry to fight.

CHAPTER 35

Astin sat on the cold stone floor of his cell with his back against the wall, staring at reddened knuckles. He had not had a chance to think through the best course of action—he had simply reacted. Something inside him had snapped. Every violent thought he had suppressed over the years had risen to the surface in one dangerous surge. He knew with certainty that if those men had not dragged him off the king, he would have beaten him to death. For Lyndal. For the merchants. For people like his sister who suffered at the hands of those kinds of men.

He looked up at the sound of footsteps and saw Harlan. The commander leaned his shoulder on the bars.

'Can't say I'm surprised,' he said. 'I'm more surprised it didn't happen sooner.'

Astin tipped his head back, resting on the wall. 'Bastard had a knife to her neck.'

Harlan nodded. 'I get it. Just wondering how you being locked up helps.'

Astin banged the back of his head on the wall before climbing to his feet. 'Do you know where she is? If she's all right?'

'She's with Queen Fayre, and Eda's confined to her bedchamber. They've put a guard outside her door to make sure she stays there.'

Astin dropped his head to the bars.

'Even if by some miracle they don't execute you,' Harlan said, 'you'll never be permitted within a mile of the king again.'

'Probably for the best.' He took a hold of the bars. 'And where was Thornton earlier? He wasn't even there.'

'He did the two most valuable things he could in that situation. He got Queen Fayre involved and removed Eda from the scene. Thornton knows what he's doing. He would have weighed up every option.'

Astin pinched the top of his nose. 'God forbid Lyndal do something sensible like leave with them.'

Harlan was silent a moment. 'She's not here for the crown. She's here for the merchants. She's already proven she'll put them ahead of her own safety when she agreed to marry the king. None of us like it, but we all understand it's her sacrifice to make.'

Astin turned and leaned his back on the bars. 'And now the merchants know about the livestock.'

Harlan nodded. 'And we brace for war.'

'And what side will you fight on?' Astin asked. 'How do you choose?'

'It's impossible. For me it's a daily choice. Which way my sword points depends on who's most at risk. Then I ask myself what the cost of my choice will be to those around me.' He shifted his weight. 'Today you chose to break the king's nose.'

Astin exhaled in place of laughter. 'Best part of my week.'

'And now Lyndal is scrambling to keep you alive because she's the only one with any real leverage.'

Astin turned back at the sound of someone jogging up the stairs. A young defender emerged, looking frantically around. He seemed relieved when he spotted Harlan.

'The warden wants you on the north wall at once, Commander. It's urgent.'

Harlan straightened. 'Urgent how?'

'English troops in the thousands a mile out.'

Astin looked at Harlan. 'How many wars can one king fight in a day do you suppose?'

'Sit tight,' Harlan said, heading for the stairwell. 'We're about to find out.'

It should have been unsettling to play across from a woman wearing a blood-splattered dress, but the queen mother was not the slightest bit fazed by Lyndal's appearance. She had sent Borin to his quarters to calm down, like one does a child, before meeting Lyndal on the terrace. Rain fell hard around them, yet that was no longer a peculiar thing either.

'I have sent for a physician to tend to your neck,' Fayre said before moving one of her pawns.

Lyndal touched the superficial cut on her throat, then moved a piece on the board.

'You were right about my son selling livestock to England,' Fayre said, taking her turn. 'I looked into it, and then I raised the matter directly with the king.'

Lyndal said nothing as she took her next turn.

'The problem with these kinds of arrangements,' the queen mother continued, 'is that they are difficult to end.' She moved her bishop. 'I think my son believed it would win him a new friend, but it seems he has forgotten that it is Edward's mother and her lover who control England at this point—and they are not looking for new friends.' Fayre leaned back, regarding her. 'Do you know any kingdom or country that could survive on forty head of cattle right now?'

Lyndal shook her head.

'Exactly. The moment this kingdom changed its name, raised its banners, built an army, and dismissed their god, we became the enemy.'

'That's a lot of enemies at once,' Lyndal said, moving her castle to the far end of the board.

Fayre watched her. 'Yourself included. It seems he knows about your little affair.'

'Yes. I think it's safe to say the charade is over. Mistakes have been made on both sides, and there's no coming back from them now.' Lyndal moved her knight, then sat back.

'And yet we must,' Fayre said, taking her move.

Lyndal stared at the chessboard. 'Your son held a knife to my throat.' She moved her bishop.

'Which saddens me enormously. I take that as my own personal failure.' She used her castle to take out one of Lyndal's pawns.

'Surely you've figured out by now that your eldest son is not fit to rule. Every merchant knows it, every farmer, every noble. And now King Edward knows it too.'

The queen took another piece from the board and looked up. 'There are English troops waiting north of the wall. I do not believe for one moment they are here to collect a few head of cattle.'

'Then why are they here?'

Fayre took her turn before replying. 'They are here to take Chadora.'

Lyndal swallowed. 'Will they succeed?'

'Check,' Fayre said, placing her knight near Lyndal's king. 'We have a strong army.'

'An army that's outnumbered.' Lyndal's eyes were on the board. 'An unfortunate time for King Borin to be out of favour with his people, because their arrival feels strangely like liberation.' She reached for her castle, paused, then moved one of her pawns. 'Checkmate.'

The queen's gaze fell to the board, her eyes widening slightly. After a long moment of silence, she sat back. 'Well, look who finally learned how to win.'

Lyndal waited to see what her next move off the board would be.

'I want you to manage the merchants for me,' Fayre said. 'We need them onside for this fight.'

Fury flickered inside Lyndal. 'You want me to pacify them until you have the capacity to crush them?'

'I want you to keep the peace until we have the resources to work through this.'

Lyndal pressed her teeth together. 'You had the resources. Your son sold them beyond the wall.'

Fayre fell silent again. 'I really admire and respect you, which is why it pains me to force your hand.'

'But you'll do it anyway.' She brought a hand up to her neck. 'Let me guess. If I play by your new rules, you'll let Astin live.'

'I cannot even promise that now. He attacked the king.'

'Who had a knife to my throat.' She saw Fayre swallow. 'Tell me. What is it you want me to do?'

Fayre tapped a finger on the table. 'Right now I need you ready to deal with the merchants when the time comes. I need the news of England's troops contained. If the merchants realise our army is fighting elsewhere, they may take advantage of the situation. And I most definitely need you to stay away from the tower. So I am afraid I must confine you to your quarters in the interim.'

Lyndal's foot bounced under the table as her mind worked. 'I see. Well, I have a request also.'

'Go on.'

'I would like Thornton to escort Eda to the nobility borough so she can be with my sister and mother while this all plays out.'

The queen mother nodded her consent, then gestured to Thornton. He walked over to the table, awaiting instructions.

'Please see Lady Lyndal to her bedchamber. Lock the door, and bring me the key.' She watched Lyndal across the table. 'We must keep our future queen safe.'

Lyndal looked up at her bodyguard. 'Then you'll take my sister to Wright House in the nobility borough.' Her eyes returned to Fayre. 'That's what we agreed, was it not?'

The queen mother bowed her head. 'It was indeed.'

Rising from her chair and curtsying, Lyndal strode from the terrace. The moment she was inside the corridor, she slowed to walk beside Roul.

'Why did you just agree to be locked in your bedchamber?' he asked.

'Because the queen mother wants to control the pieces she can, so I'm going to oblige.' Lyndal glanced over her shoulder to ensure no one was behind them. 'And you're going to follow orders because you're a defender.'

He glanced sideways at her. 'What are you scheming in that head of yours?'

'You defenders always think the worst of people. All I ask is that you let me say goodbye to my sister before you lock me up.'

He kept his gaze forwards. 'You have five minutes.'

Lyndal closed her eyes. 'Five minutes is plenty.'

Astin recognised the king's footsteps long before he appeared at the top of the stairwell. Borin paused, looked around, then strolled over to Astin's cell. The defender rose to his feet, eyes moving over his red, swollen face and crooked nose.

Borin slapped the bars, then shook out his hand as he began to pace.

'I've got an English army ready to descend, nobility asking questions, and merchants one wall over carving weapons out of sticks.' He glanced in Astin's direction. 'And instead of you being out here, keeping me alive, you stab me in the back.' Borin touched two fingers to his swollen eye. 'You once told me that your stepfather cannot be trusted.'

'He can't.'

Borin stopped walking. 'To what extent? Is he capable of betraying his king?'

'That man is capable of all kinds of atrocities.' Astin leaned one shoulder on the bar, no longer caring about standing respectfully in the king's presence. 'He's loyal only to himself.'

Borin was silent a long moment. 'He told me he would handle negotiations, so I gave him free rein to come and go as he pleased. Now there are English troops at my doorstep, despite there being no quarrel between us. And now Cooper Brooke is nowhere to be found.'

Astin almost felt sorry for the king. Almost. 'What did you give my stepfather to keep this whole thing a secret? What did you promise him? Coin?'

'Yes.'

Astin exhaled through his nose. 'And what did he *ask* for? Because I know it wasn't money.'

'He wanted a title. Obviously I could not give him that. Handing him a title would have raised all kinds of questions.'

Astin nodded as the pieces fell into place. 'So you offered him money in place of power. A man with no conscience or morals. A man with all the information one needs to take control of a small kingdom.'

Borin's face slackened. 'You think he's working with King Edward to take my kingdom?'

Astin shrugged. 'More likely Lord Roger Mortimer.'

'Is no one in your family trustworthy?' Borin said, stepping closer. 'Tell me, how long have you been in love with the woman I am to marry?'

Astin stared past the king. 'Since before.'

Borin was silent a moment. 'You know, if my mother had not shown up, I would have killed you. I would have killed you, and then I would have let her cut her own throat to save me the hassle of orchestrating her death later.'

Astin calculated the distance between them, wondering if he could reach the man in order to slowly strangle him to death.

'The merchants seem to think the sun will magically shine from her arse when that crown lands on her head,' the king continued.

Astin shifted his weight. 'War has arrived at your door. They're ready to take everything your father built. I think you have bigger things to worry about right now, don't you?'

A crashing noise in the distance made them both look to the small window. Shouting ensued.

'Sounds like the merchants have returned to the gate,' Astin said. 'And they're not coming for me.'

Borin's face fell.

'Perhaps they figured out that you've sent your army to the wall,' Astin continued. 'Smart time to act. If I were you, I'd get back to the castle as quickly as you can.'

The king's face hardened as he turned away. Walking to the top of the stairwell, he paused, eyes going to the keys hanging by the torch on the wall.

'You are right,' Borin said, looking back at Astin. 'We

are going to need every capable soldier on the wall. I think it best I send the prison guards to join the effort, so I am afraid it will just be you and the rest of the criminals here for a while.' He reached for the keys and tucked them into a pocket. Then, taking the torch off the wall, he stood observing the flame for a moment. 'I liked you a lot,' Borin said. 'I trusted you. So the betrayal stings all the more.'

'I did the job expected of me. I kept you alive.'

Borin nodded slowly. 'And now I am forced to find someone else to keep me alive.' With that, he bent and laid the torch beneath a small wooden stool that sat by the wall.

Astin took hold of the bars, watching the flames rise to meet the wood.

'I'll be sure to comfort her for you,' Borin said before disappearing down the stairwell.

*L*yndal paced back and forth past the window of her bedchamber, praying she had done the right thing.

'Tell the merchants it's their fight now,' she had told Eda. 'The king's army is on the wall, all eyes looking outwards.'

She had called up an army of merchants, knowing they were hungry for this fight. Now she listened as the gate was ripped apart, as weapons clashed, as pent-up rage flooded into the royal borough. She was done playing these games. This was their fight, and she was handing them the best chance to win.

Lyndal knew when they had reached the castle gate because the shouting grew louder. Stepping up to the window, she saw a handful of archers atop the castle wall, but only a handful. She had been right. The majority of the king's army had been sent to the outer-wall, and the king would be hiding somewhere in the castle.

Smoke drifted in through the open window, tasting of

animal fat and ash. There was only one reason the merchants had arrived with torches in broad daylight. She pressed her head against the bars of the window, trying to get a glimpse of the tower, but it was the wrong angle for it. She took comfort in the fact that the tower was filled with merchants, which made it the safest place in the royal borough at that moment. They would not attack their own.

A horn sounded, long and deep. In the distance, she saw defenders racing along the south wall.

The door rattled, and Lyndal whipped her head around. She stilled, listening, watching the handle move. A moment later, the door swung open.

Eda stood in the doorway, pressing pins back into her hair. *A little trick Harlan showed me.*

Lyndal stared at her. 'What are you doing here? You were supposed to return home after delivering the message.'

And leave you locked in here?

'How did you even get inside the castle?'

Eda tapped her nose. *That one was a little trick Roul showed me.* She threw a dress at Lyndal. *Put this on. If there was ever a time you wanted to blend in with the merchants, that time is now. They're tearing down the gate.*

Lyndal stepped out of her dress and into the faded cotton one, stilling when she heard banging below. The merchants had arrived.

God help anyone who stands between the merchants and the king they hunt.

'I need to get to the tower,' Lyndal said, rushing out into the corridor and heading for the stairs. She removed the pearl comb securing her hair and dropped it on the ground as she walked. Her hair fell down her shoulders. She glanced sideways at her sister, whose skirts were muddied all the way up to the knee. Her dark hair was pulled back in a single practical plait. No chance of anyone mistaking her for nobility.

The girls broke into a run when they reached the fountain court. The doors at the far end had a drawbar across them but did not require a key. They were almost there when a voice stopped them.

'If you are planning a visit to the tower, I am afraid you are too late,' Borin said.

Lyndal almost tripped at the sound of the king's voice. She looked back at the fountain just as he emerged from behind it, surrounded by bodyguards. The defenders already had their weapons drawn, eyes moving between the women and the doors behind them. Eda stepped up beside her sister, one hand tucked behind her back. Lyndal did not have to look to know she was holding a knife. What she planned to do with one knife against a small army of defenders Lyndal had no idea.

'I just came from there,' Borin said, 'and I am sorry to inform you that there was a small incident.'

A loud bang on the door behind them made Lyndal jump and Eda glance over her shoulder.

'A bit of a tragedy really,' Borin continued, as though hundreds of merchants were not standing on the other side of the doors waiting for their chance to get him.

'What did you do?' Lyndal asked, her stomach falling.

He tutted. 'You merchants love to blame me for everything.'

Bang.

Lyndal flinched at the noise. 'For years, Fletcher has protected you with his life.'

A nod. 'Yes. Then you came along, and now suddenly everyone wishes me dead.'

'I'm afraid I can't take credit for that. People wished you dead long before I was lured here to help clean up your mess.'

'Well, I tried to rectify that—twice.' Borin's eyes flashed. 'Fletcher was determined to protect *you* with equal enthusiasm.'

Lyndal's lungs expelled all the air they were holding. 'Oh. It was you.'

Eda looked up at her, confused.

'The fire, then the poison.' She pressed a hand to her stomach as the new information settled. 'All that effort when all you had to do was tell your mother no.'

Bang.

Borin's eyes went past her to the door. 'My mother's logic was sound. I cannot fault her there. The merchants were in love with the idea of us. I had no choice but to play along.'

Bang.

She shook her head. 'Then why try to burn me alive?'

He took a step in her direction, and she took a step back.

'Better to win their sympathy than break their hearts.'

Bang.

'You are vile,' she said, taking another step towards the door.

Borin pointed a finger at her. 'And you are lucky to

still be talking, because I am fed up with your mouth. The only reason my guards have not sliced you open already is because I made a promise to my mother, and I am a man of my word.' His eyes went to Eda. 'Of course, I made no such promise about you.'

Eda revealed the knife and did the most remarkable thing she had done in years: she spoke.

'Good luck with that.'

Lyndal sucked in a breath when she heard her sister's voice. It was the sweetest form of music. No heart had been hit harder after their father's death than Eda's. The tiny shadow had lost its person the day he died. Her voice was no longer that of a child but of a confident young woman. It was remarkable and frightening all at once.

'She speaks,' Borin said, amused. 'Is that knife for me?' When she did not reply, he said, 'Do you know what happens to people who kill kings?'

Eda raised her chin. 'Your father's killer went on to live a long and happy life.'

The darkness that descended Borin's face was chilling. 'Kill her,' he instructed. 'And take Lyndal to my quarters.'

There was not a chance in hell either of those things were happening.

One of the guards came for her, but before he had taken his second step, Eda threw her knife, striking his sword arm. The defender grunted and dropped his weapon. The king's eyes widened slightly. Clearly he had not been expecting that level of skill from her.

Door, Eda signed as she shook another knife from the sleeve of her dress.

Lyndal leapt in the direction of the exit, praying her sister had the situation under control behind her.

'If you open it, you will kill us all,' Borin shouted

Lyndal looked back as she took hold of the drawbar, watching as the second knife flew between two of the guards, striking the king in the leg.

He roared.

The door banged once more, the noise vibrating through Lyndal. The drawbar was too heavy.

'Eda!'

Her sister was at her side a moment later, throwing her shoulder into it and pushing as hard as she could while two defenders came at them.

'Don't fret, Your Grace,' Lyndal called when the drawbar finally budged. 'The merchants will show you the same compassion you've shown them.'

The women tossed the wooden plank at the defenders as the doors burst open and merchants poured in like floodwater. The guards were swept back with the force of the deluge. Lyndal and Eda pressed themselves against the wall, then squeezed around its edges.

'I need to get to the tower,' Lyndal shouted, but her words were drowned out by King Borin's screams.

The castle grounds were swarming with merchants. No one looked twice at the two women moving in the opposite direction with their unkempt hair and worn clothes. They were there for one reason only: to knock the monster off his throne.

'What are we going to do about them?' Lyndal asked, pointing to the handful of defenders atop the wall shooting at merchants below.

Eda tripped, and when the girls looked down to see what she had fallen over, they found a dead merchant man clutching his longbow. Without hesitating, Eda snatched it from his hands.

We need to keep moving, she signed.

The habit of signing in place of speech would take time to break.

As they ran towards the gate, they pulled arrows from corpses. Lyndal watched the defenders atop the wall carefully, praying their bows would not swing in their direction, because she knew they would not miss. They stopped beneath the archway to regroup, looking in the direction of the tower. Lyndal's breath caught when she spotted smoke pouring from the windows of the circular structure.

Astin.

Go, Eda signed. *I'll cover you.*

Lyndal took off at a sprint towards the tower, leaping over bodies, her dress snagging on weapons. Her wet skirt tangled on her legs, and she fell, slamming into the mud just as an arrow whistled overhead. She watched it pierce the ground in front of her, knowing another would follow.

A hand wrapped her arm, pulling her to her feet. She came face to face with Blake, and her eyes widened.

'What are you—'

'Move!' Eda shouted behind them, jogging backwards while shooting at defenders atop the wall.

Blake grabbed Lyndal by the arm and pulled her in the direction of the tower. 'She spoke!'

'A very recent thing,' Lyndal shouted back, holding up her dress to prevent another fall.

They stopped once they were out of shooting range, eyes sweeping the outer-wall to ensure there were no more arrows pointed in their direction.

'What are you doing here?' Lyndal asked Blake, her breaths coming in heaves.

Blake held her knees. 'You didn't think I was going to let you two have all the fun, did you?'

'What about Mother?'

'She's with our aunt.' Blake straightened.

Lyndal looked up at the tower, the smell of smoke

making her sweat. 'Astin's inside. I'm going to get him out.' She headed for the tower.

'What?' Blake ran after her. 'It's on fire. You can't just walk into a burning building.'

Lyndal did not slow. 'Why not? He did it for me once.'

She heard Eda swear behind her. Not overly surprising that some of her first words in years would be ones that should never come from a lady's mouth.

Eda caught her arm just before she entered. *The guards hang the keys on the wall.*

It was the one advantage of having a sister who had once been locked in there.

'This is madness,' Blake said. 'The smoke alone will kill you.'

Lyndal drew a breath, preparing to enter.

'Fine,' Blake said, 'I'm going in with you.' She pointed at Eda. 'You stay right here—no matter what.'

Lyndal pressed the crook of her arm to her nose and mouth, nodded at Blake, and then the sisters ran into the smoke-filled doorway. The haze made the darkness even more unsettling. Lyndal blinked against it as she took Blake's hand and pulled her through the smoke in what she hoped was the direction of the stairwell. Relief pulsed through her when her foot hit the first step. Then they were climbing as fast as they could.

'Open the door. Please' came a voice that did not belong to Astin. 'Let us out!'

In her rush to get to Astin, Lyndal had almost forgotten that there were other prisoners locked in the tower. The king had done this knowing others would die also.

Blake waved her sister forwards. 'Go. I'll catch up.'

Lyndal nodded and drew her first breath. Her throat closed in protest. She hurried on, coughing into her arm. Her shins smashed into the edges of the steps as she misjudged their location over and over, but she continued forwards, checking each cell she passed. Whenever she heard a cough, she made a mental note to return for them on the way down.

'Astin!'

Panic was setting in. She called for him, knowing it was a terrible waste of air and energy but unable to stop herself. He was probably already dead.

Where is the fire?

As she continued to climb, she got her answer. The smoke glowed an eerie orange up ahead, and the wall felt hot beneath her hand as she steadied herself.

'Astin!'

Flames appeared, climbing one wall and reaching all the way to the roof.

'Lyndal?'

She was so relieved when she heard his voice that she began to cry. He was alive. Now she just had to get him out.

Holding her breath once more, she ran towards the flames, the heat from them almost knocking her backwards. She passed just out of reach of them and fell to her knees in front of Astin's cell. He crawled to her on his stomach.

'Get right down,' he instructed. 'The cleanest air is closest to the ground.'

She coughed as she reached for him. 'Where are the keys?'

She knew from the look on his face that there were no keys.

'You need to leave—now. The damp walls in here are the only reason I'm not burning, but they're drying out, and the fire will spread.'

She shook her head. 'I'm not leaving without you.'

'Yes you are.' He coughed, his chest wheezing. 'Crawl to the stairwell, then get down those steps as fast as you can.'

Again, she shook her head.

'Stop telling me no and leave!'

She looked around, thick smoke in all directions. 'There has to be a way.'

'There's no time. Think about your sisters.'

She gripped him through the bars, crying.

He kissed both of her hands. 'I love you. Don't let your death be the last thing I see. It's senseless.' He coughed long and hard into his arm.

Dropping her head to the bars, she knew he was right.

Arms wrapped her middle, lifting her. Lyndal turned to see Blake's soot-covered face.

'There's no key,' Lyndal said, a sob tearing from her. 'I can't get him out.'

Blake's eyes were raw from the smoke, tears rolling down her face. 'I'm so sorry,' she told Astin. She coughed, and it was so violent Lyndal felt it through her own body.

'Take her,' Astin said, bloodshot eyes pleading with Blake.

A thought came to Lyndal as she was pulled away.

'Wait!' She reached up and pulled two pins from her sister's hair. If Harlan knew how to pick a lock using pins, then maybe Astin did too.

'We have to go,' Blake said, her voice unrecognisable.

Lyndal pulled free and stumbled back to Astin, pressing the pins into his hands and closing his fingers around them. The room spun, and she fell forwards, her cheek smashing into the bars.

'Get up,' she heard Astin say. 'I'll be right behind you.'

She looked up at him to see if he was telling the truth but could no longer see him through the smoke. Then Blake was dragging her away.

Heat hit her once more, flames ahead of them, above them. The stairwell seemed like an impossible target. When Blake hesitated, Lyndal knew it was time to take charge. She tugged her sister's hood up over her head and face, knowing the wool would protect her, then ran for the stairwell, turning her own face away from the flames.

They part ran, part fell all the way to the bottom of the steps, then headed for the light. The second they emerged outside, Lyndal said to Eda, 'Take her.' Then she took a few steps and threw up.

'Where's Astin?' she heard Eda ask.

Lyndal pressed her eyes shut and threw up again. Eda appeared at her side, pulling her away from the smoke, away from the tower. Away from him. That was when she noticed the prisoners nearby. Blake had gotten them out before coming for her.

'I'm so sorry,' her sister said, coughing and crying.

She had nothing to apologise for. The choice was one

of them dying or both of them dying, but she knew Blake would see his death as her own personal failure.

Lyndal shook her head and wrapped her arms around Blake. 'Don't. He's coming. He said he'd be right behind me.' She was trembling so badly she had no idea how she was standing.

Eda looked in the direction of the door, her expression doubtful. All three of them stared at it for what felt like twenty minutes but was probably more like twenty seconds.

Twenty eternal seconds.

'There,' Eda said as a figure came staggering out into the daylight, coughing and gasping.

Lyndal ran to him, *flew* to him, leading him away from the smoke, then taking hold of his blackened face while crying.

'It's all right,' Astin said, his voice hoarse. His reddened eyes met hers. 'I'm all right.'

She wrapped her arms around his middle while he continued to cough. 'Thank God.' When she drew back to look at him, she saw his gaze had drifted to the castle.

'They actually did it,' he croaked.

Lyndal turned just as a corpse was hoisted up the wall by the neck. Not just any corpse—the king. Knowing he was dead was one thing, but seeing it was something else. There was no sense of victory, and it was too early for hope. She felt only relief knowing King Borin would never harm another merchant again.

'I need to go to the farming borough,' Astin said, coughing into his arm. 'Cooper's the reason we're in this mess, and I need to get my sisters and mother out of the borough.'

'I'll come with you,' Lyndal said straight away.

He shook his head. 'I need you all to go to the nobility borough. You'll be safest there.'

Blake chewed her lip, then asked, 'Do you happen to know where Harlan is?'

Astin glanced at her. 'North wall. I'm guessing he thinks you're safely in the nobility borough?'

Blake shrugged. 'I'm probably safer here due to recent events.'

Astin blinked slowly. 'Remind me not to be present for that reunion.' He wandered off to collect the weapons from a nearby corpse.

'You're in no condition to fight,' Lyndal said, following him.

He strapped on the sword and slung the quiver and longbow over one shoulder. Coughing, he said, 'It's just a precaution.' He cupped her face with one hand. 'Promise me you'll go to the nobility borough.'

Nobody spoke—or met his eyes.

He looked between them. 'None of you are going, are you?'

'I doubt they would let us in anyway,' Lyndal said. 'We'll meet in the merchant borough when this is over.'

Astin searched her eyes, stifling a cough. 'I need to know you're safe.'

Lyndal gestured to her sisters. 'You of all people should know it's not the location but the company.'

His hand fell away. 'I'll come find you as soon as I can.'

Lyndal watched him jog off in the direction of the gate. A bad feeling enveloped her, but she did not get time to indulge it, because then Blake said, 'Is that Queen Fayre?'

Lyndal's eyes snapped in the direction of the castle wall. And there she was. No guard in sight and surrounded by merchants. Lyndal's heart sank as the queen mother was confronted by the sight of her own son hanging on the wall. Her feet were moving before her mind had a chance to catch up. 'We have to make sure they don't hurt her.'

Eda and Blake rushed after Lyndal.

Why? Eda signed. *She locked you in your bedchamber.*

Blake's eyes widened. 'She locked you in your bedchamber?'

'It sounds bad out of context,' Lyndal replied. 'It's not like she set it alight.'

The king did though. Eda sneered.

Blake moved in front of Lyndal, blocking her path. 'The king lit that fire?'

Lyndal stepped around her. 'He also tried to poison me, but let's not dwell on the past.'

'Tell me how you got that cut on your throat,' Blake demanded, matching her stride.

Knife to the throat, Eda signed.

Blake was fuming now. 'He's lucky he's already dead. You don't owe that woman anything. You know that, right?'

Lyndal met her eyes. 'She doesn't deserve to die for his sins.'

When they reached the castle wall, the girls pushed their way through the crowd of merchants pressed in tightly for a close-up view of the dead king. Lyndal tried not to look up. She did not want to see his lifeless eyes, the red and purple face painted with blood. It had not been a quick or painless death.

'We should string her up with him!' someone shouted. 'She's proven where her loyalties lie.'

Lyndal's eyes met the queen mother's as she emerged at the front of the crowd. Fayre gave her a resigned smile, like she had already accepted her fate. The woman had birthed a monster—there was no denying it. But his choices were not her fault. Making her pay for them was unfair. She had done her best, even if at times her best had fallen short.

Lyndal turned to the unruly crowd. 'Have you forgotten all this woman has done for us? She saved our lives that day in the square. She took a stand against her own son when he instructed his army to shoot us down like rabid dogs.'

'And hasn't spoken a word on our behalf since,' a woman shouted. 'While we've watched our loved ones starve and suffer.'

Lyndal stood her ground. 'She's been making a plan to end your suffering. I can attest to it, because I was the plan.'

The crowd quietened.

'It was Queen Fayre who brought me here, hopeful that I could make a difference. She taught me the true meaning of strength, showed me how to be the queen you all needed.' She coughed, tasting soot and ash. 'She was not sitting idle. She was hard at work.'

A man stepped forwards. 'We don't trust her.'

Lyndal nodded. 'I understand. But perhaps you trust me, and I swear to you that she wants to see the merchants thrive as much as I do.'

'You think she's going to care what happens to us now?' the man asked. 'We're the reason her son is on that wall.'

Lyndal looked to Fayre, who was not saying a word. 'It's true, she's the king's mother, and she'll grieve the loss of her son like any mother would. But she's also a queen, and one of the first things she taught me was to separate heart and mind.' Her shoulders fell. 'I wasn't very good at it, but she's exemplary.'

Queen Fayre's eyes creased at the corners.

Lyndal faced the crowd again. 'This woman will grieve and cry and fall down in the privacy of her quarters, but then she'll get up and do what has to be done.' She looked between their faces. 'Prince Becket will be coming for his crown. Don't you think the young prince has lost enough already?' Seeing that last comment hit the mark, she added, 'Don't make him return to an empty home. Every merchant here knows that kind of pain.'

She did not stop there.

'And take her son down from the wall. That's not who we are. The king has paid the price for his actions. Must his mother wait for the crows to arrive as we have all waited at some point?'

Silence fell over the crowd. There was not a merchant present who had not witnessed the horror of seeing a loved one or neighbour get pecked apart by birds.

'Let Queen Fayre lay out her son and bury him the

way many of us couldn't. *That's* who we are. You all came here for change, not revenge.'

It felt like a full minute passed before Lyndal heard a rope creak behind her. She turned as the king was lowered to the ground, the queen mother's face contorting when he landed. Taking control of her emotions, Fayre finally addressed the merchants.

'I am sorry for his death, but I am more sorry for his failure as your king. You all deserve a better leader, a better protector. I really hoped he would come to see that so I would never have to see this.' She glanced over her shoulder, lips pressed tightly. 'You owe my family and this kingdom nothing. You have endured more hardship in the past ten years than most can bear, but I am afraid I must ask more of you.'

There was a shuffle of feet as they waited to see what she would say next. Lyndal exchanged a look with her sisters and drew a breath.

'You are likely aware that King Edward's army is outside our walls. It seems they intend to stay. While I do not know exactly what that would mean for Chadora, I do know there is not enough food for us as it is.'

Birtle hobbled forwards, his wary eyes on the queen mother. 'That's because you lot have been selling it behind our backs.'

'Your anger is not misplaced' was Queen Fayre's reply. She took a step forwards. 'I know it is a big request, but I want to assure you that better times lie ahead for all of us. Prince Becket is not his brother. He is a young man with a lot of empathy and compassion. However, you will not get the chance to discover that if Chadora falls to England today.'

'So what would you have us do?' Birtle asked, arms crossed in front of him.

Queen Fayre looked around. 'Stand alongside our army. That means no more fighting within these walls. We need every defender protecting the boroughs and the rest of you ready to fight for your homes and families. You are the next line of defence.'

The merchants looked between themselves.

'Maybe we'll be better off under King Edward's reign,' a woman called.

Fayre found her in the crowd. 'Perhaps. Or perhaps the English army will storm your village and slaughter your families. I cannot speak of the king's intent.'

A murmur of voices rolled through the crowd.

'Can you promise we'll see some of the food we'll be laying our lives down for?' Birtle asked, continuing to watch her with suspicion.

Queen Fayre nodded. 'I know it is not worth much to you at present, but you have my word.'

With a hard sniff, Birtle turned to the other merchants. 'You heard her. Pick up those swords and bows, and whatever else you have tucked underneath those threadbare clothes of yours, and get ready.' He nodded at Lyndal before leaving.

The merchants turned and followed him, walking back in the direction of the gate, leaving only the queen mother and the three sisters standing there. Blake and Eda wandered a short distance away in an attempt to give them some privacy, but no one spoke for the longest time.

'This morning he was the King of Chadora,' Fayre eventually said, her voice quiet. 'Now he is just another muddy corpse.'

Lyndal looked over to where Borin lay twisted on the ground with a noose still around his neck.

'I know it is a great deal to ask…' the queen mother began.

'Of course I'll help you,' Lyndal said.

Fayre's eyes went to the tower, where smoke continued to pour from the windows. 'Did he make it out?'

Lyndal did not need to ask who she was talking about. 'Yes, he made it out.'

'Good,' Fayre said, eyes returning to her son. 'Good.'

Lyndal walked over to Borin, swallowing down the rising nausea. She did not know whether to take his arms or his feet, and Queen Fayre had not made a move in either direction.

Eda and Blake appeared, gently pushing Lyndal out of the way. They each took an end and lifted him.

'Lead the way,' Blake said.

Lyndal gave her sister an appreciative smile, then went and threaded her arm through Fayre's. She knew the queen was too proud to admit her legs were failing her. 'Let's go inside.'

CHAPTER 38

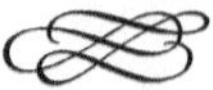

The defender at the farming gate looked Astin up and down, taking in his dishevelled appearance and filthy face. The uniform was the only reason he raised the portcullis. The fact that there was only one guard at the gate demonstrated how few soldiers they had on the ground.

'Is it true?' the guard asked. 'Is the king dead?'

Astin nodded.

The defender did not seem surprised—or emotional, for that matter.

'I'm looking for Cooper Brooke,' Astin said. 'He left the borough earlier to meet with someone on the other side of the wall. Do you know if he's returned to the borough?'

'Never heard of him. You'll have to speak with the guards at the north gate, but they're not opening for anyone right now given the English army is parked just out of shooting range.'

'The fight hasn't begun?'

'And no one's interested in talking either.'

What were they waiting for? It made no sense. Every minute the English delayed their attack was another minute of preparation for their own army. If they were expecting Chadora to surrender, someone would have surely mentioned it by now. Unless they were waiting for the war inside to play out first. With the king dead and the people divided, it would be less of a war and more of a taking control of the reins.

The realisation hit Astin like a rock to the head.

Cooper had probably leaked the news of livestock being sold outside the wall himself, knowing the outcome. The bastard had let the merchants do his dirty work for him. God only knew what other surprises he had in store. Astin needed to get his family somewhere safe until he figured out exactly what was at play.

Nodding at the defender, he took off at a run in the direction of the farm and did not stop until he reached it. He went wide, approaching from the back of the house just to be safe, and kept out of sight, listening for clues as to who was inside. Cooper's horse was missing from the paddock, but there was a quietness to the place he did not trust, so he proceeded with caution.

Approaching the window, he peeked inside and saw his mother in her chair, staring hard at her sewing. Presley and Rose were seated at the table preparing vegetables. But something looked off.

A man stepped into view and glanced at the window.

Astin pressed himself against the wall as footsteps drew closer. His hand rested on his weapon.

That was no farmer. That was a soldier.

The problem was he was not one of theirs.

He struggled to figure out how there was an English soldier inside the borough and yet no one else seemed aware of the fact.

There was only one way to get answers.

Grabbing hold of the top of the window, Astin swung his legs through and dropped into the room, drawing his sword as he landed. He pointed it at the English soldier as he turned.

'Someone start talking.'

His mother rose from her chair, gripping tightly to her sewing. Presley moved to stand in front of Rose.

'No one says a word,' the soldier said, his weapon only half drawn.

Presley looked from the guard to Astin. 'They're already in the borough, hundreds of them.'

When the soldier turned his head to look at her, Astin pressed the tip of his sword to the man's neck. 'Eyes on me.'

The balding man looked back at Astin.

'There's an entrance on the east wall,' Presley said. 'I doubt even the warden knows of it. The king had it built to get the livestock out—' She swallowed nervously. '— and now Cooper's using it to get the enemy in.'

Astin's eyes were fixed on the soldier. 'And now a question for you. What are you doing in my family's home?'

The man's face hardened. 'That's not your business.'

'Wrong answer.' Astin lunged forwards, cutting the man's throat before he had a chance to get his sword the rest of the way out. He caught the soldier, dragging him to the door and throwing him outside to save the floors.

His mother watched the dying man through the open door while Rose clung to a pale-faced Presley.

'There will be more of them,' Presley said.

Astin had to get his family out of the borough—fast. 'Saddle the horses. Let's move.'

'Cooper said they wouldn't hurt us if we cooperated,' his mother said, not moving.

Astin blinked slowly. 'I'd hoped you might have realised by now that you can't believe a thing that comes out of that man's mouth.'

'If he comes back and we're gone—'

'Mother,' Presley said, tone firm. 'The borough will soon be overrun by soldiers. We're going with Astin.'

Lari placed her sewing on the chair behind her and nodded. 'All right.'

The moment Astin stepped outside, he stopped, lifting a hand to his family behind him. Everyone froze, ears straining as they listened.

'Horses coming our way,' Presley said.

They were moving at a gallop. He guessed around six of them.

'Stay inside,' he instructed. He loaded his bow and swung it in the direction of the horses as they came into sight. There was Cooper flanked by English soldiers in helmets, chain mail, and steel chest plates. Astin took aim at his stepfather.

'I wouldn't do that,' Cooper called, gesturing past him.

Astin's eyes flicked over his shoulder as another horse appeared from behind the house, an arrow trained on him. He was tempted to shoot his stepfather anyway, but he was not sure how the soldiers would react, and he could not protect his family if he was dead.

He lowered his bow.

'Last I heard you were locked in a tower,' Cooper said, pulling his horse up a few yards from the house and looking down at the dead body at Astin's feet. 'Did the king have a change of heart?'

'The king's dead,' Astin replied. 'But I'm guessing you already knew that.'

Cooper watched him a moment. 'I think even you would agree it was time for a change in leadership. King Edward is not his father. Any defender who lays down their weapons and bends the knee will be spared.' He paused. 'I doubt the merchants will take much convincing when they realise he already has control of the food. Troops are securing the farms as we speak.'

Astin slowly shook his head. 'You absolute traitor.'

'Soon to be *Lord* Traitor.'

Every muscle in Astin's body was tense. 'Do you honestly think anyone's going to respect that title?'

'Not at first, but they will when they realise I've given Chadora a king fit to rule.'

'All you're doing is giving away our food. Nothing more. Nothing less.'

Cooper let out a breath and walked his horse forwards. 'Surely you understand that letting you live would be a big mistake. You'll fight me the whole way.'

That was true. He would.

'Don't. Please,' Presley said, stepping out of the house.

Astin calmly raised his hands, not wanting any arrows

flying his way while his sister was outside. 'Presley, get back inside.'

'No.'

He looked over his shoulder. 'Inside, *now*.'

She turned when she felt a tug on her dress. There was Rose looking up at her with pleading eyes. Presley snatched her up and carried her inside.

Astin heard the release of an arrow, a familiar noise he would recognise anywhere. There were things he could have done in that moment to save his own life, but to what end for those inside the house? He pressed his eyes shut, readying for the searing pain.

I'm sorry, he told Lyndal as she filled his thoughts. He would have done anything to spare her the grief of his death.

He flinched at the sickening thud of arrows hitting flesh, waiting for the explosion of pain that would spread like liquid through him. A scream rang out, but it did not come from him. His eyes snapped open, and he found his mother next to him, an arrow protruding from her chest. She looked down as her knees buckled, and Astin caught her, lowering her the rest of the way to the ground.

Another scream sounded, and he realised it was coming from Rose.

'Mama!'

Presley stood frozen in the doorway, face slack, holding tightly to her daughter.

Astin's eyes burned as he crouched over his mother. It was not supposed to end like this. Her protection had come far too late, and his forgiveness not at all.

'I'm sorry,' she breathed, eyes fixed on him and voice gurgling.

He had seen death up close before, but the sight of his mother desperate for exoneration as she struggled to draw breath almost broke him. He was supposed to say 'I forgive you'. That was the correct response. But the words stuck in his throat. Instead, he gave her the next best thing he could. Bringing his face close to hers, he said, 'Father's waiting for you.'

Lari's mouth turned up slightly as she exhaled and fell still. Her chest did not rise again.

Presley dropped to her knees, and Rose slipped from her hands, running over to the woman she had called "mama" her whole life.

'Look what you've done,' Cooper snarled, jumping down from his horse.

Astin lifted his gaze to his stepfather, then said to Rose, 'I need you to go inside with your sister. Can you do that for me?'

Presley was already at his side, pulling the girl away and dragging her towards the house.

Astin was not going to play nice anymore.

Reaching for the knife strapped to his calf, he shot to his feet, throwing it at the soldier who had killed his mother. It struck him just above his steel chest plate. The moment the knife left his hand, Astin was reaching for his bow. The other soldiers drew their weapons now, but they were no match for a defender. Astin released five consecutive arrows—and he did not miss. The men cried out, two slipping from their saddles and slamming into the ground. None of them would be any help to his step-father now.

Cooper's breaths came a little faster. He should have stayed on his horse. He looked around, weighing up his options.

'There's nowhere you can go right now that I won't follow, you sack of shit.'

Astin dropped the bow and walked towards him, eyes flicking to the soldiers to make sure none of them were going to try anything cunning. But it was Cooper who tried to be clever. He drew a knife, deluded enough to think Astin was going to let him use it. Astin punched it from his hand and grabbed Cooper by his tunic, throwing him to the ground. His stepfather wheezed as the air was knocked from his lungs. Astin dropped a knee onto Cooper's chest and drew his sword. Cooper struggled for a moment, then fell still when he felt the blade against his neck.

'Go on, then. Do it,' his stepfather growled, sending a spray of spit in Astin's direction. 'You'll finally get to feel like a man.'

Astin looked into his eyes, hoping to see remorse, or at the very least fear. But all he saw was hate. 'You think I need to hurt you to feel like a man? That's where you went wrong in life. Hurting people doesn't make you a man, it makes you an arsehole.'

Cooper strained beneath him, but he was no match for Astin.

'Get it done!' he shouted.

Astin stared down at him, not speaking for the longest time. Then, removing the blade from his neck, he took hold of Cooper's wrist, pinning him in place. 'You don't get an easy death. First, you must pay for her death,' he said, nodding towards his mother. 'Then all the cruelty, every beating.' He leaned closer. 'And every time you forced yourself on my sister.' He squeezed the wrists tighter. 'Then you'll pay for every merchant who has died because you gave away their food.'

Finally, some fear in his stepfather's eyes.

A horn sounded, a deep noise that vibrated around them. The sound of fighting carried on the breeze.

'You might have missed your chance,' Cooper said, his lips turning up. 'Here come the English.'

Astin looked to the road as a stampede of feet whispered along the ground to them. 'It's you who's missed your chance.' He looked his stepfather in the eye. 'Because here come the merchants.'

Panic filled Cooper's face, and he turned his head in an effort to see. Hundreds of merchants appeared on the horizon, clutching swords and homemade weapons. Astin rolled his stepfather onto his stomach, removing Cooper's belt and binding his hands together behind his back.

'Presley, Rose,' he called. 'We need to leave—now.'

CHAPTER 39

'Stay close,' Astin told Presley as he helped the girls onto one of the horses. 'We need to get to the merchant gate as quickly as possible.'

Presley nodded and tucked Rose against her chest before gathering the reins. The moment Astin landed in the saddle they were off, riding through the paddocks in order to avoid the roads where the fighting was underway. When they reached the gate, they found a crowd gathered there, women and children pressed against the portcullis, begging to be let through. The defender Astin had spoken to earlier stood on the other side, hand resting on the hilt of his sword and feet shuffling in the dirt.

'Why is he not opening the gate?' Presley asked as she pulled up their horses.

That was a very good question. Dismounting, Astin pushed through the crowd until he reached the gate. 'Raise the portcullis,' he instructed the defender.

The guard shook his head. 'There are English soldiers in the borough. The gate remains in place.'

'You can't leave women and children trapped in a war zone.' Astin punched the wood. 'Raise it!'

The defender still appeared conflicted until the warden's voice sounded from atop the wall.

'Get that gate up!'

Astin let out a relieved breath as the portcullis finally went up. He returned to his sister and niece, shoulders clipping shoulders as people moved in the opposite direction to safety.

'Astin!' Presley called. Rose was still in her arms, clinging to her neck.

He made his way over to them. 'Stay inside until the borough's secure. Understand?'

'Where are you going?' she asked, eyes searching his.

'East wall.'

She blinked and swallowed. 'You'll come back?'

'Lower the gate!' the warden shouted.

Astin pushed his sister in the direction of the portcullis. 'Go before it shuts.'

'You'll come back?' she asked again, walking backwards as she waited for his reply.

He nodded, then watched her turn and pass beneath the archway just in time.

'Move back!' shouted the defender on the other side.

And just like that the girls were gone from his sight.

Astin looked up, thankful to find the warden leaning on the embrasure, looking out over the borough. He moved closer, positioning himself beneath the man. 'Cooper Brooke is the man you're looking for. He let the

English in via an unknown door on the east wall. Let me find it, sir.'

Shapur's gaze fell to him, but before he could respond, the sound of approaching horses had everyone looking to the road. Twenty mounted defenders rode into view, coming to a stop in front of the warden.

'Half of you will travel to the east wall with Fletcher,' Shapur instructed. 'The rest of you will head north.'

The commander on the ground turned to his men. 'You heard him. Let's move out!'

Astin looked up at Shapur as he mounted his horse. 'Cooper Brooke's tied to a tree at the farm. I suggest you send someone to collect him.'

The warden nodded.

Astin dug his heels into his horse's sides and rode off, the other defenders following behind. They galloped through paddocks, jumping fences they did not have time to navigate. Wind whistled in Astin's ears, carrying the sound of weapons and dying men. Up the hill slope they rode, only slowing when they caught sight of merchants up ahead. There were around a hundred of them, fighting trained soldiers as though they had been secretly preparing for this moment their whole life. Even in their famished state, their hearts continued to beat as strong as ever.

Astin looked past them to the wall, where archers watched them down their arrows. The enemy was out of shooting range. 'We'll approach from the west, see if we can push them closer to the wall.'

He nudged his horse forwards, the collective sound of ten weapons being drawn the most comforting noise he had heard all day. They picked up speed, Astin swinging his weapon once, twice, before descending on their enemy. Merchants leapt out of the way of the horses, panting and bloodied from their efforts. The tiring soldiers could not stand their ground against fresh defenders. They were driven back by force and fear.

Astin slid from his horse as he hit the fight, drawing his dagger in the same breath and throwing it at the soldier closest to him. It struck the man's neck, stopping him in his tracks. Another was upon him a beat later, sword swinging at Astin's head. He blocked it, steel screeching, then kicked him hard in the stomach, sending him flying backwards into the mud. Astin pushed forwards, slicing and stabbing and punching. The English worked to maintain the ground they had won—and failed.

Behind their enemy, arrows protruded from the ground, clearly marking the shooting range of the archers waiting atop the wall. Astin swooped down, plucking a sword from the hand of a dying soldier. Two weapons would hurry the process along.

The soldiers began tripping over the arrows in the ground, then over each other. They seemed to lose their rhythm and confidence all at once. More arrows came, whistling through the air and sinking into the backs of their enemy, who could no longer retreat from them. Their fight was lost.

'Hold!' Astin called, not wanting his own men to be struck down in the process.

The defenders stood their ground, fighting, until every English soldier lay dead or too injured to fight.

For a moment, they were triumphant.

For a moment, it felt like a win.

But then the arrows stopped falling from the sky, and when Astin looked to the wall, he saw the archers vanish from the embrasures, their bows swinging in the other direction.

'Shit,' said the defender beside him.

Astin's gaze fell to the base of the wall, where English soldiers now spilled into the borough. At least that answered his question as to where the door was located. Whatever the archers were doing to stop them on the other side, it was not enough. Astin knew he had to get to that door, but he stood no chance with only ten men.

He looked back at the merchants defiantly gripping their weapons with bony hands. The sight might have warmed him if it were not for the fact that they were all about to die fighting a war they should never have been a part of.

Movement behind the merchants caught Astin's attention. His body went rigid, and his hand tightened around his weapon, believing for a moment that they had been surrounded by their enemy. But it was Harlan who appeared on the horizon, behind him an army of defenders. The merchants separated, and the two men locked eyes.

'Need a hand?' Harlan asked.

The corner of Astin's mouth tugged up. 'Several.'

'Merchants to the back!' Harlan shouted. 'Archers to the front!'

Astin looked to the men with him. 'Fall back.'

It was a strange thing to wash the corpse of the man she was supposed to marry, but Lyndal did it to help the woman who had tried to help everyone else. Yes, she had made mistakes along the way—they all had. The king's mistakes had cost him his life.

The queen mother brought her son's hands together, laying them one on top of the other, then straightened. The maid picked up the basin of dirty water and left the room, leaving the two women alone.

'Prince Becket is going to take some convincing to return to this place,' Fayre said. 'History always depicts second-born sons as resentful of their position in the family. My youngest has always been grateful for the fact.'

'I'm sure you'll help him transition.'

Fayre met her gaze. 'I suppose I shall have to go about finding him a suitable wife.' She lifted one eyebrow in question.

Lyndal smiled. '*Suitable* being the key word there. I imagine he'll be free to select a wife of his choosing.'

'As long as I approve.'

Lyndal bit back a smile. 'Of course.'

The queen mother pushed a loose strand of hair off her tired face. 'You would have made a wonderful queen. However, I must be content with a wonderful friend instead.'

'Don't forget superb chess opponent.'

Fayre's eyes creased at the corners.

A confession sat on the tip of Lyndal's tongue, one she was not sure she could live with. 'There's something you should know.'

The queen mother looked in her direction, waiting.

'I was with King Borin before he died. Some heated words were exchanged.' She swallowed repeatedly. '*I* opened the courtyard doors. I was the one who let the merchants into the castle, knowing they were coming for him.' It was so wrong to say those words to his grieving mother.

Queen Fayre was still and quiet for a moment. Then, wandering over to the table by the window, she picked up the arrow sitting on it and turned it in her hands.

'He threatened my life,' Lyndal continued. 'But to stand here and tell you it was an act of self-defence would be a lie. I think I would have done it anyway.'

Fayre was quiet for the longest time as she ran her finger repeatedly over the fletching on the arrow. 'Do you know what this is?'

Lyndal's brow creased at her response. 'It's an arrow.'

'Not any arrow. It is the arrow that killed my husband. Borin was quite determined to find his killer, as you well know.'

The merchants had been locked up and starved as a result. It was not something she would soon forget. 'Grief is a strange beast.'

Fayre nodded thoughtfully. 'I understand why you did it, why you opened that door. Sometimes we queens have to make difficult decisions for the greater good.'

Lyndal looked at the ground. 'Well, I'm no queen.'

'No, but hopefully I taught you to think like one.' She paused, eyebrows drawn tightly together as if pained by whatever memory she was reliving. 'I had to be a queen, not a wife, that day.'

Lyndal was lost. 'What day?'

Fayre met her eyes. 'The day I ordered my husband's assassination.'

At first Lyndal thought she had misheard, but then the queen continued.

'I remember sealing that letter and handing it to the messenger with a trembling hand. I was certain he knew what was written inside.'

Lyndal was speechless for a moment. '*You?*' Her voice barely carried the short distance between them.

Fayre placed the arrow on the table and looked her in the eyes. 'Sometimes one must throw open the courtyard door and help history run its course.' She attempted a smile, but it did not stick. 'I do not judge you for your actions today, despite the personal cost to me. And I hope you will not judge me for the things I had to do.' When Lyndal did not say anything, she added, 'I have shocked you.'

'A little.'

'A lot.'

Lyndal nodded. 'Did you tell me to make me feel better? Or did you tell me to ease your conscience?'

The queen mother thought for a moment. 'Both.' She cleared her throat. 'Might I suggest this conversation not leave the bedchamber?'

'I think that's probably very wise.'

A knock at the door made them jump.

Fayre smoothed down her dress before calling, 'Enter.'

Shapur Wright stepped through the door, his helmet tucked beneath one arm and blood covering his hands. He looked from the queen mother to the bed behind her. 'I am sorry for your loss, Your Majesty.' He paused. 'I ordered all but a handful of defenders north—'

'Stop,' Queen Fayre said, cutting him off. 'This is not on you, Warden.' Her eyes moved over him. 'I gather from your appearance that King Edward's army breached the wall?'

Shapur glanced at Lyndal. 'They appear to have been let into the farming borough via a secret entrance. The borough has since been secured and the English troops have withdrawn. The merchants insisted on joining the fight.'

Lyndal's heart lodged in her throat as she waited for a mention of his name.

'Who let them inside?' Fayre asked.

'Cooper Brooke. A farmer.'

'The farmer my son was conducting business with?' the queen mother asked.

Shapur nodded. 'He has confessed to working with Lord Roger Mortimer. He awaits sentencing.'

'Do you know if Fletcher got his family out of the

borough?' Lyndal asked, unable to hold the question in any longer.

Something in Shapur's expression made her nervous.

'I believe his sisters are safe.'

His sisters. No mention of his mother. 'Where is he?'

'He was last seen at the east wall.'

'Last seen?'

Shapur's face hardened. 'The dead and injured are still being retrieved. There are many families waiting for news.'

'Of course.' Lyndal looked to Queen Fayre. 'Your Majesty, I wonder if I might—'

'Go,' Fayre said. 'There are no locked doors, I promise.'

One corner of Lyndal's mouth lifted as she lowered into a curtsy. 'Much appreciated, Your Majesty.'

It was strange to see the gates between the merchant, royal, and farming boroughs open, people wandering freely back and forth between them. Lyndal knew the most sensible thing to do was to go to the merchant borough, because that was where she had told Astin she would be. But her gut was telling her to go east to the farming borough.

'I'll tell Birtle to open the shop up for anyone who needs it,' Blake said as they headed for the merchant borough. 'Assuming he hasn't done it already.'

Lyndal stopped walking.

What's wrong? Eda signed, looking back.

Blake sighed. 'You're going to look for him, aren't you?'

'The warden said the borough's secured. I'll be fine. You go ahead, help people. I'll follow shortly.'

Blake exhaled. 'Be careful.'

Lyndal hugged them, then watched them until they reached the merchant gate. When they were gone from sight, she headed east to the farming borough.

The first thing she noticed when she stepped beneath the unguarded archway was smoke rising in the distance and the smell of burning flesh. Covering her nose and mouth, she walked the empty road that led to Astin's farm, passing stray sheep, chickens, and oxen along the way. It was strange seeing livestock unaccounted for, but many of the fences appeared to be damaged.

Lyndal was almost there when she came upon a corpse on the road. She walked right up to it, eyes moving over the unfamiliar armour. He looked around twenty. Someone's son, brother, perhaps husband.

Another life wasted.

When it began to rain, she stepped over the blood splashed across the road and kept walking, passing a wagon travelling in the other direction. It was full of bodies. Her eyes met the defender's briefly, and then she picked up her pace.

Finally, she arrived a soggy mess at the farm, and her spirits lifted when she spotted Rose seated on a small stool next to a milking cow. Rain was a normal part of life for a girl her age who knew no difference. The sound of a hammer pulled Lyndal's attention west, and she spotted

Presley pounding away at a fence post. She made her way over, calling out so as to not frighten her.

'Only me.'

Presley paused, looked in her direction, then resumed hammering. 'He's not here.'

Lyndal stopped a few feet away, blinking against the rain. 'Are you all right?'

Presley wiped sweat from her brow with the back of her hand. 'Fine.'

Her tone reminded her so much of Astin. 'Where's your mother?'

'Dead.'

Lyndal closed her eyes. 'I'm so sorry.'

Presley continued to pound the wood. 'The soldier was aiming for Astin. Then she…' The hammer slipped from her hand and fell to the ground.

Lyndal closed the distance between them, pulling Presley into her arms.

Presley went limp against her. 'She was a terrible mother in so many ways, except today. Today she was perfect.' Her shoulders shook. 'Astin got us to the merchant borough, then went in search of the entrance on the east wall. I haven't seen him since.'

Lyndal could not think about that. Letting go, she said, 'The man has proven to be thoroughly unkillable in the past.' She forced a smile and looked around. 'Now, what can I do to help? Where are all the animals?'

Presley pushed her palms to her eyes. 'Lost. Stolen. Dead. I don't really know. We returned as soon as we could and found the place like this. I can't even go into the house because that's where she is.' Her face crumpled.

'And I'm supposed to be strong'—she gestured to Rose—'for her.'

Lyndal glanced at the young girl milking the cow. 'I passed a few animals on the way here. Perhaps they're yours.'

Presley drew a shaky breath. 'Hundreds? Did you pass hundreds?'

No. She had not passed hundreds.

Presley licked rain from her lips. 'Our bull is gone. And that's a strange thing to care about when your mother is dead in the house, I know.'

Lyndal tilted her head. 'I'm not sure whether Astin told you this, but I happen to be very good in a crisis. So this is what's going to happen. I'm going to go inside and tend to your mother. You and Rose are going to stay out here and make sure you have at least one secure paddock. Your cattle are branded, which means they'll be brought here when they're found wandering about the borough. Then I'm going to feed you both, even though you'll insist you're not hungry. Only then will I leave, because if I don't, my sisters will come looking for me.'

Presley was silent a moment. Then she bent and picked up the hammer. 'Rose,' she called. 'Come and help me with this fence.'

CHAPTER 41

Presley had not been exaggerating when she described it as a secret entrance. The door had been covered with stone so it blended perfectly with the rest of the wall. A defender walking by would have no idea of its existence except for the tracks in the mud giving away its location. By the time they reached it, hundreds of English soldiers were already inside. So Astin captured a young soldier, broke his nose, then sent him back through the door with a message for his commander.

'You tell him Cooper Brooke is in shackles. Tell him there's no way in or out now. Then you tell him that if he doesn't take his men and go home, *our* men are going to come down from that wall and collect all your heads. Did you get that?'

A dazed nod had been the soldier's only reply before Astin shoved him through the door.

Astin had then fought on the ground alongside Harlan, the other defenders, and hundreds of merchants while defenders atop the wall struck down the English soldiers left and right with their sharp aim and sharper arrows.

When the borough was secured, prisoners were taken to a holding in the nobility borough, because the tower in the royal borough was no longer an option. They were queued down the road, forced to watch their dead comrades being burned while they waited to be locked up.

The English soldiers did not get a burial. Nor would Cooper Brooke.

It was dark by the time Astin returned to the farm-house, tentatively stepping inside. He half expected Cooper to burst in the room at any moment armed with a log. Instead, he found Presley seated in a chair by the fire-place with Rose asleep on top of her.

Presley teared up at the sight of him. 'You're alive.'

He nodded. 'Sorry. There was a lot to do.' He looked around for their mother's corpse. He had carried her inside before they had fled earlier that day, but she was not there.

'She came here looking for you,' Presley said, resting a hand on her daughter's back.

'Lyndal?'

A nod. 'She took care of Mother, got her ready for burial.'

Of course Lyndal had come looking for him, and of course she had helped when finding two people in need of it. 'How did she seem?'

'Bossy.'

Astin smiled at the ground. 'Sounds about right.'

'You didn't happen to pass our bull on your way here?'

He shook his head. 'He'll show up. There's no way he'd fit through that door.'

Presley exhaled, eyes shiny with tears. 'Rose is mine now. No matter what happens, I get to keep her.'

He nodded, knowing what that meant to his sister. 'She's all yours.' His eyes fell to a sleeping Rose, far too big and heavy to be lap napping yet somehow fitting perfectly. 'Let's get her into bed.' Stepping forwards, he carefully picked her up and carried her to the bedroom. He was surprised to find only one bed in there.

'She sleeps with me,' Presley said, stepping past him and pulling back the blankets.

Of course she did. What better way to keep her safe?

After settling her, Presley heated some food up for him. Astin could tell Lyndal had prepared it. He had eaten enough of her food over the past year to recognise her cooking.

Making himself comfortable in front of the fire, he assured his sister he would be fine on the floor. He lay awake listening to her cry in the next room, but that was not the only reason he struggled to sleep. The house was filled with memories he could not sleep through. Some bad, others pure magic.

Giving up on sleep, Astin wandered outside, surprised to find stars. Change was coming. He could feel it. Exhaling long and deep, he sank down onto the chair on the veranda, knowing without a doubt that Lyndal was watching the sky with him.

Finally, he slept.

The following morning Astin hitched the wagon and

placed his mother's body in the back. When Presley hesitated to climb in, he asked her what was wrong.

'I think we should bury her here.'

Nodding, Astin removed her from the wagon.

They found a place on high ground, a spot that would get a lot of sun when it finally returned. All three of them dug the grave, with Astin doing the bulk of the work. When they were finished, they stood in silence for a long time before Rose finally said, 'I'm glad he's not going to hurt her anymore.'

Presley looked away.

'You heard from Chadwick?' Astin asked as they wandered back towards the house. 'I thought he would be here.'

Her eyes were on the ground. 'He has his own farm to worry about.'

Astin glanced sideways at her. 'You know, Cooper's not coming back.'

She nodded. 'I know.'

'So if you want out—'

'I can't run this place alone. You know that.'

'You won't have to. I'll be here to help you.'

She looked up, wary eyes on him. '*You're* going to move back to the farm? You're going to be a farmer? You, the defender?'

He chuckled softly. 'I've lived this life before. I can do it again—at least until you find a man you actually *want* to marry.'

She watched him as she walked. 'I thought I might go into the village, pick up some supplies. I'll need to make new linen for the other bed if you plan on staying. Perhaps you know a place?'

He smiled down at his feet. 'I know a place.'

The merchant borough was slow moving but alive with the smell of simmering meat. Whether that meat had been bought, donated, or stolen was irrelevant given the state of the kingdom. Every person had earned their meal. Noblewomen wandered between the shopfronts carrying baskets of food and medical supplies. There were horses tied up in the street—an act of faith. For once, it seemed like the kingdom was working together and taking care of each other.

Lyndal had stayed the night at their old house in the merchant borough with her sisters and mother. They had opened the shop to anyone who needed it, and now they had a number of children whose parents were either missing or dead. They were nothing but skin and bone and broken hearts, so Lyndal fed them to bursting, cleaned them up, played with them, and prayed people would come looking for them when everything settled.

She was sitting on the veranda with a young girl on her lap while Blake and Eda played gameball with the other children when her mother wandered out and handed the girl a small doll she had sewn that morning.

'What are you going to name her?' Candace asked, sitting down beside Lyndal.

The girl ran her fingers over the doll's face. 'Fayre.'

Lyndal smiled. 'Perfect for a doll with so much queen

potential.' Her gaze drifted down the street before returning to the game.

'Harlan said Astin is alive and well,' Candace said, watching her daughter. 'He just lost his mother and has his sisters to care for.'

Lyndal focused hard on the ball. 'I know that.'

Her mother tucked a piece of hair behind Lyndal's ear. 'Have I mentioned how proud I am of you?'

'You have.' Lyndal looked at her. 'And yet I feel sick about the whole thing. The merchants stormed that castle yesterday because *I* told them to. People died because of a fight I started.'

Candace angled her head. 'You cannot take credit for civil war.'

Lyndal heard men shouting down the street. She rose to her feet, placing the girl on the ground next to her. People were darting in every direction, and her eyes widened when she saw why.

'Everyone off the street,' she called, stepping down and ushering the children off the road.

Blake narrowed her eyes. 'Is that a... bull?'

Eda picked up the last boy and carried him to the veranda.

'There is something you do not see every day in the merchant borough,' Candace said.

Food? Eda signed.

Blake laughed, and Candace tutted.

Lyndal watched as the bull trotted past the shop, her eyes widening with recognition. 'Oh my goodness. That's him.'

Blake looked at Lyndal. 'Him?'

'That's the Fletchers' bull. He went missing from the farm.' She stepped down onto the street. 'Get me something to catch him with.'

'To catch a *bull*?' Blake called to her back.

Lyndal ran after it. The animal did not slow until it reached the end of the street, leaving confused merchants running for cover.

'Wait,' Lyndal called, out of breath. 'Remember me? From the swamp? I can take you home. I know where you live.'

The bull turned with a snort, pawing at the ground. Blake and Eda arrived a moment later with a length of rope.

What exactly is your plan? Eda signed.

'Obviously she's going to use her expert bull-catching skills to secure this enormous charging animal with a single piece of rope,' Blake replied.

Lyndal bit her lip. 'He was quite tame last time we met.' She frowned. 'Though he was stuck in mud at the time.'

Blake folded her arms. 'Well, he seems less tame today.'

Lyndal took the rope from Eda and drew a long breath. She moved slowly towards the woolly bull, careful not to startle it. She was pleasantly surprised when it did not immediately take off or impale her on one of its horns. She approached from the side to be safe, carefully slipping the rope around its neck and tying it in a knot. With a relieved sigh, she turned to her sisters with a triumphant smile.

'Well done,' Blake called. 'Now what? You going to ride it back to the farm?'

Ignoring her, Lyndal gave the rope a gentle tug to get the bull to start walking. The animal dropped its head before taking off again. Lyndal foolishly tried to keep hold of the rope and was dragged several feet before falling forwards onto the muddy street. She got her hands out just in time to stop her face from colliding with the stone. Looking up, she watched her sisters leap out of the way and the bull run off.

Instead of coming to help her, Blake and Eda doubled over with laughter while asking if she was all right.

'What if I had broken something?' Lyndal said, standing up and looking down at her mud-covered dress.

'Then we would have scooped you up in our arms and laughed all the way to the physician's house,' Eda said, speaking instead of signing.

Blake's laughter died at the sound of her youngest sister's voice. She pulled Eda to her. 'I love hearing you speak.'

'Yes,' Lyndal said, joining them. 'More of that, please.'

She looked in the direction the bull had gone and stilled when she saw Astin standing in the middle of the road, watching her. A familiar energy filled her chest and a smile spread across her face.

'I found your bull,' she called to him.

His expression did not change. 'Yes, I saw it run by.'

'Did you see the rope around its neck?' Blake asked, biting back a grin. 'That was all her.'

Lyndal turned to glare at her sister.

Blake cleared her throat and began pulling Eda down the street. 'We're going to head back to the shop.'

'But we won't be able to hear from there,' Eda whispered.

'That one was probably best said with your hands.' Blake smiled at Astin as she passed him.

Suddenly aware of the enormous distance between them, Lyndal moved closer, her hands fidgeting at her sides because she had no idea where they stood. He had told her he was done, but he had also told her he loved her. Mind you, he had been locked in a burning tower at the time. Now all the obstacles between them were gone, and yet he stood there not touching her.

'I can't believe you took on a fifteen-hundred-pound charging bull,' he said.

She shrugged. 'Honestly, he seemed nicer the first time we met.'

His mouth lifted.

Why was she so unbelievably nervous? 'I'm very sorry about your mother. Presley told me what happened.'

He only nodded. A ball hit his foot, and he kicked it back to its eager owner. 'Thank you for being there yesterday when I couldn't.'

'Of course.'

They turned and began walking slowly up the busy street, their arms bumping occasionally.

'Your shop seems busy,' Astin said, 'but not with people buying cloth.'

'It's been that way since yesterday.'

His gaze flicked to her. 'If only the borough had an almshouse.'

She smiled at her feet. 'If only.' Up ahead, she saw Presley had caught the bull and was now securing him to the back of their wagon. 'Seems he prefers your sister.'

'Don't take it personally. Even the bravest of bulls wouldn't take on my sister right now.'

Her eyes went to Rose, who was playing gameball with the other children on the street.

'How is Rose doing?' Lyndal asked. 'So much for her little mind to grapple.'

'Luckily we breed them tough in the farming borough.' He stopped and turned to her. 'I'm going to stay with them for a while, help with the farm.'

Lyndal could hardly believe what she was hearing. 'Surely the warden won't discharge you for punching the king while those responsible for his death walk free.'

'No. He was prepared to let that slide given the circumstances. It's just that my family need me more right now.' He glanced at Presley, who was pretending not to watch them.

'That's very admirable.' So why did her stomach feel heavy all of a sudden?

'I want to offer my services to you also.'

'Your services?'

'Yes. My time and labour for the building of one much-needed almshouse.'

As if she needed more reasons to worship at his feet.

Her eyes creased at the corners. 'I thought I should wait awhile before hassling Queen Fayre about that. She's had a bit of a week. But I'll hold you to your offer.'

His eyes went to the veranda, where Candace was watching them. 'Nothing quite like an audience when you're struggling to get words out.'

'What words are you struggling to get out?' There was an embarrassing amount of hope in her voice.

His hands went to rest on his hips. 'I meant what I said in the tower. I love you.' He swallowed, then cleared his throat. 'In a perilous sort of way.'

'The kind of way that makes sensible bodyguards punch the kings they're duty bound to protect in the face?'

His lips curled up. 'Yes.' He paused. 'Now that your plans with the king are dashed, I wonder if we might keep seeing one another—once life returns to some semblance of normal.'

She chewed her lip and watched the game for a few moments. 'It probably doesn't mean much now, but I lied to you the day you asked me why I changed my mind.'

A nod. 'I thought about that a lot. I couldn't figure out what she would have said that would have you lying to my face. It wasn't until I was locked in that tower that I realised what she threatened you with—me.'

Her eyes met his.

'The crazy things we do to protect the people we love,' he said. 'All I could think about while watching those flames grow higher was that I should have built you that damn almshouse a year ago and asked you to marry me before you went to Eldon Castle.'

She reminded herself to breathe. 'I probably would have said no.'

'A smart man would keep asking.'

They stood in complete silence for a full minute, watching one another. Lyndal's heart was drumming in her throat.

'I used to believe you don't get security *and* love,' she said. 'You have to choose. My mother chose love, and it almost killed her—several times. So at some point while growing up in this place, I chose security.' She flicked a piece of mud off her dress. 'I've since realised that the two aren't separate. With love comes security. There's no security without it. So when you're ready to ask, when the time is right, I'll be here waiting to tell you yes.' She swallowed. 'I've loved you for longer than I care to admit. I'm already yours. I can wait for the formal part.'

Astin wet his lips, glimpses of sun breaking through those stormy eyes of his. 'I'm not sure I can walk away after hearing that, so if it's all the same to you, I'll just ask you now.'

She could feel warm light rising inside her, heat filling her cheeks.

'Marry me,' he said. Two words. Nothing more.

A smile spread across her face, and she flung herself at him. He caught her with a laugh.

'Can I bring Pig and the babies to live with us?' she asked him.

'Yes.' He kissed her deeply, seemingly inhaling her.

Lyndal's sisters and mother came rushing over, faces lit with excitement, having clearly eavesdropped on the conversation. Astin lowered Lyndal to the ground, and her family descended on her. Presley wandered over also.

'I'm going to have to teach you how to tie a proper knot,' Presley said.

Lyndal pulled her in for a hug.

'Oh. Is this going to be a regular thing?' Presley asked, awkwardly patting Lyndal's back.

'Yes,' all the Suttone women said at once.

Astin grabbed Lyndal around the waist and tugged her back to him, kissing her again. Apparently he did not care about the audience standing a few feet away.

'What's all this?' Harlan called to them. He was shaking his head as he approached.

'Guess who's finally joining the family?' Blake said.

Harlan kissed Blake's head and hooked an arm around her, looking at Astin. 'Really? You might want to hold on to your armour, farmer.'

Blake threw an elbow into his ribs, and he chuckled.

'I think he knows what he's getting himself into by now,' Lyndal said.

The shop door opened again, and Birtle came wandering out. He looked between Astin and Lyndal. 'I've got a bottle of wine I've been saving for when we finally got some good news.' He waved everyone over to the veranda.

Candace, Blake, and Eda were already walking in that direction.

Astin turned to his sister. 'We don't have to stay.'

'I think we could all do with a bit of wine right now. Besides, Lyndal wore the bull out, so he'll need to rest for a while.' Presley signalled for Rose to join them, then looked at Astin. 'I know it probably doesn't mean much to you, but Mother would have loved all of this—especially seeing you happy.' She gave him a tight smile before walking off ahead.

Astin took hold of Lyndal's hand and brought it to his lips. A familiar sensation of invincibility ran through her.

'You're limited to one cup of wine,' Astin said. 'I've seen you drunk.'

Lyndal's head fell back with laughter, and he bent to kiss her again.

When she finally stopped, she asked. 'Does this match come with a title? I was quite fond of "Lady Lyndal the third".'

'That's fine, but only if you continue to address me as Your Superiorship.'

Smiling, she pressed her lips to his arm. 'Done.'

EPILOGUE

*L*yndal stood on the veranda of the new almshouse, trying very hard not to cry. She had promised herself that she would keep it together, but the fact that Queen Fayre had insisted on saying a few words was not helping.

'I remember how impressed I was when I first met Lyndal,' Fayre said, looking in her direction. 'She had travelled to hell and back, yet was brimming with an optimism so contagious I just knew I had to get her in a room with everyone I know and hope they caught it.' She looked behind her at the house. 'This was her idea, her vision, her understanding of what this borough needed. A piece of her enormous heart.'

Don't cry, don't cry, don't cry.

'I am so pleased to see her vision brought to life and so happy for those who will benefit from it,' the queen mother continued. 'And I am very sorry that Prince Becket could not be here to witness what a wonderful job his people are doing of caring for one another in his absence.'

The merchants exchanged glances. It had been nearly a year since King Borin died. A year of waiting for their new king—yet no such king had arrived. But because Queen Fayre was doing such a superb job as queen regent, no one was complaining.

Lyndal's eyes met Astin's. He was wearing the proudest expression she had ever seen on him. He winked at her, which only made the sting in her eyes worsen. Beside him stood his smiling niece. Lyndal had been shocked to learn the truth about Presley and Rose, but she would take the secret to her grave so Rose would never have to know just how big a monster her father really was.

'I am sure there are people Lyndal wishes to thank,' Fayre said, 'so I shall let her say a few words now.' She stepped to the side.

Finding a smile, Lyndal clasped her hands in front of her and looked out at the crowd. 'Thank you, Your Majesty. Not only for your kind words but for your personal contribution to the project.'

She went on to thank everyone who had been involved, from the merchants who gave their time, to the nobility who gave coin and materials, to the farmers who would be donating food.

'And, of course, my husband,' Lyndal said, finally losing the battle against her tears. She brushed a hand over her cheek. 'He was here every day, helping in some way. I've no idea how I got so lucky, but I'm incredibly thankful I did.'

More tears fell, and she could not wipe them away quick enough.

'Sorry,' she said. 'I promised myself I wouldn't cry, but the enormity of this moment and everything it symbolises has clearly gotten to me.' She laughed to expel some of the emotion building.

Astin stepped up onto the veranda of the almshouse and wrapped an arm around her. 'My wife wanted to build a place for people with nowhere to go, a place to fall down, to not be alone. It's a place where a mother can bring her children when the pot at home is empty. It's a place where those with enough can come and help those who are struggling. All the love and warmth this woman holds has been poured into this house. I've watched in awe.'

That only made the crying worse.

She wiped her face. 'If you, or anyone you know, is ever in need, this door behind me will open to you. And it's not just for merchants. Let's not let a few walls stop us from taking care of each other.'

The crowd applauded that last part.

'Long live Farmer Lyndal,' Presley shouted, grinning.

Laughter rolled over the crowd. Even Queen Fayre was smiling.

Lyndal walked to the door and pushed it open. Cheering ensued.

'Here it is,' she shouted above the noise. 'Your almshouse is officially open.'

~

They ate outside that night. Astin built a fire near the new farmhouse, and they roasted a side of pork big enough to feed the large group. They ate perched atop logs, cups of ale at their feet.

Lyndal loved these nights, everyone together, the constant hum of conversation accompanied by bouts of laughter. She looked across the fire at Astin and smiled. He rose when he caught her eye, walking over and sitting beside her.

'You're happy,' he said, kissing her forehead.

She nodded and put her plate on the ground, picking up her cup. 'How lucky are we to have all these people here to celebrate with us?'

Astin looked around the group. 'We could probably afford to cut a few loose, to be honest.'

Lyndal squeezed his knee. 'Be thankful my uncle always declines our invitations. He's above such gatherings.'

'I was secretly hoping his daughter would be above such gatherings,' Astin muttered.

'Don't. She's planning on volunteering her time at the almshouse.' Lyndal looked over at Kendra, who was carefully picking something out of her cup. 'She's earned her place at the fire and her cup of cheap ale with grass floating in it.'

Astin watched her a moment. 'The sooner she learns to chew her drink the quicker she'll fit in.'

Lyndal laughed into her cup, eyes going to Blake and Presley. It was not surprising the pair got along as well as they did. They were two peas in a pod.

Across the fire, Harlan and Birtle stood talking politics

while her mother sat with Kendra, ensuring she did not feel left out. Rose was playing with Garlic nearby. Astin had agreed to let the duck attend the celebration on the condition that Harlan did not accidentally leave the indoor pet behind at the end of the night.

Through the fading light, Lyndal could see Eda and Roul playing barley break. The two most reclusive people she had ever known had fallen into the most unlikely of friendships.

'She's speaking more than she's signing now,' Astin said, reading her thoughts. 'Have you noticed that?'

'Yes.'

Roul tried to pivot around Eda in an attempt to make it to the other side of the circle, but Eda dove to the ground, tagging his boot just before he reached the line. Rolling onto her back, Eda laughed. Roul accused her of cheating, which only made her laugh harder.

At first, Candace had discouraged the friendship, worried about rumours starting. But once she saw the improvement in Eda's speech and accepted that her youngest was never going to befriend the other young ladies in the nobility borough, she had let the matter go.

'Any news on Prince Becket?' Lyndal said, turning her attention back to Astin. 'Surely Harlan's father knows something.'

'He doesn't want the crown—and Queen Fayre thinks she can change his mind. But she's running out of time.'

'Meaning?'

'Meaning if the prince doesn't come sit his arse on that throne, someone else will.'

Eda appeared in front of them, out of breath and

covered in grass stains. 'Come play. It's better with more players.'

Lyndal frowned up at her sister. 'I'm quite happy to remain clean, thank you. Ask Blake. She loves the mud.'

'I'll referee,' Blake said, rising.

Lyndal sighed. 'Why can't I be referee?'

Harlan appeared behind Blake, arms going around her. 'I think you'd better explain to your sister why you'll be refereeing and she'll be rolling in the mud.'

Lyndal looked between them, then at Eda, who was smiling. 'What's going on? Why can't Blake play in the dirt like usual?' She looked to her mother for an answer.

The excitement in Candace's eyes made Lyndal gasp and shoot up, cup falling from her hand.

'What's wrong?' Astin said, leaping up.

Blake laughed. 'Nothing's wrong. I'm just pregnant.'

And now Lyndal was crying again. She went to her sister, hands going to the beginnings of a bump. 'Oh my goodness.'

'I figured it out before anyone,' Kendra said proudly.

'If you were still living with us, you would have known straight away,' Harlan said. 'She has thrown up more food than she has kept down of late.'

Lyndal hugged her sister, but not as tightly as usual. 'I'm so happy for you.'

'Thank you,' Blake said, kissing her cheek.

Lyndal released her with a dramatic sigh. 'Fine. You can referee.'

'I'll play if it gets me out of cleaning up,' Presley said, rising.

The entire group wandered over to the circle. Harlan

stood explaining the rules to Kendra, who had never heard of the game, while Birtle and Candace refilled everyone's cups.

'Look up,' Astin whispered into Lyndal's ear.

She lifted her gaze. The clouds had parted above them, revealing a sliver of black sky with bright stars. 'So beautiful.'

'Agreed,' Astin replied, but he was not looking up at the sky. He was looking at her.

'Do you see me, defender?' she asked, a smile playing on her lips.

He nuzzled her hair and breathed her in. 'I see you.'

ACKNOWLEDGMENTS

I would like to express my gratitude to the many people who contributed to this book. My biggest thanks goes to my readers. Without you guys, I wouldn't get to do what I love. Next, a huge thank you to my rock star husband who supports and encourages me even though my writing takes time away from him. I love you to bits. A big thank you to McKinley, Kristin and the team at Hot Tree Editing for polishing the manuscript into something beautiful. A shout out to Katy for beta reading, and to my proofreader, Rebecca, for catching everything I missed. A round of applause for my cover designer, Stuart Bache, for another gorgeous cover. And finally, a huge thank you to my Launch Team for your encouragement, honest reviews, and being the final set of eyes on my work. You guys are amazing.

ALSO BY TANYA BIRD

You can find a complete list of published works at

tanyabird.com/books